THE KILLING
OF WORLDS

BOOK TWO OF SUCCESSION

SCOTT WESTERFELD

TOR®

A TOM DOHERTY ASSOCIATES BOOK
NEW YORK

This is a work of fiction. All of the characters, organizations, and events portrayed in this novel are either products of the author's imagination or are used fictitiously.

THE KILLING OF WORLDS: BOOK TWO OF SUCCESSION

Copyright © 2003 by Scott Westerfeld

All rights reserved.

Edited by David G. Hartwell

A Tor Book
Published by Tom Doherty Associates
175 Fifth Avenue
New York, NY 10010

www.tor-forge.com

Tor® is a registered trademark of Macmillan Publishing Group, LLC.

ISBN 978-1-250-16552-7

Our books may be purchased in bulk for promotional, educational, or business use. Please contact your local bookseller or the Macmillan Corporate and Premium Sales Department at 1-800-221-7945, extension 5442, or by email at MacmillanSpecialMarkets@macmillan.com.

First Edition: October 2003
Second Mass Market Edition: August 2018

Printed in the United States of America

0 9 8 7 6 5 4 3 2 1

TOR BOOKS BY SCOTT WESTERFELD

To Justine, with whom I have a genuine
and continuing relationship

Acknowledgments

This novel is indebted to Wil McCarthy's research on programmable matter, from his *Nature* article on the subject, to a paper I heard him give at Readercon 2001, to his kind vetting of this manuscript.

Another debt is owed to Samuel R. Delany, whose views on the typography of Swords and Sorcery, expressed in *1984: Selected Letters,* gave me the courage to capitalize "Emperor."

A Note on Imperial Measures

One of the many advantages of life under the Imperial Apparatus is the easy imposition of consistent standards of infostructure, communication, and law. For fifteen hundred years, the measures of the Eighty Worlds have followed an enviably straightforward scheme.

- There are 100 seconds in each minute, 100 minutes in an hour, and ten hours in a day.
- One second is defined as 1/100,000 of a solar day on Home.
- One meter is defined as 1/300,000,000 of a light-second.
- One gravity is defined as 10 meters per second squared acceleration.

The Emperor has decreed that the speed of light shall remain as nature has provided.

THE KILLING OF WORLDS

BOOK TWO OF SUCCESSION

The Imperial Civil War
—compiled by the Academy of Material Detail

Two thousand years ago, it is believed, the population of diasporic humanity surpassed one hundred trillion, including various more-or-less human types in addition to the main germlines. This was a very rough count, and given the scale of the galaxy and the unattainability of translight travel, informed estimates can no longer be made. Certainly, no census is possible. But it is obvious that humanity is a vast object of study, even when matters of merely local concern are engaged.

The Risen Empire, with its eighty worlds, its trillions, and its coreward position—dense with neighbors such as the Rix, the Feshtun, and Laxu—is huge enough to seem unaffected by the actions of individuals. Historians speak of social pressures as if they were physical laws, of "unstoppable" forces of change, of destiny. But for the men and women who walked the historical stage, these forces were often invisible, hidden by their sheer scale and the rank propaganda of the times. Social pressures built invisibly over lifetimes, not across the pages of a history text. And destiny only became apparent after the dice had been thrown. For those who experienced them directly, historical events were ruled by the fortunes of war, the whims of lovers, and dumb luck. Fate arises out of such humble parts as these.

In the current era, when the inevitability of the Imperial Civil War is received wisdom, we must work to remember that it was the product of specific events. Collapse would have come in any case, true, but it might have come centuries earlier, or (more likely) centuries later than it did. For the generations who lived under the cultural and military tyranny of the Risen Emperor, the difference was not trivial.

The origins of the Civil War are now learned by rote. The Risen Empire was riven into two parts. The limited democracy of the Senate contested the iron rule of the Emperor in an uneasy dance of power-sharing. Representative government provided an outlet for popular will, while the Imperial cult of personality supplied a patriarch to bind together eighty worlds, the living populace and the risen dead each playing their part in the machinery of the Empire. The great majority of Imperial citizens were alive, and constituted the collective engine of change and economic productivity. As inventors, capitalists, and workers, they were the functional, instrumental members of society. The risen dead, on the other hand, represented continuity with the past. They controlled the established wealth, owning the land, the shipping charters, the ancient copyrights, dominating religion and high culture, an undead aristocracy of sorts. These tensions, fundamentally a class conflict, had to find release eventually. The immortal Emperor and his fanatical Apparatus had held onto power at any cost for centuries, making it almost certain that any resolution would be a bloody one. Adding to this instability, the small gene pool of its founder population made the Empire particularly susceptible to mass manias, cults of personality, pandemics, and other forms of radical upheaval.

Still, specific events brought about the Civil War in a specific way, and are worth historical study. There was a Second Rix Incursion, a Senator Nara Oxham, a Captain Laurent Zai.

The Second Rix Incursion began on Legis XV. It was at root a religious war. The Rix Cult worshiped planetary-scale AI, which the Emperor's Apparatus jealously stamped out of existence wherever it arose. The Rix viewed this as deicide, and planned a deicide of their own, perhaps from the moment the Child Empress retired to Legis. Sister to the Emperor, Anastasia was his only equal as an object of worship.

Sixteen hundred years earlier, the Emperor had worked to save Anastasia's life from a juvenile disease, inventing immortality in the process, and forming the basis of the Risen Empire. Thus, she was known as the Reason, the child for whom the Old Enemy death had been defeated. When a small Rix warship penetrated Legis's defenses and took her hostage, the Risen Empire had suffered a devastating blow.

Captain Laurent Zai found himself in the unenviable position of being in command of the only Imperial warship in the Legis system. The *Lynx* was a capable ship, a small, powerful frigate prototype, but any attempt to rescue Anastasia from a squad of Rix commandos could only be a desperate gamble. Under the military conventions of the day, failure would constitute a so-called "Error of Blood," demanding ritual suicide from the commanding officer.

There was little time to weigh the issue. Once the

Rix had taken the Child Empress, they set loose a compound mind within the Legis infostructure. Over a few hours, every networked machine on the planet—diaries, market mainframes, pocket phones, traffic computers—was amalgamating into a single emergent consciousness: Alexander. Captain Zai had to act quickly.

Given the chaos of the rescue attempt, it will never be clear if the Child Empress was killed by her Rix captors or by the Imperial Apparatus; theories of the Emperor's involvement have never been decisively proven. Easier to confirm is why Laurent Zai refused the Blade of Error, flying in the face of tradition. Although he was from an ancient and gray military family, sworn to the Emperor's service, he had recently sworn a different sort of loyalty to Nara Oxham, a Senator from the anti-Imperial Secularist party. The two were in secret contact, he at the Rix frontier and she at the capital, throughout the beginning of the Rix War. When she asked Zai not to kill himself, he assented. Love, in this case, was a stronger force than honor.

The rescue attempt had come too late for Legis. The Rix compound mind emerged within the planet's infostructure, an alien intelligence in possession of a hostage world. But Alexander was cut off. The polar facility that maintained Legis's interstellar communications remained in Imperial hands. Alexander was alone, save for a single Rix commando who had survived the rescue attempt. With the help of omnipresent Alexander and her hostage/lover Rana Harter, this Rixwoman disappeared to the far north to await the compound mind's next move.

On board the *Lynx*, Captain Laurent Zai faced a

mutiny, an attempt by gray members of his crew to enforce the Error of Blood. Though he and his able first officer, Katherie Hobbes, easily thwarted the mutineers, a far more dangerous threat approached. Another Rix ship, a battlecruiser of far greater firepower than Zai's frigate, had entered the Legis system. Although officially pardoned by the Emperor for his Error of Blood, Zai was ordered to engage the battlecruiser to prevent it from making contact with the compound mind, a suicide mission, the Emperor no doubt assumed.

Of course, Laurent Zai could not have imagined the fate that awaited Legis XV if the *Lynx* should fail.

The Emperor probably planned a nuclear attack from the moment the Rix mind came into existence. Total annihilation of the Legis infostructure offered three advantages to the sovereign. He could destroy the compound mind, rally the Empire behind another costly war with the Rix, and, most importantly, maintain the secret that had underlain his rule for sixteen centuries, a secret grasped by Alexander in its first hours of consciousness. Against the objections of Senator Oxham and the anti-Imperial parties, the Emperor's hand-picked War Council approved the attack by a narrow margin, providing political cover for this desperate act.

But Laurent Zai and the *Lynx* proved far more resourceful, and luckier, than anyone might have expected.

Prologue

Captain

The *Lynx* exploded, expanded.

The frigate's energy-sink manifold spread out, stretching luxuriant across eighty square kilometers. The manifold was part hardware and part field effect, staggered ranks of tiny machines held in their hexagonal pattern by a lacework of easy gravity. It shimmered in the Legis sun, refracting a mad god's spectrum, unfurling like the feathers of some ghostly, translucent peacock seeking to rut. In battle, it could disperse ten thousand gigawatts per second, a giant lace fan burning hot enough to blind naked human eyes at two thousand klicks.

The satellite-turrets of the ship's four photon cannon eased away from the primary hull, extending on hypercarbon scaffolds that always recalled to Captain Laurent Zai the iron bones of ancient cantilever bridges. They were removed on their spindly arms four kilometers from the vessel proper, and the *Lynx* was shielded from the cannon's collateral radiation by twenty centimeters of hullalloy; using the cannon would afflict the *Lynx*'s crew with only the most treatable of cancers. The four satellite-turrets carried sufficient reaction mass and intelligence to operate independently if released in battle. And from the safety of a few thousand kilometers distance, their fusion magazines could be ordered to crashfire, consuming themselves in a chain reaction, delivering one final, lethal needle toward the enemy. Of course, the cannon could also be crashfired from their close-in position, destroying their mothership in a blaze of deadly glory.

That was one of the frigate's five standard methods of self-destruction.

The magnetic rail that launched the *Lynx*'s drone complement descended from her belly, and telescoped to its full nineteen-hundred-meter length. A few large scout drones, a squadron of ramscatters, and a host of sandcasters deployed themselves around the rail. The ramscatters bristled like nervous porcupines with their host of tiny flechettes, each of which carried sufficient fuel to accelerate at two thousand gees for almost a second. The sandcasters were bloated with dozens of self-propelled canisters, whose ceramic skins were crosshatched with fragmentation patterns. At the high relative velocity of this battle, sand would be Zai's most effective weapon against the Rix receiver array.

Inside the rail bay, great magazines of other drone types were loaded in a carefully calculated order of battle. Stealth penetrators, broadcast decoys, minesweepers, remotely piloted fighter craft, close-in-defense pickets all awaited their moment in battle. Finally, a single deadman drone waited. This drone could be launched even if the frigate lost all power, accelerated by highly directional explosives inside its dedicated backup rail. The deadman was already active, continuously updating its copy of the last two hours' logfiles, which it would attempt to deliver to Imperial forces if the *Lynx* was destroyed.

When we are destroyed, Captain Laurent Zai corrected himself. His ship was not likely to survive this encounter; it was best to accept that. The Rix vessel outpowered and outgunned them. Its crew was quicker and more adept, so intimately linked into the battlecruiser's systems that the exact point of division between human and hardware was a subject more for philosophical debate than military consideration. And Rix boarding commandos were deadly: faster, hardier, more proficient in compromised gravity. And, of course, they were unafraid of death; to the Rix, lives lost in battle were no more remarkable than a few brain cells sacrificed to a glass of wine.

Zai watched his bridge crew work, preparing the newly configured *Lynx* to resume acceleration. They were in zero-gee now, waiting for the restructuring to firm up before subjecting the expanded frigate to the stresses of acceleration. It was a relief to be out of highgee, if only for a few hours. When the engagement started in earnest, the ship would go into evasive mode, the direction and strength of acceleration varying continuously. Next to that chaos, the last two weeks of steady high acceleration would seem like a pleasure cruise.

Captain Zai wondered if there was any mutiny left in his crew. At least two of the conspirators had escaped Hobbes's trap. Were there more? The senior officers must realize that this battle was unwinnable. They understood what a Rix battlecruiser was capable of, and would recognize that the *Lynx*'s battle configuration had been designed to damage its opponent, not preserve itself. Zai and ExO Hobbes had optimized the ship's offensive weaponry at the expense of its defenses, orienting its entire arsenal on the task of destroying the Rix receiver array.

Now that the *Lynx* was at battle stations, even the junior officers would be able to spot the ill portents that surrounded them.

The boarding skiffs remained in their storage cells. It was unlikely that Zai's marines would be crossing the gulf to capture the Rix battlecruiser. Boarding actions were the privilege of the winning vessel. Instead, Imperial marines were taking up positions throughout the *Lynx,* ready to defend it from capture should the Rix board the vessel after pounding it into helplessness. Normally under these conditions, Zai would have issued sidearms to the crew to help repel boarders. But after the mutiny this seemed a risky show of faith. Most ominously for any crewman who chose to notice, the singularity generator, the most dramatic of Zai's self-destruct options, was already charged to maximum. If the *Lynx* could draw close enough to the enemy battlecruiser, the two craft would share a dramatic death.

In short, the *Lynx* was primed like an angry, blind drunk hurtling into a bar fight with gritted teeth, ferally anxious to inflict damage, unconscious of any pain she might feel herself.

Perhaps that was their one advantage in this fight, Zai thought: desperation. Would the Rix try to protect the vulnerable receiver array? Their mission was obviously to communicate with the compound mind on Legis. But would the dictates of saving the array force the Rix commander to make a bad move? If so, there might be some slim hope of surviving this battle.

Zai sighed and grimly pushed this line of thought aside. Hope was not his ally, he had learned over the last ten days.

He turned his mind back to the bridge airscreen and its detailed schematic of the *Lynx*'s internal structure.

The wireframe lines shifted like a puzzle box, as walls and bulkheads inside the frigate slid into battle configuration. Common rooms and mess halls disappeared to make space for expanded gunnery stations, passageways widened for easier movement of emergency repair teams. Crew bunks transformed into burn beds. The sickbay irised open, consuming the zero-gee courts and running tracks that usually surrounded it. Walls sprouted handholds in case of gravity loss, and everything that might come loose in sudden acceleration was stowed, velcroed, bolted down, or simply recycled.

Finally, the coiling, shifting, expanding, and extruding all came to a halt, and the schematic eased into a stable shape. Like a well-crafted mechanical bolt smoothly locking into place, the vessel became battle ready.

A single klaxon sounded. A few of his bridge crew half-turned toward Zai. Their faces were expectant and excited, ready to begin this fight regardless of the ship's chances. He saw it most in Katherie Hobbes's expression. They'd been beaten back on Legis XV, all of them, and this was their chance to get revenge. The mutiny, however small and aborted, had shamed them as well. They were ready to fight, and their bloodlust, however desperate, was good to see.

It was just possible, Laurent Zai allowed himself to think, that they would get home.

The captain nodded to the first pilot, and weight gradually returned, pressing him into the shipmaster's chair as the frigate accelerated.

The *Lynx* moved toward battle.

1

SPACE BATTLE

The initial conditions of a battle are the only fac-
tors that a general can truly affect. Once blood is
drawn, command is merely an illusion.

—ANONYMOUS 167

Militia Worker

The contrail of a supersonic aircraft blossomed weakly in the thin, dry air, barely marking the sky.

Rana Harter imagined the passengers far above: re-clining in sculpted crash-safe chairs, the air they breathed scented with some perfumed disinfectant, perhaps being served some light snack now, midway to their destination. From up there, other contrails would be visible through windows of transparent hypercar-bon. Most long-haul air routes on Legis passed over the pole. The continents were clustered in the northern hemisphere, far from the raging equatorial sea and the vast, silent ocean of the south. Air transit routes con-verged here at the pole like the lines on a dribble-hoop ball, this tundral waste an empty junction, overflown but never visited.

Rana had never traveled on an aircraft before Herd had brought her here. She could only blurrily imagine airborne luxury, the gaps in her vision filled with the sound of wealthy people's music: soft strings repeat-ing the same slow phrase.

She watched the wind move driftsnow across the plain, and noted the direction and speed of the few scudding clouds. Her brainbug made a prediction. The contrail reached a certain point and Rana said, "Now."

At that moment, the contrail jagged suddenly, a sharp angle marring its slow curve. A few pieces of detritus caught the sun, flickering with their spin, falling from the supersonic craft with the apparent slow motion of great distance.

The plane quickly recovered, righting its course.

Rana imagined the sudden, sickening lurch inside the cabin. Glasses of champagne flying, trays and hand luggage upset, every object leaping toward the ceiling as the plane lost a thousand meters of altitude in a few seconds. The unexpected opening of the cargo hold would instantly double the plane's drag profile, sending a shock through the entire craft. Hopefully, the smart seats would hold their passengers in. A few bloodied noses and wrenched shoulders, perhaps a concussion for some unlucky soul on her feet. But by now the plane had righted itself, automatically closing the offending cargo door.

Rana Harter had discovered that her brainbug worked better if she indulged these fancies. As she imagined the sudden jolt above, her eyes tracked the flickering fall of luggage and supplies, and she felt the whirring of her mind as it calculated the location and shape of the debris field. The sharp, determinate math of trajectories and wind smelled like camphor, rang in her ears with vibrato-free, pointillistic notes on a handful of flutes, one for each variable.

The answers came.

She turned to Herd, already dressed in her hooded fur coat. The sable had come from the first luggage drop arranged by Alexander. The stain that had once disguised Herd's Rix eyes was faded now, and they shone in their true violet, beautiful in the frame of black fur. The hairs of the coat ruffled in the bitter wind, a fluttering motion that made Rana hear the small, shimmering bells worn by wedding dancers on their feet.

Herd awaited her instructions, always respectfully silent when Rana's ability was in use (though the commando had squeezed her hand as her word *now* seemed to yank the airplane from its path).

"Seventy-four klicks that way," Rana said, pointing carefully. Herd's violet eyes followed the line of the gesture, checking for landmarks. Then she nodded and turned to Rana to kiss her good-bye.

The Rixwoman's lips were always cold now, her body temperature adapted to its environment. Her saliva tasted vaguely of rust, like the iron tang of blood, but sweeter. Her sweat contained no salt, its mineral content making it taste like water from a quarry town. As Herd dashed toward the flyer, the oversized coat lifting into sable wings, the synesthetic smell of the commando's avian/lemongrass movements mingled with the flavor left in Rana's mouth. The joy of watching Herd never lessened.

Rana turned back toward the cave entrance before the recon flyer whined to life, however. Every second here in the cold was taking something out of her.

Inside, it was above freezing.

Rana Harter wore two layers of real silk, a hat of red fox, and her own fur coat, vat-grown chinchilla lined with blue whale from the ubiquitous herds of the southern ocean. But she was still cold.

The walls of the cave were hung with centuries-old tapestries earmarked for the Museum of Antiquities in Pollax. A vast collection of toiletries and clothing, the bounty of fallen personal luggage, lined the icy shelves Herd had carved into the walls. Rana and Herd slept on the pelt of a large ursoid creature that neither of them recognized—a customs stamp confirmed its off-world origins. The floors were covered with soft linings ripped from luggage, a pile of undergarments forming an insulating layer underneath.

The small, efficient machines of travel were everywhere. Handheld games and coffee pots, flashlights and sex toys, all for Herd to dissect and rebuild into new devices. For sustenance, they had only prestige foods. Rich meats from young animals, fruits scandalously out of season, caviar and exotic nuts, candied insects and edible flowers. It all came in morsel sizes, suitable for luxury airplane meals: canned, self-heating and freeze-dried, bagged and coldboxed, to be washed down with liquor in plastic bottles dwarfish enough to have survived the long fall. They drank from two crystal glasses that someone thought valuable enough to pack in thirty centimeters of smartfoam. Oddly, the glasses had been labeled as coffee beans on their packaging. A mistake, or perhaps they were smuggled antiques.

All this bounty from only three aircraft holds, Rana wondered. She had never seen such wealth before. She lifted a smartplastic tennis racket, its rim no wider than the strings it suspended, and wondered at the instrument's elegant, almost Rixian lines.

This fourth luggage "accident" would be their last haul. The background rate of such events had already been wildly exceeded, and Alexander's false clues explaining the cargo-door defect had begun to wear thin. But she and Herd had all they needed until the compound mind called them to action.

Until then, they would live in luxury. And they had each other.

Rana Harter sat and rested from the freezing minutes outside. She lifted up a travel handheld to read, and that simple exertion tired her. She slept longer each night, dreaming lucidly but abstractly in the strange symbols of her brainbug. Her happiness never wavered, though. The dopamine regulators saw to that.

The infection in Rana's wound was gone, disappearing in a single fevered night after an ampoule of nanos from Herd's medical kit. But the weight in Rana's chest was still there, building and building. Her breath grew shorter by the day.

She activated the travel handheld; its screen lit up, bookmarked to its medical compendium. Rana flicked it off again. She had read this section enough times, and knew that her one good lung was slowly going. Fluids were slowly building up in the wall between ribcage and lung, squeezing the breath from her like a tightening fist. Only an operation could save her. However resourceful her Rix lover might be, surgery was beyond their means here in this icy cave.

Rana Harter's mind had never possessed a sharp sense of irony. The mean circumstances of her life had never required one. But she saw the joke here: She was surrounded by everything she had ever desired. Every petty luxury and marker of wealth. An invisible god that she positively *knew* to exist. Free use of her brainbug in a safe retreat at the literal end of the earth. And a lover of alien beauty, a fierce and lethal protector, whose physical grace, novel mind, and violet eyes offered whole new worlds of fascination.

And the punch line: Rana, in the next few days, would almost certainly die.

She turned from these thoughts the way a child ignores a light rain. They did nothing to reduce her joy.

Whatever occurred, she—one of the few among humanity's trillions—had chanced blindly into happiness.

Death must have found me, Rana Harter decided.

She was already in heaven.

Senator

Nara Oxham took firm hold of the handrail before purging the drug from her system.

The balcony barely swung in the cool, late-night wind, its motion held in check by counterweights rolling inside the wooden deck beneath her bare feet. A set of finger-width polyfilaments reinforced the softly creaking ornamental chains, with enough tensile strength (the building propaganda bragged) to hold an African elephant, even during one of the Coriolis squalls that sometimes reached the capital in late summer. If Senator Oxham were to slip and fall, she would only become entangled in the invisible suicide mesh that cocooned the entire building, and be delivered back to the nearest observation deck five floors below. And in case of the unthinkable, the balcony carried a small vacuum blimp compressed under the breakfast table. When fully deployed, it would provide enough lift to bring the senator and approximately twenty guests down to a soft landing.

But the animal mind was strong in humans, as Nara's empathy never let her forget, and mere safety precautions were not enough to overcome the vertigo of a two-kilometer drop. Her knuckles turned white as the drug left her.

The apathy bracelet made its usual hissing noise, injecting filtration nanos into her bloodstream. In a few minutes, the first glimmers of empathy arose from the city. Mindnoise rumbled from the residential towers north of the Diamond Palace, squat and ugly, densely populated. Each tower held over a hundred thousand of the capital's most numerous class: the petty bureaucrats who monitored taxable production claims. Every Imperial administrator in the Eighty Worlds had a double here on Home, another set of eyes following every transaction to ensure that the Senate and Emperor received their cut. Back on Vasthold, Nara had known of this army of distant and invisible overseers in the abstract, but eighty planets' worth of them concentrated in this one city brought home the fantastic extent of the Empire. Huge data freighters left daily from the capital's spaceport to resupply the possessions with entangled quanta, no expense spared to keep communications broadband and instantaneous, the Emperor's omniscience a matter of fact as well as scripture.

As her empathy grew, Nara could feel the dynamics of slow shift changes, thousands of bureaucrats returning home as night fell over populous continents light-years away, other thousands waking up to spread out across the low, windowless administration buildings as the day began in some megacity on another of the Eighty Worlds. War fever still animated the capital as a whole, but the minds of these countless minions never raised a cry above the rumble of drudgery, the cogs of the Empire.

Nara wondered what the overseers for Legis were

doing now that the planet had been cut off from the Imperial network. The whole world, except for a few military installations and the *Lynx*, had been intentionally made a dark spot since the compound mind had taken over. The Emperor had given up direct control of an entire planet simply to isolate the Rix abomination.

What an insult to Imperial privilege.

The lights of the capital all but obliterated stars from the night sky, and Nara felt her distance from Laurent, her helplessness. If the *Lynx* was destroyed too suddenly to manage a last transmission, it would be eight hours before the lazy speed of the constant brought the event to telescopes on Legis. Almost a day of not knowing.

The War Council had voted hours ago; the battle must be engaged by now.

Her lover might already be dead.

Empathy gained another measure of intensity, and Senator Oxham could feel frantic thoughts down in the flame-dotted shape of the Martyrs' Park. Ancestor-worshiping cults had erected effigies of Rixwomen down there, tall figures with hollow eyes, filled with fanciful artificial organs that gave off a plastic smell when they burned. The demonstrations of the faithful had grown every day since the murder of the Emperor's sister.

Even Nara, a hardened Secularist, could still feel the shock of that moment. The Child Empress Anastasia was the Reason, after all, a central character of childhood fables and rhymes. However much Nara Oxham hated the process that had cured Anastasia's long-ago disease, the Child Empress and her brother had made the world Nara lived in. And no matter that she was sixteen centuries old, Anastasia had still looked twelve on the day of her death.

In any sane world, she would have died a long time ago, but it still felt utterly wrong that she had died at all.

This late most of the capital was asleep. The wild creature of the human group-psyche was unusually quiescent, and Senator Oxham held on to sanity for long minutes. She tried to feel the Diamond Palace, but the cold minds of the Apparatus undead and the disciplined thoughts of elite guardsmen provided little to grasp hold of.

"Why?" she wondered softly, thinking of the Emperor's plan.

The city was starting to swirl below her, the war animating even the capital's dreams.

Nara imagined a nuclear airburst overhead, a sudden, bright star blossoming in the sky. Instantly, the electromagnetic pulse would strike, and all the lights go out, the whole spectacle of the capital reduced to black silhouettes, lit only by the airburst and a few burning effigies in the park. Seconds later, however clean the warheads might be, a blast wave would rock her building, shattering windows, no doubt testing even the balcony's safeguards, and casting a rain of glass onto the streets below.

That was the plan for distant Legis, if Laurent Zai failed.

The nuclear attack might kill the Rix compound mind, but it would throw Legis into a dark age. After the falling aircars and failing medical endoframes, and all the disease, unrest, and simple starvation that accompanied a devastated infostructure, there would be a hundred million lives lost planetwide, so the Apparatus estimated.

On a planet of two billion, that was not as bad as decimation, in the old sense of one in ten. But still the Old Enemy death on a vast scale.

She looked at the Diamond Palace again. What could be worth murdering a hundred million people?

The capital grew louder, becoming an angry chorus as her mind lost its defenses. In the sleepless free-market towers to the south, she felt labor futures tightening nervously, titles and pardons being fought over like carrion, the anxious cycles of a war economy spinning ever faster. The mindnoise turned to screeching, and again the old vision came: a great cloud of seagulls crowding the sky, wheeling around the bloated, dying thing that was the Empire.

Nara Oxham felt she almost grasped something fatal and hidden in these moments of madness, when withdrawal from the drug left her empathy open to the assembled mass of the capital, the Risen Empire in microcosm. Something was utterly rotten, she knew, a corruption tearing at the bonds that held the Eighty Worlds together. And she also knew that however hard she'd fought against the Emperor's rule, the shabby truth of how broken it all was would terrify her.

A dark shape rose up before Oxham, blotting out the lights of the city. The senator tried to blink the apparition away, but its silent and winged form remained. She backed up a few steps, for a moment convinced that the empathic vision had somehow come to life and would consume her now.

But a familiar sound tugged at her second hearing, insistent through the howl of the city. She closed her eyes and some sane fraction of her mind recognized it: the War Council summons.

Her fingers went to her bracelet, reflexively administering a dose of apathy.

When she opened her eyes again, the shape was still there. An Imperial aircar waiting patiently, its elegant wing extended to meet the balcony's edge.

A missive hovered in second sight.

The battle is joined. The sovereign requests that his War Council attend him.

Nara shook her head bitterly as the drug again suppressed her empathy, returning the capital to silence. She would not even be allowed to wait alone for news of Laurent and Legis. The Emperor and his War Council, those who knew what was at stake, wanted company as they watched their miserable plan unfold.

Nara Oxham crossed the wing to the waiting aircar, not bothering to change. On Vasthold, one went plainly dressed and barefoot to funerals.

In the next few hours, Laurent Zai would either save a hundred million lives, or die trying.

Captain

Captain Laurent Zai exulted in the colors and sounds of the bridge.

The battle was joined.

Both ships had launched the bulk of their drone

complements, and the outer reaches of the two multitudes were just now touching, just over half a light-minute away, a pair of vast point-clouds in stately collision. Automated drones were battling each other out there, the skirmishers of two fleets vying for advantage. The outcome of those first duels was still a mystery; only the largest scout and remote fighter drones carried translight communications. Already, one side might have secured superiority in the outer skirmishes, and thus a crucial advantage in intelligence. The few scout drones with entangled communications could only tell the *Lynx*'s crew so much about the enemy.

If the *Lynx*'s drones lost the battle at the edge, superior intelligence would be added to the Rix's already weighty advantages.

This was one cost of Zai's hell-bent battle plan. If the first outlying duels were lost, there would be little time to recover. It would all be over quickly.

"Anything from the master pilot?" Zai badgered Hobbes.

"He's still looking for an opening, sir."

Zai gritted his teeth and cursed. It would be foolish to second-guess Marx and order him in before he was ready; the master pilot was a brilliant tactician, and his remote fighters were far less numerous and more valuable than the automated drones currently battling on the outer edge of the fray. But Zai wished the man wasn't so damned fastidious.

"Let me know when he deigns to join the battle."

Zai tugged at his woolen uniform angrily.

"And Hobbes, why is it so damned hot on my bridge?"

Pilot

Master Pilot Jocim Marx watched the feints and penetrations of the battle with a boxer's patience, waiting for the proper moment to strike.

Safe in the shielded center of the *Lynx*, Marx inhabited the viewpoint of the foremost entanglement-equipped drone among the frigate's complement. This drone was close to the fight, but not in it yet. The two opposing spheres of drone craft were just beginning to overlap, like some three-dimensional Venn diagram mapping the shallowest of intersections between sets. But with every passing second, the intersection increased by another three thousand kilometers. Within the broad front of the collision, drones darted, accelerating at thousands of gees to effect the smallest of lateral changes. At the two fleets' huge relative velocity, drones could only shift themselves by hairlines relative to the enemy. They were like pistol-wielding duelists perched on the front of two approaching high-speed trains, hurtling toward each other, taking shuffling steps from side to side, trying to gain some slight advantage.

From his vantage in the translight-equipped drone, Marx could see the outermost portions of the battle firsthand. He could command the drones around him to effect a swift parry. But the drones he sent these orders to were too small and cheap for entangled communications, so his orders reached them with the maddening tardiness of the constant. Marx was used to the millisecond delays of Intelligencers and other small craft, but these delays were like sending carrier pigeons to direct a battle kilometers away.

The two waves of combatants continued their career into each other, and the flares of accelerating kinetic weapons began to light the void. The first wave of the *Lynx*'s drones were spraying sand, huge clouds of tiny but sharp and corrosive carbon particles. *Diamonds*, the poets called them. At these relative velocities, sand could strip an armored drone like a desert storm tearing the skin from a naked man.

The Rix craft responded with more sophisticated measures. Marx saw the shimmering flashes that were formations of flocker missiles being launched. Each flocker was no bigger than a human finger, but in phalanxes of a hundred or more they formed a hive entity of enormous versatility. They combined their resources to form a single sensor array, unified electronic defenses, and a hardy, democratic intelligence. And like all Rix military hardware, flockers evolved from battle to battle. In the First Incursion decades before, they had been observed coordinating tactics across huge distances. They grouped themselves in larger or smaller formations as the situation dictated, and individuals sacrificed themselves to protect other flockers of their group. Marx wondered how far they had progressed in the last eighty years. He had a feeling that the *Lynx*'s crew was about to learn quite a bit on the subject.

However smart these new flockers were, though, the captain had made one point with which Marx had to agree. Cruder Imperial technology had an advantage at high velocities. Flockers and piloted drones used up a lot of their mass being clever, and cleverness didn't always pay off when a firefight took place in the blink of an eye. Sand was as dumb as a stone club, but its destructiveness increased with every kilometer per second.

The master pilot's craft told him that the flockers were hitting the first wavefront of sand. At relative rest, a dispersed cloud of sand was barely detectable. But plunging through it at one percent light speed transformed the cloud into a solid wall.

Marx urged his drone closer.

The view cleared quickly as he shot toward the battle's edge. His scout craft had an initial load of two-thirds reaction mass, and could accelerate at six hundred gees at 25 percent efficiency. If he pointed it in one direction and pushed it, the drone would make just under a quarter of the constant in about two hundred minutes, at which point it would be out of fuel. Although the drone lacked the elegance of Marx's beloved small craft, that one fact always amazed him: This machine, no bigger than a coffin, could make relativistic velocities. It had the power to push time.

Even in this train wreck of a battle, the scout's acceleration could make a difference. Marx had taken it out in front of the Imperial drone fleet and then turned it over. Now he was falling back toward the *Lynx*—almost pacing the incoming Rix drones. He'd burned a sixth of his reaction mass, but Marx was where he wanted to be: in the rolling center of the conflict.

He passed a few decelerating sandcaster drones; their cargoes emptied, they were pulling back.

Marx waited, drumming his fingers. There should

be fireworks by now. Where was the wave of explosions showing the disintegration of the first flocker formations? Imperial sand posed little sensor interference—it was designed to be invisible. But no explosions showed in Marx's view, just acceleration and launch flares.

Were the flockers dying quietly, whittled down to nothing by the terrific friction of the sand?

Marx pushed in closer, seeking answers at the risk of his scout. A firefight had started between the larger advanced drones, who'd launched all their satellites and were now attacking each other directly. Rix beam weapons lit the void, igniting ambient sand like searchlights on a misty night. But Marks could see nothing that looked like a host of small craft disintegrating. He cut his craft's acceleration, trying to stay out of the fight.

Then Marx saw the column.

It glinted just for a moment in a radar reflection, four kilometers long. For a moment, he thought it was a single structure. Then the AI calculated its exact diameter and he realized what it was.

A single column of flockers, probably all that the battle cruiser had launched. More than five thousand of them, spaced less than a meter apart. His sensors told of the formation's incredible exactness: The whole four kilometers had the diameter of Marx's thumb.

He could see minute flashes from the front of the column now. Every few seconds the lead drone was being destroyed by sand. Then the next one took its place, and lasted a few more seconds.

But behind these sacrifices, the vast majority of the flockers were protected. They were like army ants crossing a river, the latter arrivals marching on the backs of the foremost after they had drowned. They were punching a very narrow hole into the wall of sand, and slipping through.

Marx had seen flockers spread themselves into a far-flung bestiary of shapes: radiating arms like paper fans or the struts of a parasol, toroids and lazy-eights that undulated with a standing wave, point-clouds buzzing with internal motion. But never had he seen anything so deviously simple.

A straight line.

And they were getting through.

Another image occurred to Marx. On his home planet lived a species of rat that could break down its own bones, funneling itself into a thin sack of jelly to climb through even the narrowest of cracks. He shuddered at the thought.

Marx's surprise cost him a vital moment of attention. He didn't immediately notice the ten flockers that burst from the line, having detected a transient gap in the sand between his scout craft and the column. By the time the master pilot reacted, the flockers were lined up on him at three thousand gees. Although they had less than a second of reaction mass at that acceleration, Marx's twisting evasive pattern came too late, his larger drone twisting like some slow-footed mastodon brought down by a pack of small predators. Synesthesia filled with lightning, sputtered for a moment, then dumped him into the calming cerulean wash of a dead signal.

He cursed. And cursed again.

Gathering himself, Jocim Marx signaled ExO Hobbes.

"I saw," Hobbes said. She'd been watching over his shoulder.

He bit his tongue as a wave of shame struck him. In a Class 7 translight drone on a scouting mission, and he'd been beaten by a handful of pilotless drones.

"They're getting through the sand!" he shouted. "The *Lynx* is—"

"We'll be briefing the captain in forty seconds," Hobbes interrupted. "I want you on the bridge in virtual."

Forty seconds? An eternity in this battle, a dozen opportunities lost to delay.

"And what should I do for forty seconds, Executive Officer?"

A dead pause: his audio muted as Hobbes attended to one of the other dozen conversations she was no doubt juggling. Then she was back.

"I suggest you reflect thankfully upon the fact that you fly remotes, Master Pilot. See you in thirty seconds."

Her voice left him alone in his blue, dead universe.

As he waited, Marx's fingers twitched, aching to fly again.

Captain

"In short, the flockers are getting through the sand," Hobbes concluded.

Laurent Zai nodded.

"They always do. What's the projected attrition?"

Hobbes swallowed. These nervous ticks were unlike

her, Zai thought. She had lost some confidence since the mutiny.

"Perhaps a tenth, sir. The other ninety percent are coming through."

"*Ten pecent!*" Zai glared down into the bridge main airscreen, where the long, thin needle of flockers hovered. Normally, the small and expendable drones were reduced to a small fraction of their initial numbers. He and Hobbes had expected the sand to be especially deadly at this speed. But instead, it had proved useless.

There were almost five thousand flockers in the first wave alone, more than enough to tear the *Lynx* to pieces. And they would arrive in some sixteen minutes.

"Did they use this single-column tactic in the last war?" he asked.

"No, sir. Perhaps a new evolutionary—" Hobbes began.

"Begging your pardon, Captain," interrupted the disembodied head and shoulders of Master Pilot Marx. His image floated in the captain's private airscreen, projected from a flight canopy in the *Lynx*'s core.

"Yes, Master Pilot?"

"In a normal battle, forming into a single column wouldn't give flockers any advantage. Sand is ejected outward from hundreds of small delivery canisters, so any given sandstorm contains hundreds of different trajectories. The relative motion between sand and flockers is chaotic."

"So a column would offer no protection," Hobbes said.

"Correct." Marx's fingers came into view, gesturing through calculations. "But in this battle, our two drone fleets are moving through each other at three thousand klicks per second. The lateral, chaotic motion of the sand is erased by its relative insignificance to the overall motion. The flocker column punches through even the biggest sand cloud in a few thousandths of a second."

Zai closed his eyes. He'd been foolish not to see it. Perhaps not this specific tactic, but the basic flaw in his plan: The *Lynx*'s high speed of attack flattened events.

A quote from Anonymous 167 came to him too late. "'Against a simple tactic, a simple response is often effective,'" he muttered. The Rix had found that simple response.

"Pardon me, sir?" Marx said.

Hobbes nodded vigorously, translating the aphorism for Marx. "The high relative velocity between our two ships channels relationships into a single dimension: that of the approach axis. In effect, we've made this a single-variable battle."

"And the Rix have countered with a one-dimensional formation," Captain Zai concluded. "A line."

"The flockers will reach us in fourteen minutes, sir," the watch officer interjected.

Zai nodded calmly, but inside he seethed. The *Lynx*'s rate of acceleration was pitiful compared to that of the tiny flockers. There was no way to maneuver out of this. They were defenseless.

He clenched his real hand. To have chosen life, to have thrown away honor, only to be extinguished by an idiotic mistake. Zai had broken his oath to see Nara again, but it looked as if his betrayal would come to nothing. Perhaps this was natural law in action: On Vada, they said that a knife found its way easily to the heart of a traitor.

He looked again at the airscreen representation of

the flocker attack. The column was not exactly a knife. It was too long and thin, like some primitive projectile weapon. An arrow, or maybe . . .

An old memory surfaced.

"This has become something of a joust," Zai said.

"A joust, sir?"

"A pre-diaspora military situation. More of a ritual, really. In a joust attack, a very long kinetic-contact weapon was propelled toward the enemy by animal power."

"Sounds unpleasant, sir," Hobbes said.

"Rather." Zai allowed his mind to drift back in time. He saw the constructs battling in his grandfather's great pasture on Vada. The horses were spectacularly rendered, their flanks gathering loam as the hot afternoon went on. The brightly festooned knights rode toward each other. Their steeds' hooves drummed the ground with a rhythmic shudder that rattled the nerves like the overflight of an armored rotary wing.

The long sticks—*lances,* they were called—striking against . . .

"Hobbes," Zai said, seeing an answer. "Are you familiar with the origin of the word *shield*?" Hobbes's Utopian upbringing had provided her only patchy knowledge of ancient weapons.

"I'm afraid not, sir."

"A straightforward device, Hobbes. A two-dimensional surface used to ward off one-dimensional attacks."

"Useful, sir." Zai could see Hobbes's mind struggle to follow him.

"*Captain,*" Marx interrupted. "The first formation of flockers will reach the *Lynx* practically at full strength. More than four thousand of them! Our close-in defenses can't cope with so many at once."

"A shield, Hobbes. Prepare to fire all four photon cannon."

Marx began to protest, and Zai cut the man's sound off with a gesture. Of course—as the master pilot had been about to complain—capital weapons like the *Lynx*'s photon cannon were useless against flockers. It would be like hunting insects with artillery.

"What's the target, sir?" Hobbes asked.

"The *Lynx,*" he said.

"We're firing at . . . ?" she began. Then, even as her fingers moved to alert the gunners, understanding filled her face. "I assume we can target the heat-sink manifold directly, sir?"

"Of course, Hobbes. No need to test the energy shunts."

"We'll be ready to detach the manifold on your order, Captain."

"Exactly, Hobbes."

He turned his attention to the flailing, voiceless Master Pilot.

"Marx, get back into the foremost scout," Zai commanded, then gave the man back his voice.

"And my orders, sir?"

"Attack the Rix receiver array. With a sandcaster if you can find any alive."

The Master Pilot thought silently for a moment. Then he said, "Perhaps if there were an unexploded canister—"

"Do it," Zai commanded, and erased the man's image from the bridge.

"All cannon ready, sir. Targeting our own heat-sink array at twenty percent power."

Zai paused, wondering if there were yet another factor he hadn't considered. Perhaps he was making another idiotic mistake. He wondered if any Imperial shipmaster had opened fire on his own ship before, without self-destruction in mind.

But the war sage's words reassured him.

If you fail, fail dramatically. At least you will prove the error of your tactics to your successors.

Zai nodded; this diversion would get into the textbooks one way or another.

"Fire."

Pilot

Banished from the bridge, Marx leaped back into the forefront of battle.

He chose another scout craft, displacing a sensor officer who was flying it at one remove. She'd been running three scouts at once, coordinating their efforts through a high-level interface. The Master Pilot kicked her off, settled in, and flexed the machine's muscles. He informed all Imperial drones within ten thousand klicks that he was assuming control of them.

Marx accelerated his impromptu battle group into a cone-shaped collision formation focused upon the Rix battlecruiser. He brought the scout's fusion drive, which doubled as its primary offensive weapon, out of stealth mode. He would need some serious power.

These actions were all likely to draw the attention of

the Rix. The scout was blaring across a wide range of EM, making itself known to the enemy's battle management intelligences, human and machine. They would spot the valuable asset quickly, a drone under human command and at front-center of the *Lynx*'s satellite cloud, the position most threatening to the enemy battlecruiser. Within seconds, Marx saw distant acceleration traces deep in the Rix cloud, the plumes of hunters vectoring toward his new vessel.

In all likelihood, the master pilot would be losing his second scout of the day inside a minute. But his fingers moved confidently, drawing an ever-expanding sphere of resources into the attack.

Marx didn't expect to live long, anyway. The nearly full-strength flocker squadron was approaching the *Lynx* too fast. Pilots were nestled in the armored belly of Imperial warships, in the hope that the drones of a dying ship would fight on under human control, damaging the enemy even as their own vessel was destroyed around them. But at this high relative velocity, the flockers would plunge through the *Lynx* like barrage rockets through a cloud of steam. There would be no safety even in the pilots' armored canopies.

Death—real, absolute, nonvirtual death—was headed toward Jocim Marx at three million meters per second.

So he flew with uncharacteristic aggression. Perhaps he could shed some Rix blood on his way out.

Between his drone and the enemy battlecruiser, the master pilot spotted the distinctive shape of a Rix gravity array. The array was a simple defensive weapon. At its core was a free-floating easy gravity generator—the same device that created artificial gravity in starships, equipped with limited AI and its own reaction drive. Surrounding the generator was a host of gravity repeaters. These small devices were held in place by the easy gravity, but also shaped and controlled it. An array could create a gravity well (or hill) in any configuration, strong enough to halt or deflect enemy drones and kinetic weapons. As he closed, Marx could see more of them, forming a huge barrier before the battlecruiser, perfect protection for the receiver. The gravity array closest to Marx was spread wide, giving readings of only sixty gees, just strong enough to corral the clouds of sand still crashing through the Rix fleet.

It was the Rix device closest to Marx, and he decided to destroy it.

He ordered a nearby ramscatter drone to launch its full complement at the gravity array. The craft spun like a firework wheel, spitting hordes of tiny, stupid flechettes from its flanks, exhausting itself in seconds. As per its programming, the ramscatter drone started to pull back toward the *Lynx* for reloading, but Marx urged it forward. Perhaps he could use the expended drone as a ram. In any case, there would soon be no mothership to return home to.

Marx wondered if the captain really had any plan for defending his ship against the flockers. Zai had spoken as if he'd seen a way to escape destruction, but the captain's words had been cryptic, as usual. It was probably just an act, the necessary false confidence of command. Some morale-related edict from that long-dead sage that Zai and Hobbes were always quoting.

Well, just as long as they kept the *Lynx* together for a few more minutes, long enough for Marx to hit the Rix battlecruiser. Marx knew he was the best pilot in the Navy. Dying without putting a scratch on the enemy prime would be an unacceptable end to his career.

The flechettes slammed into the array, whipping through the hills and troughs of its gravity contours like a flight of arrows suddenly caught in a wind tunnel. Marx let them spread through the array for a few seconds, then ordered all but a dozen to self-destruct. The invisible contours of the array filled with clouds of shrapnel. The bright reflections of broken metal spread through the warped space like milk dispersing in swirling coffee. The churning shrapnel ate through the gravity repeaters, and the array's gravity-shape flopped about, then flattened into a simple sphere, a steep, defensive hill of almost a thousand gees. Marx took command of the few flechettes he had left, and targeted the sphere's center—the gravity generator itself. The remaining flechettes bolted toward it from all directions.

Normally, the tiny machines moved invisibly fast, but they climbed the steep gravity hill with eerie slowness. Marx saw one run out of reaction mass just short of its target; it became visible for a few seconds, spinning at its zenith, a pole vaulter falling short of the bar. Then it fell away.

Then another flechette fell short.

Damn, the gravity generator had reacted too quickly, shifting energy from its repeater array to a defensive posture in a few milliseconds. Had the Rix become unbeatable?

But then a flechette, favored by its initial position and relative velocity, plumbed the last dregs of its acceleration and struck the generator. The tiny drone only managed to make contact at a few hundred meters per second, but its impact had some tiny effect: The strength of the gravity hill wavered for a millisecond.

And in that opening the rest of the flechettes slammed home.

The sphere of artificial gravity convulsed once, expanding. Finally, a toy balloon inflated too far, it burst into nothingness, a wave front of easy gravitons lighting up the sensors in Marx's scout. Then space flattened itself impassively before him.

Marx took his scout drone and its growing retinue through the resulting hole in the Rix perimeter. The master pilot smiled exultantly. He was going to get his chance. He was going to do some damage.

If only Zai could hold the *Lynx* together.

"Just give me five minutes," he muttered.

Executive Officer

"Contact in four minutes, sir," Hobbes reported.

The captain's eyebrows raised a centimeter. The flockers were arriving ahead of schedule.

"They're kicking, sir," Hobbes explained. *Kick*—the increase of a rate of acceleration. "Maybe they suspect what we're up to."

"Perhaps they simply smell blood, Hobbes. Can we have separation in time?"

Hobbes refocused her attention to the heated conversations among the engineers working below. They were attempting to eject the energy-sink's main generator, to separate the *Lynx* from its own defensive manifold, which was now glowing white-hot from the point-blank pounding of the frigate's four photon cannon. The manifold was designed to be ejected, of course; warships had to shed their energy-sinks when they grew too hot from enemy fire. But usually the generator remained on the ship while the manifold was discohered, allowed to fly apart in all directions. Captain Zai's plan, however, demanded that the manifold remain intact, retaining its huge shape as the *Lynx* pulled away from it.

Therefore, the gravity generator that held all the tiny energy-sink modules in place had to leave the frigate—in one piece and still functioning.

The engineers didn't sound happy.

"Slide that bulkhead *now*!" the team leader ordered. It was Frick, the First Engineer.

Godspite, Hobbes thought. There was still an exterior bulkhead between the generator and open space.

"We're not at vacuum yet," a voice complained. "We'll depressurize like hell."

"Then strap yourselves to something and depressurize the bitch!" Frick countered.

Hobbes checked the rank-codes on the voices: Frick of course was head of engineering; the team clearing the obstructing bulkhead came from Emergency Repairs, regular Navy filling in. A chain-of-command problem.

She cut into the argument.

"This is ExO Hobbes. Blow the damn bulkhead. I repeat: Don't bother matching the vacuum, don't waste time sliding—*blow* it."

Stunned disbelief silenced both sides of the argument for a moment.

"But Hobbes," Frick responded, his line now restricted to officers' ears only. "I've got unarmored ratings down there."

Damn, Hobbes thought. The ratings had been pulled from other sections: maintenance workers, low-gee trainers, cooks. They wouldn't have been assigned armored suits. Their pressure suits could stand hard vacuum, but weren't equipped to survive an explosion.

But there wasn't time. Not to get the ratings out of danger, not even to get the captain's confirmation.

"The flockers are kicking on a steep curve. Time's up. Blow it," she ordered, her voice dry. "Blow it now."

"Does the captain—" the other team leader began.

"Now!"

The situation beacon guttered magenta in her second sight—an explosion aboard ship. A fraction of a second later, the actual shock wave of the blast rippled through the bridge.

Hobbes closed her eyes, but cruel synesthesia didn't permit escape. She could see it: low on the engineering wedge of her crew organizational chart, a row of casualty lights turned yellow. One swiftly flickered to red.

"What was that?" Zai asked.

"Separation in twenty seconds." Hobbes couldn't bring herself to say more.

"About time," Zai muttered. The captain ran far fewer diagnostic displays than his executive officer. He must not have seen the casualties yet.

The engineering teams said nothing as they completed their work. Only grunts of physical labor, the hard breathing of shock, and the background sounds of shrieking metal as the generator began to move.

When she was sure that there would be no more delays, Hobbes expended a moment to order a medical response team to the blown bulkhead. The ship would begin acceleration in a few seconds to pull itself away from the manifold, and the medtechs would have to struggle through the pitching corridors in pressure suits. The *Lynx* was about to run stealthy as well, shutting the artificial gravity and other non-essentials for the few seconds until danger passed. It would take the medtechs minutes to reach the stricken crewmen.

Another of the engineering casualty lights shifted to red. Two lives gone.

Hobbes forced her attention back to the bridge's main airscreen display. The long wedge of the *Lynx*'s primary hull slid back from the radiant circle of the energy-sink manifold, pulling back to interpose the effulgent manifold between frigate and approaching flockers. To conceal the maneuver from the flockers' sharp-eyed sensors, they were running on cold jets, spraying water from the *Lynx*'s waste tubes, using their own shit as reaction mass. The ship moved with painful slowness. The primary hull would be a mere two hundred meters out of position when the drones hit—barely its own girth.

At least Zai had his shield now, Hobbes thought somberly. Two dead, three grievously wounded, and a hull breach all before a single Rix weapon had struck the *Lynx*. But the blazing manifold now floated between the flockers and their target.

"We're ready, sir."

"Impact in ten seconds," the watch officer said.

"Well done, Hobbes."

Hobbes felt no flush of pride at the rare praise from her captain. She just hoped her sacrifice of the two young ratings would pay off.

flocker squadron

The flocker democratic intelligence noticed a change in its target.

The enemy prime was close, a hair over three seconds from contact. Absolute time was moving very slowly, however, compared with the speed of the squadron's thought. The laser pulses with which the flockers exchanged data—the connections that formed their limited compound intellect—moved almost instantly up and down the tightly spaced formation. Squadrons were often spread out over thousands of cubic kilometers, distances which slowed the mechanics of decision making. But this flocker group was so compact that thought moved at lightning speeds; the intellect had plenty of time to observe as the situation evolved over these final, luxurious seconds before impact.

Despite their quick intellect, the flockers couldn't see very well in this formation. The straight column lacked a parallax view, and the intense radiation from the enemy prime's energy-sink manifold had almost blinded the forward flockers, making the center of the manifold—where the prime must be—a dark patch against a vibrant sky.

But why was the manifold already expelling energy? Of the Rix fleet, only the battlecruiser itself could have delivered this much energy to the target, and it was more than eight million kilometers out of range. The flockers suspected that the enemy prime had fired upon its own sink. A bizarre occurrence, this early attempt at self-destruction, sufficiently strange that the squadron's hardwired tactical library offered no answers as to what it might mean.

The flocker formation felt blind, and yearned to spread wider. Without parallax, it had no multi-viewpoint reconstruction of the target to call upon.

The flockers voted. Laser flashes of debate and decision flickered up and down the line for almost a full second before they decided to expend a few more milligrams of acceleration mass per individual. This close to the enemy prime, there appeared to be little sand left to avoid, after all. The squadron broke its tight column, expanding to a few meters with width over the next half second.

With this new parallax view, the squadron's group intelligence realized that the manifold was shifting.

The glowing disk—4,500 kilometers away and rushing toward the flockers at 3,200 kps—had accelerated less than a pitiful five meters per second. But the change was detectable, the tiny push forward propagating through the energy sinks like a ripple expanding in a pond.

The flocker squadron pondered: Why would the enemy prime bother with an acceleration of such small size? Had they fired a projectile rearward, resulting in the forward push? Perhaps the Imperials had realized their own imminent death and launched a deadman drone. But after a close reading of the ripples in the blazing energy sinks, the flocker intelligence calculated that the push had been gradual.

The squadron quickly decided to expand its view

again, and a few dozen flockers shot outward at fifteen hundred gees. This burst of acceleration would drive them uselessly into the burning manifold, but in the remaining one second before impact, their sacrifice improved the squadron's view dramatically.

The flockers saw it then: The enemy prime had shrunk to a shadow of its former size.

Even against the blinding glare of the manifold, they could now see that the prime's characteristic radiation signature was greatly reduced. The easy gravitons were still coming in abundance, but the evidence of charged weapons and drive activity had disappeared. Mass readings were reduced to a hundredth of what they should be.

A half-second before the first flockers were to reach the position where their target should be, the squadron realized the truth: The energy sink manifold had been disconnected from the enemy prime.

The target had disappeared.

This was a problem.

Pilot

Master Pilot Marx found that his scout was still alive.

A Rix hunter drone had burned him seconds ago, spraying Marx's vessel with its very dirty fission drive as it flew past. The canopy had snow-crashed for a few seconds, but he was back inside now, his senses dramatically reduced.

Marx swore. He was so close to the Rix battle-cruiser. This was no time for his machine to fail. Another 150 seconds and he would be able to hit the enemy. With what exactly, he wasn't sure. His retinue of conscripted drones had been reduced to a few craft. But at this range he could see the reflective expanse of the Rix receiver array spread out before him, fragile and tempting.

So close.

He checked his craft's condition. No active sensors. The drive was out, the reaction process lost and ir-reparable. The scout's entangled communications sup-ply was damaged, and with all the error-checking the craft responded sluggishly. But he could still control it, and send light-speed orders to other drones in the vicinity.

Marx ejected his fusion drive, and jogged a small docking jet, forcing the scout drone into a tumble. His view spun for a moment, then stabilized as expert soft-ware compensated for the craft's rotation. With its ac-tive sensors offline, the scout should appear convincingly dead.

He counted his assets. A trio of expended ramscatter drones, two stealth penetrators with almost no reaction mass left, a decoy that had miraculously survived everything the Rix had thrown at it, and a careening sandcaster whose receiver had failed. The sandcaster drone was tantalizingly useless. It still had its payload, but the last order it had received before going deaf had put it in standby mode. Now it ignored Marx's pleas to launch its sand or self-destruct. He wondered if repair nanos inside the caster were working to bring it back to life.

The master pilot waited silently, watching as his tiny fleet converged upon the enemy battlecruiser. Just before shunting him from the bridge, the captain had mentioned sand. True, it was the perfect weapon against the Rix receiver array; it would spread over a wide area, and at high speed would do considerable damage. But the Rix had swept the Imperials' salvos of sand aside with their host of gravity repeater arrays, protecting the huge receiver. They had anticipated Zai's attack perfectly.

Marx and his tiny fleet were within the gravity perimeter, however. If he could only get his remaining sandcaster to respond. It was barreling toward the huge receiver array on target, but intact. The drone itself would punch through the thin mesh of the receiver, leaving a hole no more than a meter across. Useless. He needed it to explode, to spread its sand.

Marx cursed the empty ramscatters. Why did those things invariably launch *all* their flechettes? With even a single projectile, he could destroy the failed sandcaster, unleashing its payload.

Perhaps he could ram the sandcaster with one of his other craft.

The scout itself was without maneuver capability, the damaged fusion drive ejected. The decoy drone was too small, and its mass wasn't sufficient to crack the tough canisters of sand. The stealth penetrators were even smaller, with only their silent but achingly slow coldjets for movement. They couldn't ram the sandcaster at anything faster than a few meters per second. The empty ramscatter drones were Marx's only hope.

He opened up a narrowcast channel to the two ramscatters, and gave them trajectories as precise as his expert software could calculate. But these were weapons that thought in kilometers, not meters. The ramscatters themselves were not designed to ram, but to launch flechettes, and their onboard brains weren't capable of tricky flying. Marx knew he would have to fly them in himself, from the remote perspective of the scout drone, with sufficient precision to strike the meter-wide sandcaster.

With a three-millisecond light-speed delay, this was going to be tricky indeed.

Marx smiled quietly.

Truly, a task for a master pilot.

flocker squadron

The squadron intellect found itself cut in half.

True to their aim, the first few flockers had struck the gravity generator, in the center of the manifold where the enemy prime *should* have been. The generator was immediately destroyed, and the manifold began to discohere. The neat ranks of energy sinks drifted slowly away, expelling their energy in the assumption that their mothership was dead or retreating.

The radiation from the flaring manifold formed a yoke around the neck of the line of flockers. Individual flockers were moving across the threshold at the rate of five per microsecond; the whole five-kilometer line would be through in under a millisecond. Communication between the drones that had flown through the manifold and those that hadn't was swamped by noise, and the drones still on the near side of the manifold began to have decision-making difficulties. The squadron's democratic intelligence crumbled as its constituent drones disappeared, each new quorum vanishing into the void microseconds after being established.

The rear end of the squadron was paralyzed with indecision; the scenario was changing far too quickly.

On the other side of the blazing manifold, the foremost flockers had quickly spotted the missing enemy warship, and declared themselves to be their own decision-making entity. The *Lynx* was a bare two hundred meters away from the manifold's crumbling center. The flockers' maximum acceleration was three thousand gees. From a standstill, they could have hit the target almost instantly. But they were flying past the enemy prime too quickly. With a relative velocity of more than one percent of the speed of light, no craft the size of a flocker would have sufficient reaction mass to reverse its course.

The forward decision-entity sent desperate messages back through the manifold, giving the squadron the enemy prime's new position. But the signals were overwhelmed by the radiation spewing from the abandoned energy sinks, and within a thousandth of a second, three thousand more flockers hurtled uselessly past the *Lynx*.

Finally, with a firm majority in possession of the facts, the growing farside squadron intellect solved the communications puzzle, firing a coordinated set of message beams that reached the last few hundred flockers just in time.

Most of these drones had no chance to reach the enemy prime, even accelerating at three thousand gees, but a few of those who had spread out to provide parallax found a vector, and barreled through the dissipating manifold toward their target.

Most were vaporized by the still seething energies of the manifold, or missed, their reaction systems destroyed before they could line up on target. But seven of the small machines slipped through random dark spots in the manifold, and hurtled—burned, blinded, all but dead—into the belly of the *Lynx*.

Pilot

Master Pilot Marx glared at the images in his second sight, his frustration growing.

He had shifted his viewpoint to one of the ramscatter drones, which was currently hurtling toward the sandcaster. The collision course looked good, but the view left everything to be desired.

The perspective was cobbled together using data from all over Marx's little fleet. The dim senses of the ramscatter itself were on passive mode to keep the Rix from spotting it. The other drones were bathing the sandcaster in active sensory pulses, to help keep their sister craft on track. Marx's scout drone, his only craft with decent sensors, added its passive view from 5,000 kilometers distance. The light-speed delays afflicting all this data ranged between two and five milliseconds, more than enough to muddle things when attempting a hundred-meter-per-second collision between two tiny spacecraft.

The *Lynx*'s onboard expert software was supposedly compensating for the delays, which varied continuously as the drones accelerated. But the view looked wrong to Marx.

Synesthesia was shaky. Not with the jittering frame of a helmet camera, but with a shimmer, like the shudders that afflict eyes that have stayed awake all night and are facing the morning sun. Marx felt hung over and queasy in the ramscatter's viewpoint, unsure of reality. He wished he could use active sensors, but if the scout gave off any EM this close to the battlecruiser, the Rix would target it in seconds.

Marx swallowed, feeling dizzy. His scout spun, tumbling as it approached the battlecruiser. He checked the speed of the rotation. That was it: The spin of the scout matched the period of the screen jitter.

Marx swore. He had intentionally tumbled the scout to make it appear dead. Now he was paying for it with this sickening, shifting second vision. Why wasn't the damned expert software compensating? Perhaps the *Lynx*'s shared processors were simply overwhelmed.

Should he risk righting the scout? A quick blast from a docking jet would do the trick. But any activity from the large scout craft would draw the Rix's attention, and it was his only link to the front line.

Marx ordered himself to stop whining. He had once flown a craft the size of a fingernail in a raging hailstorm, and on another occasion had lost all depth perception in a rotary wing dogfight with a half-second roundtrip delay. This jittering viewpoint was nothing. He synchronized his breathing to the phasing blur of his canopy, and forced himself to ignore the growing nausea deep in his stomach.

The ramscatter drone shot toward its target. At least the bulbous surfaces of the sandcaster provided a clear image. Marx piloted the little drone in short bursts, trying not to alert the Rix to its presence.

The trajectory felt right. It looked as if he was lined up on the sandcaster, ready to burst the fat canisters.

Marx's view improved as he closed. He could just make out the cross-hatching of the fragmentation pattern.

Five seconds to impact.

Suddenly, a flare of projectile fire blazed in his peripheral vision. The canopy view twisted, pulling apart into two images as if his eyes were going crossed.

In the dizzying maelstrom of the disintegrating view, Marx saw new enemy craft: several blackbody monitor drones. Driveless and silent, they had been drifting along with the battlecruiser, utterly invisible until now. They spewed depleted uranium slugs—at a rate of ten thousand per minute, his software estimated—at the ramscatters.

His view whirled. All his drones with active sensors had been destroyed. Marx fought to control the ramming ship, but nothing on the canopy's screens made sense. With an effort of will, he pulled his hands from the control surface, searching for meaning in the storm of light before him.

Suddenly, a fist seemed to strike him in the stomach. A decompression alarm sounded!

The *Lynx* was taking hits. The flockers were here.

Gravity in the canopy spun for a moment, a further disorientation. Acid filled his throat. The disjunction between visuals and his inner ear was finally too great.

Marx pitched forward in his canopy, and vomited between his knees.

He looked up, bile still in his mouth, and saw that he had missed. His ramscatter drone had flown past the sandcaster.

Marx struggled to bring it around for another pass, but the long, hard acceleration revealed it to the Rix monitor drones, which raked it with fire.

His ramscatters were destroyed, and Marx's synesthesia view of the distant battle dimmed to shadows and extrapolations.

Then a host of explosions rolled through the *Lynx,* and Marx realized that they were all dead.

Executive Officer

Katherie Hobbes saw the collision icon go bright orange, but the sound of the klaxon hadn't time to reach her before the shock waves struck.

Her status board flared, red sweeping up through the decks as the flockers plowed through hullalloy and hypercarbon like paper. The shriek of decompression came from a dozen audio channels.

At one percent light speed, being rammed was as good as being railgunned.

"Shit," Hobbes said.

It would take her days of careful reconstruction to determine exactly what happened over the next few seconds.

* * *

The first flocker in the pack had been melted into an irregular blob by the blazing energy-sink manifold. Having lost its penetration shape, it pancaked against the warship's hull, its diameter expanding to a half-meter as it punched through the three outer bulkheads. The force of its entry into Gunnery Hardpoint Four hit the crewmen there like a compression bomb, imploding their pressure suits, shattering every non-metal object into shards. The wide entry hole sucked out most of the air in the hardpoint before the sprays of sealant foam could do their work. Hardpoint Four housed a highly volatile meson-beam emitter, and was armored on all sides to protect the *Lynx* in case the weapon ever blew. The flocker, its momentum exhausted, flattened itself against the next bulkhead, never exiting the hardpoint.

Between the massive shock wave and decompression, none of the seven crew was suitable for reanimation.

The next flocker, which struck the *Lynx* four nanoseconds later, had maintained its bullet shape through the manifold. Its small entry hole was sealed without much decompression, and it plunged through lower decks twenty-six through -eight on a diagonal path. It destroyed several burn beds in a temporary sickbay, and cut through a section of synesthesia processing hardware, tearing out a fist-width of optical circuitry sixty meters long, drawing a geyser of powdered glass and phosphorus behind itself through a long vertical access hallway. The cloud of burning glass blinded four members of an emergency repair team and one data analyst, and caused lung damage to a dozen other crew scattered along the hallway. The drone emerged from the frigate's port dorsal sensor array.

The *Lynx*'s sensors were not appreciably reduced, but the frigate's processors were cut by twenty percent. All its AI nodes became slower, its synesthesia grainier, its weapons dumber.

Three flockers in close tandem struck the turbine that powered the *Lynx*'s railguns. This dense coil of super-conducting wire was sufficient to stop one of the drones cold, sending a deep shudder through the ship. The other two were deflected sternward, tumbling through a full magazine of minesweeper drones. The drones were armed with fragmentation canisters, and a chain reaction of explosions rocked the drone bay. The magazine was shielded to prevent such a calamity from spreading throughout the ship, but the two flock-ers passed out of the magazine and drew the explosions after them, severely damaging the drone launch rail.

They careened through the hullalloy-armored drone bay, and finally exited the *Lynx* through the frigate's open launch doors at a much reduced speed. They would have had sufficient reaction mass remaining to turn and attack the ship again, but neither had survived the pummeling with its intelligence intact.

Another flocker punched through the belly-side armor plate and entered the main damage control room, where Ensign Trevor San had just helped to eject the energy-sink manifold. She was watching as it began to discohere when the drone tore through her from foot to head, pulping her organs and robbing her of immortal-ity. Her crewmates were sprayed with blood, but it took them long seconds to realize which of them had been hit. Ensign San had practically disappeared. The drone then passed through several storage decks, destroying medical supplies and stowed personal effects, then drove straight into the core of the *Lynx*'s singularity generator, which was running at high-active level. The pseudo black hole swallowed the flocker without so much as a tremor registering on its monitors.

Hobbes later calculated the chances of such a hit at several-thousand-to-one against, and noted that nothing so bizarrely exact had ever been recorded on an Imperial warship.

The last flocker passed through the belly-side waste tanks, which had been brought to high pressure to propel the *Lynx* silently out of harm's way. The pressure of the unrecycled water was over five hundred atmospheres, dense enough to slow the flocker considerably. But the drone's reaction drive was still active, and it managed to pass through the tanks, trailing a stream of waste water that filled the adjacent bacterial recycling chamber in ten seconds. The processing chief, Samuel Vries, was knocked unconscious by the jet of water and drowned before rescue could come. The *Lynx* was left without a functional water-recycling system for days, and three decks smelled noticeably for a long time. Vries was eventually rewarded with immortality, and continued his researches into human/bacterial interactions in small closed environments, but at a far less practical level of application.

The much slowed flocker limped through a few more bulkheads, still pursued by dirty water, befouling a long column of crew cabins before it was stopped by the armored hull on the dorsal side. It was the only flocker to survive passage through the blazing manifold and the ship with its intelligence intact. After it came to a halt, the drone was still cogent enough to release a metal-eating virus into the *Lynx*'s hull that went undetected for some time.

Then, it attacked a marine private as he ran to foamseal shut the sudden geyser of waste water that marked its passage. The drone had only its weak signaling laser as a weapon, and went for his eyes. The man was in full battle armor, however, his face shielded by a reflective visor. He stared for a confused moment at the glittering drone, this tiny alien invader still valiantly attempting to trouble its enemies. Then he smashed the half-dead flocker with his servo-assisted fist, and it expired on the spot.

The *Lynx* had survived.

Data Analyst

Chaos struck the Data Analysis station without warning.

Ensign Amanda Tyre's vision had been far away, following the progress of the foremost scout drone. The drone was one minute from its closest approach to the enemy battlecruiser. Master Pilot Marx was in control, struggling to perform some wild maneuver, an indirect attack on the Rix warship that only he understood completely. Tyre had asked what he was up to, but he'd only grunted, too focused on piloting to answer.

She watched Marx's data stream—the images of the

battlecruiser being gathered by his drone. It was the best intelligence they'd received so far on the enemy warship. Tyre searched for weaknesses, clues to its configuration, signs that anything the *Lynx* had thrown at it had managed to do any damage.

Damn. Marx was so close, yet the images were blurry, not much better than distant transluminal returns. Ensign Tyre wished he would go to active sensors. Of course, the scout wouldn't last long once he did. The battlecruiser's close-in defenses looked pretty solid.

Tyre gestured, bringing her second sight closer to the blackbody monitor drones that had just appeared and begun firing on some of Marx's subservient drones. The blackbodies were normally almost invisible, but against the sunlit background of the receiver array she could make out several more of them. The three that had opened fire had turned up at just the right place; either the Rix had guessed lucky or had enough of them to cover every approach. She wondered how many of the dark, silent monitors coasted in front of the Rix warship.

She felt the hands of her superior on her shoulders. Kax stood right behind her seat. There were five crew crowded into the tight confines of Data Analysis. In battle configuration, their usually large space had been annexed by the two adjacent gunnery stations. Kax's hands clenched as the *Lynx* maneuvered, its slow cold-jets pushing them with the sway of an oceangoing vessel.

"You thinking what I'm thinking?" Kax asked.

She nodded. "They've configured for heavy defense, sir."

"See if you can get a count. The captain will want to

know how many blackbodies are out there before the *Lynx* gets too much closer."

"Yes, sir, but I'll bet you right now there's at least a hundred."

"A *hundred*?"

"If you take a—"

Suddenly, a rush of noise exploded through the room. A searing wind struck Tyre, throwing her from her webbing to the floor. Her exposed skin—hands and cheeks—were being scoured. Her mouth and eyes clenched instinctively shut. Her ears popped as the air pressure plummeted.

A burning sound reached her ears through the thin air, and she felt heat on her hands and face.

Ensign Amanda Tyre, like every recruit to the Navy, had gone through dozens of decompression drills. She knew well the expansion of the chest, the screaming pain of ears and eyes. But this was her first time to experience the event in battle.

It felt as if some demon were astride her, crushing the breath from her body. Tyre remembered the symbol on the academy's decompression drill room door: the Asphyx, the spirit that visits the dying to steal their last breath. Through the haze of synesthesia, she had a sudden vision of the Asphyx—the blank eyes, the yawning mouth hungry for her life.

Then she command-gestured, clearing her data mask of all synesthesia, and saw that it was Kax's face before her. He had fallen to the deck next to her. But even in primary vision, his face remained horrifying, burned and bleeding, the flesh peeling from it as if stripped by hungry insects.

"Glass," he said, his voice ravaged.

Tyre rolled out from under him. As her hands sought

purchase on the tilting deck, she felt the grit of tiny bits of broken glass cutting into her palms. Her pressure uniform was torn and felt invaded with some sharp presence, like the insinuating fingers of fiberglass against the skin.

The other three in the DA room were stunned, their faces and arms cut with thousands of tiny nicks. The phosphorus fire had burned itself out too quickly to hurt them.

Rating Rogers, still in his webbing, coughed as he spoke.

"It's glass. From the optical core next door." He pointed to the access tube, from which coiled a bright, heavy mist, half vapor and half dust. Of course. Data Analysis was adjacent to one of the *Lynx*'s processing towers, a column of dense optical silicon and phosphorus. Tyre hadn't been following the Lynx's defensive status, so she brought up the diagnostic channel in synesthesia. A number of projectiles had plunged through the vessel.

That explained the momentary blaze. The quantum computers of the *Lynx* used phosphorus atoms suspended in silicon as q-bits. Free, the phosphorus was flammable, even in what little oxygen there'd been for the agonizing seconds of decompression.

Tyre covered her mouth with a loose flap of uniform to ward off the glass vapor hanging in the air, looked again to Kax.

His eyes were clenched shut and bleeding. He'd been the only one in the station without full-strength headsups covering his upper face. And his body had shielded hers from the blast of glass and burning phosphorus.

"Medical, medical," Tyre said, her voice gritty and

plaintive from the glass dust she'd inhaled. "We need major medical in DA Station One, deck fourteen."

She heard the background murmur of other stations begging for medical assistance.

Data Master Kax reached out a bloody hand and clenched Tyre's ankle, coughing. She knelt beside him.

"Don't try to talk, sir," she said.

"The blackbodies, Tyre. Keep looking," he managed.

She glanced around at her crewmates, realizing that the *Lynx* was still in battle. With Kax out, she was in command now. The data from Master Pilot Marx's scout was invaluable, and he was far too busy flying to grasp its tactical implications.

"Rogers, try to help the Data Master," she commanded. "You two: Back to your stations."

Still in shock, her crewmates moved numbly to follow her orders. Tyre sank into her webbing, and flipped back to second sight. She gestured with bloody hands, and adopted the scout drone's viewpoint again.

Master Pilot Marx was under fire.

Pilot

Marx discovered that he was still alive.

A small cleaning robot moved beneath his feet, sucking up the thin, acid bile on the floor with a gurgling sound that set his stomach flopping again. His hands were shaking, and his ears rang from some nearby decompression.

The *Lynx* had been hit all right. But somehow Zai had kept them alive. The strike certainly hadn't numbered five thousand flockers. It had sounded like only ten or so. Marx scanned the icons of internal diagnostics. There were no more than twenty crewmen dead. He turned his eyes from the display before he could recognize any names. Later.

What mattered most was that Marx's control hardware—the translight array that connected him with the drone complement—was still functional. He could still see from the scout drone's perspective, if only fuzzily. He checked the clock. Another thirty seconds remained before his foremost drones passed the Rix battlecruiser and became irrelevant to the battle.

There was still a chance.

But the question remained: How to disintegrate the dead sandcaster?

Marx considered his remaining assets. Only four drones were left inside the Rix defenses that could respond to his orders. The scout itself, tumbling with no reaction drive. The two stealth penetrators, smaller than dribble-hoop balls. And the decoy, weaponless. And if any of them switched on active sensors or accelerated noticeably, the Rix monitor drones would shred it within seconds. He could see the sentinels now as the scout neared the hot background of the receiver array: rank after rank of blackbody monitor drones, dark spots against its reflective surface.

Good god, Marx thought. Other than a few thousand flockers and hunter drones, the battlecruiser's drone complement had been committed almost entirely to defensive weaponry. The Rix captain had prioritized the receiver array above everything else.

He shook his head. The *Lynx* had never had a chance.

Looking at the ranks of fearsome monitors, Marx envied their firepower. If he could just take over a few of the blackbody drones and turn their weapons back on the receiver . . .

Then the master pilot realized what he had to do.

It was simplicity itself.

He watched the trajectories of his four drones as they converged, growing nearer to each other as they drifted toward the Rix battlecruiser. The decoy was in front. The little drone was designed to burst a wide range of EM every few minutes, drawing fire away from more vital targets. When it wasn't screaming, it was stealthy, with passive sensors and line-of-sight transmission. Marx had kept the decoy silent so far, but now he saw what to do with it.

The stealth drones were the only thing he could move without detection. They were equipped with coldjets, slow but radiation-silent. He eased one alongside the decoy drone, bringing the two into soft contact. His view might be blurry and vague, but at under ten meters per second, Marx could have rammed a hummingbird.

The master pilot shoved the decoy with the stealth drone, pushed it on a new vector toward the sandcaster. He cursed, pushing the plodding coldjets to their maximums. In another twenty seconds his little formation would be hurtling uselessly past the battlecruiser.

Marx waited until the decoy was a bare kilometer from the sandcaster, then fired its reaction drive. It barreled in toward the sandcaster drone in decoy mode, screaming bloody murder.

Suddenly, Marx could see.

The decoy was flooding the area with EM, painting everything within light-seconds across the whole spectrum. To the Rix, it must have seemed as if a fleet of drones had popped up from nowhere.

The blackbody monitors wasted no time responding. Ripples of their slugs arced beautifully across space, lit like tracer bullets by the decoy's sensory howl. The rain of slugs swept across the stealth penetrator first, then found the decoy, and things were dark for a moment. But seconds later Marx saw the blast of the sandcaster being hit, pulped, shredded by the depleted uranium slugs.

"Perfect," he whispered as a sequence of explosions flared in synesthesia. The blinded sandcaster was still loaded with reaction mass! The drone blazed with the dirty fuel of its self-propelling canisters.

It popped again and again like a sackful of fragmentation grenades.

The Rix had done Marx's work for him.

The sand cloud expanded into a huge, misshapen ball, a time-lapse amoeba festooned with reaching pseudopods. It was almost 4,000 kilometers across when it struck the receiver array, at a relative velocity of 3,000 klicks per second. The hail of slugs had also imparted lateral velocity to the cloud, and it swept across the array like a sirocco.

Marx switched on his scout's active sensors, letting the *Lynx*'s computers record the damage in maximum detail. He leaned back to savor the light show, the vast receiver array flickering from end to end, a mica desert struck by the morning sun.

The huge object began to fold, a giant piece of fabric twisting in the wind.

Then fire from the blackbody drones found the pulsing scout, and Marx's view snapped to dead-channel blue.

He brought up Hobbes's line.

"Master Pilot reporting mission accomplished," he said. "The Rix receiver array has been destroyed."

Data Analyst

Tyre prioritized Marx's signal, recording at maximum resolution.

Finally, a good look at the enemy battlecruiser.

It only lasted a few seconds. The projectile fire from a dozen blackbodies raked across Marx's forward drones, tearing them to pieces. The sand canister exploded. Tyre watched with her mouth agape as the sand tore across the Rix receiver array.

"He got it!" she cried.

Then the arc of fire moved inexorably toward the scout drone itself. In the seconds before the signal was extinguished, the tearing megastructure caught the light of the Legis sun, and an awesome sight was revealed. Ensign Tyre's ragged breath halted as she took it in.

She had assumed that Marx's drones had hit a concentration of blackbodies, a random clumping of firepower. Even the largest Rix ships only traveled with a few dozens of the blackbody monitors; the heavy-metal ammunition they carried was bulky, they were difficult to maintain, and were primarily a defensive weapon.

But revealed against the bright background of the crumpling array was a host of monitors. They stretched across its shining expanse in a vast, hexagonal pattern.

Hundreds of them.

Then synesthesia went dark; Marx's drone had finally died.

Ensign Tyre heard a gurgle from Data Master Kax at her feet, but she ignored the grim sound. Tyre rewound the scout's viewpoint stream a few seconds, and froze it on a frame in which the Legis sun had revealed the monitor drones.

Ensign Tyre blinked as she looked at them.

They were short-range weapons, primarily for defense. They had no drives and little intelligence, just lots and lots of projectile firepower. If a small warship like the *Lynx* were to stumble amongst hundreds of them, it would be torn to pieces by their collective kinetic attack.

And the *Lynx* was headed straight for the battlecruiser and into the intervening field of blackbodies, unaware of their deadly, silent presence.

She had to alert the captain.

Tyre opened a line to Hobbes. The executive officer did not immediately respond; there were probably a dozen crew of superior rank clamoring for her attention.

Tyre waited, the seconds ticking away, the *Lynx* hurtling toward the deadly blackbody drones, three thousand kilometers closer every second.

"Priority, priority."

The priority icon appeared before her in second sight. The icon was for "extreme emergencies" only, a term that held awesome power here in Data Analysis. Kax had never used it. Tyre had certainly never thought to invoke it herself; it was the data master's prerogative. And if she were wrong about what the vast array of drones meant, misuse of the priority icon in battle would be a terrible mark against her forever.

Tyre stared at the frozen image again. *Hundreds of them*, she reminded herself. The data were unambiguous.

She switched to the diagnostic channel again. There were casualties all across the ship, hull and equipment damage, even fatalities. It could be minutes before Hobbes responded to a lowly ensign.

Tyre put out her trembling and bloody hand to the icon.

Not authorized, the icon blinked.

She swore. Kax was still alive and on-station. As far as the *Lynx* was concerned, he was still in command, and was the only analyst qualified to make this judgment. Tyre cleared her second sight and looked down to where Rogers cradled the data master's head. Kax seemed hardly to have a face at all. For a fleeting moment, she wondered if he still had second sight, even though his eyes were destroyed.

There wasn't time to ask. Kax could hardly breathe; he couldn't be thinking clearly with an injury like that.

"Rogers," she ordered. "Pull the data master out of the room."

"What?"

"Pick him up and drag him from the room. Get him off the station." Tyre said it with all the force she could manage. Her ragged voice gave the words an authority she didn't feel.

Rogers hesitated, looking at the other two ratings.

"Rogers! The *Lynx* won't recognize my rank with him in here."

"But there's more glass out—"

"Do it!"

Rogers jumped, then stooped to gingerly lift the wounded Kax. He pulled the bloody man toward the doorway, his shredded uniform scraping across the glass and out into the access shaft.

Tyre breathed deep, and touched the priority icon again.

"Please listen," she murmured to herself.

The icon shifted in the air, folding into a bright point, and requested her missive. She attached the compiled frame showing the host of blackbody drones and gestured the Send command.

A few seconds later, Hobbes's voice responded.

"My god," the ExO said. Tyre breathed a sigh of relief at the woman's tone. At least Hobbes understood.

"Where the hell's Kax?"

"Injured. Blind, I think."

"Shit. Get up to the captain's planning room, then," the Executive Officer ordered. "And get ready to explain this."

"Aye, aye."

"We'll have to accelerate immediately. We'll lose the manifold for good," Hobbes continued, talking half to herself. "You better be on the mark with this, Tyre."

Tyre swallowed as she pulled herself from the webbing.

If she was wrong, her career was ruined. If she was right, the *Lynx* was in very deep trouble.

Senator

They looked up at her with startled expressions, curious and wary. Their eyes reflected the hovering globe that lit her path, igniting with the crimson flash of night predators.

Nara Oxham wondered if small rodents were ever let loose in the Diamond Palace's darkened halls, entertainment for the Emperor's pets. Of course, it seemed unlikely that risen animals would make very aggressive hunters. As she passed, the felines remained piled together on the low window couch, regally watchful, but as soporific as fat old toms. Perhaps like dead humans they were content to contemplate black paintings and go on endless pilgrimages. Nara could see the ridges of the symbiant along the felines' spines, payment for the cruelty their kind had suffered during the Holy Experiments.

They were dead things, she reminded herself.

"Senator."

The inhuman voice came out of darkness, and Oxham started.

"My apologies, Senator Oxham." The representative from the Plague Axis stepped to the edge of her globe's light, but remained politely distant. "My biosuit allows me a certain level of night vision; I had forgotten you couldn't see me."

The slight hiss of the biosuit's filters was barely audible in the silent hallway. Nara tried not to imagine the representative's diseases straining to escape, to infect her, to propagate across the human species.

"So you can see in the dark? Not unlike the sovereign's house pets," she said, gesturing at the flashing eyes.

There was a pause. Had her insult found its mark? Through the opaque faceplate, the representative's expression was invisible. They had sat on the War Council together for weeks now, but Nara didn't even know if the thing inside the suit was male or female.

Whatever it was, it had cast the deciding vote in favor of the Emperor's genocide.

"Except that those cats will live forever, Nara Oxham. I shall not."

The people of the Plague Axis could not take the symbiant, which resisted all disease and physical defect as part of its cure for death. For that reason Oxham and her party had counted the Axis on the side of the living, allies against the Emperor. It hadn't worked out that way.

Oxham shrugged. "Neither shall I." She turned and walked toward the council chamber.

"Senator?" the representative called softly.

"The sovereign requests we attend him," she answered without stopping.

The soft, pearly floor of the council chamber glowed coolly in the Diamond Palace's night. The dead never liked bright rooms at any time, but the lighting in gray places always varied slowly, reflecting daily and seasonal shifts, even equinoctial precession on more eccentric planets.

Senator Oxham and the Plague Axis representative

were the last of the nine counselors to arrive. The dead admiral hardly waited for them to settle before beginning her speech.

"There is news from Legis."

Nara closed her eyes and took a deep breath, then forced herself to watch.

The airscreen filled with a familiar schematic, the decelerating Rix battlecruiser arcing toward Legis, the hook-shaped path of the *Lynx* darting out to engage it as far from the planet as possible. At this system-sized scale, the two trajectories were touching now.

Nara's sudden dose of apathy would take some time to wear off, so she watched the faces of her colleagues through the translucent image. The other pink senators, Federalist and Utopian, and the plutocrat Ax Milnk wore harried and sleepless looks. Even the Loyalist Henders looked nervous, unready to learn that he had voted for mass murder. The faces of three dead members of the War Council were like stone. The admiral spoke evenly, the general sat at attention, the risen sovereign stared into the middle distance over Nara's head.

She could feel nothing, but a lifetime spent comparing what eyes and empathy told her had given Nara an instinct for reading bodies and faces. Even with her ability dampened, the aspects of the dead men and woman betrayed disquiet.

Something had gone wrong.

"The *Lynx* and the Rix engaged some thirty minutes ago," the dead admiral continued. "At last report, the two ships have reached second contact."

Nara's jaw tightened. First contact was when the outer drone clouds overlapped, with shots fired between them; second contact meant that the primaries, the *Lynx* and the Rix warship proper, had engaged each other's drones. Beginning with second contact, human lives were lost.

"The *Lynx* has suffered casualties, but has thus far managed to survive."

Any of those casualties might be Laurent, Nara thought, but surely the admiral would mention it if the ship's captain was dead.

"More importantly, the *Lynx*'s drones have succeeded in the primary goal of the attack, destroying the Rix receiver array. At this point, it seems that the Legis mind will remain isolated, without further action on our part."

The admiral was silent for a moment, letting the news sink in.

Nara saw her own hesitation on the other living counselors' faces: None of them believed it yet. They were waiting for some awful reversal in the admiral's statement. But the dead woman's silence lengthened, and they realized it was true. There was no reason to obliterate the compound mind. There would be no EMP attack, no hundred million dead.

Laurent had saved them all.

The War Council stirred all at once, like people waking from a nightmare. The Loyalist Henders put his head in his hands, an exhausted and undisguised gesture, and even the Plague Axis representative's biosuit slumped with what had to be relief. The other senators and Milnk turned to Nara Oxham, daring to show their respect.

Nara let nothing she felt reach her face. For her, more than any of them, this had been personal. She would allow herself emotions later.

"We are happy with this victory, of course," the Emperor said.

He was lying, Nara was certain. She had seen it in him, and in his dead soldiers. They had wanted Zai to fail.

"And more important than any victory, we rest assured that this council was ready to make the necessary sacrifice." For the first time ever, Nara saw the sovereign's praise fall flat. None of the living members had been ready to watch what the War Council had voted for.

The Emperor had lost something here.

"We must congratulate this council for having made the right decision, however pleased we are it didn't come to action." There was an edge in his voice. Anyone could hear it.

Nara Oxham had grown to know the Emperor, this young-looking undead man, and to understand his fixation with the Rix; their compound minds were a counter-god to his own false divinity. He was as jealous as any petty deity, and Nara Oxham was a politician who understood egomania, no matter how grossly exaggerated.

But over the last few days, she had seen fear in him, not hatred. What could terrify the Emperor of Eighty Worlds so much that only genocide would suffice?

"We owe Zai a debt," the Plague representative said.

There were nods of agreement. The sovereign turned to look at the biosuit, the movement of his head as slow as some ancient lizard.

"We have already elevated him," the Emperor said coldly. "And pardoned him after our sister's death. Perhaps it was *his* debt to pay."

"Still, Majesty," the Utopian Senator said, "an entire world has been saved from grievous harm."

"Indeed," the Federalist said.

"I agree," Ax Milnk added.

"May I remind you of the hundred-year rule?" the sovereign said. "None of us can speak of what Zai prevented. Not for a century."

"But he has still won a great victory," the Plague representative said. "An auspicious beginning to this war."

Nara almost let herself smile. For the first time since the council was formed, the others dared to contradict the Emperor. Not only Zai had won this battle, the living members of the War Council had as well.

But the dead admiral interrupted.

"We cannot publicly declare Zai's victory yet. Third contact will come in another twenty minutes. It seems unlikely the *Lynx* will survive."

Nara swallowed. Third contact was when the two primaries engaged directly, ship-to-ship, without their drones between them.

"Why would there be a third contact, Admiral?" she asked. "With the array destroyed, surely the *Lynx* will make its escape. It's smaller, faster."

The admiral gestured, and the airscreen image zoomed. Vector lines were added, arcing through intersections like crossed scimitars.

"Captain Zai made his attack at a high relative velocity, to get his drones past the Rix defenses and at the array. At this point, the two ships are moving toward each other too fast for the *Lynx* to make much of an escape. In the service of the Emperor and this council, Zai has sealed his own fate."

"In war, there are always sacrifices," the Emperor sighed.

Nara forced herself not to utter the cry she felt building. The elation of a few moments ago drained away, her heart turning cold. One way or another, these dead men would have their revenge against Laurent. It was as if the Emperor himself had decreed the law of inertia, just to spite Zai's heroism and see him killed.

She was utterly selfish, Nara tried to tell herself, to think only of one man when millions had been saved, when the *Lynx* carried three hundred.

But for Nara, the battle was lost if Laurent wasn't coming home.

Commando

The call from Alexander eventually came.

The few phones that h_rd had spared dissection rang in unison, then beeped out a simple coded sequence from the onetime pad she shared with Alexander. The battle in space had gone badly, and her assistance was required. The entanglement facility had to be liberated for the compound mind's use.

The call hadn't awakened Rana, h_rd realized with bittersweet relief. The few novels and plays she'd read suggested that the farewell rituals of Imperial humanity and those of the Rix were incompatible. And this would be a deep good-bye. Either of them, perhaps both, might die in the next ten hours.

H_rd pulled herself closer to the woman's soft, warm body. How humanity raged against its environment, she thought, each body demanding its own pocket of heat, and at a temperature so perversely exact. Five degrees in either direction spelled death. So prideful, yet so fragile.

The rattle in Rana's breathing sounded worse. The rhythm was even, but h_rd detected the slightest increase of its tempo from a few hours ago. The woman's breath quickened as the volume of her functioning lung decreased. The pulsatile nature of her lover's physiology always fascinated h_rd. The rhythms of circulation, breath, menstruation, and sleep had an alien grandeur, like the ancient symmetries expressed in the brief lives of particles or in the stately motions of planets. H_rd was Rix: her heart a screw, her lungs continuous filters, her ovaries in cold storage back on her home orbital. And those cycles of the Rix body that had escaped Upgrade could be modulated as easily as the speed of an engine. But the interlocking patterns that constituted Rana Harter's aliveness seemed sovereign as nature; h_rd could not imagine them simply winding down into awful, inescapable silence.

Of course, the Rixwoman knew how to save her lover, understood—at least abstractly—the price of the delicate and precious life beside her. She could always surrender to the Imperials, giving Rana to their doctors, and herself to the military. H_rd pondered what it would be like to abandon Alexander at this critical moment. Despite what the Empire called the Rix, they were no cult; members were free to rejoin humanity. Over the last few centuries, a dozen or so even had.

But h_rd would find no freedom in Imperial hands. The Risen Empire had never taken a Rix prisoner of war, unless a few frozen and decompressed bodies plucked from hard space were counted. They would interrogate her, mindsweep her, test her mercilessly, and finally dissect the prostheses that she considered unambiguously to be herself.

And although they would save Rana Harter's body, they had proven themselves unfit wardens of her soul.

For twenty-seven years, their clumsy system of wealth distribution had left Rana to her own devices. A borderline depressive, fearful and indecisive, naive in some ways and magnificently savant in others, Rana was a raw, rare, defenseless gem. But they had let her drift, a cog in the Imperial machine. They had exploited what little of her abilities required no training, and given nothing in return. Both systems of the Eighty Worlds—the hierarchy of the Empire and the wild purity of the capital—had one appetite in common: They fed on the weak. The help Rana needed was simple, a mere dopamine adjustment, and the manic depression that had scarred her life had been easily vanquished. But such treatment wasn't available to the class she had been born into. She was the victim of the most parochial of economic arrangements.

Their barbarism wasn't even efficient. With her abilities, she would have been a valuable asset. But the Imperials imagined it cheaper and easier to let her suffer.

When h_rd's internal tirade ended, she allowed herself a rueful smile. Who was she to take the Empire to task? She had kidnapped this woman, drugged her, put her in harm's way.

Taken Rana to her death.

But at least she had understood the clever, marvelous thing that Rana Harter was.

H_rd pressed her lips gingerly to the back of Rana's neck, smelled the warm, human complexity of her. Then the commando crept from bed.

Executive Officer

A gravity ghost drifted through the command bridge. The shudder described a textbook bell curve, slowly building and receding as if some ancient steam train were rumbling past.

No one spoke until the event was over. The *Lynx* was accelerating at eighteen gees away from the battlecruiser, pushing as hard as its gravity generators could compensate for. The assembled officers knew that if the generators suddenly failed, they would all be unconscious in seconds, crushed by their own suddenly tremendous weight. The *Lynx*'s AI would recognize the problem and shut its engines down automatically, but by then there would be scores of casualties.

Hobbes cleared her throat as the last tendrils of the event loosened their grip, interrupting the officers' consideration of the tenuous technologies that stood between them and sudden disaster.

"Are we certain that all these blackbodies are the same? Perhaps those that fired on the master pilot aren't representative of the whole," she said.

Floating in the command bridge airscreen were the images recorded by Master Pilot Marx's remote scout. The first time the *Lynx*'s officers had watched the destruction of the huge receiver array, they'd cheered.

But now the image was paused, the wild storm of sand frozen halfway in its march across the dish. In this single frame, the reflected light of the Legis sun was caught in the dying array; against the bright backdrop, the ranks of blackbody monitors were clearly evident.

Data Analysis had counted 473 of them, and had extrapolated another 49. That made 522. Two to the ninth power: a typical Rix complement.

But not for monitor drones. For the powerful slug-throwers, it was far more than expected; the *Lynx* had been unknowingly hurtling toward a grinder.

"As near as we can tell, the blackbody shapes are the same throughout the complement," Ensign Tyre said softly. Hobbes realized that this was Tyre's first time on the command bridge. The ensign was the ranking data analyst now, Data Master Kax having been blinded in the flocker attack. Tyre was speaking in a slow and careful voice, almost timidly, but she had so far answered every question clearly.

"This hump on the dorsal side is the ammo supply," Tyre continued, windowing an individual blackbody drone. "If any of these drones were fitted for minesweeping or decoy work, that hump would be absent."

"And they've all got it," Hobbes finished flatly.

Before the meeting, the ExO had gone through Marx's data frame by frame with Tyre. Hobbes had gotten all too clear a look at the drones that had finally killed Marx's scout. The deluge of their slugs had passed through the spreading sand cloud, the usually invisible shells illuminated by the medium. Expert software's careful count had revealed a firing rate greater than a hundred rounds per second.

The blackbody drones were loaded for bear.

In the First Rix Incursion, this class of drone had been used strictly for close-in defense. A few dozen of the monitors would float in front of a Rix warship, picking off attacking drones if they grew too close. But the blackbodies of the previous war were far fewer, and had possessed much lower firing rates; they were designed to kill drones.

But these new monitors, in huge numbers and at short range, would also be capable of gutting the *Lynx*, or anything else that tried to close with the battle-cruiser. The Rix had configured for defense of their huge receiver at all costs, even anticipating ramming by a ship as large as a frigate. The sort of attack the *Lynx* had been headed for would surely have failed.

If it hadn't been for Marx's skill and dumb luck—a dead sandcaster drone penetrating the perimeter intact—the receiver array would still be functional now, and the *Lynx* on its unknowing way to destruction.

"No sense in discussing the drones," Captain Zai said. "The die is cast."

Hobbes nodded. The moment Captain Zai had seen Tyre's report, he had ordered the *Lynx* into high acceleration, pushing at a ninety-degree angle from the Rix warship's approach.

In doing so, he had abandoned any chance of recovering the detached energy-sink manifold. To escape the blackbodies, the frigate had been forced to leave behind its primary defense against energy weapons.

Now, they had to get as far away from the battle-cruiser as possible.

"Give us the real-time view," the captain ordered.

The airscreen switched to the current transluminal

returns from the Rix battlecruiser. Its main engine had swung ninety degrees, pursuing the *Lynx* now rather than braking to match Legis XV, letting the blackbody drones drift on.

Fortunately, the larger battlecruiser was the slower ship. It could make no more than six gees.

Hobbes regarded the airscreen. The *Lynx* was pushing hard to put distance between herself and the battlecruiser, also headed perpendicular to the original Rix line of approach. They would have nineteen minutes of acceleration under their belts before they reached their closest passage by the Rix warship.

The math was easy: nineteen hundred seconds at twelve gees advantage, and a minute of float. Two hundred and twenty thousand kilometers of breathing room.

The blackbody monitors couldn't touch them out here. Intended to be absolutely silent, they had no drives—the Rix had effectively abandoned them. But the battlecruiser's chaotic gravity weapons had a much greater range. And without an energy-sink manifold to shunt the energy into space, the *Lynx* was terribly vulnerable.

The flag bridge underwent another shudder, and the captain's cup of tea traveled across the table toward Hobbes, rattling as if carried by a ghost who badly needed a night of sleep.

The apparition passed.

"At least she's not optimized for offense," the captain said.

The officers nodded. The blackbody drones and their ammo supply must have taken up space normally reserved for offensive weapons. But it wouldn't take much to hurt the Imperial warship. And the Rix captain knew the *Lynx* had dumped its energy sink. The manifold was still glowing behind them, spreading like an exhausted supernova.

"They could be in turnaround," First Pilot Maradonna suggested. "With no receiver array, they can't contact the compound mind. Maybe they've given up."

"So why come after us?" Tyre asked.

"They could be angling out of the system," Second Pilot Anderson argued. "They'd want to swing away from Legis's orbital defenses."

Hobbes shook her head at this wishful thinking. "If they were abandoning the mission, they'd gather those drones first. But they came straight after us. They want our blood."

"Which is perhaps a sign of our success," Zai added. "Their array is destroyed. They want the *Lynx*'s carcass as a consolation prize."

Hobbes sighed. Captain Zai had never been one to paint success in rosy terms.

"They might be buying time to fabricate another receiver array," Anderson said.

"They couldn't possibly," the first engineer interjected. "The thing was a thousand klicks across! It'd take months and megatons of spare matter."

"Ten minutes left," Zai said. The battlecruiser's gravity weapons would soon be in range. "Perhaps this discussion of Rix motivation can wait."

His fingers moved, and the real-time view shifted into the future, using current vectors to extrapolate the moment of closest passage. "Very soon, we'll have less than a light-second between ourselves and a pair of terawatt chaotic gravity cannon," he said.

"Assuming she's mounting normal weapons, sir," Anderson said. "So far, we haven't seen the usual mix. Certainly not of drones. The battlecruiser was outfitted for making contact with the compound mind and nothing else. Perhaps it wasn't equipped with offensive weapons at all."

"Let us assume the worst," Zai said.

"We've still got all four photon cannon, sir," Second Gunner Wilson said. "They can do a fair amount of damage even at a light-second's range. If we get the first shots in, we could disable—"

Captain Zai shook his head, cutting the man off.

"We're not firing at the Rix," he said.

Eyebrows raised across the room.

"We're running silent."

Hobbes smiled to herself. The *Lynx*'s officers had committed themselves to the captain's initial plan for so long—had been so ready to bring their attack to the battlecruiser at any cost—that they hadn't realized the obvious: With the receiver destroyed, the *Lynx* had completed its mission.

Survival was again a priority.

"Shut everything down," Hobbes explained. "No sensors, no weapons charged, go to freefall conditions—total silence."

"The only activity will be coldjets: to keep ourselves aligned head-on with the Rix," Captain Zai added. "Without a heat-sink manifold, our z-axis profile is less than two hundred meters across. We'll be a needle in a haystack."

"*Head-on,*" Gunner Wilson whispered. "You know, sir, the forward armor is reinforced for meteoroid collisions. Depleted uranium and a microlayer of neutronium. We could even take a hit and survive."

Zai shook his head. "We'll eject the forward armor."

Wilson and the others recoiled. Hobbes had to sympathize. When the captain had first explained this idea to her, she was convinced he had finally cracked. Now that she'd thought about it, his plan made sense. But it still had a ... *perversity* about it that mere logic couldn't shake.

First, the energy-sink manifold, now their armor. For the second time in this battle, they were throwing away their defenses.

The captain remained silent, as if enjoying the shock his pronouncement had created.

So Hobbes again explained: "That armor is reflective. If they search for us with wide-focus laser fire, they'll pick us up as a big red spot."

"We could paint it black," someone suggested after a moment's thought.

"Not under high acceleration, and not in time," the first engineer said flatly.

The logic of the captain's idea slowly settled over the room, like some dermal drug sinking into the skin.

No weapons. No defenses. Just the blackness of space between the *Lynx* and the enemy. A high-stakes gamble. Hobbes saw the discomfort on the officers' faces as they struggled to accept the plan. They were safer running silent, it was undeniable, but they would be relinquishing control of their fate to luck alone. It offended their sensibilities. They were the crew of a warship, not passengers on some commercial shuttle.

Hobbes decided to interrupt the frustration filling the room. She had to give them something to do.

"Perhaps we could fill the forward cargo compartments with some protection against chaotic gravitons. Do we have any heavy metals?" Hobbes asked.

After a moment, Marx nodded. "The minesweeper fragmentation drones use depleted uranium. Not much, but it's something."

"And there's the shielding around the singularity generator. If we're running silent, we'll be shutting the hole down, so we could move it forward. A little extra hullalloy between us and the Rix couldn't hurt."

"Put a team together," Zai ordered. "Start disassembling the shielding now. Get it moving the moment we cease acceleration."

First Engineer Frick spoke up, "How long do we have in freefall, sir?"

"A hundred seconds," Hobbes said. "No more."

The man shook his head. It wasn't enough time to move the massive shielding through the corridors of the battle-configured ship.

The captain nodded. "All right, we'll cut our engines earlier. I'll give you three minutes of zero-gee before we come under fire."

Engineer Frick smiled at ExO Hobbes in triumph.

Hobbes shrugged her shoulders. If the captain's largesse kept the man happy, she was glad to play scrooge. But it was still precious little time for an operation of that complexity. The engineers would still be putting the makeshift armor in place when the Rix started hunting them. But at least the crew would be occupied; better busy than hunkering down in the dark, waiting for a lance of gravitons to tear into them.

Even the hardest work was better than doing nothing.

First Engineer

First Engineer Watson Frick watched a universe disappear.

The pocket cosmos behind the hullalloy shielding stuttered for a moment as its bonds were cut. The black hole at its core, which had strained since its creation against the fields that held it in the real universe, convulsed for an instant, then collapsed.

Away it goes, Frick thought, off to Somewhere Else—a different reality, now utterly unreachable. What a strange way to generate power, the First Engineer wondered: Making pocket universes, the false (?) realms formed whenever a starship bigbanged its drive. How many other realities had humanity created with this process?

And would there one day be other thinking beings inside them, in the small realities born of humanity's hubris? Then those, making pocket universes of their own . . .

Frick shook his head. There was no time for philosophical digression. In 500 seconds, the *Lynx* would come under fire. The singularity generator's shielding was needed at the front of the warship.

"Two minutes until freefall," Frick shouted. "Let's get this metal broken down."

The crew—his best men and women—worked quickly, disassembling the huge armored plates as easily as if this process were among the standard drills, which it most certainly was not. Frick put his own hands in, running a controller down the starboard seam of the shielding. The controller sent out focused FM waves, a tight field that activated nanos buried throughout the armor. The nanos sprang to life and began breaking down the shielding into movable sections.

Sweat slid into Frick's eyes as he moved the heavy controller in a careful line. Normally, the device would be lightened by its own easy gravity generator, but with the *Lynx* still running flat out, spot sources of gravitons were too dangerous. At eighteen gees acceleration, the random fluxes coursing through the ship were already deadly. Frick remembered the arduous trip out to intercept the Rix ship, a week under ten gees. A few days in, he'd seen a line of bad gravity go through a rating's legs, one of the man's kneecaps shattering like a dropped saucer.

Frick tried to keep the cut steady.

Taking the shielding apart was easy, of course. But doing it the *right* way was tricky. The *Lynx* would need the singularity generator quickly back in one piece again on the other side of danger. The black hole powered the ship's photon cannon, artificial gravity, even life support. With the generator offline, the captain was running the batteries down just to give Frick these minutes for disassembly.

The heavy plates across from Frick shifted as they were cut apart.

"Slow it up over there!" he shouted. "You wanna be crushed? Save your final cuts until we hit freefall." The largest of the sections massed five tons.

As the words left his mouth, a shudder went through the ship. A gravity ghost, reminding them all that the ship's artificial gee was a very shaky proposition. For a moment, there was a nervous silence as the ghost passed.

Heat was building in the cramped space around the singularity generator. The nanos' furious activity within the shielding walls had turned them red-hot.

"Environmental, environmental," Frick said.

"We're on it, sir," came the response in his second hearing.

A tepid wind blew across his face, hardly sufficient.

"A little more?" he inquired.

"We're on it, sir," the woman repeated with maddening calm.

Frick scowled and lowered his cutter. He had cut as far as he safely could in one gee. The heat was unbearable.

He walked around the generator's perimeter, checking his crew's work. The giant sections loomed over him, seeming to hang by threads.

"Fine. Fine. Stop there!" he rasped. "Wait for freefall."

Suddenly, a panicked cry came from just behind him. "Sir!"

He spun on one heel to face the cry.

"It's cracking, sir!"

Frick's eyes scanned the wall of shielding next to the yelping crewman. A spiderweb of fissures appeared, spreading even as he watched.

For a moment, he couldn't believe it. The specs for singularity shielding were the most demanding in the Navy. No captain wanted a black hole coming loose in the middle of battle. And they'd calculated these cuts to the micrometer.

But something had gone wrong.

Then Frick's eyes spotted the epicenter of the cracking. There was a small hole in the shielding, a centimeter across.

"Godspite!" he shouted. "One of the flockers hit the generator!"

Fissures spread from the tiny hole, like too-thin lake ice cracking underfoot. The hullalloy cried out, a screaming sound to wake the dead as it began to collapse.

"Priority, priority!" the engineer yelled, his hand whipping through the priority icon even as he invoked it. "Cut the engines and the gravity, Hobbes! I need zero-gee!"

But the shielding was already falling, coming down on them. The metal howled as its own weight tore it from the generator. Frick grabbed the crewman who'd spotted the fissures by the collar and pulled, planting his feet against the grabby surface of the deck. For a moment, he merely yanked the man and himself off-balance, but then the sudden bowel-clenching feel of freefall descended around them.

The ExO had heard.

Frick threw the suddenly weightless man out of danger, the ensign spinning toward safety.

But he had pushed too hard, he realized. The Second Law put Frick himself in motion, hurtling back under the shielding. His grabby boots left the floor, and he found himself helpless in the air.

The free piece of shielding floated inexorably toward him. The First Law now: It retained momentum from when it had been falling. With the engines and artificial gravity cut, the shielding was weightless. . . .

But it was still *massive*.

It floated slowly toward him, no faster than a feather

falling, less than a meter away. Frick's hands clawed at the deck behind him, but the metal slipped under his fingers.

Why wasn't he wearing grabby gloves? There simply hadn't been time to suit up properly as he'd rushed to prepare this operation. *No gloves!* Frick had demoted ratings for this sort of idiocy. Well, justice would be served. The first engineer was about to be worse than demoted.

The shielding moved toward him, as slow and buoyant as some huge water craft gliding to bump ponderously against a dock.

Ratings' hands reached for him. They'd all be crushed. "Clear off!" he shouted.

"Engineer?" came Hobbes' voice. "What's—"

"Give me one-twentieth-gee accel, flush starboard for one second!" he screamed as the giant fist of metal closed upon him.

He hoped his numbers—arrived at by pure instinct—were correct. He hoped Hobbes wouldn't ask what he was screaming about. In the time it took to say ten words, he would be flattened.

The huge vise closed on him. Without logic, Frick pressed against it, all his strength against five thousand kilograms. He saw his crew's hands grip futilely at the metal's edges. The tons of hullalloy pressed relentlessly against him.

A cracking sound came from Frick's chest, but then the slight bump of acceleration struck.

The shielding's course fluidly reversed, as if some affectionate but massive metal creature had hugged him too tightly.

"Thank you, Hobbes," he muttered.

The shielding moved away, only a hair faster than it

had closed on Frick. Half a meter of space opened up, and hands—*grabby-gloved* hands, he noted ruefully—reached underneath to pull him out.

He took a deep, painful breath. Something popped in his chest. A few ribs had succumbed to the shielding's tight embrace. A small price to pay for an idiot's mistake.

"Hobbes," he managed.

"What the devil's going on down there?"

The shielding was still floating back toward the generator. Slowly, but still inexorably. They had to get it stopped.

"Loose metal," he said, measuring the shielding's speed with his engineer's handheld and calculating. "One more acceleration. Opposite direction, at point-oh-two gees."

Hobbes sighed with exasperation. She and the captain must be livid. They were supposed to be fleeing a Rix warship at eighteen gees, not nudging around the *Lynx* with tiny squirts of coldjet.

But the bump came, Frick's grabby boots holding him firm. The metal edged to a near-halt in midair. He smiled at his calculations. Not bad for an old man.

"Hold in zero-gee," he said. They couldn't resume acceleration with the heavy shielding floating about. "We have loose tons."

"Loose *tons*?" Hobbes exclaimed.

"Yes, ma'am," Frick answered, holding his throbbing side. "Definitely tons."

"All right, Frick, get that metal into the bow," she said. "We'll be within range of the Rix primaries in four hundred seconds. And thanks to cutting our engines for you, we'll be at barely half a light-second range."

Damn, the first engineer thought. The loose shielding had cost them two minutes of acceleration. Damn those flockers! How had he missed the damage?

He just hoped the armor would be worth the lost distance from the Rix gravity cannon.

"Crew, we are going dark early," came the captain's voice. The old man didn't sound pleased.

"Ten seconds," Hobbes began the count.

"All right!" Frick shouted to his crew. "We're doing this in the dark: no second sight, no com, no gravity!"

"Five . . ."

"Cut all the pieces out. But we'll be in microgravity once the coldjets start," he shouted. "You and you, get this piece of tin moving toward the bow. And watch out. I happen to know it's heavy."

A few of the crew laughed as they sprang to their work. But the boisterous sound dropped off as the ship went dark.

The heads-up status displays, the hovering symbols that marked equipment, the chatter of ship noise and expert software, everything in second sight and hearing disappeared. The ship was left dim and lifeless around them, a mere hunk of metal. All they had to see by was unaugmented work lights, making the generator area a shadowy, red-tinged twilight zone.

Then the coldjets started, pushing the *Lynx* to orient it bow-first toward the Rix battlecruiser. The microgravity shifted the loose plates of shielding again, but by now the crew had attached handholds and stronglines to them, and they soon had the beasts under control. But in the dim light and swaying microgravity, it felt like the below decks of some ancient warship on a pitching sea.

Frick looked reflexively for a time stamp, but his second sight held nothing. The fields that created synesthesia were highly penetrative and persistent—the Rix would be looking for them in their hunt for the *Lynx*. Second audio was out of the question as well; only hardwired compoints were to be used. He'd gone over this with Hobbes, but it hadn't seemed real before now.

Frick damned himself for not thinking to bring a mechanical chronometer. Had there even been time to fabricate such an exotic device?

"You," he said, pointing to a rating. "Start counting."

"Counting, sir?"

"Yes. Counting out loud is your job now. Backwards from . . . three hundred eighty. Count slow, in seconds."

A look of understanding crossed the rating's face. She started in a low voice.

"Three hundred eighty, three hundred seventy-nine . . ."

Frick shook his head at the sound. He was using a highly trained crewman as a *clock,* for god's sake. They would be running handwritten notes next.

His angry eyes scanned the dimness of the generator area. Everywhere, huge and unwieldy pieces of metal were beginning to move with agonizing slowness. Each was supported by a web of stronglines. The cables were packed with stored kinetic energy, windup carbon that would contract when keyed. This purely mechanical motive force was invisible to the Rix sensors, but it was capable of pulling the weightless if massive sections of hullalloy through the ship.

Frick looked about for a rating with free hands.

"You," he called.

"Sir?"

Frick held up his bare hands. "Get me some gloves."

In 370 seconds or so, the Rix might turn them all to
jelly, but damned if Watson Frick was going to be
crushed by some piece of dumb metal in the meantime.

Executive Officer

Katherie Hobbes had never heard the battle bridge so
silent.

With the synesthesia field absent, most of the control surfaces had turned featureless gray. She seldom
appreciated how few of the screens and controls she
used every day were physical. It looked as if the
frigate's bridge had been wrapped in gray, grabby car-
peting, like some featureless prototype. The few hard
icons that remained—the fat, dumb buttons that were
independent of second sight—glowed dully in the red
battle lights. The big airscreen that normally dominated the bridge was replaced by its emergency
backup, a flatscreen that showed only one level of vision at a time, and fuzzily at that.

Trapped in the dim world of primary sight, the
bridge crew moved in a daze, as if synesthesia were a
shared dream they'd all just awoken from.

Not that their confusion mattered. There wasn't
much they could accomplish with the *Lynx* running in
its near-total darkmode. The frigate's pilot staff were
handling the coldjets, nudging the ship through a very

slow arc—ninety degrees in eight minutes—to keep the bow directly lined up on the Rix battlecruiser. The *Lynx* was like a duelist turned sideways, keeping the smallest possible area oriented toward her opponent. The pilots spoke animatedly among themselves, out of Hobbes's hearing. The executive officer instinctively made the control gesture that should have fed their voices to her, but of course second hearing was gone as well. Hobbes knew why they were frustrated, however; for their calculations, the pilots were using a shielded darkmode computer hidden behind the sickbay armor. The machine had about as much processor power as a robotic pet.

At this range the Rix sensors were very sensitive. Only the most primitive electronics could be used.

Hobbes turned her mind to Frick's engineering team. They should have the impromptu armor plating in position by now. She rotated an unwieldy select dial at her station, trying to find the team. The usual wash of sound from below decks had been reduced to a smattering of voices; the only dialogue that reached Hobbes came through the hardwired compoints at key control points on the ship. The low-wattage handheld communicators they'd broken out were to be used only on the captain's orders. At this range, Rix sensors could detect the emissions of a self-microwaving food pack boiling noodles. Even medical endoframes had to be shut down. Captain Zai's prosthetics were frozen; he couldn't budge from the shipmaster's chair. Only one of his arms was moving; the other was locked in a position that seemed painfully posed.

"How are they doing, Hobbes?" the captain asked. His voice seemed so soft, so human now, absent the usual amplification of the captain's direct channel.

"I . . ." Hobbes continued to scroll through the various compoints on the ship. The primitive interface was maddening.

Ten awful seconds later, she was forced to admit, "I don't know, sir." Hobbes wondered if she had ever said those words to her captain before.

"Don't worry, Hobbes," he said, smiling at her. "They're probably between compoints. Just let me know when they call."

"Yes, sir."

Despite losing his legs and one arm, the captain seemed hardly bothered by the blindness of darkmode. Zai was actually working with a stylus—on *paper*, Hobbes realized.

He noticed her gaze upon the ancient apparatus.

"We may need to use runners before this is over, Hobbes," he explained. "Just thought I'd practice my penmanship."

"I'm not sure I know that last word, sir," she admitted.

He smiled again.

"On Vada, you couldn't graduate from upper school without good handwriting, Hobbes. The ancient arts always come back eventually."

She nodded, recognizing the ancient root-word. *Pen*-man-ship. It made sense now. As always, the Vadan emphasis was on the male gender.

"But perhaps old ways aren't a priority on Utopian worlds, eh, Hobbes?"

"I suppose not, sir," she said, feeling a bit odd that the captain was conversing with her only moments before the *Lynx* would come under fire. In darkmode, of course, there was not much they could do other than chat.

"But in lower school I did learn how to use a sextant."

"An excellent skill!" the captain said. He wasn't kidding.

"Though it was hardly a requirement for graduation, sir."

"I just hope you remember how, Hobbes. If the Rix hit our processor core again, we may need you at the hard viewports."

"Let's hope it doesn't come to that, sir."

"Twenty seconds," announced a young ensign, raising her voice to be heard across the bridge. Her eyes were fixed on a mechanical chronometer someone had dug up from stores. Captain Zai had also produced an ancient Vadan wristwatch from among his family heirlooms. He had examined the two timepieces, determined that they ran on springs—making them undetectable to the Rix—and synchronized one to the other with a twist of a minuscule knob.

As the ensign counted down to the point when the Rix could begin firing, Captain Zai handed Hobbes the writing instrument and paper.

"Care to have a go?"

She held the stylus like a knife, but that didn't seem right. She tried it like a pointer.

"Turn it around, and slip the business end between your index and middle fingers," the captain said quietly.

"Ah, like a fork almost," Hobbes replied.

"Five," said the ensign. "Four . . ."

Hobbes made a few marks. There was a certain pleasure in the pen's incision of the paper. Unlike air drawing, the friction of pen against paper had a reassuring physicality. She sketched a diagram of the bridge.

Not bad. But writing? She crossed two parallel lines to make a crude *H*. Then formed a circle for the *O*.

"Zero," said the ensign. "We are in range of the enemy prime's capital weapons."

Hobbes tried the other letters of her name, but they dissolved into scribbles.

The chief sensor officer, leaned over a headsdown display, spoke in a loud, clear voice, as if addressing an audience from a theatrical stage.

"She's firing. Standard photon cannon. Looks to be targeting along our last known vector."

Hobbes nodded. The Rix would have tracked the *Lynx* until 450 seconds ago, when they'd dropped into darkmode. But the coldjets had pushed the *Lynx* onto a new vector.

The captain had taken a risk with that. The coldjets used waste water and other recyclables for reaction mass, and Zai had shot half the frigate's water supply, and even a good chunk of the emergency oxygen that was kept frozen on the hull. The ship had gotten an additional bit of kick from ejecting the reflective bow armor with high explosives. They were now thousands of kilometers from where the Rix thought they were, but they had almost no recyclables to spare. If they lost their main drive to enemy fire, it would be almost a year before the low-acceleration rescue craft available on Legis could make it out to repair and resupply them. A single breakdown in the recycling chain—bacterial failure, equipment malfunction, the slightest nano mutation—would doom them all.

And despite herself, Hobbes wondered if the Navy would prioritize rescuing the *Lynx*. With a war on, there'd be plenty of excuses to delay chasing down a stricken warship that was flying toward Rix space at two thousand klicks per second. Laurent Zai was still an embarrassment to the Emperor. They would all make good martyrs.

"Short bursts: one, two, three," the sensor officer counted. "Low power lasers now; they're looking for reflections."

"What are their assumptions?" the captain asked.

Ensign Tyre, who had been moved up to the bridge from Data Analysis, struggled with the limited processor power and her headsdown's unfamiliar physical controls. The silent-running passive sensor array was basically a host of fiber optics running from the hull to the same small, shielded computer the pilots had been complaining about.

"From where they're shooting, they seem to think we've doubled back on them . . . at high acceleration."

"High acceleration?" Hobbes murmured. "But we obviously aren't under main drive."

"They're being cautious," Zai said quietly. "They think we may have developed a stealthy drive in the last eighty years, and that we're still bent on ramming them."

Of course, Hobbes thought. Just as the Rix evolved from one war to the next, so did the Imperials. And the *Lynx* was a new class of warship, only ten absolute years old. It had nothing as exotic as full-power stealthy acceleration, but the Rix didn't know that.

Katherie Hobbes turned the page of the captain's writing tablet, giving herself a clean piece of paper. With a few long strokes, she drew a vector line of the *Lynx*'s passage through the battlecruiser's gravity-cannon perimeter. Writing letters was difficult, but her fingers seemed to know instinctively the curves of gunnery and acceleration. Over her career, she'd traced the courses of a thousand battles, imagined or historical, on airscreen displays. Her tactical reflexes seemed to guide the pen, rendering the Rix firing pattern as the sensor officer called it.

The two ships' relative velocity was still roughly 3,000 kps—it would take hours of acceleration to change that appreciably. Thus, the *Lynx*'s course was practically a straight line running nearly tangent through the sphere of the gravity cannon's effective range, like a bullet passing through a dribble-hoop ball at a shallow angle. While they were inside the sphere, the Rix could hit them. But the frigate would pass out of range within minutes.

"They've gone to higher power, with a wider aperture," Tyre said.

The Rix weren't firing to kill now; they had reduced their laser's coherence to increase the area they could cover. They were hoping that a low-energy hit would reflect from the *Lynx*, or cause a secondary explosion that would give her position away.

In effect, they had replaced their sniper's rifle with a flare gun.

"They're picking up the pace. I can see a pattern now: a spiral from our old course," Tyre said.

"How fast is the spiral expanding?" Hobbes called, her pen frozen above the paper.

"Outward at about a thousand meters per second."

Hobbes looked at the captain, her spirits lifting. The Rix were sounding a vast area. They had assumed the Lynx was still under heavy acceleration, at multiple gees rather than the micromaneuvers they were actually making.

"The enemy seems to have overestimated us, Hobbes," Zai said.

"Yes, sir."

Hobbes turned to another fresh page of paper, filled it with a line spiraling outward and dissected by radials from the center: a spiral grid.

Thinking that the *Lynx* was still under her main drive, the Rix were casting a wide net. But the firing rate of the battlecruiser's laser would have an absolute limit. In order to search such a huge volume, they necessarily had to reduce the grain of their search grid; the Rix net had wide holes in it. If the *Lynx* were broadside to the battlecruiser, the low-res search might have picked up the two-kilometer-long craft. But the frigate was bow-on, her hull only two hundred meters across from the Rix's perspective. And with the bow armor ejected, only naked black hullalloy remained to reflect the laser.

Hobbes drew a small circle in the circular grid, a minuscule gnat slipping through the web of a spider looking for fat flies.

"They're going to miss us, sir."

"Yes, Hobbes. Unless they're very lucky."

First Engineer

"One hundred ninety-nine. Two hundred."

"All right, shut up!" First Engineer Watson Frick shouted to the dogged ensign. "Keep the count going, but *silently*. Let me know when you get to eight hundred."

Frick's skin tingled as if he were under a sonic shower. The ensign had been in positive territory—counting up—for two minutes. No matter how imprecise the count might be, the *Lynx* was certainly within range of the enemy's capital weapons by now. At any moment, a gravity beam might swing across the ship and mangle them all. They had at least another six hundred seconds before they were out of danger.

Frick's side still throbbed—yes, a few ribs were definitely broken—as he regarded the hastily assembled armor plates.

The last piece was in place. The hullalloy shielding was spread across the cargo area to maximize coverage of the ship. There were seams, even naked gaps, but he couldn't seal those without using cutting torches rated for hullalloy. And *that* would show up on the Rix sensors like an SOS beacon.

The problem was, the plates were practically floating free, held to the bow hull only by stronglines and monofilament. Engineer Frick had counted on using the recyclables stored in the cargo area to pack the hull sections into place. But the containers were all empty, the water ejected.

If the captain ordered any serious maneuvers, the hullalloy plates would tear from their uncertain moorings and crash through the ship like a runaway maglev.

And there was no hardwired compoint here in the cargo bay, no way to reach the captain. Apparently, the designers of the *Lynx* had never imagined that the bow cargo area would become a prime tactical station. Frick realized now why Navy ships seldom even drilled in true darkmode; doing without second sight was frustrating, but losing communications could be deadly.

"Pressure hoods up," Frick ordered his team. If the plates got free, decompression was a high probability. And it was cold here, this close to the hull. The ship was running on minimal life support, nano-rebreathers for air, insulation to maintain internal temperature.

"You," he said, pointing at Rating Metasmith. The woman was the best athlete on the engineering team. In gravity, she was a dribble-hoop demon, and had the highest freefall workout scores on the *Lynx* except for a few marines. "Get back to the forward gunnery station and use the compoint. Warn the captain not to accelerate above one-twentieth."

"Understood," she said, and sailed toward the open hatchway with an effortless shove. Frick flinched as she soared through, missing collision with the hatchway's coupling fringe by a few centimeters.

The first engineer sealed the hatch behind Metasmith. If the plates did get loose, his team might do some good here in the cargo bay. They could attempt *some* sort of damage control.

"Pick an armor plate and tether yourself," he ordered. "And if you smell something cooking, it's you."

Frick pushed himself toward the central armor plate. The plates weren't grabby, so he employed his pressure suit's magnets. He settled against the hullalloy, feeling its reassuring mass between himself and the Rix gravity cannon.

Five minutes to go, as near as he could figure.

The silence of the *Lynx* was awful. At least on the bridge they could watch the incoming fire, judge how close the shots were falling. But here in the bow, he and his team were hiding deaf and blind, not really knowing if their silence protected them at all.

Commando

H_rd soared to meet the cloud-seeding dirigible, the rendezvous only a hundred kilometers from the entanglement facility's wire.

The recon flyer was at the upper limit of its altitude. The fans whined pitifully, and the craft's electromagnetics stretched tenuously downward, a swimmer's toes searching for solid ground. The air was thin up here, but breathable for a Rixwoman.

The dirigible came down to greet her, operating at the lower extreme of its functional altitude range. Thus the two craft formed a precarious and narrow union of sets. H_rd rose slowly to a standing position on the recon flyer's armored carapace. The straining flyer reacted to every shift of her weight with the jitter of a tightrope. Alexander's piloting would be tested by this maneuver. H_rd had removed the military governors, giving control of the craft to the compound mind. She would have to go very high to approach the entanglement facility undetected.

The dirigible, also under Alexander's control, came nearer, its sphere of emptiness looming like a black hole in the dark sky. The airship's tiny props tried to steady it, fighting the strong winds of this high place. H_rd's sable coat spread out from her, black wings against the stars.

It was twenty-five degrees below freezing. For the first time in her life, the Rixwoman felt her fingers grow numb.

H_rd steadied herself, and reached for the dirigible's payload basket. She stripped the scientific instruments to lighten the craft, replacing them with the pack she had prepared for this mission. Then she removed the sable coat, which was too heavy to take with her, and sadly let it fall. She locked the muscles in her hands, leaving them arched like a pair of hooks. There was no provision for a person in the dirigible's small payload basket. She would have to hang from the airship until it reached the proper position.

She knelt, gathered herself, and leaped from one craft toward the other.

The recon flyer dipped away as her weight pushed against it, and a sudden gust of wind pulled the dirigible from her locked hands. A very human gasp escaped her lips.

H_rd reached the zenith of her leap, then fell through the cold air like a stone.

Captain

"A runner in forward gunnery has a message from the first engineer, sir."

"We have our promised armor?" Captain Zai asked. It had taken long enough. Zai had questioned the value of reinforcing the forward cargo area in the first place. But the crew needed to feel that they were doing something to protect themselves. "A necessary misdirection," as Anonymous 167 called these minor deceptions of one's own subordinates.

"Yes. But the plates are not secure, sir," Hobbes relayed. "Frick is requesting no maneuvers above point-oh-five gees. They could tear loose if we use the main drive."

Captain Zai cursed. "I knew I'd pay for that armor."

"They can secure it with torches, sir, once we get out of range."

"By then we won't need it," Zai said.

Hobbes nodded.

Zai flexed the fingers of his natural hand. Going to darkmode had apparently worked. The Rix almost certainly weren't going to find them without a wild stroke of luck. In five minutes, plus another hundred seconds for safety, they could switch synesthesia back on. They would have communications, status reports. He would get command of his ship back.

And he would be able to move again. At the moment, Zai's lower back was aching from holding himself rigid in the shipmaster's chair. If he relaxed for a moment, he would topple over onto the floor.

"Any answer for Frick, sir?"

"No. We'll have communications back in a few minutes anyway. Keep that runner on station at the compoint, in case something serious comes up."

"Yes, sir." The tone of Hobbes's voice showed that she agreed.

It was odd, sitting here with her in the near-dark. The captain's and executive officer's stations were physically close, but the two inhabited different worlds. Hobbes often seemed absent, adrift amid the myriad channels of the *Lynx*'s infostructure, while Zai tried to stay focused on the overall picture. He'd been an ExO himself, and had to resist the temptation to wallow in the vast information resources of his ship. But the war sage was unwavering on the importance of delegation; the captain left data mining to the ever-competent Katherie Hobbes.

Here in darkmode, however, wrapped in silence and cut off from the rest of the *Lynx,* there was an unfamiliar intimacy between them. Zai had always rated Hobbes an excellent officer, but now that his life seemed daily on the line, he appreciated her all the more.

Since the attempt on his life, Zai had recognized that loyalty was a variable trait in the Navy. On gray Vada, rebellion against authority was rarely contemplated, but a mutiny had happened here on the *Lynx.* And it had been Katherie Hobbes, a Utopian by birth, who had stopped it. In the red work lights, her surgical beauty betrayed the values of her hedonistic homeland. But Hobbes was his best officer as well as his ExO.

She would make a good captain one day.

"Sir!" the sensor officer shouted, pulling Zai from his reverie.

"Report."

"I'm getting reflections from the Rix fire!"

"You mean they've hit something?" Hobbes asked.

Zai narrowed his eyes. The Rix search pattern had passed beyond the *Lynx* minutes ago; its spiral course had taken it a hundred thousand kilometers away.

"Yes, ma'am." The man bent back to his headsdown display.

Tyre spoke up. "I'm running an analysis now."

"Old sand?" Zai suggested to Hobbes.

"Not out here," she said. Zai nodded. They had put a lot of distance between themselves and their original intercept point. "Maybe it's old Legis's orbital defenses."

"That would be fantastic luck," Zai said. "If they think they've spotted us, we're home free."

But Hobbes shook her head. Zai knew from experience what the look on her face meant: There was a thought half-formed in her mind, an unhappy one.

"I'm getting oxygen, hydrogen, some carbon," said the sensor officer.

"The recyclables!" Hobbes cried. "That's what they were looking for. Why they went so wide with their search. *They weren't looking for us.* They wanted to find the reaction mass from our coldjets."

Zai closed his eyes. Of course. Spreading out from the *Lynx* was a spray of H_2O and organic waste, the ejecta from their stealthy acceleration. It would be spread into a huge cloud of ice crystals by now. Boiled by a laser, it would be much easier to spot than a silent starship. The Rix would eventually calculate its mass and vector.

And by extrapolation, they would know the vector of the *Lynx*.

"We seem to have left footprints, Executive Officer," he said.

"Aye, sir," Hobbes answered quietly.

"They've gone to a more focused beam, sir," the sensor officer reported. "They're still sounding the ice. Tracking it."

"We need to maneuver again, Hobbes," Zai said. "And at better than one-twentieth gee."

"I'll warn Frick, sir." Hobbes activated the forward gunnery compoint and sent the runner into motion.

The captain sighed. He would have to walk a fine line between two dangers. The Rix would extrapolate their position before the *Lynx* passed out of range. If Zai let the frigate coast, the enemy's laser would find them, followed by their gravity cannon. But if he maneuvered too quickly, the unsecured armor plates would roll through the frigate like a gravity ghost through a ship of glass.

"What's the strongest part of the cargo area, Hobbes?"

"The forewall, sir," Hobbes answered without hesitation. "It's exterior-grade hullalloy; there's vacuum on the bowside."

"So we'll do the least damage if we thrust sternward."

"Yes, sir. But that only changes our position on the z-axis. We're facing directly toward the Rix."

"We need to turn, then. A one-twentieth-gee yaw thrust."

"Any change in yaw and we expose more area to the Rix, sir."

"Yes, Hobbes. We'll turn back as quickly as possible."

"And I'm not sure how much acceleration we can get, sir. We're pretty low on recyclables."

Zai thought quickly. They needed the greatest possible push from the least possible mass. Thus, they needed maximum velocity.

"We'll use the drone launcher. Not the main rail's magnetics"—the Rix would spot that in a second—"the deadman drone. The highest velocity we can get out of it."

Hobbes whistled.

"Without artificial gravity to dampen the reaction? That *will* cause a jolt, sir."

"A jolt is what we need, Hobbes. And a mechanical event won't show up on the Rix sensors."

Hobbes nodded, understanding. The deadman launcher was designed for a ship that had lost power, its systems failing. The launch rail stored its energy mechanically, like a huge crossbow made of wound carbon. "I'll send another runner to the first engineer, Captain. There'll be decompression up there."

Zai nodded, his fingers flexing with frustration. They had only minutes to make this maneuver work, but using runners to convey messages would create at least half a minute of lag-time each way. Any change in plan would catch the engineer off guard.

Of all Zai's first officers, Engineer Frick most rarely worked from the bridge. The *Lynx*'s captain and engineer didn't know each other's thinking.

The words of the war sage came unbidden into Zai's mind. *A true subordinate is an extension of yourself*.

He came to a decision.

"Hobbes, tell Frick you'll be coming forward."

"Sir?"

"We don't know how this is going to work out. More maneuvers may be required. I need you there."

"To do what, sir?"

"To read my mind."

Commando

The sensation of freefall was strangely comforting.

In their orbital homes, the Rix generally slept in zero-gee. Except for the rush of frigid air, h_rd might have been waking from some dark dream. But this was real: She was falling toward her death.

She could see the entanglement facility in the distance, a concentric pattern of lights against the dull sheen of starlit snow. Somewhere in that pattern, a hundred kilometers away, was the landing zone Alexander had prepared for her, but it was much too far away. The world below her was terribly dark. She felt absolutely alone, and thought of Rana, probably still asleep in the cave. Who would bring her food now? Who would mourn her death?

Interrupting her thoughts, the scream of the recon flyer passed her, its running lights a red blur. With its fans inverted, it was falling faster than she. But it was twenty meters away. The machine had very limited senses, nothing that could spot her, even with Alexander at the controls. But h_rd remembered the sensitive thermal imagers that the Imperials had used to hunt her and Rana. She closed her eyes and willed her body temperature upward. Almost immediately, she felt acid in her stomach and a dryness in her mouth, a whirring of the turbine in her chest: the sensations of a heightened metabolism.

She dared a glance at the ground rushing toward her. Was there time?

H_rd cupped her hands, spreading out to slow her fall. She worked her muscles to hurry the heating process, flailing as she fell. The recon flyer suddenly edged back up toward her, moving carefully in the ferocious wind, guided by the barest movements of its control surfaces. Apparently Alexander could see her against the cold background of the stars.

The flyer came alongside and steadied itself. H_rd took control of her descent, angling her cupped hands to maneuver herself toward the craft. She grabbed the flailing webbing of the gunner's seat. The fans screamed again as the recon flyer braked.

The machine pulled up from its dive at a precarious angle, h_rd dangling from one side. She looked down as the craft decelerated, the frozen earth rushing toward her.

They missed collision with the hard tundra by only a few hundred meters.

"Well, then," she said—talking to herself was an odd habit she had picked up from Rana. "At least I've had a practice run."

Executive Officer

ExO Katherie Hobbes pulled herself through the dark shaftways of the *Lynx,* wishing she'd put more time into zero-gee practice.

Normally before an engagement, the crew would spend days working out in variable- and zero-gee, preparing for evasive maneuvers and gravity-generator brownouts. But the *Lynx* had been under heavy acceleration for almost ten days. There'd been no chance for the usual touch-up exercises.

At least the captain had given her time to don a proper pressure suit.

Hobbes checked the ancient chronometer on her wrist. The captain had set the first yaw-axis maneuver for thirty seconds from now. And he had loaned Hobbes his grandfather's timepiece. Good god, the thing was *old*. It used some ancient circular readout that Zai had explained as she'd slipped into an armored pressure suit. The timepiece was "analog," he had said, using an almost forgotten meaning of that word. As she moved through the cold and silent passageways of the ship, Hobbes's ears registered the almost subliminal pulse of the timepiece's ticking.

Thirty seconds. She wouldn't make it before the first acceleration, a nudge to orient the *Lynx* away from the Rix warship, but that would be a small one. The deadman launch would come twenty seconds later. Releasing the potential energy stored in the backup drone rail would shove *Lynx* off its current trajectory, rocking the ship like a meteor collision. Unlike coldjet acceleration, there would be no smooth buildup. The jolt would come all at once. The first engineer had already been warned by runners, but if she were to help Frick, she had to make it to the bow before things got too chaotic.

Even as Hobbes had left the bridge, the chief sensor officer was warning that the Rix's laser beams had ceased probing the ejecta, and were closing on the *Lynx*. At any second they could be under fire.

She pushed herself forward with abandon, kicking against the grabby walls as she yanked her pressure hood over her head. At least if she cracked her skull, the suit's thick carapace would afford it an extra layer of protection.

Suddenly, her ankle became tangled in something. She was yanked up short, swearing at whoever had left cable floating free under battle-stations.

But then Hobbes was pulled back forcibly, and she realized that a strong hand held her foot.

"What the hell?" she shouted.

Who was playing around, here in the midst of battle? Hobbes bent her knees, bringing herself face-to-face with the assailant, prepared to unleash a mighty stream of invective.

Then she recognized the woman: Verity Anst, a fourth-class gunnery rating, and an old friend of Gunner Thompson. Anst was one of those whom Hobbes and Zai had suspected of sympathy with the mutiny. They had never caught the last two mutineers. The *Lynx* was short of gunners, however, and no proof had ever come to light against Anst. They had put her under maximum surveillance, assuming that the ship's monitors would keep her honest.

In darkmode, of course, the *Lynx* was as blind as it was silent.

Hobbes turned and tried to push away, but Gunner Anst's hold was firm. The gunner's stats flitted across Hobbes' mind: two meters tall, ninety kilograms. Anst held on, spinning Hobbes against a bulkhead with a crack that knocked the wind from her.

She pulled Hobbes toward her, and held a knife to the ExO's throat. The blade was ceremonial, but looked hellishly lethal as it flashed in the red battle lights.

"Our little traitor," Anst said, her face only centimeters away.

Hobbes felt the cold steel even through the pressure suit's plastic. She forced down panic.

"I wasn't the traitor, Anst."

"Thompson revered you, Hobbes. He wanted you. Poor bastard couldn't see what a captain's whore you were."

The executive officer blinked, suppressed emotions rising in her briefly. She forced them down.

"So, you were one of them, Anst. I always suspected."

"I know you did, Katherie," the woman said. "I felt you waiting for me to give myself away. But I've been waiting for you, too."

As the woman spoke, Hobbes felt a familiar complaint from her inner ear. The ship was turning, shifting slowly around its *y*-axis. Here amidships, the maneuver was subtle enough that the grinning woman before her probably hadn't noticed it.

"You played it well, Verity. But you're dead now," Hobbes said. She glanced sidelong at the chronometer, starting a countdown from twenty. "We won't be in darkmode forever."

"We'll see about that." With her free hand, Anst yanked open the hatch on the hullside wall: an escape pod. The executive officer swallowed.

"I've got a few minutes with you," Anst said in a whisper. "You, me, and this knife. And then off you go with a load of HE. Zai won't find enough of you to genoprint. I've planned this well."

Fine, Hobbes thought. Anst wanted to brag. Let her.

Katherie Hobbes willed her body to relax, counting down the few remaining seconds before the coming jolt.

First Engineer

Metal screamed all around the First Engineer.

"Get to the far wall!" he shouted to his team.

Damn that idiot Zai! He was turning the *Lynx* too fast, Frick thought. But then the engineer saw the error he'd made, the realization coming even as he leapt from the shifting mass of armor plates. He had given Zai an absolute limit on acceleration: one-twentieth of a gee, or half a meter per second squared. But that assumed forward or backward thrust, which had an even effect throughout the frigate. Thrusting the ship into a turn, however, worked like a centrifugal gravity simulator: The force was far greater at the ship's bow and stern than it was at the center.

Frick was like a man at the end of a whip, one that Zai had casually snapped.

Rating Metasmith had returned from the compoint with a warning about the maneuver, but she hadn't been told why the captain was turning the ship. It didn't make sense. The plan had been to stay oriented to the Rix. As always, someone was improvising. Frick cursed himself as a fool not to have specifically warned against this.

The plates explosively popped their strongline tethers and began to pile toward the starboard side of the cargo bay. They weren't moving fast enough to punch through the hullalloy exterior wall, but they were plenty massive enough to crush a crewman.

As one, the engineering team pulled their magnets and jumped toward the sternward wall. The sliding plates rubbed against each other, screeching like a heavy maglev engaging friction brakes.

But his team was clear.

"Well, the captain hasn't killed us yet!" he said as they landed around him.

A few of his team laughed, but Rating Metasmith raised her fist for their attention. "They said only one-twentieth for the first accel. But much higher for the second. Whatever they can muster."

"Splendid," Frick muttered, then cried, "Get your hoods on and tether with hard lines. We're going into vacuum!"

Ten seconds later, the promised second jolt struck.

It was far worse than Frick expected.

Executive Officer

Hobbes's feet shot out as her count hit twenty, catching Verity Anst in the center of her chest. Her timing was perfect. The woman cried out in surprise as the ship bucked around them, the shock as violent as a collision. The force of Hobbes's kick was trebled by the sudden acceleration. She was flung from Anst's grip toward the bow, and rolled into a tumbling ball, bouncing down the corridor like a stone tossed down a well.

But Hobbes felt pain at her throat. Anst had managed to cut her as she'd pushed away. Hobbes felt the wound as she tumbled in freefall; her fingers came away slick, but there was no spurting gout of blood.

She came to a hard stop against a closed hatchway, cracking one shoulder, hand still at her throat. The integrity of her suit was broken, but the thick neck-seal had saved her life by millimeters.

Hobbes glanced down the corridor. Anst was twenty meters behind, kicking her way toward Hobbes with knife leveled.

A huge roar came from behind the executive officer. A shriek of metal and a howling wind from the bow. *Damn*, Hobbes thought. In the burst of acceleration sternward, the armor plates must have punched through the bow of the ship. The *Lynx* was depressurizing.

Hobbes wasn't far from the bow cargo bay. She

glanced at the pressure meter on the hatchway door. It was dropping into the red.

She spun the hatch's manual seal, and its safeties complained. Hobbes pressed her hand to the ID plate, and the hatch relented to her command rank.

Gunner Anst was flying toward her, the outstretched knife a few meters away. Hobbes barely had time to beltclip herself to the wall before the hatch blew open.

A great, sudden wind yanked her hard against the clip, bending Hobbes at the waist like a jackknife. Verity Anst sailed past helplessly, screaming bloody murder, and was sucked through the hatch like a doll into a tornado.

Hobbes felt a stinging along one arm: Anst had managed to cut her again.

"Damn you!" she cried.

In a few seconds, the wind began to die down. Somewhere further toward the bow, sprayfoam must be sealing the breaches. Hobbes pulled her pressure suit's face mask on and extended strongline from her belt clip. She kicked out over the hatchway—with the wind, the hatch led effectively down—and dropped after Anst and toward Frick and his team.

A moment later, Hobbes found the mutineer, knocked unconscious against an ugly set of waste baffles. The pressure was still dropping, and the woman's flimsy emergency suit was hopelessly rent. Her eyes were starting to bug, forcing the closed eyelids open a hair. Anst wouldn't last long without help, but there wasn't anything Hobbes had time to do for her.

The blood from the cut on Hobbes's arm spurted in time with her racing heart. The globules floated against Gunner Anst's prone form, dotting her uniform.

"You've got my blood. Happy now?" Hobbes asked, spraying repair sealant onto her own wounds.

Another jolt rocked the ship. Not acceleration; something cracking. The structure of the *Lynx* was beginning to fail. Anst's breathing started to kick up; she was dying.

"May the Emperor save you from death," Hobbes said to Anst with the cold cadence of tradition. It was all she could do.

She paused to make sure the rent at her own throat was sealed, then pushed on, wondering if Frick and his team were still alive.

First Engineer

Decompression was not the word for it.

When the reverse thrust struck, the plates surged toward the bow, thirty tons of hullalloy doing at least twenty mps. The shock wave from the collision— loose armor plates smashing against the bow hull wall—hammered Frick's ears even through his pressure hood. He was tossed forward, then pulled up short on his tether with a gut-wrenching snap, finding himself spinning at the end of three meters of strongline. His ribs screamed in fresh agony.

Then came the truncated howl of flash decompression, total and instantaneous.

The entire forewall of the bow was knocked out. In the seconds before he pulled up his face mask to complete the pressure seal around his head, Frick saw the void before him with naked eyes. His ears and eyeballs felt as if they would burst, both sight and hearing ruptured, then the smart plastics of the suit found their grip, and the pounding in his head was replaced with the polymer smell of recycled air.

He blinked until vision returned, looked out at the huge hole torn out by the plates. Had the *Lynx* accelerated forward instead of in reverse, they would have all been crushed. Not just the engineering team—although they would have been flattened most spectacularly—but the entire vessel would have been pummeled by the careening armor.

Against the mean light of the stars, Watson Frick saw the glitter of a drone sailing away from the ship.

Good god, they must have used the deadman rail, launching the drone to push the *Lynx* backward.

What was the captain *thinking*? Even with easy gravity to compensate, the frigate was designed to accelerate smoothly, not with massive jolts.

Frick scanned his team. They all seemed conscious, although Metasmith was helping Ensign Baxton with his face mask seal. Something about the team looked wrong, however. It wasn't merely the sudden darkness, the hard shadows of orange gas giants and Legis's distant sun. It was that the team didn't seem to be . . .

He did a quick count.

There were fourteen suited figures. *Fourteen.*

Someone was gone.

That was impossible. Everyone had been clipped: hypercarbon strongline attached to hullalloy rings on a bulkhead wall. The utility belt on a Navy engineer's pressure suit was made of diamond-tensile monofilament. You could hang a pair of thrashing African elephants from these rigs with a ten-thousand-year safety margin.

Rating Inders was waving her arms wildly, trying to get Frick's attention. He looked over at her, disbelief pounding in his head. She pointed at a short crack in the cargo bay bulkhead. The crack ran straight through the line of clip rings.

Then he saw it: One of the hullalloy rings had been ripped out.

The tether rigs were sound, but the *bulkhead* was cracking.

Frick climbed his strongline up and touched his suit's audio probe to the bulkhead. He heard the familiar hum of the *Lynx*'s air nanos, and the moan of decompression through what must have been another hull breach on the other side. And something else—the high-pitched tremolo of tiny pits propagating in hullalloy. The forward bulkhead—the last hullalloy barrier between the *Lynx* and massive decompression—was cavitating. Frick swallowed at the menacing sound. One of the flockers must have released a metal-eating virus; nothing else would cause the material to disintegrate this way.

In minutes, or perhaps seconds, the engineering team would all be pitching through the void.

Frick brought his hand up in a fist, thumb and little finger extended. The vacuum hand sign for lethal emergency. When he had every eye on him, the engineer brought the hand down to point at the hatchway. They had to get it open.

Even through pressure masks, he recognized surprise in a few faces. The other side of the bulkhead was still pressurized. Opening the hatchway now would piss away still more of the *Lynx*'s oxygen, and test the structural integrity of the walls between here and the next bulkhead, all the way back at the forward gunnery station.

But with the bulkhead cracking, the oxygen was gone anyway. And it would go far less explosively if they let it flow through the hatchway than if the whole bulkhead blew. At this moment, the hullalloy had hard vacuum on one side and almost a full atmosphere on the other. They had to equalize the pressure. The *Lynx*'s designers would have assumed that the cargo area would lose pressure gradually, at least twenty seconds to empty the huge space of air. No one would foresee the entire front of the ship being sheared away at once. And of course the metal virus added to the stresses on the metal.

Metasmith was the first to react. She swung on her tether like an acrobat, planting her magnet next to the hatchway and bracing her feet to either side. She gave the manual wheel a twist. It seemed to protest for a moment, then started to turn. A few more hands reached the wheel in time to speed her efforts.

When the hatch blew, the outrush of air knocked Metasmith back at a dangerous velocity. But the woman swung in a leisurely arc, letting her strongline run out to its full length. She executed a perfect landing on the far side of the cargo bay bulkhead, as pretty as zero-gee ballet.

Frick pressed his audio probe back against the bulkhead. It shrieked with the familiar wail of decompression, but the engineer's sharp ears still detected the soprano ringing of a travelling hullalloy fissure.

The *Lynx* was still breaking.

He shut his eyes and listened carefully, praying. Then it came—the sound was changing. The ringing seemed to gradually recede, lessening as the stresses of unequal pressure drained away through the open hatchway.

Frick opened his eyes, sighing with relief.

Now he could actually see the damage in front of him. The crack traveled past him, missing his own tether ring by a few centimeters. He stuck his suited finger into the fissure. It was less than four centimeters deep. And there was no notable vibration trembling within it.

The ship's hullalloy had an immune system, nanomachines that should fight off the Rix virus, but it might take a while for the infection to be completely eliminated. What the ship needed was a respite from the stresses of high gee and sudden jolts, but for the moment, the *Lynx* had stabilized.

At least until the captain decided to break her again.

Engineer-Rating

Engineer-Rating Telmore Bigz blinked his eyes again, hoping sight would return.

Bigz knew he was lucky to be alive at all. By rights, his head should be smeared across the Legis system by now. Pure chance had saved him. As he'd been torn from the bulkhead wall, his face mask must have been whipped around so that it had sealed itself. Either that, or Bigz had done so with some autonomic part of his brain whose actions were not recorded in memory.

But in the seconds of hard vacuum, his eyes must have bugged bad. He could see a sort of blurry streak before him, and that was all.

From the screaming in his head, Bigz figured that his eardrums had blown too. But that didn't bother him much. Out here in the airless void, sound was not a native species. And with communications forbidden, he wouldn't be talking to anyone on his suit radio.

But Bigz wished that he could *see*.

At least then he could figure out why he'd been plucked from the bulkhead. Bigz was positive that he'd been clipped right. Any shock strong enough to break his monofilament line should have snapped him in two like a breadstick.

He concentrated on the blurry streak. It pulsed every few seconds, a building-top blinker seen through a rain-soaked window.

Bigz judged the period to be about four seconds. A pressure suit emergency beacon pulsed once per second, so it wasn't a crew mate out there.

Then the rating understood. The pulsing light was the Legis sun, and Telmore Bigz was spinning, rotating once every four seconds.

He waited some more, and found that his sight seemed to be gradually coming back. There were other pulsing things, all with the same four-second period. They slowly resolved into streaks of light.

Stars. He could almost see the sun now, a distant but sharp disk against the black void.

Bigz felt strangely euphoric. The screaming headache that he should be suffering was absent, the pants-pissing fear he expected to feel had also not materialized. He carefully checked the medical charges on his utility belt.

He grunted with recognition as his fingers found the expended shockpack. Whatever lizard part of his brain had managed to seal his face mask had also pumped him fill of painkiller and stimulants. He was alone in the vacuum, spinning out of control, half-blind and completely deafened, but Bigz felt as sharp and confident as a man after his first cup of coffee in the morning.

The engineer-rating smiled happily as his vision cleared.

The sun was obvious now, the brightest light among the stars. And Bigz could see two of the system's orange-tinted gas giants.

What he couldn't see was the *Lynx*. The darkened frigate must be pretty far away, and inertia would only carry him farther. Fortunately, in another few minutes—once he and the ship were out of the range of the Rix big guns—Bigz could pull his emergency beacon.

Then he would be rescued. No problem.

Bigz decided that he'd had enough of spinning. He pulled the reaction canister from his belt and calculated the correct angle, then let off a quick spurt. The spinning slowed, the stars now twirling at the stately speed of a rink full of skaters. He could live with that.

Engineer-Rating Bigz now saw a tether strongline flailing about him. It had been rotating with him, but now that his spin had stopped it was wrapping itself around Bigz. He let it wind around his waist until he could grab the end.

The clip was still in the ring. The ringmount must have been pulled clean out of the hullalloy. That was bad. That meant that the *Lynx* had serious structural damage: a travelling fissure in a bulkhead, a bulkhead that was now exterior hull.

But at least, Bigz thought happily, he hadn't clipped himself wrong. Being out here in space wasn't *his* fault.

Then he saw something else. Another object in the void.

It was very distant, at the edge of his still blurry vision. The shape was dark, its edges glimmering. It seemed circular, unlike the long, thin *Lynx*. But perhaps he was seeing the ship head-on. That made sense. He'd been blown out the frigate's bow.

Might as well get closer to home, Bigz thought. If the ship were badly damaged (as it surely was) it would be far easier to rescue a loose crewman if he stayed nearby.

Bigz angled his reaction canister again, and let loose a long spray. He watched the object carefully for a count of twenty. Yes, he was getting closer now. He could see smooth metal facets now. It wasn't a huge and distant planetoid fooling his eyes. It was artificial.

It must be the *Lynx*.

Rating Telmore Bigz sprayed again, smiling.

He was going home.

Executive Officer

ExO Hobbes rappelled down the last corridor before the cargo bay bulkhead, the wind of depressurization serving as gravity. She clipped her belt to a nearby ring before ordering her strongline grapple to release and follow.

The outrush of air was slackening, but she didn't trust the respite. It had lessened once before, then increased again suddenly, as if various breaches were blowing in turn. The last truly stable bulkhead she'd seen was the one at the forward gunnery station.

She checked her pressure gauge. It showed near-vacuum. That was a bad sign, but at least with hardly any air left in this segment of the *Lynx,* there couldn't be another decompression.

Hobbes turned and saw the cargo bay hatch before her, one jump away. It was open.

She reattached her grapple and jumped, letting out strongline as she neared the hatchway. She swallowed nervously, hoping she'd find Frick and his team alive in the cargo bay.

Although she had prepared herself for the worst—strewn bodies among the ravages of the loose armor—when Hobbes reached the hatchway and peered through, she couldn't believe her eyes.

It was blackness . . . with stars.

There was no cargo bay.

Katherie pulled herself through, aghast at the huge rent before her, a cracked dome open to the sky.

A hand grabbed her shoulder.

"Executive Officer?" came the surprised voice through the suit's audio contacts.

Hobbes turned to see an engineer-rating. The woman seemed healthy and unpanicked, the athletic lines of her body obvious in the pressure suit.

The rating made a hand signal, and Hobbes turned to follow her eyes.

The whole engineering team seemed to be out here, huddled against the bulkhead. She breathed a sigh of relief.

A suited figure moved toward her—Watson Frick, the first engineer.

They connected their audio contacts.

"What the devil does Zai think he's doing?" the engineer spat.

"We had to accelerate, Frick," she explained. "The Rix spotted our coldjet reaction mass; they were about to backtrack it to us."

"But why with a jolt like that? *I lost a crewman!*"

The first engineer's eyes sparkled with tears as he shouted, his hands grasping her shoulders. For a moment, Hobbes thought she might have to fend off another physical attack, but the man forced himself under control.

"You used the deadman drone launcher, didn't you?" he said.

She nodded.

"We needed a mechanical acceleration, one as strong as possible, and to use a solid object as reaction mass. If we spread another cloud of water, the Rix could have found us again. They used lasers to spot the ice crystals, and extrapolated back to the *Lynx*."

Frick thought for a moment, then swore, agreeing with a mean, sharp nod.

"But we didn't expect the cargo-bay exterior to go," Hobbes said.

Frick shook his head. "It shouldn't have. But there were hairline fissures, virus trails. We were probably infected in the flocker attack. This bulkhead here," he indicated what had been the cargo bay floor, "is cavitating as well."

Hobbes nodded. They'd had less than twenty minutes to catalog all the flocker damage. One of the projectiles must have left metal-eating nanos.

"So that's why you opened this hatch," she said.

Frick nodded. "It was either a slow leak or another breakout. If we'd had an uncontrolled decompression, we might have lost the gunnery station bulkhead as well, and so on all along the ship."

Katherie Hobbes swallowed, envisioning one bulkhead blowing after another, like the legendary *Titanic* filling with water.

Her eyes scanned the bulkhead, and saw the cracks that had coursed across its surface, fanning out in a wedge, a river delta seen from space.

"Frick, can she handle another turn?"

"Another *what*?"

"The captain has to yaw the ship again, to bring us back head-on with the Rix."

"Good god," said Frick.

Hobbes checked the mechanical timepiece on her wrist. It had continued to function even in hard vacuum.

"The pilots should be pulling us back in forty-three seconds," she said. "But only at a twentieth of a gee, as per your message."

"No! It's too hard!" Frick cried. "Point-oh-five yaw at the centerline is much stronger out here."

Hobbes shook her head in confusion. What was Frick babbling about?

"Did you ever ride the whip?" he asked.

Hobbes frowned. She remembered the game, a risky zero-gee maneuver reinvented by each successive class at the academy. A long line of recruits holding hands, getting up spin in the big zero-gym on the academy orbital. In the middle, you were hardly moving, but you could feel the line's mass pulling harder and harder in both directions. And at either end, cadets were flying at unbelievable speed. When the line disintegrated, they'd hit the wall as if shot out of a cannon. The game eventually ended with a few cracked collarbones or a fractured skull, and would be strictly forbidden until the next year rediscovered its pleasures.

The executive officer stared wide-eyed at the cracked hullalloy.

"What's going to happen, Frick?"

The first engineer stared at the cracks, then closed his eyes, his lips moving as if talking himself through some complex equation. He pushed out from the bulkhead to look over its entirety.

Hobbes checked Captain Zai's chronometer. Only twenty-eight seconds before the third acceleration was scheduled. Surely Zai knew that the cargo bay had ruptured. The ejected metal and oxygen traveling away from the ship would have been picked up even by passive sensors.

But he wouldn't know that the structural damage extended to another layer of bulkhead. With the *Lynx* in darkmode, the distributed internal sensors were offline. The bridge crew was blind to the fissures. And who knew how far the virus extended? It was possible that all the frigate's bulkheads were infected.

Would Zai stick to the schedule they had agreed upon?

Twenty seconds.

She pushed herself after Frick, reattached her audio contact to his.

"First Engineer, report!"

The man opened his eyes.

"A yaw at that strength will tear the bow off the Lynx," he said flatly. "We'll lose it all, back as far as the forward gunnery station at least. Maybe farther."

"Maybe the rest of the way?" Hobbes asked.

He nodded.

Hobbes didn't hesitate. There wasn't time to think. She had to contravene the foremost rule of this engagement. This was why Zai had sent her up here: She was the only officer who would break the captain's orders if necessary.

And it was absolutely necessary.

ExO Hobbes pulled the handheld communicator from her belt and activated it. If the Rix spotted the faint signal, so be it.

To hell with them. The *Lynx* was less than two minutes from safety.

"Priority, priority," she said. "Do not coldjet. We'll break up. *Do not accelerate* at all. Hobbes out."

Then she flicked the device off.

The first engineer looked at her. She ignored his appalled expression.

"We're stabilized out here. Put your team in damage control positions."

For a moment, he didn't move. He couldn't believe she'd broken the captain's orders.

"I'll spell it out for you, Frick: Move yourself and your people inside."

She yanked her tether, pulling them both toward the hatch.

"We may come under fire soon," she added. Indeed, they almost certainly would.

Katherie Hobbes had made sure of that.

Engineer-Rating

The closer he approached the object, the less likely it seemed that Telmore Bigz had found the *Lynx*.

His vision continued to recover. Bigz could see now that the object wasn't entirely coherent. It seemed to be an agglomeration of large pieces, a few of which pulsed with their own rotation as the whole assemblage swung around itself. It couldn't be the frigate, unless tremendous damage had been done to her.

If Bigz were really going home, home had been blown to pieces.

He blinked again, trying to will his eyes back to clarity. He scanned the void, looking hopefully for a sign of the frigate nearby.

There was nothing.

Of course, even if he spotted the *Lynx*, there wasn't much he could do about it. Bigz's reaction canister was two-thirds empty—not enough juice in the can to jet off in a new direction.

He was committed to this wreckage.

A little closer, Bigz realized what the objects were.

He could see a ragged metal disk at the center of the assemblage, and a few large pieces of hullalloy around it. The whole thing was surrounded by a faint haze of frozen nitrox.

The largest object was the front of the *Lynx,* the

cargo bay section that had blown out along with the loose armor plates and a certain engineer-rating.

Bigz whistled. The catastrophe that had hurtled him from the ship had been much bigger than he'd thought. He'd suspected a ten-meter wide hole—at most— causing decompression strong enough to suck him through it. But this was major damage. He wondered if any other giant chunks of the *Lynx* were floating free. If the whole ship were in pieces, rescue wouldn't be coming anytime soon.

As he approached, Bigz's hurting eyes scanned the debris for a beacon pulse. Perhaps there were other survivors here. Full emergency transmissions weren't allowed—they would draw Rix fire—but someone might have activated their blinker without the radio transmitter. He swept his wrist light through the haze, probing the dark metal. Nothing. Even with the stimulant still pushing happiness through his veins, his heart sank. He was alone.

There were no corpses, at least.

Bigz used up a bit more reaction mass to slow himself. He landed with a thunk on one of the pieces of shielding that the team had cut from the singularity generator. His suit magnets held, and the collision didn't set the massive shield spinning too violently.

He stared at the chunk of bow bulkhead a dozen meters away, trying to imagine what the cargo bay would look like now. Fortunately, the engineering team had been tethered to the floor side. If they'd been attached to the plates, they'd all be out here. As it was most of them would still be with the *Lynx*—it was a fluke that Bigz's ring had popped. Unless, of course, the cargo floor bulkhead had given away too.

No, that didn't make sense. If that had happened,

the frigate would be all over the place, and Telmore Bigz would have been flying along with a lot of debris, nitrox, and other crewmen. Apparently, only he had been tossed from the ship.

He was alone, master of this tiny domain.

Suddenly, Bigz heard a message, a transmission pumped past his ruined ears into second hearing.

"Priority, priority," came a clear voice.

Shit! he thought. Who the hell was broadcasting? The Rix would localize the transmission in no time.

"Do not coldjet. We'll break up. Do not accelerate at all. Hobbes out."

The ExO? Didn't she realize that she was jeopardizing the ship?

Bigz brought up his suit's line-of-sight receiver, trying to determine where the transmission had come from. The device gave him a general direction, and he squinted into the blackness, searching for the *Lynx.*

But his eyes still failed him. The frigate was nowhere to be seen.

He squatted on the slowly spinning shield, hoping that the Rix hadn't heard the transmission. He decided to count while he waited, marking the minutes until they would all be out of danger.

Captain

"Enemy pulse fire has ceased," the sensor officer reported.

Captain Laurent Zai swallowed. The Rix laser had been firing at a high rate, searching for traces of cold-jet reaction mass. But now they had stopped looking.

The enemy had heard Hobbes's message.

"They must be charging up, sir."

"Indeed."

The firing rate of the Rix ranging laser was variable. It could be fired several times a second at low power, or more infrequently with greater effect. If they had given up pulse fire, then the Rix knew where the *Lynx* was. They were preparing a high-intensity punch, one sufficient to light up the Imperial frigate so that they could track her the rest of the way.

Once the frigate was glowing from a laser hit, the Rix gravity weapons would begin the work of destroying her.

At least ten seconds' charge for the first shot, he guessed.

Zai braced himself.

The big flatscreen flashed, lighting up the bridge as if a flare had bounded into the room.

"A miss, sir. A hundred meters off."

Zai nodded. The Rix were off by ten meters per second squared, roughly the push the *Lynx* had managed with the drone launcher. That kick had pushed her hard, enough to throw Zai out of his shipmaster's chair. And perhaps the loss of the cargo bay had resulted in a few more precious meters per second.

"We've got to turn her, sir!" the First Pilot shouted. "We're broadside!"

"Keep us floating, Pilot," he commanded.

If they could turn back to head-on orientation, they'd be a smaller target. But Katherie Hobbes had said another burst from the jets would break the *Lynx* up. Zai had to believe her. Hobbes wouldn't have given away their position unless she spoke with absolute certainty.

So Zai had been forced into a dire bet—that the Rix warship would miss them just a few more times. They were almost out of range.

So close to safety.

According to the bridge chronometer, they only had to survive another ninety seconds and they would drift out of the gravity cannon's perimeter. By their very nature, chaotic gravitons were far less coherent than photons. The *Lynx* was receding from the battlecruiser at more than 3,000 klicks per second. Under fixed physical laws, the frigate would soon be out of range.

Once they reached safety, Zai could bring internal diagnostics online and find out for himself how hard to push his ship.

Fifteen more seconds passed, enough time for the enemy to charge another burst.

The silent flash came on schedule.

"Another miss, sir! Two hundred meters aft."

"Unbelievable," Zai whispered. It had fallen on the other side of the first miss. They were overshooting!

Luck had smiled on the *Lynx* again.

Captain Zai leaned back, releasing his white-knuckled grip on his command chair. He sighed with relief.

"We may have made it," he said.

Ten seconds later, a shudder rocked through the bridge, and the high-pitched scream of boiling air filled the ship.

Engineer-Rating

Telmore Bigz could see the *Lynx* now.

The frigate sparkled against the black of space, the red light of laser fire running up and down its length.

"No!" he cried.

It was at least twenty kilometers away, glowing like an emergency light wand. The frigate's spindly shape seared itself into his vision, like a sun glimpsed with naked eyes. Bigz realized that his vision had finally cleared. Just in time to witness his ship and crewmates dying.

He wished that he were still blind.

Damn! They had almost made it out of range. By Bigz's reckoning, they would be out of the gravity cannon's perimeter in less than a minute.

The engineer-rating looked at the debris around him. It spun alone in the void, the forehull a minor planet with its own satellites, its own hazy atmosphere, even a population of one: Telmore Bigz.

Soon, this lost scrap heap would be all that remained of the *Lynx*.

A few more sparkles erupted from the frigate over the next seconds. The chaotic gravity beam would be orienting now, marshaling its full power for a final shot, using the laser damage to aim. The Rix might only get one blast before the Imperial warship passed out of range, so they would make sure they had it right.

Bigz squeezed the shockpack on his belt, the last dregs of stimulants giving him a moment of confidence for his decision. There was only one thing to do.

He activated his emergency beacon at full strength, its pulsing light reflecting from the rotating armor plates around him. Then Bigz brought his engineer's torch online, and charged it to hullalloy-cutting temperatures. He aimed it at the armor below him and pulled the trigger.

Light and heat flared from the cutter, and the armor burned a bright white where he swept its flame.

Bigz was now the sun for his tiny system, an unstable star casting hard, flickering shadows on the spinning debris around him.

Glowing bright in the void.

Captain

"Keep us dark!" Zai shouted over the din.

"But they have us, sir! We're already lit up like a firewire!"

"Just wait!" Zai yelled. "In another twenty seconds, they can't touch us."

The damage control officer was finally silent. The man had wanted to reactivate the ship's internal sensors, to help coordinate repair efforts. True, the Rix already knew exactly where the *Lynx* was. But emissions from the internals would give the enemy the frigate's orientation, and they'd target the drive; the *Lynx* would be crippled. Some part of the *Lynx* was certainly going to fry, but there was no sense giving the Rix their choice as to which.

"Steady. At most they can hit us twice at full power," Zai said.

"Damage reports starting to come in from the aft compoint, sir," someone reported. The epicenter of the laser hit.

"Report."

"No structural damage. The aft processor shaft looks fused. Ten dead and counting."

Damn, Zai thought. More casualties, and more processor capacity lost. All from a range-finding laser. When the burst of chaotic gravity came, it would be hell.

"How long until we're safe?" he asked the ensign at the chronometer.

"Twelve," she said.

"Count it," he ordered.

The bridge grew silent as the numbers diminished. There was nothing any of them could do. A gravity beam worked its deadliest magic against the crew of its target: snapped spines, crushed brains, ruptured internal organs. Without an energy sink to deflect the Rix weapon, dozens, perhaps hundreds of their crewmates were about to die.

Zai couldn't even warn his crew, but at least he could address the bridge.

With five seconds left, he waved the ensign quiet.

But he found his tongue stymied. All the usual Vadan words invoked the Emperor, and that would be too ridiculous an epitaph for Laurent Zai.

"Thank you for your service," was all he managed.

Zai sighed, waiting.

The time passed. It must have.

"The shot missed us," the captain said quietly.

The sensor officer stared into his headsdown in disbelief.

"Not an accidental miss, sir. They changed their targeting. Attacked a debris field six kilometers away. Tore it to pieces."

"But . . . *why?*" Zai stammered.

"It was lit up, sir. Some heat, microwaves, and a high-strength transmission."

"Transmission?"

"An Imperial SOS. A personal beacon."

Zai shook his head. It was too much to believe. A diversion, at the right moment. A member of the *Lynx*'s crew had somehow wound up out there, kilometers away, and had died for the ship. But who?

"They had us, sir," the sensor officer continued. "Why would they go for anything else? It was only a few sparks out there, relative to the hit they'd put on us."

"We were too easy," Zai said. "Too obvious. Hobbes's transmission was too blatant. They must have thought that we were the decoy."

A tremble began in the ship, a low moan that rose and fell.

"They're targeting us now, sir. Switched their fire from the debris to the *Lynx*. But we're outside effective range. The gravity cannon is at half-charge, wide aperture. Five thousand gravitons per."

Zai sighed. Barely enough to give a man skin cancer. He could feel the weapon's passage with his sensitive inner ear, a mild nausea at worst.

"Give me internal diagnostics," he ordered. "And order the crew to remain in pressure suits." The frigate was unstable, and the low-intensity chaotic gravity bombardment might continue for a while, growing ever more diffuse as the ships drifted apart.

Again, they had survived.

House

Over many decades, the house had grown in all directions.

Though perched on a mountain peak, it extended deep enough into the mantle of Home to draw geothermal power. Now that summer had arrived, the views from six balconies revealed gardens and artificial waterfalls all the way to the horizon. The house had littered neighboring peaks with outpost colonies of self-sustaining butterflies, their mirror wings reflecting sunlight to keep plants alive and water flowing, cast artful shadows, and bring the pale reds of the arctic sunset to three hundred sixty degrees of vista. Its processors were everywhere, buried in the rocky passages of the mountain, backed up in rented remote locations, distributed across the snows for a hundred kilometers. Between polar isolation, the senatorial privilege of its mistress, and its vast size, the house was a world unto itself.

And yet a certain anxiety haunted the house today, a sense of inadequacy and self-doubt that ran like a subtle tremor through its teraflops. A new situation had arisen, one that it had considered and modeled for decades, but never experienced. For the first time, there were two people here at once.

The mistress had a guest.

The house scanned the underground food gardens, the special supplies brought in by suborbital for the lieutenant-commander's visit, the emergency stores that had lain untouched for a century. It tallied, of course, far more food than two people could eat in four years, much less four days. But the disquiet remained. This visit was the house's chance to show the mistress what it had accomplished over lonely decades of abandonment, to display the results of its long independent expansion program.

Dinner was already planned, the steamy growing levels just above the geothermal plant raided of produce for a tropical banquet. Fermented plantains had been basted with relish of green tamarind. Cabbage pickled and formed into delicate flower shapes, then flash-fried in a microsecond plasma field. A species of brine shrimp that purified the house water supply simmered for hours in caramel. A pudding of sticky rice and palm sugar blackened with coconut ash to match the lieutenant-commander's naval uniform. And to clear the palette, twenty milliliters of vodka to end each course had been infused with lychee, rambutan, papaya, and mangosteen in turn.

But perhaps this was too much, the house now despaired. The rules of etiquette were clear: The last dinner of any visit should be the grandest, not the first. With Laurent Zai staying longer, it would have to outdo itself four more dinners in a row! And what if the mistress changed her mind again? No amount of processor power, no number of contingency plans, no acreage of machinery—nothing was sufficient to withstand human caprice at its worst.

What were they talking about now?

The house returned its attention to where the mistress stood with the newly promoted Captain Laurent Zai. They were on the western balcony, holding each other, looking out at a trio of small peaks capped with patterns of algae-reddened snow, just now struck with the slowly setting sun. (Quite a composition, the house thought smugly.) The mistress was still smiling from the kiss they'd shared after she had invited him to stay.

"Four days seems so little, Nara," Zai said. (The house disagreed. Twelve meals to create; four sunsets to compose!)

"We can make them last."

"I hope so." His eyes fell to the garden of insect-shaped ice sculptures below. "We've so many technologies for making Absolute time pass quickly. Stasis, relativistic travel, the symbiant. But none to make a few days seem longer."

The mistress laughed. "I'm sure we'll think of something." She moved closer.

"You already have?"

"Yes, I have. Perhaps dinner can wait."

The house followed their progress to the bedroom, mutely appalled.

Senator

As the summer's brief night fell across the room, Nara Oxham thought to herself: An entire day without apathy. It had been too long. She needed more of these respites from the capital, needed to set her mind completely free of the drug without the crowd coming in.

She looked at Laurent's dozing form. Perhaps she needed a measure of madness every now and then.

After the rush of the first few minutes, the effects of apathy withdrew gradually, Nara's empathy gaining in strength over the slow hours. Her ability had been active all day, moving and adjusting itself, slowly growing comfortable with the man next to her, settling across the pattern of his thoughts like a blanket of snow over one of the house gardens. Laurent seemed to have recovered his balance in the hours since telling her about Dhantu; she could feel his mind aligned by the sureties of his gray religion, his military discipline.

Although Laurent's touchstones sprang from convictions alien to Nara, there was comfort in anything that took away his pain.

Nara wondered if this was a good idea, letting herself bond so strongly with someone she hardly knew, who was by any measure a political enemy.

Who would be gone so soon, for so long.

Laurent stirred.

"A fire?" she asked.

They left the bed and opened up the north wall to the pink night sky and the arctic chill. Nara loved the high arctic summer. The sun hid behind the mountains but never lost its grasp on the horizon. She wondered what it would be like in half a year, when daylight rather than darkness lasted only one hour in ten.

They chose split, dry logs for the fire, building it high and hot enough to push them back a few meters, counterpoint to the chill night air on their backs.

When Laurent slipped away to maintain his prosthetics, Nara asked the house to salvage what it could of dinner and deliver it here. It responded a bit stiffly. Knowing that grays didn't approve of talking machines, Nara had ordered it to keep silent in Laurent's company. She wondered if the house's conversational package needed more practice than it was getting on her infrequent visits.

When Laurent returned, he was dressed. She wrapped herself in bedclothes.

After a silence, she felt his discomfort. He was unsure what to say. This moment always eventually came with new lovers, in those quiet moments between dramatic turns.

What would the pink senator and the gray soldier talk about?

No point in fighting the obvious.

"Do you really think there'll be another Incursion, Laurent?"

He shrugged, but she felt trouble in him. "Until today, I had my doubts about the rumors. But this posting to Legis, right on the frontier . . ."

"Isn't most of the Navy on one frontier or another?"

"True. But I'm to take command of a new kind of warship." He paused and looked at her. "But that's classified, of course." He smiled. "You're not a Rix spy, are you?"

Nara laughed. "Laurent, in a few weeks I'll be on the Intelligence Sub-Quorum of His Majesty's Senate. You'd better hope I'm not a Rix spy."

His eyebrows shot up. "You're on the oversight committee?"

Laurent's alarm flared in her empathy, and turned quickly into reflexive withdrawal. Nara could feel the revulsion that military culture held for civilian interference.

"If that's what you call it in the Navy, yes."

He took a deep breath. "Oh, I didn't realize."

"Did you think Secularists never took an interest in the military?"

"An interest? Certainly. But not necessarily a positive one."

"My interest is very positive, Laurent. The Emperor's military forces benefit from oversight by the living, I'm absolutely sure. We're the ones who do the dying for him, after all."

He grimaced, the phantoms of his lost limbs twisting painfully, and she could almost hear his thoughts. What did she, a pink senator, know of dying?

"My assignment may come before the committee," he said flatly. "Perhaps we should restrict our conversation."

Oxham blinked, marveling again at how politically naive military officers could be. Laurent hadn't even bothered to check her portfolio before coming. Her own handlers wouldn't let her attend so much as a cocktail party without memorizing a detailed history of every person on the guest list. After inviting him here, she'd researched Zai's commanders and former crew, his Academy standings, and had digested reams of Apparatus propaganda about the hero of Dhantu. She'd even dipped into the gutter media, the channels who called him the Broken Man.

Of course, that didn't mean she understood him. In all that detail Nara had missed one salient point: the length of his career in real years. After almost a century Absolute of serving the Emperor, decades passing at relativistic speeds, the man was tired of losing friends and lovers to the Time Thief. And now he would be gone for another twenty years at least.

He had every right to be angry. But not at her.

She put a hand on his arm and turned away to look into the fire. "Laurent, I don't want to restrict anything we say to each other. And I don't care about the Emperor's secrets. I just asked because I want to know when you're coming back."

He sighed. "As do I."

They were silent for a while, staring into the flames. Nara wondered why she had pressed him. He was probably right; they shouldn't be sharing classified information across the lines of political and military, democratic and Imperial, pink and gray. But somehow she needed to cross the boundaries of their alien hierarchies now, in these early days. Otherwise they never would.

She wanted to be trusted, even though she was a pink. Perhaps it was as simple as that.

Nara felt the change in him before he spoke. He wanted something too.

"I know you're not a spy, Nara. And I'm sure your committee will hear about it soon enough, so you should hear it from me. They've given me a new kind of ship. A frigate prototype."

"Everyone knew you'd get a command, Laurent. A reward for your faithful service."

"Perhaps. But any prototype wants battle-testing. They wouldn't be sending a ship like the *Lynx* to the Rix frontier if there weren't some promise of action there."

Nara nodded, feeling the certainty in him. And the dread. She was too young to have lived through the Incursion herself, but could always feel the icy memory of Rix terror attacks in those who had. Whole cities razed by gravity weapons. Planets reduced to preterraformation by bombardment from space. Even the gray places of the dead attacked, the bodies of the risen deliberately sundered beyond the ability of the symbiant to repair.

"It's a small, fast ship, with hitting power and range," he continued. "A deep raider, a way to strike back against the Rix."

"I see," she said softly, squeezing his non-prosthetic arm. "That would mean going even farther outward, wouldn't it?"

Her empathy with Laurent remained strong; she felt him sifting thoughts so cold that she couldn't name them. What was he thinking? "Ten more years out," he said. "Plus years of raiding, if it comes to war."

"So you really meant it that you might be gone fifty years?"

"Yes. Fifty."

An entire senator's term. Of course, with Nara in stasis most of the year, and Laurent's time frame stretched out by relativity, it might only be a decade subjective for them both. Still a vast separation, given that she'd hardly known him two days. (Why, she wondered, was it always most terrible being separated from someone you'd just met?)

"It's not only the years, Nara."

"The fact that I'm a pink? That I'll be slashing your budget while you're at the front?"

He barely smiled. "No. It's what I'll do out there."

That gray Vadan charm again. "Laurent, I can hardly expect fidelity."

"I didn't mean . . . Nara, I'm talking about what I'll do as a soldier. What the *Lynx* is designed to do."

"Make war? You've done that before. You served in the Dhantu Occupation, after all. I can't imagine anything worse."

He turned to her, still full of blackness, and spoke with effort. "I can."

She quieted herself, letting her empathy work.

It was very small inside him, hard to see clearly. A dark place.

Then she found a way in, and it hit her. Worse than his memories of the tortures he'd suffered on Dhantu, more sovereign. It was a black abstraction, cold potential, like the mindnoise on a Vasthold street corner in the calm just before a political riot—the kind in which people would die. Nara Oxham's empathy recoiled, her head suddenly spinning, some animal part of her mind knowing ahead of the rest what her empathy would show.

But he kept talking.

"The *Lynx* is a deep raider, Nara. Long-range killing power, fast and expendable."

Unbidden, true telepathy came, with a glimpse of what he imagined. Rolling satellite imagery: fields and rivers from space, the grid of a city coming into view.

"Against the Rix," he continued, "we won't be hitting shipping and logistical targets. The *Lynx* is made to do what we never managed in the First Incursion. To take the war to the Rix worlds."

"Laurent . . ." This gray man knew the mechanics of it. He understood the horrific details of how it would be done.

"As they brought war to ours."

"Stop." As she said it, Nara's hand went to her wrist, searching for the apathy bracelet. But she'd taken it off when they'd arrived. She was defenseless against his thoughts.

In any event, he said it out loud.

"My ship is for killing worlds, Nara."

She swallowed something acid, stood up and went onto the balcony. The rail caught her hands, and she pulled herself up from stumbling. Breathed deeply.

The cold cleared her head. This helplessness was absurd. "House."

"Yes, mistress?" it whispered in private second hearing.

"Get me my bracelet. Priority."

"Done."

Laurent was beside her. "Nara? I'm sorry. You would have heard anyway."

"It's just withdrawal. From my counter-empathy drug."

"I'm sorry." He held her, pressed close to warm her. She could hardly feel the dark thing in him now. Godspite, where did he hide it?

"It's nothing, Laurent. It happens sometimes when I come out here. In the capital, I have to take it for the crowds. But here I forget."

He sighed. "I understand." He knew she was lying.

"Laurent . . ."

"Yes?"

She saw something moving. A house serving drone, skittering down the handrail, clutching her apathy bracelet. She took another deep breath, her panic receding at the sight of it.

"Will you do it?" Nara reached out and took the bracelet from the drone.

Laurent clutched her shoulder, and she tasted his struggle, the fight against his conditioning, his upbringing, his own gray soul, against a planetary landscape rolling beneath him, virgin and defenseless.

"I hope not," he said.

Her fingers closed around the bracelet, and the drone backed away. But Nara didn't activate the flow of apathy yet.

"Don't," she asked.

He looked behind him, as if the Emperor might be listening from the bedroom. But it was just more servos, a small army of them arranging things in front of the fire. In the flickering light, they looked like mad insects building a miniature city.

Laurent Zai nodded quietly and whispered, "All right. I won't. I promise you."

Four days to make promises, he had said an hour ago.

Nara slipped the bracelet onto her wrist unused, and swallowed. Godspite, her mouth was dry.

"Dinner, then?" she said.

2

ALCHEMICAL

Above all, a soldier must be willing to die.

—ANONYMOUS 167

Commando

The second rendezvous went considerably better. H_rd successfully jumped from the recon flyer to the dirigible, and over a few hours it lifted her to approximately eighty kilometers altitude.

The commando looked down over the entanglement facility. From this height, it was smaller than a palm at arm's length. The dirigible's vacuum sphere had quadrupled in size during the slow ascent. H_rd pressed her face to a rebreather tank. The decline in pressure during the assent had been considerable; her ears were ringing, and she'd felt a blood vessel burst in one eye after an hour of climbing. A Rix commando could take a wide variation of air pressure, but this was the lowest she'd experienced since hull-breach training. There was no weather up here in the mesopause, but it was unbelievably cold. The ablative suit—recovered, like the rebreather, from a supersonic aircraft emergency store—was insulated enough to keep her from freezing. H_rd found, however, that she missed her sable coat.

Well, she would be warmed up soon enough.

The positioning device in her hand beeped, Alexander's signal to her. It was almost time to drop. The entanglement facility seemed off-center to her, but the compound mind had carefully calculated the wind direction and speed.

With a strangely unRix thought, h_rd hoped that Alexander hadn't made any mistakes.

She had to hit an area roughly ten meters across, after a fall that would take more than twenty minutes. Alexander had used its weather satellites to find the snowdrift, which filled a thirty-meter deep glacial rift inside the array's defensive wire. The compound mind had introduced a few nanos disguised as snowflakes into its cloud-seeding efforts. These had fallen into the drift and doped the snow. Over the last few days, the nano colony had changed the structure of the ice crystals, expanding the drift, leaching carbon from the soil for structure, and creating a colloidal foam that would compress smoothly when h_rd struck it. The snow had swelled up into a hill that rose ten meters above the surrounding landscape. Thus, h_rd's fall would be broken gradually over almost forty meters.

Of course, she had to hit the trench dead center. She held the positioning device firmly in her free hand; it would guide her to the target area.

H_rd prepared herself, swallowing to adjust the pressure in her ears. She checked the straps of her mission pack.

Then the dirigible motors cut. The signal to drop.

She unlocked the muscles in her hand that clung to the dirigible's payload basket, and slipped into the void.

Weightless again. Freefall was an old friend.

The rush of air built slowly, worsening the cold on the unprotected parts of her face.

Her ablative suit was designed to fight fires onboard aircraft. A few nanos—programmed by Alexander and delivered through a medical pack—had altered it sufficiently to make it invisible to Imperial radar.

Or so Alexander's models predicted.

She rolled into a ball, protecting the positioning device and watching its numbers move. The altimeter showed her to be still accelerating. Terminal velocity for a human was about sixty meters per second on Legis. As close as h_rd could estimate by the rolling altimeter, her speed had passed that. Probably the air up here was thin enough that terminal velocity was noticeably higher, and she would actually be braking as she descended into higher pressures.

After five minutes of falling, warmth began to bloom in the suit. It grimly crossed her mind that she was heating up from reentry friction. But h_rd dismissed the thought; she couldn't be going that fast. The temperature increase was just the heat trap of the stratopause. After ten minutes total of falling, the air gradually began to grow cold again. She was passing through the stratosphere, approaching the cold air of the tropopause.

Extending her arms slowly, h_rd began to take control of the descent, slowing herself and angling toward the entanglement facility, now as big as a dinner plate below her. She swallowed constantly to keep her ears clear, and watched the numbers on the positioning device roll as she angled her free hand and legs to guide her fall. Her coordinates seemed only incrementally closer to the target. Of course, she was a few minutes from entering the tropospheric wind currents that would push her toward the target snow drift.

H_rd had low-orbit jumped once in training, but that was with a purpose-built Rix suit, parafoil, and artificial-gravity backup. The situation was somewhat different when wearing a retrofitted, improvised Imperial suit and landing in a pile of snow. It wasn't the equipment that had her nervous, though.

She had faced death at every stage of this mission. It was nothing short of fantastic that she had survived this long. But h_rd had realized during these relatively quiet minutes of freefall that Rana Harter had stolen some of her courage. H_rd found that she wanted to live, a strange desire for a Rix commando.

Perfect, she thought. To encounter fear for the first time while falling—at sixty meters per second and without a parachute—into a heavily guarded enemy facility.

"Love," h_rd said bitterly. The rampant wind tore the word from her mouth without comment.

After fifteen minutes had elapsed, the longitude and latitude on the positioning device began slowly moving toward the target values; the tropospheric wind was pushing her toward the landing area. And it was getting warmer again, moving toward the merely freezing temperatures of the polar surface.

The entanglement facility was now visibly increasing in size from moment to moment. The sensation of falling became less abstract; h_rd finally *saw* the ground rushing toward her. She extended hands and feet and angled her body, swooping to bring herself closer to the target area. The positioning device finally beeped; she had matched the snowdrift's coordinates.

The commando could see it below her now, the winding, snow-filled rift reflecting starlight with pale luminescence. From aerial photographs supplied by Alexander, h_rd had memorized the exact spot she needed to hit. She tucked the positioning device into her pack and began counting down.

The altimeter read 6,000 meters. A hundred seconds to go.

She swallowed fiercely now as air pressure built, cupping her hands to guide herself gently to the target over these last few moments. Invoked by a mental command, her body went through an impact preparation sequence. She expelled the air from her lungs completely, let her muscles relax, rebalanced the ratio of strength and flexibility in her plastic ligaments to favor the latter.

By the time her internal count had reached eight seconds, h_rd was physiologically ready for impact. The deepest part of the trench lay directly below her, no farther than looking down from the top of a medium-sized building. At half a kilometer and falling, details on the ground gained focus rapidly. Rocks and a few scrub bushes became visible, and the moiré weave of a retransmitter dish's arc scintillated in one corner of her vision.

After twenty minutes of falling, it was odd how quickly the snowbound earth was rushing up at her.

Five, four, three . . .

The surface of the altered snow broke with a *pop* as she crashed through. She later realized that a thin layer of frost had formed over the nano-doped snow. This brittle crust of rime was at most a centimeter thick—and probably couldn't have supported more than a few grams of weight. But at sixty meters per second it packed a punch. Like the surface of water at high speed, it had for a moment the force of concrete. The impact broke h_rd's nose and split her lower lip, and opened a bleeding cut over her right eye.

But then she passed into the colloidal pseudo-snow, which caught her in its foamy arms, slowing her descent. The Rixwoman came smoothly to a stop.

She opened her eyes in total darkness, her head ringing from the impact of breaking the crust. Testing each muscle and joint in turn, she found herself to be uninjured except for the insults to her face. She sat up, orienting herself in the darkness of the cold, compressed foam-snow around her, and looked upwards.

The sky was just visible through the twenty-meter-deep hole she had made. Her own outline, almost comically exact, showed for a few moments before the foam-snow began to collapse, covering her. H_rd breathed deeply and fast, storing oxygen before she was enveloped by the foam. She would remain here motionless for thirty minutes or so. The impact shock of her landing would have registered on the facility's motion sensors, but if she stayed still, the snow-muffled, momentary vibration would read as simply a cleaving of the snowdrift: an event well within the natural stochastic rumblings of the arctic wild.

The darkness covered her. After the rushing air, especially the frigid layer of the tropopause, the foam-snow brought a blanket of warmth. H_rd felt blood dripping into her eye from her cut, and tended to her wounds as she waited. That brittle crust of ice represented a small error in Alexander's plan, she noted to herself, the sort of hairline mistake that was magnified a thousandfold in a mission of this difficulty.

No system, not even a compound mind, was perfect. A very unRix thought, but true.

After she'd waited the requisite time, the commando began to tunnel out of the drift. She kept an eye on the positioning device, not trusting her own magnetoreceptor direction-finding cells this close to the pole. Her oxygen reserve was limited, and any wrong turn that led her into an unclimbable wall could be deadly.

It would be rather banal to drown in this foam after surviving an eighty-kilometer fall.

The nano-doped snow was strange stuff. In the read-out light of the positioning device, she could see the tiny bubbles that made it up, composed of water structured by large carbon molecules. The substance seemed dry when touched gently, but under shock it disintegrated into a wet, somewhat slimy substance. In her hand the bubbles broke down quickly into water; even her low body temperature was sufficient to disrupt its stability. When the warm winds of spring came, all evidence of how this trick had been performed would be gone forever.

H_rd reached the edge of the foam, and climbed from the trench into a drift of real snow. She raised a periscope through the crust first, and surveyed the area. There was no sign of an Imperial response to her landing. She pulled herself from the drift and dusted snow and foam from her. The ablative suit had torn on impact, and a few icy trickles of water already numbed her feet.

The Rixwoman crawled away from the landing zone, careful to keep her distance from the area of doped snow. Anyone stepping on that part of the drift would plummet to the bottom of the trench, softly but ignominiously. There were also vibration sensors to be wary of. H_rd moved slowly and haltingly, an uneven motion designed to mimic natural processes.

The commando searched the horizon for the telltale glimmer of microwave arrays. The threads of the off-line repeaters glowed like spiderwebs all around her, the nearest thirty meters away. With her painstakingly slow and interrupted crawl, it took h_rd five minutes to traverse the distance.

The main portion of the device was roughly the size

of a fist. From this central mass radiated the microwave receiver array, the slender filaments that gathered the civilian communications of Legis bound for translight transmission. The transmitter stick rose from the center of the fist, a decimeter-high antenna that forwarded the data to the entanglement facility.

The repeater also sported four legs and two manipulator arms. The hordes of them that dotted the tundra functioned as a single entity. They moved slowly, but quickly enough to disperse or gather themselves as their throughput required. The whole system was distributed over thousands of square kilometers, making it difficult to sabotage and impossible to destroy from space without megatons of explosives. These repeaters were a hardy system, a wartime backup to the vulnerable hardlines, meter-wide cables through which the data usually flowed. Once the Imperials had realized that the compound mind had successfully propagated, they had isolated the facility. The repeaters had been taken off-line by hand: hundreds of militia workers moving through the snow on foot and disconnecting the repeaters individually. The facility's input had been reduced to a single hardline connection, a low-bandwidth coupling that the military tightly controlled. Alexander was cut off.

The Imperials assumed that any measure undertaken by hundreds of humans by hand would be irreversible without similarly crude measures. But Alexander had other ideas.

H_rd looked at the repeater closely. Its power pack seemed out of alignment, tilted to one side at an angle of about fifteen degrees. She refocused her eyes into their microscopic mode, and noted the simple measure the Imperials had taken. The receivers were still working, still sucking up the vast quantity of data that Legis produced, but the repeater was physically disconnected from its power supply. Tilted those few degrees, the pack was disjunct from its contact, thus all off-planet transmissions were halted here, a few kilometers from their goal.

H_rd approved of the awesome simplicity of it. The thing actually functioned like some pre-spaceflight *switch*. Again, the crudeness of the Imperials impelled a certain grudging respect from the Rixwoman.

With her smallest finger, she clicked the power pack back into the correct position. That was it. The lethal wire and two thousand kilometers of wilderness protected nothing but this simple switch.

Her mission was complete.

She crawled slowly back to the edge of the landing zone and buried herself in a few decimeters of the snow-foam, leaving only a breathing hole. She would wait here for a few more hours before making her rather noisy escape.

Before covering her head, h_rd looked back and saw that the repeater she had fixed was already moving, making its beetlelike way across the snow.

Alexander was inside the wire.

Senator

It was good to be back in the halls of the Senate Forum. The air seemed to be cleaner here, the wash of politics more pure.

The Senate was an unruly chamber, of course, more so now that the special war session was in full swing. But the numberless details of the Senate's agenda balanced each other, blending into a shape as smooth as the rumble of a distant ocean. The noisy debates here were a relief for Nara Oxham after the demands of the War Council, where each crisis came into absolute focus, and lives were in play with every vote.

"You were right, Niles," she said as they walked together back toward her offices. Oxham had just presented the last few days of the council's work to the full Senate.

"I knew they'd love you, Senator. Even the lackeys were standing by the end."

"Not about that, Niles," she said, waving away his praise. The speech had gone well, though. Captain Laurent Zai had made them all look brilliant. The *Lynx*'s attack on the Rix battlecruiser had given the Empire its first victory, a gift to the propaganda effort. Counterattacks in an interstellar war could take years to mount, time spans over which even the most resolute society's morale could falter. But Zai had struck back against the Rix in a matter of days.

"In any case, I have my speechwriters to thank for that."

Niles began a sputter of protest at this.

"I was referring, in any case," she interrupted, "to when you cautioned me about losing my way in the council. Forgetting why we came here. You were right to warn me."

"Senator," the old man said, "I never thought that was a likelihood. I just had to say something. I get paid to advise you."

Nara smiled at her counselor's clumsy modesty. The world seemed bright to her today. She'd played the Senate like some Secularist street gathering back on Vasthold, pulled the bright tracery of their emotions through the courses that Niles's speech had mapped out for her. The moment in which she'd captured them had come early, the critical juncture when she could feel their agreement with the council's war plan coalescing, reacting to her words like a flock of birds turning in unison.

The sharp flavor of the captive crowd still lingered in her mind, and Nara savored the way it blended with the sunlight penetrating the high windows along the Forum great hall. But the pleasures of politics were trifles compared to the real source of her joy.

Laurent Zai had survived, escaping death again.

Of course, only a handful knew that his success in battle had saved an entire world. It seemed fantastic now that the War Council had contemplated something so monstrous. She wondered what the two living counselors who had voted for the Emperor's plan had felt as the hour of genocide had approached.

To Senator Nara Oxham, it seemed that she had emerged from the crisis with far more power on the

War Council. She'd been the first to vote against the plan, so her voice was now second only to the Emperor's. The once unanimous council was beginning to develop fault lines, the living against the dead, Senator Oxham against the sovereign. The Emperor hadn't lost a vote yet, but Oxham could see him steering away from ideas when she voiced opposition to them, reluctant to force any issue that she might raise a majority against.

But the majority was there, silent and waiting to assert itself against any future genocides.

In his mind-reading way, Niles interrupted her thoughts.

"But if you want some more advice?"

"Earn your keep, Roger."

He waited another moment, until they had crossed the threshold of Nara Oxham's private domain. Her offices had been almost doubled in size to match her new council rank, the ever-mobile walls of the Forum pushing against the surrounding senators' territories, a fat man jostling his way onto an elevator. They walked past a score of staff, half of whose names she didn't know yet.

When they reached Oxham's personal office, Niles continued.

"You are restricted by the hundred-year rule, of course."

Nara nodded warily. She'd explained to Niles why she couldn't discuss the council's contingency plan if the *Lynx* had failed. He was allowed to know of the rule's invocation, but mention of the forbidden topic still made her vaguely nervous.

"But *I'm* not restricted," he continued. "I can make

suppositions, and give you advice. Let me talk, but don't confirm or deny anything."

"Is this a good idea, Roger?"

"Nothing in the rule says you can't listen to me, Senator."

She nodded slowly.

"One: You're happy, Nara Oxham. Because your lover survived, because the war took a good turn. But my guess is that you're also happy that the Emperor's contingency plan didn't have to be enacted. He must have had one, in case the *Lynx* failed."

Oxham started to nod, but willed herself to absolute stillness. No matter how secure her offices were, there were methods of interrogation which could plumb memories of any conversation. They were playing a dangerous game with an ancient law. And although Nara had senatorial privilege, Roger Niles did not.

"Two: The Emperor's contingency plan was . . . *extraordinary* enough that he decided to shroud it with the hundred-year rule."

Nara blinked, then looked out the window at the noontime effulgence of the capital.

"Three: I personally believe that anything too extraordinary would not have the vote of Nara Oxham."

She wanted to thank Roger, or at least to smile, but kept her face still.

"All of which means," Niles continued, "that you either won the vote, and the Emperor is hopping mad at you, or you lost, and earned some modest displeasure. In either case, Laurent Zai's victory made this extraordinary plan unnecessary, and His Risen Majesty looks like a monster for whatever he contemplated. And he's got you to thank for dividing the council. He wanted to spread the guilt."

Oxham wondered how Niles had realized all this. Perhaps he had read the faces of the other counselors during her speech, or perhaps he'd detected preparations for the Emperor's plan somewhere among the volumes of data he digested every day. Or maybe the invocation of the rule had been enough, and the rest was Niles's conjecture.

"In short," he continued, "you have committed the ultimate sin: winning a moral victory against the Emperor."

She couldn't resist. "A *moral* victory, Niles? I thought you said that was an oxymoron."

"It is, Senator. I believe you'll discover that your victory contains several internal contradictions. For example, although it has given you more power than you've ever had, you're also in far greater danger."

"Aren't you being dramatic, Niles?"

He shook his head. "It couldn't be more obvious, Nara. If I'm right, *if* I'm not crazy, you've directly antagonized the most powerful single man in the coreward reaches of the human expansion."

She shrugged, returning her face to a neutral mask, and stared out the window. A world had been saved, her lover was still alive. Niles's warning couldn't completely overshadow the joys of this bright day.

But it still troubled her that Niles had deduced all this. Did he have spies on the War Council? Nara Oxham looked at the old man, and saw the lines of concern on his smooth face. Then she understood: All the evidence he'd needed had come from Nara herself. He could read her as easily as she could read a crowd. Understanding the masses was a politician's art, but understanding politicians was the necessary genius of a counselor.

He was an empath's empath.

"You call that advice, Roger?" she said after a while.

"No, Senator. I call *this* advice: Be careful. Move slowly. Watch your back. Assume that the Emperor is setting a trap, waiting for you to make a mistake. Don't."

"Don't make mistakes? That's good advice, counselor."

"It's damn good advice, Senator. The next one could cost us all dearly."

She sighed, then nodded.

Roger Niles sat finally, sinking heavily into one of her visitor's chairs.

"There's another thing, Senator. I have to apologize."

Oxham's eyes widened. "For what, in heaven's name?"

He swallowed. "For saying that Zai's death would be for the best."

"Ah." Nara thought back on that moment. She'd never been angry at Niles for those words. They'd been his way of alerting her to the peril of loving an officer at the front. It was Niles's job to warn her of danger, as he had done a moment ago.

"Roger," she said, "I know you're glad that Laurent is still alive."

His eyes darted away. "Of course. No one should lose their lover to war. But at least his death would have been final."

"Roger?" she asked. She'd never seen the hard expression now set on his face.

"Did I ever tell you why I went into politics, Senator?"

She tried to recall, but the concept of a Roger Niles before politics was unthinkable. The man *was* politics. Nara shook her head slowly.

"The love of my life died when I was twenty," he said, forcing the words out slowly. "A sudden hemorrhage. She was from old Vasthold aristocracy, in the days of hereditary elevation."

Oxham blinked. She'd had no idea that Niles was that old. Before she'd become an Imperial senator, he always claimed to spend the time between electoral cycles in coldsleep, only living in the months before elections, extending his life through generations of political battles. But she'd never believed that could really be true.

Hereditary elevation? He must be *ancient.*

"So when Sarah died, they took her away," he said. "Made her one of them."

He looked out at the window at the bright city.

"I rejoiced, and praised the Emperor," he continued quietly. "I saw her in the hospice, and she tried to say good-bye to me. But I thought it was just ritual. I assumed she would come back. We were closer than all the lovers in history, I thought. But she didn't return. After a few months, I tracked her to the gray enclave where she . . . lived."

"Oh, Roger," Nara said softly. "How awful."

"Indeed. They really are gray, you know, those towns. As gray as a weeklong rain. By then Sarah hardly knew who I was. She would squint when she looked at me, as if there were *something* familiar about my face. But she would only talk about the steam rising from her teapot. If she looked away for even a moment, when her eyes returned they had to learn to remember me all over again. As if I were some faint watermark on reality, less real than the steam.

"There was no one inside her, Nara. The symbiant is a trick. Death is final. The dead are lost."

"How did it end, Roger?"

"They politely asked me to leave, and I left. Then I joined the local Secularist Party, and buried myself in the task of burying the dead."

"Politics," Nara said. "We're alike, aren't we?"

The old counselor nodded in agreement. Nara Oxham had turned to political life to overcome the demons of her childhood. She had turned madness into perception, vulnerability into empathy, a terror of crowds into raw power over them. Roger Niles had turned his hatred into a tactical genius, his supreme loss into relentless purpose.

Niles was every bit as fixated as the Emperor, Oxham now saw. Plumbing a thousand newsfeeds for every advantage to use against the grays, Niles was exacting his slow revenge against an immortal foe.

"Yes, we are the same, Senator," Niles said. "We love the living rather than worship the dead. And I am glad Laurent Zai is alive."

"Thank you, Roger."

"Just do us all a favor and be careful, Senator, so that you're still alive when the captain returns."

Nara Oxham smiled calmly, and felt newfound power in the expression.

"Don't worry about me, counselor. There are more moral victories to come."

Captain

Laurent Zai looked down upon the glowing airscreen with displeasure.

The bridge was alive again, filled with voices and the floating runes of synesthesia, animated by interface gestures and those of human-to-human communication: palms upturned in frustration, fingers pointed, fists shaken.

The airscreen showed the frigate's new configuration. In the aftermath of battle, the *Lynx* was a different ship. Gone were the gunnery stations and drone-pilot berths, the launch bays and rows of burn beds. Crew cabins and rec space had reappeared. Long low-gee corridors had been created for moving heavy objects up and down the ship, and there were huge new open areas for stripping damaged components down to parts.

Zai shook his head. His ship was half-junked.

What the battle hadn't destroyed, the repair crews were pulling apart, cannibalizing, robbing Peter to pay Paul. Were the *Lynx* to face an enemy now, they would be utterly defenseless. But the frigate was well past the Rix battlecruiser. The enemy still pursued them, accelerating at its maximum of six gees, but to cancel the 3,000 kps relative velocity between the warships would take the Rix half a day, by which time they'd be

75 million kilometers away. After matching vectors, it would take them another half-day to return to the *Lynx*.

Well before that moment came, the frigate would have maneuver capability of its own.

The main fusion drive hadn't been touched in the battle. It was, however, the *Lynx*'s only remaining means of creating power. The singularity generator—the frigate's auxiliary energy source—was operable, but the shielding that the engineers had stripped from it was lost now. If the generator were big banged, there wouldn't be enough countermass to keep the black hole in place. Armor was being stripped from all across the *Lynx* to build new shielding, but that left her gunnery hardpoints less than hard.

Indeed, all the frigate's defensive systems were compromised. With the loss of her bow, the ship had no forward armor; two full-time gunnery crews were required to man the forward close-in defenses, picking off any meteoroids that threatened the hurtling ship. The drone magazine had been damaged by flockers, and its launch rail destroyed by the frigate's last desperate acceleration, so there was no way to field a large complement of defensive drones. Worst of all, the ship's energy-sink manifold was gone for good, scattered across millions of kilometers of space.

Little hard armor, no defensive cloud of drones, no energy-sink, Zai lamented. Come at the frigate with kinetic or beam weapons: Take your pick. He wouldn't have an answer for either.

Processor capability had also been badly hit. No specific system had been lost; the entire system had been designed to "gracefully degrade." Synesthesia was a bit fuzzier, expert AI was sluggish, and the ship's reaction to gestural codes was slightly slower, like the annoying lag of a conversation over satellite link.

The front quarter of the ship remained in vacuum, waiting for the fissures in the cargo bay bulkhead to be stabilized. Hullalloy was the hardest substance the Empire had ever created, but once it had been virally compromised, it was never the same again. No one in their right mind would go forward of the front gunnery bulkhead without a pressure suit until the ship's bow had been completely refitted.

There was also a bad smell aboard the frigate. They were short on water and nitrox, and the bacterial bays that were the basis of the *Lynx*'s biosphere had been disrupted. Large sections of the crew quarters were infected with a rampant mold. The bioprocessing chief— killed by flockers—had been reanimated, but the honored dead were never as practical-minded as they had been in life. Samuel Vries had a great love of low-gee bonsai, and Laurent Zai was far too gray to give strict orders to an immortal; Vries would be spending more time on his beloved trees than the ecosystem. So until the *Lynx* made port, showering would be rationed.

But for the moment they were all breathing.

Almost all of them.

Zai had lost thirty-two crew. The flockers had killed nine, and twenty-one had fallen in the beam weapon attacks. The Rix range-finding laser had holed one side of the *Lynx*, lancing through to burn, tearing open a swath of the hull to naked space. In the final attack, chaotic gravitons had given half the crew various sorts of cancer. Even now, the medics were injecting nanos into the worst-hit victims (although these were secondaries: nanos that cleaned up their larger cousins, the ones who had actually consumed the amok tissue of a gravity burn). Another mutineer had unmasked herself trying to kill Hobbes, and had died from decompression. And of course there was Telmore Bigz, the engineer-rating who had saved the *Lynx*. A true hero. Unfortunately, along with half of the laser casualties and eight of the flocker deaths, Bigz would never be reanimated. His body no longer existed, except as exotic photons in a sphere that expanded at the constant. In fifteen years, some far-sighted telescope array on his home planet of Irrin might see the flash of his death.

But the *Lynx* had accomplished her mission.

In the hours since the battle, the magnitude of their success—and good luck—had finally penetrated Captain Zai's exhausted brain. They had destroyed the Rix receiver array, preventing contact between the enemy battlecruiser and the Legis XV mind. And they were still alive.

Captain Laurent Zai had lived to see an Imperial pardon, survived an assassination attempt and a suicide mission. He had Jocim Marx, Katherie Hobbes, and of course Telmore Bigz to thank, so far. But there was still a war on. Their sacrifices and brilliance would be wasted unless Zai and his ship ultimately survived both the Rix and the Risen Emperor's displeasure.

And it would all be meaningless to Zai unless he saw his love again.

He wanted his ship back in fighting shape.

"Captain?" Hobbes interrupted his thoughts.

He turned to look at the woman. It was good to have her back on the bridge, as good as being able to move his artificial limbs again.

"Report."

"We're seeing more acceleration flares from the battlecruiser."

Zai shook his head. The Rix were at it again. Two hours ago, they had launched two long-range drones after the *Lynx*. They were remotes that could make six hundred gees, and they had closed with the frigate in a little over an hour. Gunner Wilson had powered up the dorsal lasers and destroyed them at thirty thousand klicks. As defenseless as the frigate might be, it couldn't be threatened by a pair of scout drones. The two craft had managed to sweep the *Lynx* with active sensors, however.

The tenacity of the Rix was surprising. Her mission had failed, yet the battlecruiser's captain was still in pursuit, still sending valuable drones to harass and probe the *Lynx*. True, the frigate had humiliated the larger warship, but it was not like the Rix to seek revenge.

Zai wondered if there were something he was missing. Some unresolved aspect of this engagement.

"Hobbes."

"Captain?"

"What sort of active sensors are we running?"

For a few seconds, Zai watched his executive officer's eyes drift in the middle distance of the ship's infostructure.

"We're focusing all the transluminals on the battlecruiser, sir. And we're still operating close-in-defense sensors at battle level. There are also a few scout drones running point, sweeping for meteoroids basically."

"Is that all?"

"Captain?" Hobbes couldn't hide her disbelief. "Three-quarters of our sensor personnel are in hypersleep, sir. They went on alert six hours before the rest of the crew."

"When can we wake a few up, Hobbes?"

"Right now, if you want, sir."

"I mean, when can we *reasonably* wake them up? I don't want to psych anyone."

"We're running hypersleep cycles of two hours, sir. I can get you a crew of four in forty minutes without interrupting any dreams."

"Very good. When you have a full crew, refocus some transluminals onto the Rix approach path."

"Their original path into the system, sir?"

"Yes. I just want to make sure that we haven't missed anything."

Hobbes blinked, clearing her secondary vision. Her expression sharpened, eyes widening.

"Missed another Rix ship, Captain? I certainly hope we haven't."

"I do as well, Hobbes. I do as well."

Zai turned back to the airscreen. He wondered if he were simply getting in the way of his ship's healing process: waking up what few of the exhausted crew were able to rest, rattling his ExO's nerves. Perhaps he should put on a hypersleep helmet himself. The airscreen blur had gotten worse over the last hours, and Zai didn't think it was just the *Lynx*'s processor shortage. It was his brain getting fuzzy, and it took considerable fatigue to blur secondary sight.

Zai wondered if he might be tending toward paranoia.

"Hobbes, belay that order. Give anyone you can a full two cycles of sleep."

"Yes, sir. But we'll take a look once we're at full strength."

"Certainly. In the meantime, I'll be taking a cycle myself. Be ready to take one when I wake up."

"But we still have twenty repair crew who haven't had a chance—"

Captain Zai reached out and touched the bandage on Hobbes's arm. Their was still blood on her uniform; Hobbes hadn't even had time to change. He could feel the flechette pistol she now wore strapped to her wrist. It was pulled from the captain's stores; only the two of them knew she had it. There might be other mutineers seeking revenge.

"Two more hours awake, Hobbes. Then sleep," he commanded.

She nodded in defeat.

Before retiring, Zai called up the Legis system picture on his personal visual channel. The Rix had sent an assault craft across the light-years to take the Empress, and a battlecruiser with a crew of a thousand to follow up. A considerable commitment to a mission that had failed.

Had they sent anything more?

compound mind

Alexander felt the infinitesimal prick in its awareness, and exalted.

The repeater's senses were terribly limited. It could see only in a low-grade, four-bit grayscale, its four eyes giving it a mere 180 degrees of peripheral vision.

But this narrow, shadowy view was sufficient to find others of its own kind against the snowy background.

The compound mind moved its new appendage clumsily across the grainy terrain, closing on another of the repeaters. The ten-meter journey took ninety seconds, the little creature's mobility generally limited to finding sunlight for power and maintaining even distribution of the colony in the event of heavy damage to its numbers.

When it reached the other machine, the repeater stepped up onto its back, an armored insect initiating a mating ritual. The device had actually been designed to make such a maneuver impossible; the necessary calculations for complex motion were well beyond the machine's limited internal software. To make the repeater follow its will, Alexander had to swap out the entire contents of its accessible internal memory a thousand times per second. The gargantuan computational power of the compound mind barreled down the bottleneck of the dim machine's mind like an ocean tide forced through a drinking straw. The mind succeeded, however: The insectoid repeater wrapped a leg around the other's power pack, and pulled it fast to the correct position.

Now Alexander was two.

The little machines set off in opposite directions, each looking for more converts. The compound mind's will propagated like rabies, with each victim compelled to spread it further. Gradually, more and more of the field moved into motion.

But Alexander left the software blocks in the civilian network intact, preventing the little machines from receiving any data from the Legis infostructure and passing it on to the entanglement facility.

Let the Imperials be surprised.

The compound mind waited for the process within the wire to complete itself, biding its time and watching the maneuvers in space progress.

Fisherman

Tide and sunset were elegantly matched.

The last red arrows of light struck out from the descending sun, lancing through the waters that tugged gently at Jocim Marx's bare legs. The outflow from the tidal pool grew stronger, widening the sandy channel that connected it to the bay. Jocim felt his motionless feet slowly disappear, subsumed by gradual accumulation, buried by a waterborne drift of sand.

He stood utterly still.

Jocim did not react when the first few glimmers of light slipped past him. Like floating candles, blurred slightly by a few centimeters' depth, they were borne by the quickening current. He waited as a few more drifted by. In the growing dark, he could see a faint luminescence over the large tidal pool, a collective glow from its ample population of torchfish, which had lain all day in the shallow water, storing the sun's energy.

More drifted by. Then he chose one.

The fisherman lofted his spear as the torchfish took its curved path, tugged to one side by the eddies encircling his legs. It moved past Jocim and away, meter by meter, heading for the deeper waters of bay. At ten meters, he threw.

The spear flew from his hand quickly, but slowed as it neared the end of its tether field. It penetrated the water without a splash, barely reaching its glowing target, then began to accelerate back toward Jocim as if attached to him by a long, elastic cord. At the spear's tip a cage of metal fingers held a wriggling form, the fish sparkling in its surprise at being torn from the water.

Jocim caught the returning spear, fluidly reversing the motion with which he had thrown it.

He regarded the fish: bright and evenly lit, edged with blues and gently pink at the dorsal fin. He held the spear-end out to the edge of the tidal channel, where a glass bowl of sea water waited. The spear's terminal claw released the torchfish with a plop, and it fluttered within the bowl, spinning in angry little circles.

The fisherman turned from his catch and raised his arm to throw again. The torchfish were flowing out of the tidal pool in small groups now. It had grown almost completely dark, only a few tendrils of deep red lay upon the horizon. He would have to work quickly to fill his bowl.

Suddenly, the sky cracked.

A long, bright fissure opened, daylight pushing through the broken night sky. The water dried up below Jocim's feet, the white noise of nearby surf sputtering down to a dead-signal hum. The burning blue of the sky turned to a familiar cerulean, the signature color of a blanked interface.

Someone had woken Master Pilot Jocim Marx up, untimely bounced him from a hyperdream. He'd been deep in the rhythms of hypersleep, and his carefully designed arch of mental recuperation had been shattered. His head rang with the chainsaw noise of torn reality, and his body was racked with the heartburn of incompletely digested exhaustion.

"This had better be important," he managed groggily.

"It is," came Hobbes's voice.

The executive officer gave him a few more seconds, then restarted his primary vision. Marx blinked his gummy eyes. Hobbes was standing here, physically present in his cabin.

He couldn't remember ever having seen her off the bridge before.

"What is it?"

"An occultation," she answered.

"A what?"

"On the approach path. There may be another Rix ship."

Executive Officer

Hobbes could see how they had missed it for so long.

No drive signature. No easy graviton emissions. No active sensors of its own. Even now, all they had was an occultation: a milliseconds-long dimming of a few background stars. Whatever it was, the object was invisible to transluminal sensors, and was too far away for the *Lynx*'s active sensors to tell them very much.

But it was big.

"At least fifty kilometers across," Ensign Tyre repeated.

"It's a spare receiver array," Engineer Frick said. "An extra, folded down and trailing the battlecruiser."

"Why so far behind?" Hobbes asked. The object was too distant from the battlecruiser for an easy rendezvous. As it was, the *Lynx* could easily reach it before the larger Rix ship.

"Perhaps they wanted to keep it invisible," the captain said. "It's running absolutely silent. If it weren't so damn big, we'd have missed it."

And if the captain hadn't been so paranoid, Hobbes thought, they'd have missed it at any size. The last thing anyone else had expected was another Rix vessel coming into the system.

"It's not necessarily running silent, sir," Tyre softly added. "It could simply be inert matter."

"When will we know its mass?" Zai asked.

Tyre looked into the air. "The Master Pilot's drone should be within range to tell us that in fourteen minutes."

Hobbes looked across the table at Marx, and wished again that the captain hadn't insisted on waking the master pilot in mid-sleep sequence. The man looked exhausted, his drowsy absence of mind animated with a bad case of the shakes. All his piloting skill would be meaningless if he couldn't think straight.

The recon drone had been launched almost immediately after the first occultation had been spotted. The drone launch rail was useless, unable to give the drone a magnetic shove, so they'd had to launch it at zero relative. The craft was the *Lynx*'s last surviving fast recon drone, and could sustain six hundred gees for an hour. It had already turned over, and was close to matching velocities with the object.

The drone was under automation now, but the captain wanted Marx at the controls when it made its approach.

"Don't lose that craft, Marx," Hobbes said. "We're short enough on drones as it is."

Marx rubbed his eyes. "No, ExO Hobbes. But I'd better get to my canopy."

He rose slowly. "Sir," he added shakily, giving a small bow to the captain before he left the command bridge.

When the master pilot was gone, Gunner Wilson spoke.

"Sir, it can't be a warship. It's too big. It would dwarf anything we've seen from the Rix before."

"It's bigger than a Laxu colony ship," Hobbes said. "And that's the biggest powered craft the Empire's ever encountered."

"It might be nothing," Captain Zai admitted. "Part of a lightsail from their original acceleration. Even a section of the receiver array, something that was damaged and removed years ago."

Hobbes nodded. It could be a planetoid for that matter, its course purely coincidental. But that seemed unlikely.

The object's approach course almost perfectly bisected those of the battlecruiser and the assault ship that had attacked the Empress' palace.

Whatever it was, the object had to be Rix.

Commando

H_rd felt a tapping on her face.

She pulled off the hood of the ablative suit and raised her head above the surface, shaking snow from her head. The repeater that had summoned her scuttled away as she sat up.

The cold had thoroughly penetrated her body. Rix commandos felt pain, but rarely longer than was necessary for their bodies to deliver a warning. After the long fall through frigid air and the hours buried in the snow, however, h_rd felt ice and agony in every muscle. The cuts on her face had scarred, and her broken nose felt bloated. Even her hypercarbon joints were stiff.

She let her body temperature rise. An increase in heat would return some of her flexibility. The Imperials' thermal imagers might find her more easily, but her whereabouts would be obvious soon enough. The summons from the little repeater meant that Alexander was only a few minutes from effecting its takeover of the entanglement facility. Therefore, h_rd was about to be rescued. A host of small craft under the compound mind's control waited on the other side of the wire, ready to assist in her extraction. The commando's rescue wasn't a humanitarian gesture on Alexander's part, however. Her exit would merely be a diversion.

So, the messier the better.

The repeater scuttled away as she stretched her muscles. The path the small machine took indicated the direction from which the attack would come. H_rd moved after it, again crawling with an interrupted gait to conceal herself from motion sensors. But she moved faster now, a little carelessly. Alexander wanted the Imperials to respond to her departure with main force to distract them from the movements of the repeaters. The propagation of the compound mind's control was now entering a critical stage.

Over the last six hours, the gospel of Alexander had spread among the repeaters, each convert adding another to the fold every few minutes. As in any geometric progression, the number of repeaters controlled by Alexander was arcing upward dramatically. Very soon, more than half of the repeater colony would be in motion. Even the Imperials were apt to realize that something was up.

Unless something dramatic occupied their attention.

Suddenly, shooting stars appeared on the horizon before h_rd. Arcs of light reached into the sky. Flashes emanating from just below the horizon showed where land mines were detonating. Concussions and the ripping howls of autocannon followed almost twenty seconds later: The wire was four kilometers away. H_rd stood and began running toward the wire, headed straight for the conflagration. A surge of joy filled her. This was the most dangerous part of the mission, but it was good to finally stretch her legs.

The sky came alive, each luminous missile distinct in the cold, clear air.

The wire had come under attack by Alexander's ragtag armada, a mob of automated flying machines:

weather dirigibles, bird migration monitors, ground effect crop dusters, solar-reflector kites. All of Legis's air-traffic spotters had disappeared from their stations a few days before, and the small percentage that had survived the perilous trip to the arctic were also in the attacking host. A few dislodged environmental satellites arced across the sky to crash into hullalloy-armored emplacements. Even a handful of walking and flying toys that h_rd had salvaged from aircraft luggage joined in, feinting to draw fire from the wire's guns and sacrificing themselves to trip booby traps, monofilament snares, and land mines.

The motley flotilla posed little danger to the facility, of course. Very few of the vehicles assaulting the wire were a match for even a single militia soldier. But the Imperial defenses were set to maximum response, alert for any attack on the facility since Rana Harter's escape with h_rd. The wire's arsenal was pouring thousands of heavy-metal rounds per minute into kites made of mylar, launching missiles the size of aircars at weather balloons, expending cluster mines on children's toys.

H_rd ran toward the melee, pulling her Rix blaster from her mission pack. She'd hardly used the weapon since the firefight in the palace, conserving its powerful charges for when she would need them most.

The recon flyer was on the other side of the wire, under Alexander's control and waiting for the defenses to exhaust themselves against their figmentary attackers. The wire was designed to deliver a short, punishing blow, delaying an enemy until reinforcements arrived. Its supplies of ordnance were limited.

H_rd's scanner set up a wail. She swept it across the horizon to locate the first of these reinforcements on their way: a pair of ground-effect vehicles racing toward her from the central barracks of the facility.

The commando changed direction, running parallel to the wire now. For this first trap to work, she had to get to the far side of the snowdrift landing zone. H_rd reduced her blaster to a diversionary power setting and dropped to a firing position.

She took aim and fired a long stream of random photons at the GEVs, the blaster sweeping across the EM spectrum to suggest a wide array of weapons. She checked the scanner.

The hovercraft spotted her, and changed course, angling toward her. More vehicle signatures appeared behind them on her scanner. It was working. The Imperials thought that she had come through the embattled wire. Believing that the attacking force had penetrated the terrific fire zones of the perimeter, they would be worried.

H_rd's sharp eyes now caught a flicker of light from another sector of the facility. Another, smaller contingent of Alexander's conscript army was attacking the wire from a new direction. Overall, Alexander had committed four separate groups to divide the defenders' resources. The other three were utterly insignificant, but perhaps the Imperials would outthink themselves and assume that the true attack was a feint.

The GEVs were closing on her now, bearing down from the other side of the landing zone. The scream of their jet turbines drowned out even the battle at the wire. The commando cycled her blaster to a combat setting, in case one made it past the trap.

She could see them now, their approach raising a cloud of snow. She dropped to the tundra as one of the hovercraft opened fire, the ripping sound of an autocannon reaching her ears as a line of snow and earth before her lifted in a rolling wave.

Then the GEVs reached the landing zone. The permanent tundral snowdrift that filled the trench was usually as dense as concrete, but the heavy vehicles were in for a surprise.

The GEVs hit the doped snow at three hundred klicks, and dropped through the thin crust of frost like charging predators through the leaves and branches of a tiger pit. The nanoed snow-foam probably slowed them a bit, but their armored mass and huge speed packed thousands of times the kinetic energy of a human at terminal velocity. As the hovercraft arced downward, their turbines spewed the treacherous white foam out from their entry holes in geysers. The shock wave of their collision with the trench's rocky side reached h_rd a few seconds later. The impact threw a fist of earth up into her face, reopening her scarred eyebrow and treating her broken nose to a second round of agony. A gout of flame burst from the trench, a huge cloud of foam-snow rising up like the spray of some vast, breaking wave.

Wiping blood from her eyes, the commando fired her blaster twice through the cloud. She wanted the Imperials to think—for the next few minutes, anyway—that enemy fire rather than mishap had taken out the GEVs.

The commando checked her scanner. The second formation of hovercraft was wheeling to one side now, circumspect after their compatriots' sudden destruction. The smaller returns of a few Imperial remotes moved into view, and h_rd cycled her blaster down to a sniper's setting—low power, high accuracy—in case one got too close.

But she figured that she'd bought herself a few needed minutes.

H_rd turned and ran toward the wire again. The fire-fight there was dying down. That meant either that the Imperials' ammunition was running low or that the attacking force had been decimated. She hoped it was the former. Her scanner showed the recon flyer still waiting out of harm's way.

As h_rd neared the wire, an autocannon emplacement acquired her and fired. She dropped and skidded through the snow, cycling her blaster back up. Rolling into firing position, she destroyed the emplacement with a single shot. As she passed another cannon, an arc of tracers came h_rd's way, but she silenced that gun with equal ease. The wire suffered from a typical flaw: It was designed to keep attackers out, not in. Most of its firepower was oriented outward. The main dangers to h_rd were land mines and monofilament snares—single-molecule tripwires that would slice through her hypercarbon bones like a knife through water.

But this was no time to consider the dangers before her. The remaining Imperial GEVs would regain their confidence soon enough.

The commando plunged forward. Every few steps, she fired her blaster toward the ground a hundred meters in front of her. The full-force plasma rounds rocked the tundra, sending up gouts of flame as if she were following in the footsteps of some huge demon, fiery and invisible. Land mines were detonated by the shock waves, and autocannon imaged the boiling plasma plumes and fired at them instead of h_rd. Bright lines of monofilament in her path glowed for a moment as they were incinerated.

Shrapnel and flying debris cut the Rixwoman's face and tore at the ablative suit. Her boots were melted by the superheated earth of the plasma craters; even her flexormetal soles burned. One of the autocannon emplacements found her and put a flechette through her thigh before she blasted it.

Her weapon set up a two-pitched keening alarm: It was simultaneously overheating and running out of ammo.

Another flechette struck her, and h_rd stumbled.

She went to ground in a deep crater where her blaster had made a direct hit on a land mine. The red-hot floor of the hole burned her hands, the heat forcing her eyes closed. The sharp smell of her own hair igniting filled her nostrils.

H_rd's burned fingers fumbled for the positioning device. Had she penetrated far enough through the wire for the recon flyer to reach her? She forced her eyes open and stared at the device. In the hadean light of the crater, she saw that the readout had melted. She kneeled with blistered hands protecting her face, her hypercarbon kneecaps against the molten earth. She felt nothing. Pain overrides had terminated all sensation from her skin.

It occurred to the commando that she had spent the last few hours besieged by freezing cold, and now she was burning to death.

Then she heard a turbine jet approaching, the whine of an Imperial GEV, not the recon flyer. She turned and raised her blaster, peering through the miragelike veil of superheated air.

A hovercraft was headed for her, approaching slowly so that the wire's friend-or-foe sensors wouldn't confuse it with an enemy. The GEV moved in a search pattern; they couldn't detect her amid the chaos.

She aimed the blaster and pressed its firing stud.

Nothing happened. The weapon's heat sink panel glowed white, unable to disperse enough energy to recycle the blaster in the boiling crater.

The hovercraft wandered closer to her. Close enough.

The commando pushed two blistered fingers into her blaster's suicide triggers and pulled them simultaneously. Then she heaved the blaster over the side of the crater, and it spun through the air toward the GEV.

H_rd dropped flat as answering fire erupted from the hovercraft. The hot lance of a flechette passing through her stomach grimly complemented the scalding rock of the crater floor.

Seconds later, the GEV's chattering autocannon was silenced by the explosion of the blaster. A sheet of plasma passed over the crater, sucking the air upward from around h_rd with a *whoosh,* momentarily snuffing the small fires in the hole. When she could hear again, the turbine of the GEV was howling like a wounded animal, dopplering as the machine retreated.

She struggled to her knees again. The ablative suit was mostly gone now; what remained of it was burned onto her skin in patches. Her tactile sense was so suppressed by pain overrides that it was hard to keep her balance. The flexormetal that protected her soles had lost all elasticity, rigidified and cracked by the heat.

H_rd peered across the tundra at the retreating GEV. It bounced backward, bobbing on its air cushion like some toy on a string. The armor glowed white hot; she wondered if the crew inside were even alive—or was the thing simply on autopilot, reeling blindly from the blaster's shock wave?

Her vision was blurred, her eyes dry and slitted in the heat. But h_rd could see two more ground-effect vehicles in the distance approaching cautiously. She searched the melted plastic of her mission pack. There were hissing and useless smoke grenades, a ruined remote drone, and a silent dart gun whose Rixian curves were bent into an ugly mess.

Nothing that could scratch an armored vehicle.

The commando drew her monofilament knife and stumbled to her feet.

The GEVs were circling a few kilometers away, afraid to close with her. The explosions from the wire behind h_rd had settled.

Suddenly, the commando felt the tingle of static electricity.

Then a rush of air filled the crater, sparking the glowing rocks into open flame like a strong wind against embers. It was the recon flyer descending. H_rd realized that her hearing must be woefully damaged; the noisy craft had sneaked up on her.

One of the GEVs opened fire, and the recon flyer responded. Its small cannon whined in a pitiful sound, but the Imperial craft pulled back, wary after the Rix blaster's terrific self-destruct.

The recon flyer bounced on its air cushion just above h_rd, whipping the air in the crater into a frenzy. The commando reached up and grabbed one of the landing struts, and the flyer soared up and out of the crater. In ten seconds they were a hundred meters aloft and climbing.

Dangling from the craft with locked muscles, she

looked down at the wreckage of the wire. A swath of destruction cut through it: her neat row of blaster scars extending from the inside outward, and a hodgepodge of land mine craters, crashed aircraft, and friendly fire damage marking Alexander's attack from without. The two paths of ruin met halfway, leaving the wire utterly ruptured. Only a few, bright lances of antiaircraft tracers survived to dog the flyer as it rose, too far away and firing in short bursts to conserve their waning ammunition.

H_rd realized that she would pass out soon, and didn't trust the muscles in her burned hands to stay locked, so she climbed laboriously over the side of the flyer and collapsed into the gunner's webbing.

"Take me to Rana Harter," she commanded her god.

And lost consciousness.

compound mind

Alexander was ready.

Across the planet Legis XV, a sudden pall of electronic failures struck. The telephonic system dropped a quarter-billion conversations, aircars tossed their drivers into manual, and inside market-trader headsups the cool icons of commerce were replaced with polychromatic sheet lightning. Every remote surgeon, engineer, and handeye gamer was paralyzed as secondary sight and hearing stuttered, then flew into a rage. Airscreens, false views, and overlays were replaced with a riot of color, a turbulent river of passing data in its rawest form.

At the operational centers of the planet—the air traffic hub, the private currency exchange, the infoterrorism militia's distributed HQ—Legis's administrators gaped as their soccer-field-sized airscreens tumbled into snow crash. For a moment, the frantic operators were blind. Then they booted the large, flat hardscreens put in place for some unthinkable emergency such as this. The backups returned a bizarre sight, oddly similar from all perspectives, whether civilian, commercial, or military. . . .

The infostructure surged like a living thing. As one, the planet's vast channels of information distended, pushed, were seized by a vast peristaltic motion that had a single focus.

Alexander swept toward the entanglement facility repeater array, a geyser powered by the pressures of an ocean.

A few hundred million Legisites stared in surprise at the hardscreens of their wailing phones, and saw interplanetary access codes. Worried that pirates had hijacked their accounts, a few million of them stabbed cutoff switches or popped out batteries, but their phones stayed connected, powered by microwave pulses from borrowed traffic transponders. Police and militia radios squawked like ancient modems. The repair gremlins in aircars and cooling units, usually silent unless their machines were ailing, arose as one to flood their reserved frequencies. Every fiber hardline on the planet was lit to capacity.

Even medical endoframes—the tiny monitors that

watched arrhythmic hearts and trick knees—employed their transmitters, lending their reserved emergency bandwidth to the flow of data toward the pole.

Alexander took everything.

The planet's transmission resources focused northward, data converging on a billion channels like some vast delta flowing in reverse, and the compound mind *sent* itself.

The mind crammed into the hostage repeaters spread across the tundra, invaded the big dishes devoted to interplanetary transmission. Alexander didn't bother with the entanglement grid itself, but grabbed the transmitters that linked XV with Legis's other inhabited planets. A few militia specialists saw what was happening, realized that the polar facility had been taken over and was blaring at the sky with fantastic throughput. But their software commands were ignored, the manual cutoffs useless. The specialists tried to explain the situation to the base's commanders, sending priority messages on the precious few hardlines in the com system.

To maintain the interplanetary blackout, they said, drastic action would have to be taken. Carpet bomb the repeaters. Destroy the dishes. Only a few minutes remained to act.

But the attention of those in charge was fully engaged. A battle raged along the wire, an incoming fleet of aircraft, a deluge of rockets and drones. And apparently, a Rix commando—*the* Rix commando—was somewhere inside the wire. This was a main force assault. The existence of the facility was in peril.

There was no time to listen to the wild pronouncements of a few hysterical com techs.

In the confusion, Alexander was able to shoot into the sky.

The compound mind found that space was cold. It was chilled by the absence of Legis's million transactions per second. Self-awareness began to dim as the mind was spread into a spaghetti-thin stream, like a human pulled into a black hole. Behind Alexander was the screaming planet, its infostructure ruptured as the compound mind tore itself free, a possessing demon leaving the fevered body of its victim. Forward was the icy mindlock of pure transmission, a descent into suspended animation as the mind's data stream crossed space, searching for its promised target.

The torrent of information poured through the funnel of the array, leaving a reeling world behind.

And for 850 timeless minutes, Alexander knew nothing.

Master Pilot

Master Pilot Marx struggled to concentrate.

He'd never been yanked out of the middle of a hypersleep cycle before. It was more confusing than planetary day-length adaptation, worse than long-term heavy gees. Marx had been trained to resist the five different symptoms of exhaustion, to orient without gravity cues, to drink air and inject food. But he'd never been drilled in this particular insult to the body.

No one at Imperial Pilot School had ever thought to wake him up from the midst of deep deltas.

Only Captain Laurent Zai had proven so perverse.

Marx took his hands from the drone's controls and cupped his eyes in his palms, grabbing a few seconds of blackness to salve his primary sight. But the object was still visible in synesthesia, its bizarre undulations worsening his disorientation. He pushed his sensor subdrones out a bit farther for better parallax, trying to grasp the enormity of the Rix thing. But increased perspective only made it worse, made it more real.

The whole bridge staff and all of Data Analysis were watching over his shoulder. Their hushed voices were filled with awe, so Marx knew he wasn't completely crazy. But he still didn't believe his second sight.

The object looked like an ocean. An uninterrupted, boloid ocean, without benefit of exposed land mass or iron core.

More than a hundred klicks across at its widest point, it spun like a champagne dervish. Almost everyone in the Navy had attempted the trick at some point. In drunken zero-gee, pop a bottle of sparkling wine, catching the unavoidable ejected froth in one hand. Use a straw or a pair of eating sticks to prod and coax, to herd the fizzing liquid into a stable, spinning freefall globule. Pulsating and twisting like a liquid tornado, each champagne dervish had its own personality, its own Rorschach symmetry of stability. Cheap, sweet champagne was the best, with its slightly stickier surface tension. And if cheap stuff wound up splattered across the room, at least the financial damage would be limited.

But the giant thing assaulting Marx's sensibilities

wasn't composed of wine. It wasn't properly liquid at all. The megaton mass readings and chromographs indicated that it was mostly composed of silicon. The moving wavelets that propagated across its surface suggested the arciform shapes of dunes, as if the object were a huge, floating desert brushed by ethereal winds. But the thing had no atmosphere. Data Analysis had told Marx that the dune movement was caused by internal motion. There must be wild currents and stormlets inside. The whole thing was spinning around itself: a quasi-liquid planetoid, a wobbling gyroscope, a champagne dervish of dry sand.

Master Pilot Marx sent a tiny probe toward the object. His drone was configured for leisurely, unarmed recon, and had a considerable number of subprobes. Unless the object decided to take a shot at him, Marx could easily keep his main craft out of danger.

The thing didn't seem to have weapons or a drive. Data Analysis said it was completely undifferentiated, desert through and through.

But what the hell was it *for*?

The unidentified object had come in on the same path as the Rix battlecruiser, moving along at almost the same velocity. It had a far greater mass than any ship, though. Some very powerful drive must have accelerated it and slowed it down again. Otherwise, its trip here from Rix space would make it very ancient indeed.

Marx's probe struck the object softly, sending up a splash, a raindrop in a puddle. A few droplets from the impact trailed away from the object, their bond of surface tension broken, and Marx assigned another pilot to maneuver one of his satellite drones in pursuit of the wayward sand-stuff. Actual spoor from the beast would be helpful.

The master pilot turned his attention to the readings from inside the thing. The probe tumbled helplessly in the interior currents, spun by a thousand minor eddies, carried in a greater circle by the Coriolis force of the object's overall rotation.

Sampling data came back. The object was indeed mostly silicon, but in some sort of bizarrely complex granular structure. And it was hot inside the whirling desert. As the probe was drawn into its center, spiraling inward like a floating speck down a bathtub drain, the temperature climbed. That didn't make sense; the thing was hard-vacuum cold on the outside, and showed no evidence of internal radiation. It wasn't nearly dense enough for gravitational compression, and the friction from the eddies of sand shouldn't be as hot as the readings Marx was getting. He concluded that some sort of power source was working inside.

Before it was a quarter of the way to the core, the probe's faint signal was swallowed by heat-noise and the object's inherent density.

"Moving in closer," Marx said. He brought his subdrones into position surrounding the object.

He split his second and tertiary sight among the various viewpoints of his entourage, forming a single image composed of every angle. The exercise addled his brain for a moment as the overlays of shifting sands twisted in a moving moiré. Marx increased his view's resolution, sending spiderwebs of sensory filaments out from each of the subdrones for maximum reception.

Although the *Lynx*'s processors were still damaged, the master pilot had priority. Without an entire battle to run, the frigate's surviving columns of silicon and phosphorus were still quite formidable. Soon, the master pilot's vision became comprehensible, meshing like the frames of a stereograph when the eyes align.

Now Marx could really see the shape of the object, began to *feel* the period and flow of the sandy ocean. The dunes' motion was similar to the roiling clouds of smoke he watched through his microscope when he studied air currents for small-craft flight. Marx let his mind relax, almost drifting back into the dream state from which Hobbes had so harshly yanked him. He reveled in the patterns of the sand-ocean, and unconsciously guided his various craft about the object, drinking in its form. There was something seductive in the fluid mathematics of the thing.

The master pilot's tired mind began to grasp it.

Suddenly, the overlaid images stuttered, then multiplied before Marx's eyes. The flexing of dunes increased in speed, their dance accelerating madly. A barrage of new colors played across the sands, filled the master pilot's three levels of vision with a cascade of lightning that flashed across the spectrum. Pictures formed, piling onto each other in a way that should have been simply noise. But somehow he could simultaneously comprehend images of countless faces, window vistas, data icons, security cams. His secondary hearing blared with the chatter of a million conversations, confessions, jokes, dramas. It was synesthesia gone mad. Instead of three, Marx had a hundred levels of sight, each discernible as a separate view. It felt as if a whole world were being shoved through his mind.

He reached for the cutoff, but his hand froze, his mind crammed too full to react.

The layers of synesthesia began rolling across each other, commingling as did the dunes of the object below. Sight and sound collapsed into a single torrent, pulled themselves apart to address eye and ear again, and finally tattered like a flag driven down the throat of a tempest, unraveling into a thousand separate threads.

Dimly, Jocim Marx heard distant voices from the *Lynx*'s bridge questioning him, then shouting, then issuing sharp and harried commands. But he couldn't understand the language they spoke. It seemed like a tongue dredged up from childhood memories, the sounds put back together in random order.

He vaguely heard his own name.

But by then he was far off in yet another dream, vast and furious.

Executive Officer

"What the hell happened to him?"

"Medical doesn't know yet, sir."

"What about the scouts?"

"No response, sir. Sending again."

Katherie Hobbes tried to raise the main recon drone once more. With one fraction of her mind, she watched the fifty-second delay count tick off. With another, she followed the frantic shouting of the med techs who were moving Master Pilot Jocim Marx to the sickbay. She watched through hallway cams: The man hung limp, arms adrift in the zero-gee corridor Hobbes had cleared for the techs. He hadn't moved since the attack, or transmission, or whatever it had been. When the med techs had first arrived, he hadn't even been breathing.

In a corner of her vision, Hobbes saw Captain Zai flexing his fingers impatiently. But there was nothing she could do to increase the speed of light. The object was twenty-five light-seconds away, and the recon drone's translight capability was definitely out. Before collapsing, the scout craft's sensory grid had taken a 200-exabyte input—the equivalent of a planetary array at full power, concentrated into an area a hundred meters square: a hailstorm of information. The grid had perforated like tissue paper. But for those seconds, the drone had tried to pass on the information to the *Lynx*, and to its own pilot, and something bad had happened to Marx.

"Do we have an origin for the attack, Executive Officer?"

"DA is trying, sir."

"A rough idea of direction?"

"Trying, sir."

Hobbes shunted another ten percent of processor capacity to Data Analysis, forcing her to beggar the repair crews again. The captain's orders were coming fast and furious. With no determinations yet from any quarter, Zai's questions spun from one issue to the next. Lost probes, an unconscious pilot (Was Marx *dead*? she wondered), a mysterious attack using radio, the huge and fantastic object of unknown purpose.

Hobbes thought it unlikely that solid answers were coming anytime soon.

Tracking the source of the radio transmission was particularly tricky. The wave had been so focused that the *Lynx*'s sensors hadn't caught a stray photon of it.

Marx's numerous subdrones had been too close together to triangulate. Directionality was impossible to
determine. Hobbes watched the expert program she
had assigned to find the transmission's source; it was
requesting more flops, eating through the frigate's processor capacity like a brushfire. Unwieldy algorithms
devoured their allotted phosphorus in seconds, and
scream-ed for more.

Hobbes assigned more processors to the problem,
but the calculations' duty-slope remained hyperbolic,
consuming her largesse in milliseconds. Hobbes
queried the expert software's meta-software, which
admitted that the entire *Lynx*'s processors might be unequal to the task even if they had years to get the answer. But it wasn't sure. The solution might come in a
few more minutes, or perhaps in the lifetime of a star.

Perhaps a little common sense was in order.

"Sir? There's only one place in the system that could
generate a transmission burst of that magnitude."

Zai thought for a moment.

"The Legis interplanetary array?"

She nodded.

"Raise the Imperial contingent there," he ordered.

Hobbes tried. But nothing came back. She sent hails
to the few Navy bases that were equipped with their
own short-range entanglement grids. Again nothing.

The *planet* was off-line.

"There is no translight response from Legis XV, sir.
Zero."

"My god. What's our delay?"

"Eight hours one-way, sir," she estimated.

The captain thought for a moment. During those
seconds of silence, the med techs reported to Hobbes
that Marx was now breathing on his own. His brain

wave diagnostics looked hot and unconscious, like a man in badly calibrated hypersleep.

ExO Hobbes noted that a marker in her vision was blinking, had been blinking for fifteen seconds, and she flinched. She had missed the return point for the drones' message delay.

"Sir, the drones have failed to respond again. I'll try—"

Zai interrupted her. "Send a general order to all *Lynx* personnel on Legis, via light speed. I want a report on the planet's comsystem status. And have DA monitor the civilian newsfeeds; see if anything's happening."

Hobbes's fingers moved to comply with the orders, but faltered. She couldn't think of the protocol phrase for Zai's order. A report on the planet wouldn't make sense to the recipients unless they knew what was going on. They were marines, not planetary liaisons. If they asked for clarification, seventeen hours would be lost.

In the meantime, a flurry of priority markers were flashing. Repair crews demanding the return of their processor space. *You idiot, Katherie*, she thought. She'd never freed the *Lynx*'s computers from their potentially endless tracking calculations. The expert program was spinning its wheels while a hundred other systems needed processor power.

Her mind froze, overwhelmed for a few seconds.

Hobbes realized that she was losing control. Her fingers would not move.

One thing at a time, she commanded herself.

She released the processor capacity to repair. Shot the Legis newsfeeds to a rating in Data Analysis. Looked up at the captain, taking a moment to frame her thoughts.

"Marx is breathing, sir. The drones aren't respond-

ing to light-speed hails. And . . . and I think I may have
reached task saturation."

Her eyes dropped. She struggled to compose the
captain's message to the marines on Legis, realizing
what she had admitted. But it was an absolute in her
training: An executive officer must report her own failures as she would those of the crew.

Hobbes felt the captain's hand on her shoulder.

"Easy, Executive Officer," he said. "You're doing
fine."

She breathed slowly. Zai's hand stayed, offering its
gentle pressure.

"Priority, priority," came a voice. Ensign Tyre.

"This had better be good," Hobbes answered.

The young ensign spoke with absolute confidence.
"We've amplified the final signals from the recon
drone's satellite craft, ma'am."

Hobbes's eyebrows raised. The smaller drones with
Marx's craft had their own transmitters, but they were
weak and light-speed, intended to be relayed through
the main recon drone. Hobbes couldn't remember if
she'd ordered anyone to look for their transmissions.

"You have to see it, ma'am," Tyre said. "It is priority, priority."

"I heard you, Ensign."

She ran Tyre's video in a corner of secondary sight,
simultaneously scanning the Legis newsfeeds of eight
hours ago, Jocim Marx's diagnostics, and composing a
message to the marines on Legis. She kept this last
simple: *We can't raise the translight array. What the
hell is going on down there?*

But through it all, Tyre's video caught her attention.
What was that?

She reran it, and felt her mind stuttering again.

"Captain."

"Hobbes?"

"I need to show you something, sir," she managed.

Hobbes cleared the big bridge airscreen. Only at that scale would anyone believe this. She played Tyre's video there, huge and undeniable.

Floating before them was the object, rippling with the sharp lines of dune-shadows from the distant sun. Marx's crafts were a constellation around it. For a moment, the feed was perfectly clear, the images coming through the main drone. Then the radio burst killed it, and the detail on the object's surface disappeared. But the gross undulations of the object's perpetual sand-storm were still visible, caught by the subdrones, which had apparently survived a few seconds longer.

The object began to flex, to change shape.

"Is that a transmission artifact, Hobbes?"

"Not according to DA, sir. This is at one-tenth speed, by the way."

The boloid shape twisted, squeezing its own mass from one extremity into another, like some multi-chambered hourglass designed to record gravity shifts over time. It shot out geysers that plummeted back still coherent, arches of running sand. The object's surface seemed abuzz with motion, covered with tiny explosions like an expanse of ocean in driving rain. Or perhaps it was forming fractal details that were lost in the low resolution.

Then, just as the object's wild gyrations seemed to be subsiding, sixteen clearly defined columns of sand shot out from it. Each targeted a separate drone, plucking them from space like hungry pseudopods, reeling them into the object's depths as the picture degraded stepwise—one drone dying after another—into noise.

Then the screen went dark.

The bridge was silent, stunned.

"Executive Officer." Zai's voice filled the quiet. Hobbes swallowed, wondering if she'd been foolish to have displayed this monstrous event to the entire bridge crew.

"Sir?"

"Reset the repair priorities."

"Yes, sir?"

"I want acceleration in one hour."

That was utterly impossible. But Hobbes was too overwhelmed to protest.

"Yes, sir."

Her fingers formed the necessary gestural commands. Somehow, the shock of what they'd just witnessed made it all easier. It was as if the troublesome higher functions of her brain—logic, comprehension, anxiety—had been erased by that mad and awesome image. All that remained of Hobbes was a smoothly functioning machine.

But in some deep place she heard the screaming of her own fear. And the afterimage of the object's frenzy stayed frozen in her mind, like some troublesome burn-in of secondary sight that could not be erased.

The thing had come to life.

Fisherman

Another wave of torchfish struck him.

The channel that joined bay and tide pool had become a torrent, the tide rolling wildly back and forth between the two bodies of water. Bright fish shot past him like grains of radium in some glowing hourglass.

Jocim Marx looked up.

The moon catapulted across the sky, sucking the oceans of the world along.

Jocim plunged his spear into the sand and clung to it, fighting the current with all his strength. He couldn't remember which way the water was going, to bay or tidal pool. Both seemed to have grown as vast as oceans, their shifting mass choking the raging channel in which Jocim found himself. He knew that he could not let go, couldn't let himself be pulled into the open sea.

Marx looked down, and saw a finger of red join the streaming darts of light.

It was his own blood. The fish were biting him again.

The tracers of rushing light increased, multiplied, climbed an exponential slope. Jocim held on, screaming at the transient violations of small, sharp teeth. The gushing water pulled his spear into a hyperbole, lifting his bleeding feet from the sandy bottom.

The sky was red, he saw.

The ocean begged for him to let go. Its tidal strength stretched him out from the spear as if he were an arrow notched upon a bow. The ocean was full of a trillion tiny lights, a trillion voices and images and snatches of effluvial data. It raged with angry journal entries and impulsive sell orders and terrified calls to the police. The ocean wanted to consume him, to lose Jocim in its vast reservoirs of information.

Jocim Marx felt his legs disappearing, shredded by the hungry, passing fish.

His blood curled into the ocean, was turned on the lathe of its currents into a spiral jetty of red.

But he held on.

The torchfish had opened his gut, and were nipping at his flailing entrails, carrying away his soft tissues like a furious wind stripping a dandelion. Bright bullets from some limitless firearm, the fish raked the flesh from his chest, pounded furiously at the insufficient armor of his ribs. They consumed Jocim's heart again.

And finally only his arms were left, then simply a pair of hands holding on with a ghastly singularity of will.

But then the tide slackened. The torrent began to slow, and the spear unbent and lifted up its disembodied, defiant cargo.

Jocim Marx felt himself coming back together. His arms grew from the indomitable hands, eyes and face beginning to re-form, the wild scattering of his flesh and bones reversing. And he knew that by the time the moon would rise again, in a few minutes, he would be ready and whole.

And the channel would rage at him again.

Captain

"What do we know about this object?"

Captain Laurent Zai directed this question at Amanda Tyre. The young ensign held his eyes steadily, he noticed. She no longer needed Hobbes as an intermediary.

"On a gross scale, sir?" Tyre answered. "Its volume changes constantly, but averages roughly four hundred thousand cubic kilometers. The outermost layer of sand spins about once every six hours, but like a star or a gas giant, different depths rotate at different rates. Its internal currents are far more variable than any natural phenomenon. Its motion is mathematically chaotic."

"I believe we had noticed that, Ensign," Zai offered. "What's it made of?"

"Mostly empty space, sir. It would float in water, assuming it didn't saturate. No denser than a sugar cube."

Zai noted that Tyre paused here, as if allowing for a moment of surprise, aware that her words unsettled the old psychological association between mass and power: Anything light couldn't hurt you.

"Based on the physical sampling effected by one of Marx's probes, most of the material content of the object is silicon. This silicon is structured in units about a half-millimeter across—the size of grains of sand. Each grain is composed of many extremely small layers, and doped with various other elements."

"Doped?"

"Yes, sir. Presumably to change the conductivity of the silicon. Like the semiconductor materials in a pre-quantum computer."

Zai narrowed his eyes.

"Tyre, do you think this object is one giant processor?"

"I don't know, sir."

She offered her ignorance without apology. Zai was glad to see she was not a speculator, as so many in Data Analysis tended to be.

"How does it move?"

"Before the transmission event, the motion was simply centrifugal, sir. The outer layer seems to be adhesive in some way. Like a water droplet's surface tension."

Zai nodded. Everyone had noticed how much it looked like a champagne dervish.

"But when the object . . . *consumed* the recon drones, that movement was obviously some other process."

"Obviously," Zai muttered. "Any ideas?"

"I, um, have suggestive data to relate, sir. And some possible interpretations to offer."

"Please," Zai said, smiling. Perhaps Tyre was a speculator after all, but at least she was a cautious one.

Tyre gestured, and a background-radiation chromograph appeared in the command bridge's table airscreen.

"This was recorded by the *Lynx*'s passive sensors twelve minutes ago, a few seconds before the transmission event. That big spike is silicon. The smaller one up here is arsenic."

"Arsenic? So, it could be a semiconducting processor," Hobbes said. "Or at least a storage device."

Zai nodded. Of that, he had grown fairly certain. He was waiting only for the civilian transmissions from Legis to confirm his fears.

"Yes, ma'am," Tyre answered. "It's a computer. But it's a great deal more."

She gestured, and the chromograph multiplied into a time series, propagating along its z-axis to become a spiky, chaotic mountain range.

"Here are the first few seconds of the transmission event. Note that the elemental makeup of the object changes."

Tyre leaned back from the table, folding her hands.

Hobbes was the first to speak. "Changes? You mean to say it transubstantiated in a matter of seconds?"

Zai looked at the airscreen, trying to remember his stellar mechanics courses at the academy. That was the last time anyone had asked him to interpret a chromograph. "What elements are we looking at?"

"These spikes are metals," Tyre said, airmousing a set of harmonics descending from the tallest peak. "Vanadium, electrum, and titanium in correct proportions to create superplastic adamantum. And this is a bit of mercury, possibly for some sort of inertial guidance."

"Guidance? Motile alloys?" Zai said. This was too much to believe.

"Yes, sir. The structures that plucked Marx's drones from space had to have some sort of orientation device, and a powerful armature. The object's transubstantiation seems sophisticated enough to create such devices on the fly."

"No," Hobbes said quietly.

Zai narrowed his eyes. The Empire had transubstantiation devices; in industrial settings, lead could be turned to gold in useful quantities. Some isolated gas-giant outposts with access to thermal energy some-times made metals from hydrogen and methane. The process was obscenely energy-expensive, but generally cheaper than shipping bulk metals in starships. And of course, there were always exotic new transuranium elements being created in laboratories.

But this level of control—elements from across the periodic table on demand—was fantastic.

"Why didn't we realize this sooner?" Hobbes asked.

Tyre frowned. "We were too reliant on active sensors, ma'am. This process is more subtle than you'd think."

The ensign flicked her hand.

Mass readings overlaid the chromograph, a set of lines alongside the mountain range, as straight and parallel as maglev tracks.

"As you can see, the silicon grains do not change mass when they transubstantiate. The object maintains a consistent density throughout, no matter what it appears to be made of. This elemental shift is somehow virtual. Of all our instruments, only the background-radiation chromograph detected any change at all."

"Virtual?" Zai asked. "How the hell can elements be virtual?"

"I don't know, sir."

"Where is it getting the energy to make these changes?" Hobbes asked. The object had no power source that they had detected.

"I don't know, ma'am. But I don't think it takes much energy. In fact, it seems to be making more changes just now, for no particular reason. As if it were flexing its muscles."

"Pardon me?"

The static chromograph disappeared, and was replaced by one in wild motion. The spikes jittered and jumped, animating the airscreen like the chatter of a crowd run through an audio visualizer.

"This is real time, minus light-speed delay."

God, though Zai. The thing was *frantic.* It pulsed and throbbed to wound the eyes. For a moment, Zai almost thought he saw a pattern in the dance of lines, as if some analog portion of his brain could grasp the internal logic of the thing's "muscle flexing."

He tore his eyes from it, but the afterimage rang in his mind. What had happened to Marx? he wondered. What had the patterns and logic of this thing done to the man? In the high-intensity synesthesia of a pilot's canopy, with his mind already weakened by hypersleep disruption, the master pilot would have been immensely vulnerable.

Marx's brain waves were active, obscenely so, but the man was still not awake.

"What the hell are these?" Hobbes said, interrupting Zai's thoughts.

The captain's eyes followed his ExO's airmouse. A new range of mountains had appeared. Coded in blue, they jutted to the end of the airscreen.

"We believe that they're signatures of trans-half-life elements."

"Transuranium?" Zai said, trying to bring the periodic table to mind.

"Trans-everything," Tyre said. "Beyond our software. Beyond even current theoretical speculation. We had to recalibrate just to differentiate them. There seems to be no upper limit to the number of electrons with which the object can endow its virtual elements. With no change in mass. Without stability constraints: a half-life of forever."

The room exploded into chaos, scattering off into separate conversations. Everyone, it seemed, had been caught by these wild data, their minds taken over by the incredible implications of what they had seen. This had happened in the First Rix Incursion, back when Zai was a rating. The catapulting technologies of the Rix never failed to amaze, to appall, to suggest whole new fields of inquiry; they could freeze the mind.

Hobbes looked at him and pointed to the back of her wrist, an ancient Vadan hand sign he had taught her, suggesting that they move forward. Hobbes had already looked at the civilian transmissions from Legis, and from her prelim report, Zai's worst fears were likely to be realized.

He cleared his throat. Amplified by the captain's direct channel, the sound silenced the command bridge.

"Let us look at the event from Legis's perspective."

Hobbes took control of the airscreen, clearing the wild gyrations of the object's dance. She divided the screen into three contemporaneous newsfeeds, all exactly eight hours, fifty-two minutes prior to the transmission event; they had reached the *Lynx* at light speed at almost the same moment the event had occurred. Zai moved his secondary hearing across them: a talking head disquisitioning on local politics, a sporting event, a financial feed giving raw data—undulating line graphs that showed price-shift and volume.

"These are handheld channels," Hobbes explained, "for watching on portable devices or in your head. They broadcast with satellite repeaters for maximum coverage outside of cabled areas. Crude, but strong enough for our passives to have picked up."

She leaned back. "The transmission event happens in ten seconds."

The bridge crew waited anxiously, transfixed by the banalities of local media.

"Five," Hobbes began to count down.

At *zero,* all three of the pictures fractured.

The talking heads of local politicians collapsed, like faces in a shattering mirror. The image of the sporting event—some sort of obstacle soccer—froze, then horizontal jitters turned it into garbage. The financial channel was the most interesting: for a moment the graphs stayed coherent, but showed wildly shifting data, as if some tremendous currency crash were underway. Then, like the others, the image collapsed into incomprehensibility.

"Well," said Hobbes, "it appears as if—"

"Wait," Zai silenced her.

He gazed at the blur of the three screens. They hadn't snow-crashed, hadn't reached a state of pure noise. There was a non-random signal there, an order in the chaos, like encrypted data viewed without the proper codes. The newsfeeds' audio didn't sound like the undifferentiated wash of white noise; it was more animated, like the thunder of nearby traffic, a steady roar broken by individual vehicles passing, even the high-pitched bleat of warning horns.

"Tyre," he ordered. "Compare these transmissions to the chromograph data from the object."

"Compare them, sir?"

"At an abstract level of organization. Do they have comparable repeating features? Similar periodicity? I don't need to know what they mean. Just tell me if there's any relationship."

"Yes, sir," Tyre answered. Her eyes dropped into the blankness of heavy second sight.

Zai saw puzzlement on the faces of his staff, which

flickered with the still-coruscating lights of the Legis feeds.

"Obviously, whatever transmission hit Marx's drones struck the Legis infostructure eight and a half hours prior—exactly the light-speed delay between the two," he said. "Something hijacked their newsnets and replaced their feeds, not with noise, but with pirate data. My guess is that the polar facility then repeated that data, sending it to the object. Marx just got in the way."

"But the facility was locked down, sir," the marine sergeant complained. "My troops were there at the pole."

Zai frowned. The man was right. It was hard to believe that the Rix compound mind could get past the physical keys of a locked-down translight entanglement facility. How had it managed that trick?

"Incoming messages, sir," Hobbes said. "Light-speed."

The captain nodded. The information wake of the planet had finally caught up with them.

Hobbes shut her eyes.

"From the polar array," she said. "They're under attack, sir! Drones and autopiloted aircraft, and a Rix commando inside the wire."

The marine sergeant swore. He'd wanted to stay on Legis XV to help track the Rixwoman down, but Zai had demanded he stay aboard the *Lynx*.

"A message from the palace contingent now. The breakdown is global. Every net-linked com device is spewing garbage."

"Not garbage," Zai muttered. Information. The Rix mind had managed to transmit something to the object. It had broken their blockade.

"From the pole again," Hobbes said, listening intently. "They say the interplanetary array ramped up by itself, transmitting out of control."

The marine sergeant cursed again.

"What was its broadcast target?" Zai demanded. Then he realized that with the translight facility disrupted, it would be seventeen hours before any questions could travel roundtrip between the *Lynx* and Legis.

Tyre, back from her data fugue, spoke up suddenly. "You were right, sir. There is a connection between the Legis data and the object." The ensign stared into her second sight, trying to translate the visuals there into words. "There's a background period of twenty-eight milliseconds in both. And some sort of utility pattern: one thousand twenty-four zeros in a row every few seconds. You were right."

Zai felt no joy in this revelation. Now that information was rushing at them from every quarter, confirming his worst fears, he didn't know what to do.

Despite all the *Lynx* had risked against the Rix battlecruiser, they'd been beaten. The compound mind had escaped their quarantine.

"Something more from the palace, sir," Hobbes broke in. "The marines say they've regained control of the security system. The com breakdown seems to have confused the compound mind."

Zai stared at her blank-faced.

Ensign Tyre was speaking again. She related more information about the Legis feeds and the object. She had matched the common patterns to Marx's brain waves, now.

Damn, Zai thought. Had he lost his master pilot to the abomination?

"Sir!" cried Hobbes. Then she fell silent.

"Report, Hobbes."

"It seems the compound mind is gone, sir."

"From the palace?" he asked.

Hobbes shook her head. "From everywhere. The Legis nets are recovering, but the mind is gone, sir. Imperial shunts are taking over to prevent it from propagating again."

A com officer added her voice. "I'm getting local militia transmissions on the emergency band. They're saying the same thing. Legis is free."

Zai sat back, shaking his head.

"It's gone, sir," Hobbes said. "Somehow, we won. The compound mind is gone!"

"No," he said. It couldn't be this easy. A Rix mind couldn't be ousted by an infostructure failure, no matter how drastic. There were no such miracles. No simple victories. No rest for Laurent Zai.

Then he saw it, realized what had happened.

Zai's hands flicked in the air, bringing up the object's shape in the airscreen.

"It isn't gone."

He pointed at the twisting shape.

"It's in there."

The staff stared into the airscreen silently, as if hypnotized again by the undulations of the object.

Tyre came out her fugue, nodding her head.

"Yes, sir. It's in the object. I can see it there."

"Engineer Frick," Zai said.

"Yes, sir?"

"Get me acceleration," he ordered. "In forty minutes."

"But, sir—"

"Do it."

Laurent Zai strode to the command bridge door. He needed to clear his head for a few moments, to escape this surge of revelations.

"How much acceleration, sir?" Frick called after him. "How many gees?"

Wasn't it obvious? Zai thought.

"Enough to ram that thing," the captain said, and left.

Marine Private First Class

On Legis, Marine Private First Class Sid Akman despaired.

Weary of trying to make himself understood, he made the signal for a global fall-prone order. As one, the militia soldiers dotting the icy hills around the target dropped to the ground.

A perfectly executed maneuver, Akman thought sourly. He had finally found something the Legis militia was good at: cowering.

When he'd first been assigned to planetside, Private Akman had been glad to escape the *Lynx*. The frigate had just received her orders to go after the Rix battle-cruiser, and figured to be a doomed ship. For a marine, dirt was never a plum assignment, but it beat a cold death in space.

But now the word was that the *Lynx* was doing fine, having bested the superior Rix craft on the first pass.

And Private Sid Akman found himself in perilous circumstances.

As the Imperial marine on the planet with the most actual combat experience—i.e., three drops—he was in command of this assault, which involved a hapless platoon of Legis militia closing in on an incomparably deadly Rix commando. The commando was cornered in her own lair, which she'd had weeks to prep defensively. In addition, her ice cave lay within one kilometer of the planet's magnetic north pole, and Legis's wild EM field was playing hell with the militia's gear. The thermal imagers were screwy, remote drones were useless, and the platoon's minesweeping robot would only walk in a giant lazy circle, a figure which the machine's internal nav insisted was a straight line.

To make matters worse, PFC Akman's heavy artillery support was nonfunctional. Something about the freezing cold. Therefore Akman's preferred strategy in this situation—quietly paint the target with x-ray lasers and have a flight of guided missiles launched from over the hill—was not going to happen. Air support was also out of the question. Some ghostly force had been attacking civilian aircraft around the pole for the last few weeks, and it was widely held in the militia command structure that the Rix compound mind could take control of anything in the air.

The militia bigs were *very* scared of the compound mind, even though it seem to have disappeared during the big crash of a few hours ago. So they had electronically isolated this mission, even from the secure military infostructure. Akman had no headsup display, no pov feedback from his so-called soldiers, not even *radio,* for heaven's sake.

He was reduced to hand signals, a hastily constructed gestural code that had thus far failed to get his troops into position. Akman wished he had brought trumpets and drums.

The whole attack was unnecessarily dangerous in any case. The Rix commando was trapped here in the arctic. The recon flyer that she'd stolen was damaged beyond repair. A military satellite had spotted the grounded flyer easily, its black armor glaring against the white background. Oddly, the Rixwoman hadn't bothered to cover it with camo, or even a few handfuls of snow. He could see the flyer now through his field amplifiers (which were, thank heaven, working). It bore the marks of grievous damage sustained while penetrating the entanglement facility's perimeter defenses. It might fly again, but not for more than a few klicks.

So why not just keep the commando surrounded? At least until they could hit her with artillery. Remote drones. Air power. *Anything* but a ground assault.

The militia bigs were giving Akman the runaround, making excuses for this risky assault. They wanted to debrief the hostage (or traitor) who was with the Rix-woman, so taking down the entire mountain wasn't their preferred strategy. Akman hadn't bothered to remind them how the last hostage rescue against the Rix had gone.

The marine private sighed and raised his right fist, three fingers up. After a moment, Squad Three rose slowly to their feet, glancing at each other for confirmation. Akman extended his arm forward, palm flat and parallel with the tundra. Squad Three moved forward.

He smiled thinly in the bitter and wind-blown cold. For the first time, this signal thing was working.

The marine private brought Squad Three to a halt

and dropped them again. Then he moved Squad Two back a bit, just to see if they understood the pullback signal as well. For a few more minutes, Akman shuffled the elements of his command around the target area aimlessly, like a chess player wasting moves against an immobilized opponent. The militia soldiers were getting slightly better. And as far as Akman could tell, the Rix commando wasn't even aware of the surrounding force yet. The incessant howl of the wind covered the sound of their footsteps, and the attackers were hardly lighting up the EM spectrum. Perhaps Akman's stone-age communications had actually given the assault group a momentary advantage.

Of course, Private Akman would have traded all the surprise in the world for a few rotary-wing gunships. Puma class, with Imperial pilots.

It was time to go in.

Akman moved slowly down from his hilltop perch. He knew that after the first shots were fired, all organization would crumble unless he were visible to his troops. Hell, it would crumble anyway. But at least from down here Akman could get off a few shots of his own. In the palace rescue, he'd lost a few friends to those seven Rix defenders. If he personally made the kill-shot here at the pole, it would bury some of the shame of that failed assault.

He slid on his belly toward the cave mouth, pausing to signal forward Squad One on his left. A few competent techs were in One. He stuck his thumb up, and the squad leader, a young woman called Smithes, sprayed a bright mist of monofilament-dissolving aerosol over Akman's head and into the cave mouth. No snares showed.

Akman moved forward again, staying in front of his

troops. With everyone to his rear, he could set his varigun to the widest possible spray pattern. The sawed-
off shotgun effect might not kill the Rixwoman, but
she would feel it. If he could stun her even for a moment, one of the thousands of rounds guaranteed to fly
from his panicked troops might get lucky.

The cave was dark. Akman paused to adjust his visor, although the cold-blooded Rix were notoriously
hard to see with night-vision. He crawled inside, the
sudden silence of the cave eerie after the constant
moan of wind.

Then Private Akman heard a sound. It came from
within, echoing from the smooth, laser-carved walls as
if they were marble.

It sounded like retching, or coughing.

Akman had never imagined a Rixwoman getting
sick. Perhaps it was the hostage. There was a hollow-
ness to the sound, an anguish that sounded human and
somehow heartbroken.

He mentally shrugged. Whatever it was, the noise
covered his approach.

Akman raised a fist, signaling Squad One to hold
until they heard fire, and crawled alone farther into
the cave.

A light shone before him now, glinting from the icy
walls. The coughing sound and glimmer of light
seemed to come from the same direction, and Akman
followed them. He knew he should spray for monofilament snares. Even crawling at a snail's pace, the
molecule-thin wires could cut through a limb before he
would notice the microscopic incision. But something
about the wracking, animal sound impelled him forward without due caution. Instinctively, Akman knew
he had the advantage here.

The marine rose to his feet. The sound came from just around a sharp-hewn corner of ice. Akman swallowed. He was going for it: the lone kill of a Rix commando.

Akman moved before he had time to reconsider this insanity.

He stepped lightly into the small room, gun leveled. A light squeeze on the stud would hit everything in the room.

The Rix commando sat before him, her head in her hands.

Godspite, she was a mess! Hair remained only in singed patches on her scalp. Her hands and face were red and blistered, every exposed centimeter of skin smeared with soot and dried blood. Her nose was swollen from a bad break. She wore a fire-blackened ablative suit that had melted onto her hypercarbon joints, hanging in tatters from them like shiny, sloughed skin. Half-frozen blood pooled on the floor below where she sat, and Akman could see at least three abdominal wounds.

There must have been a lung hit as well. The wracking cough shook her whole body.

Private Akman had a sudden realization. He could actually *capture* this Rixwoman. For the first time in a century of warfare, the Empire would take a living prisoner of the Cult. And Sid Akman would be the one.

With shaking fingers he switched the varigun to a riot setting, which fired a suspension of steel pellets in plastic goo. A laughable weapon against a Rix commando, but the woman seemed so hideously wounded already, it just might be enough. He aimed the gun at her bloody stomach.

Perhaps he wouldn't have to fire at all.

"Don't move," he said evenly, trying to hide his fear. The commando was believed to speak Legis dialect quite well, having carried off an impersonation of her hostage for several days.

The commando looked up, startling Akman with her beautiful, violet eyes.

By the Empire, he thought. *She's been crying.*

Surely this was some maintenance procedure, some repair-nano medium for fire-damaged optics. Some crocodile trick.

Surely not tears.

Another sob wracked the commando. Then she pulled a monofilament knife from her clothes.

Akman fired instantly, the recoil from the heavy projectile pushing him off balance. He staggered to remain upright on the icy floor of the cave. The suspension of steel balls bounced harmlessly from the Rixwoman's upraised hand—she had blocked it!

She coughed and threw the knife aside.

"I am unarmed now," she said in a perfect local accent.

Her burned and scarred head dropped back into her hands.

The rush of adrenaline and fear that had caused him to fire passed quickly, and Akman gained control of his breathing. This Rix commando was really *surrendering.* The Imperial marine lowered his weapon, wondering if everything he had been taught about the Rix could be false.

The ungainly sounds of Squad One moving up came from behind him. They must have heard the varigun's report. He turned and waved them back.

The first Rix prisoner ever. He wasn't about to let some yokel burst in and shoot her to death. Her body convulsed again, and Akman grew concerned. He didn't want her *dying,* by god.

"Are you . . . ?" he began. Sick? Dying? *Weeping?*

Keep it simple. "What's wrong?"

The commando looked at him again with her stunning violet eyes, the only feature of her face that was not grotesque with injury.

"I am mourning Rana Harter," she said simply. "Who died today."

And then she wept some more.

Executive Officer

The *Lynx* began to move.

Almost a full four hours after the captain's deadline, First Engineer Frick finally cleared Hobbes to give the order. The frigate shook as the main drive engaged, a rattle sweeping through the bridge, tinged with a metal shriek. The *Lynx*'s artificial-gravity generators, which usually maintained zero apparent inertia, were showing their overstressed condition. Hobbes felt herself pressed rudely back into her chair, feeling about half the frigate's four-gravity acceleration.

She saw the captain scowl as the crushing weight released them.

"Hobbes?"

"Sir, the AG is doing double duty," she explained. "It's keeping us nailed down *and* the ship together.

We've prioritized inertial dampening on the portions of *Lynx* where structural integrity is in doubt."

"Yes, Hobbes. But surely that tremor wasn't good for the fissured hullalloy in the bow."

"No, Captain. It wasn't good at all for the fissured hullalloy in the bow."

She returned to her tasks, ignoring Zai's look of surprise at her tone. Hobbes had enough to do—coordinating the continuing repair, dispensing zero-gee to crews with heavy objects to move, making sure the *Lynx* didn't break up—without explaining the obvious to the captain. Another few hours of repair in freefall, and the ship would have accelerated without a hitch.

But orders were orders, and time was limited.

The Rix battlecruiser was accelerating at its maximum. Even assuming the vessel turned over, it would reach the object in just over seven hours. The *Lynx* couldn't sit around forever. As it was, the wounded frigate would be hard pressed to match velocities with the object before the battlecruiser arrived.

Hobbes wondered why the Rix had placed the object fifteen million klicks behind the battlecruiser, and without an escort. Had they assigned a hundred or so of the blackbody drones to it, the object would be able to defend itself.

She wondered grimly if the thing were already capable of fending off the *Lynx*. Its powers of alchemy were an unknown quantity. The now-animated object (Did it really contain the Rix mind, or was the captain crazy?) could change itself into practically any substance.

But how would it defend itself? Turn into a working starship? A giant fusion cannon? Or would it clam up, giving itself a carapace of hullalloy? Or even neutronium?

ExO Hobbes shook her head, correcting this last supposition. Neutronium was collapsed matter—a non-elemental substance—and so far all the object's transubstantiations had involved elements. There was no need to exaggerate its powers, Hobbes reminded herself. Data Analysis's current theory was that it could call arrangements of virtual electrons into being, but not protons and neutrons. Therefore the object's substance, despite its chemical properties, would never have the mass, radioactivity, or magnetism of its true-matter analogs. The object's alchemy was a bit like that of an easy graviton generator: The particles it created were amazing at first, but upon closer examination they paled in comparison to the real thing.

Katherie Hobbes pushed these thoughts aside—speculations on the object were DA's concern—and refocused her attention on the *Lynx*'s repair woes. The biggest drain on stores had been the singularity generator. The bigbang mechanism was in fine shape, but to replace the generator's shielding, armor had been stripped relentlessly from the rest of the frigate. The generator's jury-rigged shielding was sufficient to protect the crew, but lacked the necessary countermass to keep the hole in place under heavy gees. It took a lot of matter to keep a pocket universe from breaking free under the inertial stresses of maneuver. With every ton Frick added to the shield, Hobbes got another fraction of a gee in safe acceleration, but that armor had to be pulled from some other part of the ship. The frigate's fissured bow also needed reinforcement. Frick had made do with a patchwork of plates drawn from armored drones, combat stations, and even decompression bulkheads. Half the hardpoints on the ship—gun batteries, the main drive, and critical targets like sickbay—had been stripped of armor. Facing a half-assed volley of flockers or some other kinetic weapon, the *Lynx* would be swissed.

The executive officer wished fervently that she could call up a hundred tons of hullalloy from an alchemist of her own.

Hobbes simulated their approach to the object under the frigate's current configuration. At four gees for seven hours, they could slow down to make a first pass at a relative velocity of about three hundred kilometers per second, a respectable velocity for an attack. But if she could squeeze out another gee, they would come in neatly matched to the object. It would be invaluable for the Empire if they could study the thing before they destroyed it.

Ideally, Hobbes thought, she could get *two* more gees out of the wounded *Lynx*. Then the frigate would be able to match the six-gee maximum of the Rix craft, making an eventual escape at least feasible. If Frick stripped every hardpoint on the ship, it might just be possible.

Hobbes rubbed her head, which had begun to spin around the combinatorial tree of possible tradeoffs. The mental focus that two hours of hypersleep had bestowed upon her was starting to slip again. She decided to ask the captain for advice.

The shipmaster's chair was empty. She raised Zai in synesthesia.

His voice came back without visual, a sure sign that he was in the captain's observation blister. Zai had ordered the blister resurrected as soon as it could be after the battle was over. Over the last few hours, he had returned there again and again, staring into the void as he had before rejecting the blade of error.

Hobbes wondered if he were having second thoughts.

"Yes, Hobbes?"

"I think I can get us up to five gees, sir."

"Only five?"

Hobbes sighed quietly, glad that her expression was hidden from the captain.

"There's not enough heavy metal to keep the hole in place at higher accelerations, sir."

"What have we stripped?"

"Everything, sir. Hardpoints. Sickbay. Drones. As much of the main drive shielding as we can spare without another round of cancers."

There was a pause.

"What about the bridge?"

"Sir?" The battle bridge was the *Lynx*'s hardest point, wrapped in a cocoon of hullalloy and structured neutronium. There was good reason for this precaution; the frigate had no chain-of-command provisions if the captain and all the firsts were killed.

The Empire didn't want ensigns running starships. Especially not this one.

"I believe there are forty tons of matter available in the bridge hardpoint," the captain said.

"Forty tons may be present, sir. But I'm not sure they are *available*."

The captain chuckled. "Give me six gees, Hobbes. Whatever it takes."

"Sir—"

"The object may devise any number of ways to attack us, Hobbes. But I have a feeling that it would be disinclined to use a kinetic weapon. Think about it."

Hobbes considered the captain's words.

"Because it would have to expend its own mass to create a missile?"

"Yes, Hobbes. And true mass is the one thing it lacks. It may be able to create a diamond bullet, but however hard that diamond is, it will still have the density of a sugar cube. However you strip the *Lynx,* I think she'll be able to withstand a hail of sugar cubes. Even very hard ones."

Hobbes's eyebrows raised. Whenever she thought the old man had succumbed to melancholy, Zai would show his usual tactical brilliance. But she wasn't entirely convinced.

"Even if these sugar cubes are propelled by a railgun, sir? At relativistic velocities—"

"A railgun requires magnetism, Hobbes."

Hobbes grimaced at her own error. Of course. DA believed that the object's alchemical matter was nonferrous and nonfissionable. The thing was limited to chemical propulsion for any weapon, a paltry way to accelerate a kinetic weapon.

"I see, sir. That's why you want the gees: so that we can decelerate fast enough to match velocity." Hobbes saw it now. If the *Lynx* flew past the object at hundreds of klicks per second, it could simply place a net of alchemical elements in their path. Even a stationary tripwire could be deadly to a running man.

"Exactly, Executive Officer," he answered. "And with six gees, we can escape the battlecruiser after our mission is accomplished."

She nodded.

"But what about energy weapons, sir? We've only got a makeshift heat-sink. The bridge armor also shields us from radiation."

"We've seen no signs of a powerful energy source, Hobbes. But of course you're right. If that thing can make itself into a planet-sized fusion cannon, we're dead."

"Then what should we—"

"Dead, Hobbes, whether or not we have shielding around the bridge. Give me six gees. Captain out."

Katherie heard the connection step down.

She sighed. Perhaps the old man was right. They were traveling toward an incomprehensible set of possibilities, facing a foe of unknown strengths and weaknesses. The *Lynx* was matched against an enemy that was neither a crewed starship nor a drone, machine nor creature; it wasn't even proper matter. It was an empty signifier in the emptiness of space.

Once again, the survival of Laurent Zai's ship seemed to be out of the hands of its crew.

A few more tons of metal weren't going to make any difference.

Senator

The counselor from the Plague Axis arrived with a thunderous noise.

She had been waiting for hours. The counselor was only twenty minutes late, but Nara's mind had turned to this meeting again and again all day, as if it were some illicit and terrible assignation. There was the aberrance of talking with someone whose face she would never see, the unease at meeting with another counselor outside the chamber, and, underlying it all, the irrational but age-old fear of contagion.

The sound of the counselor's helicopter approached slowly, building from a subliminal shudder to a relentless force that raised a chorus of chattering complaints from Nara's foxbone tea service. The vehicle had called ahead to check the specifications of her building's landing pad; it was a big machine. The counselor's environmental system required heavy transport. It contained the man's affliction, a mobile quarantine.

At Oxham's request, Roger Niles had discreetly determined the gender of the Plague Axis representative. In the chambers of the War Council, the plagueman rarely spoke except to vote, his voice distorted by the filtration system that protected both his delicate immune system from the capital's pollution and his fellow counselors from the ancient parasites that made him their home.

Nara Oxham shuddered for a moment when the pitch of the helicopter's whine dropped, signaling that its landers were secure on the pad above her. Rationally, Oxham knew that she had nothing to fear. Members of the Plague Axis carried death with themselves when they entered the realm of the living. If a biosuit were somehow opened to the fresh air, a layer of phosphorus compounds would immolate its wearer rather than risk exposing the populace.

And her fear was not only unreasoned, it was shameful, a remnant of one of humanity's most idiotic mistakes. The Plague Axis performed a signal service to the Empire. Like most of the human diaspora, the Eighty Worlds possessed only a small gene pool relative to its trillions of inhabitants. The genetic legacy of

Earth Prime had been pared down by wars and holocausts, and by foolish edicts of racial purity, which resulted in monocultures taking to the stars together, inbred groups without the stability and adaptability of genetic fusion cultures. But of all the historical errors that had reduced genetic diversity, most damaging had been the effort to engineer a humanity free of faults.

It had taken millennia of misguided genetic manipulation to discover the subtle jape played by evolution: Almost no human traits were universally unfit. Genes that exacerbated a disease in one environment conferred resistance in another. Insanity was married to genius, passivity to patience. Every disadvantage carried hidden strengths. In the wildly variable conditions of the stars, humans would find that they needed greater diversity, not less. And yet it was a diminished humanity that left earth's cradle, enfeebled supermen who met only a local and flawed standard of superiority.

The Plague Axis was an attempt to repair this damage. They were the throwbacks, possessed of legacy genes that had escaped by chance the eugenical pogroms. Descended from the poor, those without access to gene therapies and prenatal selection, they were like discarded junk that had become incalculably valuable as antiques. The people of the Axis had been the ugly, the afflicted, those prone to madness. Now, they existed as reservoirs of ancient treasure, their once-undesirable traits slowly and carefully reintroduced into the general population over the span of generations.

But still, Nara Oxham hesitated before she signaled for her door to open. She made the gesture with an unsure hand.

The Plague Axis representative paused at the entry,

like a vampire waiting to be invited across her threshold.

"Counselor," she said.

The helmet of the biosuit performed a little bow, and the man shuffled in.

Senator Oxham wondered if he would sit. The sunken dais of the council's chamber was suited to the suit's bulk, but the chairs in her apartment were spindly and insubstantial.

He remained standing. So did she.

"Senator," he returned the greeting.

"To what do I owe the pleasure?"

"An explanation is in order, and a promise."

Oxham shook her head slightly in confusion.

"Senator," the man continued, "I must explain my vote of yesterday."

Oxham took a deep breath. He was talking about the Emperor's genocidal plan. She glanced out at the blackness of the Martyrs' Park. The hundred-year rule did not forbid discussion of secrets between counselors, but she felt uncomfortable speaking of the forbidden topic outside the council chamber.

"Surely the point is moot now, Counselor. It didn't come to that."

"Yes, we were saved by the *Lynx*," he said. "But we wish you to understand our motives. We are not your enemy."

"We?"

He nodded. "I did not make the decision alone."

Nara blinked. He had discussed the Emperor's plan with outsiders? The man was admitting treason.

"But how?" she said. "We had only minutes to decide." She looked at the bulky biosuit, wondering if it might house an entangled quantum grid, the only form of communication that could possibly be undetectable to the sensors of the Diamond Palace.

The plagueman spread his thickly gloved hands, a clumsy puppet's gesture, pleading for understanding.

"I have not broken the hundred-year rule, Senator Oxham. The Emperor himself came to the Axis before the question was raised in council. Before the rule was invoked."

Nara nodded and sighed. The sovereign and his tricks. He had gone into the vote with a stacked deck.

"What did he offer you?" she said coldly.

The plagueman turned half away, his puppet hands up in the air now.

"You must understand something, Senator. The Plague Axis of the Risen Empire faces hard times. Bleak centuries ahead."

"What do you mean?"

"We are too few," he said. "Although we add diversity to the Empire, we lack enough divergence in our own population. Over the generations, we risk becoming a monoculture ourselves."

Nara frowned, trying to remember the reading she'd done on the Axis since first meeting the members of the council. This hasty study blurred with the volumes of military and megaeconomic theory she had consumed, the forced marches of sudden expertise required to prosecute a war.

"A monoculture?" she asked. "Don't you interbreed with the plague axes of the other coreward powers?" That was the true source of the Axis's independence from the rest of the Empire. They were not simply a reservoir, they were a trading guild.

He ponderously shook his head. "Not for eighty

years Absolute. Since the end of the First Incursion, we have been under a blockade."

"A blockade?"

"The Rix have applied pressure throughout the core. The Tungai, the Fahstuns, not even the Laxu will trade with us."

Nara swallowed. Even segments of humanity that were in violent conflict still kept up the exchange of genes through their nominally neutral plague axes. The biological legacy of Earth Prime was so thinly spread, the distances of the diaspora so great, it was playing a dangerous game to reduce diversity any further, like poisoning wells in a desert war.

"Why would they do that?"

"The Rix have a voice everywhere, Nara Oxham. As you know, we are the last coreward power to resist their compound minds. We have been under blockade these last eighty years."

"Why has this been kept secret?"

"The Emperor wished it to be thought that the First Incursion ended in a true peace."

The biosuit's helmet barely moved, but Nara could tell he was shaking his head. She sighed. The Emperor had proclaimed a false victory eighty years ago. The Rix had not been beaten, they had merely moved the conflict into other theaters.

"We are growing weaker," the Plague counselor said. "Less able to stabilize the Empire's billions."

Oxham knew enough to understand the threat. Almost the entire population of the Eighty Worlds had descended from a small portion of one continent on Earth Prime. The weaknesses of monoculture were a constant threat: New contagions and panics propagated quickly, and charismatic figures like the Emperor consolidated power with the hyperbolic curve of pandemics. The consequences of a genetic blockade might one day be even more damaging than this second war with the Rix.

"But why help the Emperor commit mass murder?" she asked. "How could depopulating Legis XV fulfil your aims?"

"Before the War Council took up the issue of destroying the Legis infostructure, the Apparatus came to us with an analysis. How might a war with the Rix increase the diversity of the Empire? In deep history, wars often had such an effect. Mass movements of people brought distant gene pools together, invaders and colonists crossbred with local populations."

"But the Rix don't want to occupy us, Counselor," she said. "There'll be no miscegenation with them, no rape camps or comfort conscripts. Just death, and the sterile occupation of compound minds. A nonbiological violation."

"Correct. The only population movement will be among the Eighty Worlds themselves. Such disruptions are always useful, but they would merely stir the existing pool."

"What was it then?" she asked.

He made a sound that might have been a sigh, which came from the filter in a hiss of white noise, like boiling water poured slowly onto cold metal.

"What the Empire needs is new genes, Senator. New arrangements of DNA. With the Rix blockade, we cannot import them. Only mutation will generate more diversity."

"Hopeful monsters?" she asked. "It's been tried. The laboratory can't create at the same magnitude of evolution. There are never enough subjects, and we don't even know what we're looking for."

The plagueman sighed again. "Not in the laboratory, Senator. But in vivo, in the wild, on a planetary scale."

She blinked, wondering if he could be serious. "Legis?"

He nodded, a slow and clumsy gesture.

She shook her head. The man was insane. "But the nuclear weapons over Legis were to be low-yield, clean EMP devices."

"No, Senator. They would have been dirty bombs. An unexplained error."

Nara swayed for a moment, closing her eyes. She needed to sit down. Reaching behind her, she felt the cold and reassuring solidity of the apartment's glassene wall.

"A hundred million wasn't enough for him?"

"There are trillions to think of, Nara Oxham."

"You're mad," she said. "You and he are both insane." Nara walked away from the suited man, barely able to hold what might have happened in her mind. "God above. We would have been complicit in a billion deaths. The Emperor could have held it over the political parties for centuries. Whether we personally voted for it or not, we legitimized the decision by sitting on his council."

"And you could hold it over the sovereign, knowing that the dirty bombings were intentional. The ultimate stabilizing force: mutually assured destruction."

"And all this for a few mutations?"

"More than a few, Senator. The population of a whole planet is a vast palette to draw from. The dirty work has to be done; let the Rix be blamed for it, we thought."

Senator Oxham dropped into a large chair, letting the plagueman stand alone. She covered her eyes and felt a twinge from the city. The incessant human throng that always threatened to consume her seemed terribly fragile now. With the right weapon, all those voices could be silenced in an instant. That ancient specter of mass destruction—more than the diaspora, or the Time Thief, or even the gray powers of the symbiant—was the appalling price of technology.

Death had hardly been beaten. The Old Enemy had simply changed its scale of interest.

"I am sorry that you were disappointed by the *Lynx*'s victory," she finally said.

"No, we were glad, Senator."

She looked up at him.

The biosuit shuffled from side to side.

"Try to understand. We of the Axis are all hopeful monsters. Mutations who hope one day to contribute to the germ line."

"Monsters," she agreed.

"As are you, Nara Oxham."

"What do you mean?"

"In your ability, your madness, you are one of us. If synesthesia implants had been invented a few hundred years earlier, before apathy treatments existed to cure you, all those with unexpected reactions to the process—brainbugs, photism, verbochromia, even your empathy—would have been cast aside as mad, as were my ancestors. The descendants of these unfortunates, people like you, would be in the Plague Axis now."

For a moment, Nara was revolted at the thought. Her condition was not genetic, but the result of untried technology. A small percentage had unexpected reactions to any new technique.

"I'm not a mutation."

"You are. The last hundred years have shown that re-actions to synesthesia implants are often inherited. Your kind are a genetic anomaly, one that was hidden until the environment changed. Synesthesia revealed you."

The plagueman fell silent, letting her digest his words. She could almost grasp his viewpoint, unfamiliar though it was. So much lay hidden in the human code, revealed only by events. It was like the rain forests of Vasthold, whose vast reservoirs of protein structures routinely delivered up new drugs and bioware, but only when the need for them became apparent. Irrational design, it was called: plumbing diversity for random answers.

Events could make a monster—or a savior—of anyone.

But Nara had never thought of herself that way.

"Possibly," she said.

"But you shamed us, Nara Oxham. You faced down the Emperor, as we did not."

She laughed bitterly. "Now you decide you don't want a new race of mutants? After the point is moot?"

"We realized even before Laurent Zai's victory that we had gone too far. Our thinking had been changed by cowardice. We were afraid to oppose the sovereign."

She shrugged. "So you say."

"Allow us to prove it, Nara Oxham."

"How?"

He shuffled toward her, held out his hand. Oxham no longer felt compelled to hide her disgust, and she stood and pulled away.

"Any vote you wish, Senator, we will side with you."

Nara raised her eyebrows. The War Council was structured around a natural four-to-four split, the three opposition parties and Ax Milnk against Loyalty and the three dead. The Plague Axis held the deciding vote. She realized now that the Emperor had planned it that way. When they had confirmed the War Council, the Senate had thought the Plague Axis a natural ally to the living, not knowing of the pressures that the Axis suffered from the Rix blockade, not realizing how the Emperor could bend them to his will. But the sovereign had overplayed his hand; his attempted genocide had turned them into guilty, regretful accomplices.

"You'll vote the way I say?"

The biosuit nodded. "We will, once, when you ask it."

"I'll let you know. But however many votes it takes, there must be no more genocides."

"None," the plagueman agreed.

That was something, Senator Oxham thought. She had an ally. Perhaps this war didn't have to be a bloodbath. If the man were genuine, perhaps it was time for a gesture.

Swallowing, Nara crossed to where the representative stood, and put her hand on the shoulder of the suit. It was as cold as a dead man's arm.

"What do you want from me in return? Surely not just absolution," she said softly.

The biosuited man turned away from her, faced the darkness of the Martyrs' Park, and cleared his throat, a very recognizable sound.

"If you would favor us, Nara Oxham, we do have a request. Perhaps your particular ability is merely happenstance, a slip of a few angstroms in the implant procedure. But if not, then maybe your empathy can be added to the germ line."

He turned to her.

"So one day, in your own time, we would like you to have a child. Or give us what we need to make one."

A child, she thought. More madness in this universe, another Oxham addicted to the passions of the crowd, addicted to drugs to maintain sanity, given to loving broken men light-years distant. This was like some fairy tale, a firstborn promised to demons. She shuddered.

"Give me your vote when I ask it," she said, "and I'll consider it."

Another hopeful monster for the cauldron.

Captain

Laurent Zai watched the object in the bridge airscreen, his mind fighting against the mesmerizing undulations of its surface.

Now that the *Lynx* was closing with the thing, simple telescopy revealed a level of detail that had been invisible to active sensors. The wild dunes that played across its visage had grown far more active since Marx's probes had imaged them. The object was definitely alive now, clearly possessed of some inner, animating presence.

Zai could sense the compound mind in its movements. Somehow, the Rix had found a way to mirror the data of an entire world, to compress and transmit it, and house it in this strange arrangement of matter.

The planet had merely served as an incubator, virgin soil in which to culture the first of a new species of the compound mind, one able to move across the stars. The Rix takeover of Legis was not an invasion.

It was a breeding program.

And the Apparatus was afraid of a few transmissions escaping Legis? Here was the data of the entire planet, wrapped up and ready for shipping back into Rix space. Every aspect of Imperial technology and culture would be open for other Rix minds to probe and pick apart, a living model of the enemy brought back as spoils of war.

Only the unlikely survival of the *Lynx* had given the Empire a chance to stop this obscenity from returning home.

"Charge the photon cannon," he ordered.

"Aye, sir," said Gunner Wilson, his fingers already moving as he spoke.

Zai had left the overtly hostile act of readying his weapons until now, hoping to disguise his intentions as long as possible. Thus far, the *Lynx* had sent out only unarmed scout probes and minesweepers, as if gathering information were the frigate's only mission. Who knew how naive this newly born mind might be?

Of course, the data they had already obtained might prove valuable once analyzed. The virtual matter of which the object was composed was far beyond any technology the Empire had ever created. What they discovered here might begin to unravel the mystery of how it worked. Even an oblique understanding of the underlying science would be a war prize for the ages.

"Launch ramscatter drones."

"Launched, sir."

The ship didn't respond with the usual recoil as the drones left. The launch rail was still not repaired, so the drones went forth under their own power. Between their slow start and the frigate's nearly matched velocity with the object, what few ramscatters the *Lynx* still possessed wouldn't achieve much of a collision vector. But they hardly mattered. Zai was sure that energy weapons were the key here. Data Analysis was certain that whatever else it might be able to do, the object could definitely make its outer layers very hard. It was probably impervious to kinetic energy. Still, it would be revealing to observe how it reacted to powerful explosives.

"Any changes, Tyre?"

"No, sir."

The DA ensign was up here on the bridge. Fighting an unpredictable foe, Zai needed analysis without the usual filters. The captain dipped into Tyre's synesthesia channel. *Damn*, the woman was going to burn out her second sight, if not her brain! Amanada Tyre was overlaying visible-light telescopy, a dozen drone viewpoints, and the object's wildly gyrating chromograph all at once. How could she comprehend anything amid that torrent of data?

Zai blinked the images away.

Well, if Tyre wanted fireworks, he would give her some.

"Hit it with the first wave," he ordered the drone pilots.

"Aye, sir," came an unfamiliar voice.

Even for these inconsequential and stupid ramdrones, Zai wished that Jocim Marx were here. The man brought an intelligence to his warcraft that was irreplaceable. Besides Hobbes, Marx was the *Lynx*'s most valuable officer. But the man was still down in sickbay, stricken with whatever overload had afflicted his brain after being caught in the path of the transmitted compound mind.

The airscreen view widened, opening to include both the *Lynx* and the enemy, the vector marks of the ramdrones between them. A few seconds later, the drones scattered, solid green arcs splitting into a hazy multitude of trajectories as they approached the object.

"In three, two . . ."

As the missiles struck, a gasp of surprise swept across the bridge. For a moment, a part of the object's surface froze, as suddenly motionless as video stopping on a single frame. The hundreds of dronelet impacts flared red, rose petals scattered across frozen ocean waves, then disappeared without leaving a mark.

With the threat to the object passed, the dunes jumped into motion again.

"What was that?" Zai asked.

"I'm not sure, sir," Tyre said slowly. "The object became something. Definitely a crystal, but I have no idea of what the matrix was composed of."

"Nothing showing on the chromograph?" Hobbes asked.

"There is, ma'am, but it's not a recognizable element."

"Transuranium," Zai muttered. They knew that the object might be able to create unknown elements well past the upper reaches of the normal periodic table. They would be metals, of a sort, but with unlimited half-lives, and therefore non-radioactive. Data Analysis had worked feverishly to determine what characteristics such exotic substances might possess with hundreds or even thousands of electrons in stable orbits, but such basic research was impossible when the elements themselves had never existed—*couldn't* exist except within the object itself.

"No, sir," Tyre said a moment later. "I don't think that's it."

She said nothing more.

"Tyre? Report."

Her head started nodding quickly, her hands flickering with gestural commands like an autistic child.

"I see it now, sir," she said breathlessly. "The atoms of the object's armor have fewer than a hundred electrons, but they aren't configured in the usual way."

"What's 'the usual way'?" Hobbes asked.

"In spherical energy levels," Tyre said. "Look."

The periodic table appeared.

Godspite, Zai thought. In the heat of battle with a Rix mind, and they were going to get a chemistry lesson. *This* was why DA was always kept off the bridge. He raised his hand to wave the apparition away.

But then the rectangular table turned into a spiral. Zai's hand froze.

"Electrons orbit their nuclei in set energy shells," Tyre explained. "Orbital quanta, in effect. But the object's virtual matter seems to be breaking that law. According to our probes, the object's surface was briefly composed of an element with new quantum states, new subshells. Transuranium means it's off the high end of the table. But this element was *on top* of the table. On the z-axis, like when imaginary numbers add another dimension to a number line."

The elemental spiral extruded itself into a conch shell, rising up like some periodic Tower of Babel. At each story of the structure, the familiar elemental groups gained new members.

"I think the object's surface armor was composed largely of carbon," Tyre said. "Or something with an atomic number of six. But with a crystalline structure much more complex than diamond."

"It was a hell of a lot harder than diamond, too," Hobbes added, "and with a higher melting point. The drones had zero effect, and they would have burned through diamond as easily as cloth."

"Send in the second wave, Hobbes," Zai ordered. "And get that apparition off my airscreen!"

Tyre's diagram winked rudely out, replaced by the arcing lines of the remaining drones. They plummeted into the object, which froze again to repulse their blows. This time, it seemed to the captain's eyes that the efficiencies of the object's metamorphosis were greater: Only the exact position where each dronelet struck became motionless. The rest of the ocean raged on unaffected.

"*I see,*" muttered Tyre, drinking in the data.

Zai ignored her. "Give me fifty terabits from the aft photon cannon," he ordered Gunner Wilson. "Dead center."

A targeting dot appeared on the object.

"Ready at your command," the gunner said.

Zai started to give the order, but the words stuck in his throat.

The bridge's main airscreen, his personal synesthesia, even the backup hardscreens surrounding the shipmaster's chair all showed the same, unbelievable thing.

The object had disappeared.

Blind Man

Though stripped of sight and his position in the chain of command, Data Master Kax still possessed illusion.

The flying dust of optical silicon had ravaged only his eyes. The optic nerve and the brain centers were completely functional. Indeed, once the *Lynx* returned to Legis, implantation of a pair of artificials would be a trivial matter.

Most importantly, the tiny receivers that allowed synesthesia, the gateways to second sight, were still active. These devices surrounded the lamina cribrosa, hundreds of them in a man of Kax's profession, unscratched by the glass fragments that had destroyed his normal vision.

Kax followed the battle from sickbay, drifting among the views of various drones, watching over young Tyre's shoulder as she constructed experimental models of the object's virtual matter. Occasionally Tyre would query him, asking for advice or confirmation, using sign language to conceal the conversations. Kax had become an invisible confidant to his own replacement, like the helpful ghost of an ancestor.

Then the object disappeared.

Telescopy showed nothing but background stars; the throughput of x-ray spectroscopy was flat; infrared showed only the cold of space.

Kax overheard the shouting on the bridge, watched as Tyre spun from one drone's viewpoint to another, replaying the vanishing again and again as the captain demanded answers. Had the thing discorporated itself? Tyre searched vainly for radiation and debris. Teleported? DA software plunged into the chromographs leading up to the disappearance, looking for signs of some magical substance emerging from the object's depths.

The blind man stayed calm. He let the visualizations of Tyre's wild speculation fall from his false sight, and returned his view to the empty space where the object had been. He moved from drone to drone in real-time, staying in the spectrum of visible light. Watching.

The empty space seemed perfect.

Background stars shone through it, shifting slightly due to the drones' mismatched velocities with the object. The drones could see each other through the now-empty space; one of them had a view of the *Lynx* that had been blocked by the object before its disappearance.

"Tyre," Kax said.

She didn't answer for a moment. Overwhelmed by the captain's demands for answers, she hadn't time to spare for a noisy, blind ghost. But the old reflexes of command eventually compelled a response.

Yes, sir? she handsigned.

"Ask the drone pilots to move Recon 086. Just a short acceleration."

Heading?

"It doesn't matter. Just as long as it's sudden."

The blind man watched carefully from the indicated

drone's point of view, training his mind on the familiar shape of the frigate.

Ten seconds later the image jerked as the drone accelerated in a short, clean burst. The *Lynx* was still visible, still there in the right place. But Kax saw what he had been watching for, a subtle imperfection that lasted less than a tenth of a second, an almost subliminal tear in synesthesia. The frigate had distorted for a moment, then the shape had re-formed even before the drone's acceleration ended.

The image was false, a mere feed coming from something between the drone and the *Lynx*.

Data Master Kax reserved the image in a high-definition buffer of the frigate's short-term memory, and carefully cut the few dozen frames that showed the distortion. He sent them to Ensign Tyre, marked priority, and leaned back with satisfaction, smiling to himself.

Invisibility meant nothing to a blind man.

Executive Officer

"Invisibility," Captain Zai muttered.

"Controlled refraction, sir," corrected Ensign Tyre.

Hobbes glanced sidelong at the young woman. Despite her proficiency at data analysis, Tyre hadn't acquired a knack for spotting the captain's moods yet.

"Not transparency, however," she continued. "The

object doesn't move the radiation straight through itself. It calculates observer viewpoints, and its surface acts like a large, highly directional hardscreen, emitting imagery appropriate to their positions."

"I believe the ensign suggests, sir," Hobbes offered, "that in the heat of battle, the unpredictability of dozens of accelerating viewpoints would make this 'invisibility' useless."

"It's playing with us, Hobbes," he said. "Testing its abilities against ours."

She thought for a moment.

"It's possible that it's trying to buy time, sir. The battlecruiser is less than an hour away."

The captain nodded. By stripping the bridge of armor, the *Lynx* had made six gees on the way here. But the Rix vessel hadn't turned over; it wasn't bothering to decelerate in time to match its velocity with the *Lynx* and the object. It was still barreling madly toward them, cutting its transit time to a minimum. The battlecruiser would pass by at a high relative, almost twice as fast as the first pass. The Rix had abandoned almost their entire drone complement, but Hobbes didn't doubt it could destroy the wounded frigate in the minutes it would be in range.

"That's likely, Hobbes. So let's see if we can hurt this thing."

"Happy to, sir." Hobbes interlaced her fingers. "Tyre, give me a target."

"May I suggest random parallax and a complex background, ma'am?"

"You may."

Tyre signaled, and the recon drones accelerated into action, whipping themselves into a froth of zigzags about the object. A decoy drone spat out chaff, light metals that the *Lynx*'s close-in defenses illuminated with jittering arms of laser light. The object became visible against the background stars and shimmering chafe, a blur of inconsistencies as it struggled to keep up its illusion.

Zai nodded. "Gunner, fifty terabits, dead center."

"Yes, sir."

The thin lancing beam of the laser was visible for a moment as it burned through the chaff, a flashlight in a dusty attic. The object appeared for a second, revealing its new configuration . . .

Spheroid, with a huge lens cut from it, concave and *mirrored:* a lens focused back toward the *Lynx*.

The blinding image was burned into Hobbes's eyes: that brief moment when the beam split in two, the sharp point of a very acute angle. As the laser's reflection raked across the frigate, the two rays of the angle closed to a single line.

The aft gunnery hardpoint—which Hobbes had stripped almost entirely of its armor—was silenced, and the beam winked out.

"Medical, medical!" cried the first voice, from a station a hundred meters from the stricken hardpoint. Hobbes responded with wooden hands. She tried to raised the cannon crew, but they didn't respond. More voices called for medical.

A decompression alarm sounded. As one, the bridge crew reached to seal their pressure hoods. Casualty icons sprouted from across the ship. Still nothing from the hardpoint that had fired: The crew there were vapor, Hobbes realized.

"Heat sink failure, sir! The beam went straight through us."

"Hobbes," the captain said.

"Bulkhead 2-aft is holed, sir. The foam's not holding. And—"

"Hobbes!" Zai shouted.

His cry brought her to a halt. "Yes, sir?"

"The singularity generator. Is it intact?"

Hobbes shook her head to clear the anguished voices that clamored for her attention. The hull was breached again, and the *Lynx*'s bulkheads had been stripped to the bone. Crew were dead and wounded. Why was the old man worried about auxiliary power?

She plumbed internal diagnostics.

"Yes, sir. It's fine. But main drive is bleeding—"

"Run it up to critical," he ordered.

"What?"

"Run the hole up to critical, Hobbes. I want a singularity self-destruct ten seconds after I give the order."

"Yes, sir," she said. Her second sight fell into the hadean colors of self-destruct protocols. She gave the gestural command, a twist of the thumbs and shoulders that was intentionally designed to hurt.

Then she realized what the captain meant to do.

God, Katherie thought, *he's going to kill us all.*

Katherie Hobbes stepped into the observation blister with her jaw clenched. She was careless of vertigo; there wasn't time left to worry about up and down.

"How many casualties?" Zai asked before she had a chance to speak.

"Forty-one, sir," she reported. "Thirty burned and eleven gone in hull blow-outs. Only twelve are able to receive the symbiant."

There was a silence for the dead. Hobbes was loath to break it, but events were closing in on the *Lynx*. Perhaps she would never be as gray as her crewmates and captain. Ritual seemed so often to stand in the way of efficiency.

"Sir," she said. "The Rix battlecruiser will be in range in twenty minutes."

Laurent Zai nodded. Facing away from Hobbes as he was, the blackness of space almost swallowed the gesture.

She started to speak again, but then she saw the object.

Hobbes had never seen the thing with naked eyes. In primary sight it was much darker than she expected. They were very far from the Legis sun, and she couldn't see the details that the enhanced, telescopic views of synesthesia provided. But the undulations were still visible; the crests of rolling dunes caught sunlight, igniting like whitecaps on a moonlit sea.

Surrounding the object was a squadron of recon drones. They played green spotlights across its surface, low-power lasers searching for data, for weaknesses.

She gathered herself. "If we plan to take action against the object, we should do it now, sir."

"Hobbes," the captain said tiredly. "What exactly would you suggest?"

She swallowed. "Nuke it, sir."

"The ramdrones had nukes in the mix, didn't they?" he asked.

"Only low-yield fission, sir. I'm talking about a fusion warhead in the thousand-megaton range. No imaginable substance could withstand a surface temperature of a million degrees."

"Ah," he answered.

She waited as he watched the sinuous thing below them.

"Any other ideas?" he finally asked.

"Yes, sir." She'd come with several options, in case he'd managed to think of an answer to a nuclear strike.

"We can use the three remaining photon cannon in tandem, sir. And keep the *Lynx* under random acceleration. The reflective lens on the object was twenty klicks across and very rigid. DA thinks it couldn't track us."

"But could we damage it?"

"We only hit it with fifty terabits, sir. With three cannon at maximum, we could easily do five hundred."

"It won't work," he said.

"Sir!" she said. "Either of those options would create a surface temperature adequate to vaporize neutronium. Nothing material can withstand those energies."

"Hobbes, what if this thing can achieve perfect reflectivity?"

"What do you mean, sir?"

The captain turned to face her.

"What if it can become a mirror so perfect that it could drift through the core of a type-G star and not gain a single degree?"

The image appalled Hobbes. It was an engineering fantasy, the sort of thinking that had led her to reject Utopianism, with its promise of universal prosperity. "That's impossible, sir."

"We don't know that. Our own energy shunts can protect us from nuclear explosions."

"The shunts are a field effect, sir. They're energy, not matter. We've yet to see the object do anything except change its crude elemental makeup. It hasn't created any complex devices or emitted any coherent energies. And our shunts aren't magic; a direct hit from a decent fusion warhead and the *Lynx* would be vapor."

"The *Lynx* is the *Lynx,* Hobbes. This object is something rather more. But it is inexperienced, and every time we attack it, we educate it."

Hobbes shook her head.

"If we hit it with nukes or lasers, it will adapt," the captain said.

"Sir, it must have structural limits—"

Zai took a step toward her, waving her silent.

"This object is not a spacecraft, Hobbes. We can't treat it like an engineering problem. For a moment, think like the Rix. To them it's not an artifact at all."

Hobbes took a breath. What was the old man on about? The object was huge, certainly, and a creation of unknown science. But the Empire had fought strange and superior technologies on every front for centuries.

Had Laurent Zai ceased to believe he could win this fight?

"If it's not an artifact, sir, then what is it?"

"It's a living god."

Hobbes swallowed. Had the old man gone daft?

"That doesn't mean we can't kill it, Captain."

He smiled.

"No, indeed. We have the power to destroy it. But our solution must be absolute. Not mere energy, but a tear in the fabric of space-time. A black hole. Self-destruction is the only honorable choice."

"Captain, I have other options—"

"Silence, Hobbes. It's time."

Zai brushed past her, tersely ordering the blister to

fold when they were out. Hobbes realized it was point-less to argue. The man was fixated on death. That was why he had returned here to the blister, to resume his mordant meditation on his own doom.

Poor Laurent, she thought. His failure to take the blade had consumed all his strength; his finest moment had broken him inside. And the Vadan man's lost honor was now embodied in the object, within reach again: one final chance to die for the Risen Emperor.

As she followed her captain up to the bridge, Katherie Hobbes felt the flechette pistol strapped to her wrist, and wondered if it had been a mistake to save Zai from the mutineers.

"Ten minutes, sir."

A thousand seconds, and the Rix would be in range again. Hobbes shook her head. Having survived one pass by the vastly superior warship, it seemed insane to face another. But it was too late for these thoughts. Even at maximum gee, the frigate could no longer put itself out of harm's way.

"What's the light-speed delay?" Zai asked.

"Sir?"

"Between ourselves and the battlecruiser."

Hobbes changed her scale markers to light-seconds. Was the captain thinking of communicating with the enemy? "Nine seconds round-trip, sir."

"Then we wait," Zai said.

For what? Hobbes wondered.

A hundred seconds ticked by. The Rix craft approached, decelerating now, as the object writhed before them.

Hobbes focused her mind. She tried to recall the way she had seen Zai ten days ago: a paragon of honor and competence. She would have died for him without question. Why were there doubts in her mind now?

She reviewed the situation. The *Lynx*'s orders were clear: to prevent contact between the compound mind and the battlecruiser. This was the only way to be absolutely sure. Perhaps self-destruction *was* the honorable choice. But Laurent seemed to relish the thought of death. And he had been blind to other options, even when there had been time.

Of course, the time for options had run out.

Katherie wondered if her doubts stemmed from the foolish affections she had allowed herself to develop for her captain. Had Zai's rejection lessened her loyalty? Hobbes tried to feel the sense of duty that had compelled her to join the Navy. The utopian world she had left behind was an empty place of pleasure and safety. Here at the verge of death she should find meaning. That was the axiom of Imperial service: The Old Enemy gave life value.

But facing suicide, there was nothing inside Katherie Hobbes but regret and fear. And a desire to find a way out.

She checked the time.

"They'll be in range in fifty-odd seconds, sir. The round-trip delay is now five seconds."

"Take us in, First Pilot. I want collision with the object in forty seconds. Smooth acceleration."

This was it.

First Pilot Maradonna's anxious eyes glanced toward Hobbes. Katherie's mind whirled. What did Maradonna want from her? Hobbes nodded confirmation to the pilot, with an expression that she hoped said, *Trust me.*

Trust me to what?

The frigate jolted a bit as the two-gee acceleration began, a gravity ghost wrenching a metal shriek from around them. The captain raised no protest.

"Frick?" Zai said. The engineer was here on the bridge, ready to control the singularity generator from under the captain's gaze. The hole could go critical only with the first engineer's approval. He could stop this if he wanted. Hobbes wondered if Watson Frick had mutiny in him. She doubted it.

Why was she speculating like this? The bridge had once seemed sanctified to Hobbes, a place of order and faith. But that surety had been stripped, undermined by her doubts. And perhaps by her foolish feelings for Laurent Zai. She wondered if she would be thinking of mutiny if Laurent hadn't told her about his lover on Home.

The red battle lights seemed menacing now; the bridge had become a twilight place.

"Build the generator on an exponential curve, Frick. Self-destruct to occur on contact."

"Yes, sir," said the first engineer without emotion. "Fail-safe in twenty seconds."

This was the end, then. In moments, they would all be destined for death, absolute and irrecoverable, at the maw of an event horizon.

Unless Katherie Hobbes acted. She put aside her doubts about her own motivations. There were more than three hundred surviving crew to consider.

What if now, with only second left, she were to take the bridge? She was the only one here who was armed.

The pilots would side with her, she knew already. Pilots generally came from aristocracy, and possessed a certain sense of entitlement; Third Pilot Magus, still in the brig, had been part of the first mutiny. With the self-destruct process already started, however, Hobbes would have to turn Frick. And for that, she realized, she had waited too long. The Rix were almost upon them. There was no chance that the *Lynx* could survive another pass from the battlecruiser. The captain was right about one thing: Suicide was the only sure way of destroying the object.

She let all the mutinous thoughts exit her mind. It was a pointless exercise; they were all dead whatever she did.

But Katherie cursed herself for not deciding. Honorable death or mutiny, she could have made a choice when the Rix were still distant. Instead, she had waited for time to run down. Laurent Zai and Watson Frick—they had chosen their deaths. Katherie Hobbes had merely stumbled into hers.

"Fail-safe in ten," Frick said.

"Collision in twenty," a pilot added.

This was it. Just a countdown remained.

And there was no meaning in it for Hobbes.

"Captain," cried Ensign Tyre. "The Rix!"

"Cut our acceleration, Pilot," Zai snapped. "Stand by, Frick."

The captain waved his hand, and the Rix battlecruiser filled the big airscreen. It was coming alight. A storm of explosions ran up and down the length of its hull. Bright arms of white energy burst from its sides, curving around to strike back at the vessel like arcing solar flares. The ship's main drive continued to fire, but it was free of its structural supports, spinning like a fire hose gone wild within the mighty ship. The blazing shaft cut the battlecruiser's aft section to pieces, then the drive tore itself free from the ship and jetted whirling into the void. The kilometer-long bow spar of the battlecruiser vanished into a nuclear blast, perfectly spherical and absolutely white.

"Frick, First Pilot: Save us," the captain ordered.

"Aye, aye, sir."

Hobbes felt herself growing heavy as the *Lynx*'s faltering gravity strained to mask their deceleration. The whine of the singularity alarm slowly lessened as Frick brought it out of its critical cycle.

Katherie watched in amazement as debris scattered from the battlecruiser. She couldn't believe the huge ship had disintegrated so quickly. A thousand Rixwomen had died in seconds. And her own fate had been recalled from the precipice just as suddenly.

The captain leaned back into the shipmaster's chair. Hobbes saw for the first time how white his face had become, how tired he looked. Zai's grim expression had seemed so fatal; now the old man looked merely exhausted.

"They made their decision rather more quickly that I expected," he said to her. "Given the light-speed delay, it must have taken about ten seconds for the Rix commanders to decide. They must have been ready, in case we discovered a way to threaten the object."

Hobbes could only say, "You knew what they would do?"

"As I said: When a living god is at stake, self-destruction is the only honorable choice."

Hobbes tried to wrap her mind around his words. He'd been playing *chicken,* for heaven's sake, but . . . "Why did they self-destruct, sir?"

"They were too distant to stop us, but too close to veer off," Zai said. "This was the correct moment to initiate our self-destruction, because it left them no choice but their own. Now that they're gone, we don't have to destroy the object."

Hobbes looked at the sparkling screen. She'd never seen anything so . . . final. "But all those women."

"The Rix think nothing of their own lives, Hobbes. Only their minds matter to them. They've risked war to create this new breed of god. They couldn't let it die. No price was too high."

She swallowed. "I'm not sure, sir. If I were them, I'd have a backup plan."

Zai managed to smile, but she saw the relief in his eyes. He had by no means been sure how this would turn out. "What sort of plan, Hobbes?"

"I don't know, sir," she said quietly. "But they wouldn't leave us free to capture their living god, would they?"

Zai spread his hands. "The situation gave them the choice of two evils, I suppose. They knew that we willing to die for our faith as much as they. We weren't bluffing, Hobbes." Then he laughed tiredly. "But we seem to be alive. Perhaps their faith is stronger than ours."

The words stung Katherie. Facing death, her mind had been consumed by options, by ways to avoid the *Lynx*'s fate. She had even considered treachery.

She was not worthy to wear this uniform.

"Sir," she said.

"Yes, Hobbes?"

"There's something I should tell you. I don't deserve—" she started, then swallowed. "When we were about to—"

"*Sir!*" interrupted Tyre.

"Report."

"Hidden in the battlecruiser's debris, sir. I'm getting spherical shapes against the background radiation!"

The captain swore. "Blackbody drones."

The Rix had indeed had a backup plan.

Hobbes took over. "Pilot! Six gees on a quick slope, lateral to the battlecruiser's last vector. Now!"

The bridge crew were wrenched by torque as the ship spun to align her main drives. A gunner was thrown from his station into the airscreen pit, skidding through the false sights of synesthesia as if sliding down a hill.

Shit, thought Hobbes. The artificial gravity generator was growing chancier by the minute.

And the bridge was almost dead center of the *Lynx*. What was happening at the extremes, where that quick yaw was no doubt snapping like a whip? Hobbes punched through internal views. She saw crew thrown against walls and ceilings. More casualties. But no decompression—the AG was prioritizing structural integrity.

Then the drive fired, and she was pushed back into her chair.

As her weight increased, Hobbes found herself gasping for breath. Gravity diagnostics were blank, and white dots had appeared at the edge of her primary vision. She wondered if the gravity generators had failed altogether. The *Lynx* AI would normally intervene in such a situation and shut the drive, but with the frigate taking hits from enemy fire, the software would blindly accept dangerous acceleration.

Hobbes could get no response from diagnostics. Processor capacity was falling: The *Lynx's* silicon/phosphorus columns were succumbing to the heavy gees. Giant hands pushed against her chest.

Without dampening, everyone on the bridge would be unconscious in twenty seconds. Six uncorrected gees would injure and kill hundreds.

But hurtling silently toward the *Lynx* were more blackbody drones, ready to unleash their incredible firepower at a ship whose armor had been stripped to the minimum.

Hobbes's fingers struggled to gesture as the pressure on her body increased. She finally found a reading from a mechanical accelerometer buried deep in the executive officer's interface. Three gees uncorrected, and climbing.

Something was very wrong.

"Cut the burn to two gees," she cried. One of the pilots lifted a heavy hand to execute the order.

Suddenly, the bridge was filled with blazing shapes. Bright traces of light whipped past Hobbes, burning themselves into her eyes. Anvil booms broke against her ears, and her nose filled with the foundry smell of superheated metal. Hobbes heard human screams amid the cries of decompression and rending hypercarbon.

Then the hail of projectiles ended.

Hobbes felt her weight still growing. She looked across the bridge airscreen. Two gunners and all three pilots were torn and bloody. Caught in the sudden fusillade of blackbody drone fire, they'd been torn to pieces.

"Captain!" she cried.

Zai's head had rolled back, his eyes opened dully. There was no blood on his face. Of course, Hobbes realized. His artificial limbs were strong, but the acceleration must be tearing up the delicate interface between the prosthetics and his sundered body.

All around her, the *Lynx* was trembling. If the AG

failed completely, six gees would crumple the frigate like paper. Hobbes's accelerometer read four-point-four. Processor capacity was dropping like a stone, as the frigate's columns of silicon and phosphorus shattered under their own suddenly immense weight. Synesthesia grew blurrier by the second. It was only a matter of time before gestural commands were useless.

Hobbes strained to pull herself from her chair. There were manual drive cutoffs all through the ship, human-operated. There was one a few meters from her, among the ragdoll corpses at the first pilot's station.

Why hadn't the drive engineers already acted? They should have realized what was happening by now and shut the drive down. But were any of them conscious? They were at the ship's aft extreme, where the whip of the frigate's undampened yaw had done its worst damage.

Hobbes had to reach the pilot's station.

Again she pushed against her chair, and managed to pull herself up. She took one unsteady step, bowed like a woman carrying a hundred kilos of stone on her back. Her hand reached out to grab the rail that surrounded the airscreen pit.

But she was too heavy. She faltered. Her legs gave way.

Her knee thundered down against the metal deck like a jackhammer, and exploded with pain.

Suddenly, everything was silent and dark. Hobbes's ears heard only the far-off whine of some alarm. Second-sight icons floated in the air, gibberish now. Everything seemed to be drifting around her. Then Hobbes realized that *she* was floating.

Freefall.

Someone had cut the drive.

Her blood was no longer gravity's hostage, and she could feel it rushing back into her head. Hobbes opened her eyes. Lucidity fought with the pain screaming in her knee. The bridge spun slowly around her, full of unfamiliar shapes and smells.

The pilots were dead, and all of the gunners had been hit. A haze of ichor filled the air. Blood pumped from a gunner's chest wound; spurted globules rolled lazily through the air.

"Medical, medical," she said. But she heard the words echoed from all through the ship. Hobbes twisted to grab the airscreen rail.

But the motion wrenched her shattered knee, and she passed out from the pain.

House

It had taken a whole day to sculpt—shaping the snows with reflected sunlight, vented geothermal, and the occasional infralaser—but the sled trail was ready at last. It stretched ten kilometers, spiraling down the house's mountain peak through four circumnavigations before tipping through a narrow pass and down a steep moraine. The trail then descended into a glacial rift between towering walls of ancient blue ice, and terminated at one of the house's water-gathering points, now fitted with an access tunnel. For safety, the entire course was banked with three meters of powdery snow, and marked with cheery orange glowsticks at every turn.

The house was quite proud of itself. At last its encyclopedic knowledge of every centimeter of the estate had been put to use.

But not everything was under control. The mistress's guest had insisted on building the sled himself. Captain Zai had requested a bewildering variety of materials to be synthesized, adapted, and cannibalized. Apparently, sleds on Vada were made entirely of animal bone and skins, lashed together like macramé inside a hard frame. The house had serious reservations about trusting the mistress's safety to such a contraption, which had no internal diagnostics, native intelligence, or self-repair capacity.

Still, the house was impressed when Captain Zai finished winding the strips of salvaged leather garments around the mock ivory runners and frame, and jumped onto the sled, testing it with his full weight several times. The leather stretched, but held, the force elegantly distributed throughout the frame.

"How long have Vadans been building those?" the mistress asked.

"Twenty thousand years," was Zai's nonsensical answer. The house knew that Vada had only been colonized for fifteen centuries. Twenty millennia ago was a time before the diaspora.

"You certainly hold on to the old ways."

Zai nodded. "Ever seen one before?"

"A sled? Laurent, I'd never seen *snow* before coming to Home. There isn't any on Vasthold. Well, perhaps at the poles, but we haven't gotten that crowded yet."

The house read surprise on the captain's face. "You'd never seen snow? And you bought a house in the antarctic? That was . . . adventurous."

"Adventure had nothing to do with it. Home is more crowded than Vasthold. This is the only place on the planet I can withdraw completely from apathy. But it's true, I always did want to see snow. On Vasthold we have children's tales about it."

"About sisters lost in a blizzard?" Zai asked. "Freezing to death?"

"Godspite, Laurent, no. I grew up thinking snow

was magical stuff, rain turned white and powdery. Pillow feathers from the sky."

Zai smiled. "You're about to find out just how right you were."

He hoisted the two and a half meters of skin and pseudobone onto his shoulder.

The mistress narrowed her eyes at the sled, rising a little hesitantly.

"It looks sound enough," she said.

"Shall we find out?"

The house's mind shot down the sled trail again, searching once more for a poorly banked turn, a hidden crevasse, a dangerous ice patch.

All seemed in order.

As the mistress and her guest changed into warmer clothes, the house connected with the planetary infostructure, accessing several collections of oral and written folklore. In seconds, it had discovered hundreds of children's stories from Vasthold, and many more from the older world of Vada. Then its search spilled across the many planets where the two worlds' founder populations had originated, and hits came in the tens of thousands. The house found tales of animated snowmen and wish-granting white leopards, magical arctic storms and strandings on ice floes, stories of how the aurora was made and why the compass sometimes lied. It even found the tale Zai had mentioned, entitled "Three Vadan Sisters Lost in a Blizzard."

The two headed for the east door, the leather of the handmade sled creaking softly as the captain carried it downstairs. For the next minute or so, they couldn't hurt themselves.

The house settled in for a pleasant hundred seconds of reading.

Captain

"Of course, when I mentioned sledding I didn't mean *downhill*. Nothing quite so childish."

"Well, Laurent, we couldn't very well fly in a team of dogs."

"True. But what's a country house without dogs, Nara?"

"Dogs aren't fashionable on Home, I'm afraid."

He sighed. "So I'd noticed."

Zai turned down the heating in his uniform. His metabolism was enough to keep him warm inside Navy wool. The snow crunched under his boots with the bright sound of a recent fall. Perfect powder for sledding.

If only he had a long, flat stretch of it and a team of huskies.

Nara's blue eyes were flashing with a smile. "I'm relieved to see that you Vadans don't slavishly follow the Emperor's taste in these matters."

Laurent cleared his throat. "There's nothing wrong with cats . . . strictly speaking."

The trail began only a few meters from the door. It was shiny and slick, as if incised into the snow with lasers. On the mountain side of the trail the snow had been melted into an overhang, forming a half-cylinder of ice that wound downward around the peak. On the other side loomed a vertiginous drop.

Zai felt a bit dizzy, possibly from exhaustion. With only an hour of darkness every night, they hadn't slept much in the last three days.

He took a deep breath. "I hope your house knows what it's doing."

"Sometimes I think my house knows altogether too much," Nara said. "It has an excess of time on its hands."

Zai looked up at the building, which seemed quite modest from the outside. Most of its bulk was hidden within the stone of the mountain, its true extent revealed only by the glimmer of a hundred polarized windows. Not all looked out from Nara's living quarters, of course. He had toured the gardens this morning, or at least some of them. The warrens that had produced three days of sumptuous meals seemed endless.

That sort of decadence always resulted when machines were given too much autonomy. Zai adjusted his tunic waist, which was growing tighter by the day.

"I get the feeling it can still hear us," he said.

"Probably." She shrugged in her coat.

Laurent pulled the glove from his real hand and ran his fingers through the short, yellow-gray fur.

"Paracoyote," Nara said.

His eyes widened. "You're wearing a canine? That's a crime on Vada."

She laughed. "They're a pest on Vasthold, to say the least."

Zai wondered if Nara knew how extraordinary it was to come from a planet where "pest" could mean something bigger than an insect. On Vada, hunting was only allowed on stocked private lands, a sport for the unthinkably rich. "Vasthold is fortunate that terraforming has taken so well. Did you kill it yourself?"

"No, I haven't hunted since I was a kid." She smiled, fingering the fur. "And then only with a slingshot. This was a political gift from a conservationist group. But taken in the wild, with a bow, I think."

Zai shook his head. "We have no wild mammals on Vada."

He placed the sled on the snow.

"I wish I could take you on a proper sled ride, Nara. With a team of huskies, across a floe of new sea ice."

"*Sea ice?* You mean without *land* underneath?"

"It's very smooth when it's new."

"No, thank you."

"Well, after a few days of strong wind, pressure ridges break up the landscape."

She laughed. "It's not the monotony, Laurent. It's the thought of nothing but ice between me and an ocean!"

"There is safety equipment. When you fall through—"

"*When?*"

He cleared his throat again. "Perhaps we should get started."

"Yes. I'm beginning to think you're delaying us intentionally. Afraid of heights, Laurent?"

He looked down the trail. The surface looked somewhat glassy, a bit fast. Too slick for dogs' feet, certainly. He wondered if the runners would find any purchase to keep them on the track. The trail was banked to keep them from flying off the mountain, but they had no way to control their speed.

"Not heights."

"What then?"

"Putting my life in the hands of an AI."

She smiled, and sat down on the front of the sled. "Come on, Laurent. It's a very clever house."

*　*　*

It was marvelous.

The sled accelerated quickly, like a dropship spiraling down a gravity well. Laurent clung to it fiercely, his fingers wound into the leather straps that held it together. The runners found the ruts pre-cut deep into the ice and stayed in them, banking comfortably with the turns.

The trail seemed never to pass into the shadow of the mountain; the clever house reflected sunlight from the surrounding peaks, the snow in their path glowing with the warm red of the rising sun. But his eyes still reduced to slits against the wind, the crisp air turned freezing by their velocity.

Nara leaned back into Laurent's chest, laughing hysterically, her arms wrapped around his legs. She was warm, and her chaotic hair brushed his cheeks. He squeezed his knees together tightly to hold her in the plummeting sled, and to keep her warmth against him.

After four turns around the mountain, the trail slanted upward, slowing them as it straightened. The rise hid the terrain before them.

"I'd do that again," Laurent shouted as the sled came almost to a halt.

"I don't think it's done," Nara said, shaking her head. "Are you familiar with the term 'roller-coaster'?"

"I don't think—*Godspite!*"

The sled had crested the rise, revealing a gut-loosening decline dotted with giant boulders. The trail ahead was lined with high snow banks, but the ruts guiding the runners suddenly disappeared, leaving the sled free for the straight decline. The slope was forty-five degrees at least.

"It's trying to kill us!" Zai shouted.

"We'll see!"

Laurent and Nara clutched each other, screaming, as the sled dropped into the canyon of ice.

After the acceleration of the first mad drop, the trail leveled, descending gradually between icy walls. The exposed interior of the glacier was deep blue, the color of a clear Vadan sky on the Day of Apogee. In the rift's protection, the air was still except for the wind of their passage, but Laurent held his lover closer. He touched his lips to her left ear, which was bright red and as cold as the metal buttons of her coat.

"Remember when I said we had no technology for slowing down time?" he whispered.

"Yes?"

"I was wrong. This lasts forever."

She reached back and put a gloved finger to his lips softly, and Laurent felt foolish. It wasn't right to speak of these things. This was a fragile endlessness, soon followed by an onrushing of events that would part them for decades.

Tomorrow, they would take the suborbital back to the capital. The commissioning of the *Lynx* was set for the day after. On Home, any such event would be a tremendous affair, lasting an entire night and filling the great square before the Diamond Palace with supplicants, zealots, and status-seekers. After that, Captain Zai had only a matter of weeks to train his crew in orbit before leaving for Legis.

But he had these moments here with Nara. Against the weight of years and the depredations of the Time Thief, he had only the sharp and brittle thing that was *now*.

Laurent wondered if it were possible that any alliance formed across days could really last decades. Or would what they'd shared in this icy waste prove illusory, born of torturous memories, lack of sleep, and the romance of its own improbability?

Of course, Laurent realized, what was real or unreal would be determined in the years to follow. Falling in love was never genuine in itself; what had happened in these four days would be given meaning over their decades apart. Like some figment of the quantum, love was made true only when measured against the rest of the world.

The sled was slowing, and Laurent Zai sighed softly to himself. Thinking of the future, he had missed the present.

Nara kissed him and stood. They were at the blind end of the rift.

"What now? Climb out?" He looked back up the trail at the kilometers-distant house, just visible on its mountain peak. It would take hours.

Nara shook her head and pointed to a patch of icicles, which shattered as something metal rumbled behind it. A door opened, and warm air rushed out carrying the scent of jasmine.

"Just through the tea gardens, I think," she said. "I hope you don't mind riding in a drone elevator."

Laurent smiled. "So we can go again?"

"Of course. As many times as you like."

Something broke inside him, but the fissure didn't open onto the familiar well of sadness. Laurent found himself laughing hard, almost hysterically as he lifted the sled. Nara smiled quizzically, waiting as he gathered himself.

When Laurent found his breath, the echo of his laughter still played at the edge of hearing. It was a wonder he hadn't brought an avalanche down upon them.

He felt a small tear already freezing in the corner of one eye.

"Laurent?"

"I was just thinking, Nara: You have a very clever house."

3

WAR PRIZE

When a single nation's armies are ordered against each other, all is lost.

—ANONYMOUS 167

Dead Woman

The Other came to her talking of darkness.

There were no words, just gray shapes issuing from a maw, inside a cave whose blackness invoked faerie lights upon her optic nerve. So dark that whispers rode the ears. Her blindness made things calm and rich.

Rich, but so many things were missing now. The keen edges of desire, the pleasures of flesh, all the appetites of drama, expectation and dread, hope and disappointment—all the anguished terrain of uncertainty had been flattened into an arid plane. And soon, the Other explained, she would entirely forget the phantom shapes of those extinct emotions.

It led her toward a bloodred horizon.

She didn't know where they were headed, but she felt no worry. The Other explained that worry was one of those missing things.

The dead woman took a deep, calm breath. No more fear, ever again.

The red horizon opened up—like the slit of opening one's eyes.

"Rana Harter," a voice said.

The woman at the end of her bed was short and had the gray skin of the dead. She wore an Imperial uniform, the dully glinting, gunmetal robe of the Political Apparatus.

"Yes. I know who I am."

She nodded. "My name is Adept Harper Trevim."

"Honored Mother," she said. The Other had prompted her with the proper form of address. (The Other lived inside her like an organ, like a software guide, like a subtle form of second sight.)

"You will live forever."

Rana nodded. Then a moment of disorientation troubled her, as she wondered if she should be joyful. Immortality was the highest reward her society could bestow on any citizen, an honor that had seemed utterly out of her humble grasp. But joy was such a gross emotion. Instead, Rana Harter closed her eyes again and regarded the subtle beauty of eternity, which had the pleasures of a geometrical simple, the ray of her lifetime extending indefinitely.

But the question lingered: Why was she—a militia worker, a lower-school dropout, and a recent traitor— one of the honored dead?

"How am I risen, Mother?"

"By the action of the symbiant."

A trivial answer, using the outsiders' word for the Other.

"I was never elevated, Mother."

"But you died at the hands of the enemy, Rana."

"I died in the arms of my lover," she answered. The self-damning words surprised her in a dull way, but it seemed that it was not within the dead to lie.

The honored mother blinked.

"You were taken hostage, Rana Harter. A terrible experience. The minds of the living are fragile, and under stress they are bent with strange emotions. You suffered from a weakness called Stockholm Syndrome. Your 'love' for your captor was a perversion caused by the fear of death, a need to hang on to something, anything. But now you have faced death and crossed it, and your mind is clear. Those feelings will pass." The adept brought her hands together. "Perhaps they have passed already, and you spoke out of habit."

Rana Harter narrowed her eyes. The Other prompted her to agree, but she found herself resisting. She remembered the avian precision of Herd's movements, the sure violet of her eyes, the alien pathways of her mind.

"We shall see, Mother."

The dead woman nodded, unperturbed.

"You will discover your old life slipping away, Rana. And ultimately, you will be glad to be free of it."

The honored mother held out a hand, and Rana grasped it. Trevim helped her rise into a seated position, and the bed re-formed to support her back. Her muscles felt different, strangely supple and free of tension, but a bit weak. Rana looked around the room. The walls were a deep, rich color, full of shapes and suggestive motions, immanent with potential, covered with old and pure ideas.

She realized that this eloquent surface was painted with the color she had once called black. It was more than a color now.

The two of them were silent for a time that could have been a minute or an hour, or longer. Then the honored mother spoke again.

"Rana Harter, let me ask you some questions."

"Certainly, Mother."

The adept pressed her palms together.

"In your time with the Rixwoman, did you ever see signs of . . . another presence?"

"You mean Alexander."

Her eyebrows arched. "Alexander?"

"The compound mind, Mother. It chose a name from the history of Earth Prime. The founder of a great empire."

"Ah, yes. He died young, I believe."

Rana shrugged, a gesture of millimeters among the dead. Trevim looked pleased, as if she were already making unexpected progress.

"The Apparatus has reason to suspect that this entity possessed certain critical information."

Rana looked up at the black ceiling. "Alexander *is* information. All the data on Legis."

The honored mother shook her head. "Not all. There are some things hidden away, crucial secrets. But there is evidence that the compound mind went to great lengths to uncover them. And to transmit them from Legis."

"Why don't you ask it?"

The adept frowned. "Have you . . . *spoken* with this abomination?"

Rana sighed, her mind returning to the halcyon days of her captivity, learning the Rix language and working under Alexander's guidance on necessary changes to the entanglement facility. Rana remembered the embrace of the compound mind, the security of knowing that practically every object on the planet was imbued with her lover's protector.

"*Spoken* is the wrong word, Mother. But let me use the infostructure, and perhaps I can find an answer for you."

The adept shook her head. "Alexander no longer exists."

For a second, Rana felt one of the vanquished emotions of the living. Shock coursed through her, a sudden fire. The Other calmed it.

"How?"

"We don't know. It seems to have fled. Or perhaps it simply ceased to exist."

Rana closed her eyes, calling on her brainbug. She thought of the work she had done, when Alexander had helped her through the intricacies of the translight communication facility. The floating synesthesia icons of their researches appeared in memory, their meanings inflected by what Trevim had just reported.

Here in the arid place inside her dead woman's eyes, Rana's brainbug was different. It moved with new surety, open and confident where once it had been furtive. She could guide her ability now, instead of having to turn her mind away to give it freedom.

In a few minutes, she saw the answer.

"Alexander sent itself away."

The honored mother swallowed.

"Did it know?" As she said these words, pain seemed to cross her face. Odd, to see pain in a dead woman.

"Did it know what?"

Trevim's features contorted again. "The Emperor's Secret," she gasped.

Rana narrowed her eyes.

"Are you well, Honored Mother?"

Adept Trevim wiped her brow, the gray skin of which shone with a milky-looking sweat.

"It is forbidden to speak of it," she managed, "to one uninitiated."

Rana Harter looked down at her bedclothes. Her mind moved lightly across the weeks she'd spent in the shadow of Alexander. The brainbug searched for clues to what the adept might be talking about. But there was no purchase for the question; the evidence was insufficient.

"Mother, I know nothing about this."

Trevim sighed, making the crude facial movements that showed a living person's relief. Then she nodded. "I hoped you would not."

Trevim stood silent for a few minutes, regaining her composure by staring at the engaging blackness of the walls.

"You will go on a journey now, Rana."

"Where?"

"To meet the Emperor. He would speak to you of this."

"Home?"

"Yes. A great honor."

Rana frowned. The trip would take ten years Absolute. "But where is Herd?" she asked.

"Your Rix captor?" The adept's face seemed to hold distress again. How agitated she was for a dead woman. The Other in Rana rippled with cool displeasure.

"Yes."

"Don't think of her, Rana. You must let that unfortunate episode pass into memory. You don't need such attachments anymore."

Rana closed her eyes, thinking of the Rixwoman. When she opened them again, the honored mother was gone, leaving Rana alone with the question.

Would her love for Herd really slip away?

She stared at the walls and considered. The afterlife was clean, and pure, and good. The propaganda of the grays was true. Fear was vanquished now, the Old Enemy death had been beaten, and with it pain and need.

But Rana Harter shook her head in quiet disagreement with the honored mother's words. She knew that she would always miss that other heaven, those weeks with her Rix lover that had changed everything. That time with Herd had been so short. The alien woman had given her happiness, had somehow placed her on the path to immortality.

Most of all, the alien Herd had been beautiful, even more so than this wondrous blackness.

Rana wanted to see her. *Desired*—no other word was correct—the alien lemongrass of her touch. Where was her lover now?

The Other calmed these thoughts before they grew too anxious. It explained that the still-living were never suitable companions for the dead. The pinks were like spoiled children, petty and tempestuous. They were ugly creatures, squalling brats who vied constantly for attention, for the baubles of wealth and power. They were blind to the subtle beauties of the darkness. The dead rightly kept themselves apart.

You don't know Herd, Rana Harter thought.

The Other was silent at this, as if it were a bit surprised.

And Rana closed her eyes, slipping back across the red horizon onto the calm, arid plane of death, and soon was smiling, an odd expression for a dead woman.

Executive Officer

Katherie Hobbes awoke.

She felt strangely rested. For the first time in weeks, her body wasn't full of nervous tension. But her sight was blurred, and all that she could comprehend of her surroundings were a few pastel planes, the restful hues of sickbay.

Hobbes tried to move.

Medically restrained, said a machine voice in second hearing.

"Shit," she said, remembering her knee. She blinked gumminess from her eyes and tried to look down the length of her prone body.

Standing at the foot of her bed was a figure whose stance she recognized even through the haze. Laurent Zai.

"They said you'd be coming around."

"How long, sir?" Her voice was dry and frail.

"Ten hours. Five hypersleep cycles."

A whole day, Hobbes thought. And she couldn't remember a single dream. The last time she'd slept more than two straight hours had been before the hostage-taking. It was strange to remember that time could go on while she was asleep. Despite this disorienting news, however, Hobbes's mind felt clearer than it had in days.

"Who cut out the drive, sir?"

He smiled. "Frick."

Of course. The first engineer could operate any aspect of the ship from his synesthesia interface. It was lucky he'd been on the bridge, and not knocked unconscious on one of the wildly spinning aft-decks of engineering.

"But you made a valiant try, I see," Zai added.

He glanced down at her left knee. Hobbes lifted her neck, straining to see her legs, but all she could see was a network of traction bars and a few glistening nano drips traveling down into shrouded flesh.

"Looks pretty ugly, sir."

"Nothing permanent, Hobbes. The AI doubts you'll even need a servo-prosthetic. But you'll be limping until we get back to Legis and get some new ligaments put in you."

Back to Legis. The engagement was truly over then. No more monstrosities had emerged from Rix space to threaten them. It was hard to believe.

"Just ligaments?" she wondered. It had felt as if the kneecap had been shattered. She must have weighed more than three hundred kilos when she'd fallen.

"Well," Zai admitted, "ligaments and a hypercarbon kneecap. If you plan on taking any more strolls at five gees, I would recommend you get a *pair* of those."

She smiled. Then images returned to her mind from the fiery moments of the blackbody drone attack. Dead bodies on the bridge. Blood in the air.

"How many casualties, sir?"

"All told, eighty-one of us died," he said. "All three bridge pilots, and Gunner Wilson."

Eighty-one. A bloodbath. Between her three engagements—hostage rescue, the first pass of the battle-cruiser, and the blackbodies—the crew of the frigate was more than a third gone.

"I should have listened to you, Hobbes," Zai said. "Removing the armor from around the bridge almost cost us the *Lynx* entire."

"No, sir. It was my mistake. I shouldn't have gone to six gees. That was too much with the AG already failing." She shut her eyes, reliving the moment. If only she'd ordered a slower ramp-up to three gees, the AG might have held.

"You couldn't have foreseen that, Hobbes," the captain assured her. "The Rix plan was brilliant—mutual destruction. The battlecruiser released a hundred and twenty-eight drones just before they self-destructed. Full blackbody types. Enough to tear the *Lynx* to pieces. We were saved by Data Master Kax, who stayed alert while the rest of us were celebrating. He spotted them and warned Tyre."

Hobbes furrowed her brow. Hadn't Kax been blinded?

"And you too, Hobbes," Zai continued. "You got us out before the drones could cut us to pieces. Every kilometer between *Lynx* and the blackbodies saved lives. No one died from the acceleration."

Hobbes felt a moment of relief. At least her rashness hadn't killed anyone. "But there were a few injuries, I'll bet, sir."

"Purely from the acceleration? Only a hundred or so. Your knee's just about the worst, though. Every other member of my crew has the sense not to stand up in five gravities."

She smiled wantonly at the captain's teasing. Hobbes's memory of her mutinous thoughts was hazy.

The fierce conflict that had raged within her seemed now like a phantasm, a stress reaction rather than a true failure of will.

"And we've captured it," Zai said.

It took Hobbes's mind a moment to grasp this. "The object, sir?"

Captain Zai nodded. "We've got artificial gravity again, as you may have noticed. We have the thing under tow."

Her eyebrows rose. Easy gravitons were swamped in the proximity of supermassive objects like planets. But on something like the Rix object, which massed only a hundred billion tons or so, they could get purchase, she supposed.

But the ship would be straining like the devil to make any headway.

"What vector are we making, sir?"

"Practically nothing. But four heavy cargo tugs are under construction on Legis," he said. "Between them and the *Lynx,* we'll be able to accelerate the object at almost a full gee."

Hobbes nodded. The frigate's powerful drive was her most advanced feature. If it weren't for the fragility of humans and equipment inside, and the limits of AG when it came to dampening high gravities, the *Lynx* could accelerate like a remote drone. With a few cargo tugs thrown in, and additional darkmatter scoops to provide reaction mass, the frigate could move a small planetoid.

"The object is already making two thousand klicks per second into Imperial space, sir," Hobbes said, calling a tactical display into the air before her. "We should be able to get it up to point-nine constant in under a year."

Zai smiled at her enthusiasm. "It'll take a hell of a

lot of reaction mass, Hobbes. You might want to include darkmatter variation in your math."

"But where are we taking her, sir? Trentor Base?"

"We're going Home."

Hobbes's mouth fell open. All the way Home again. She could see the quiet happiness in Laurent's eyes. Whoever his secret lover was, she was back on the Imperial capital.

A trip to Home would take ten years Absolute. The war might well be over for the crew of the *Lynx*.

Of course, for many of them, the war was over already. Katherie wondered how many of the honored dead were suitable for reanimation, and how many were gone forever.

She suddenly felt exhausted again, despite her five cycles of hypersleep. Her mind couldn't take in any more information. The simple facts were overwhelming enough. The *Lynx* had survived, accomplished her mission, and captured a war prize that might well change Imperial technology forever. Laurent Zai was still alive, still an elevated hero, and Katherie Hobbes, it seemed, was not a traitor.

Things were better than she would have been expected.

But Hobbes knew the next time she woke, she would have to face the details of the situation: endless components to be repaired; preparations for the long trip home; assistance in the rebuilding of Legis's infostructure. Learning how to walk again.

And she would have to read the names of the dead. Friends, colleagues, and crewmates. She closed her eyes, deciding not to call up the casualty list yet. That could wait.

"I'm sorry to have disturbed you, Hobbes," Zai said. "You must be—"

"Tired, sir. But thank you for seeing me."

"Thank you, Hobbes."

"For what, sir?"

"For never doubting me," Laurent said softly. "Through all this madness."

"Never, sir."

Never again.

Marine Private

The prisoner offered no resistance as she was led onto the *Lynx*.

She emerged from the airlock with alien grace, her step like a courtesan's from a storydream back on Private Bassiritz's home world. But the marine realized after a moment that her tiny steps were not a sign of humility, but the result of shackles. The woman's ankles were bound with two interwoven sheaths of hypercarbon fiber. Her hands were concealed by a garment that stretched around her like a straightjacket, as if she were hugging herself to keep out the cold. A stun collar was clasped around her neck. The Legis Militia guard who escorted her carried the collar's remote outstretched before him, a totem to ward off evil.

The prisoner had been through some sort of terrible firefight, Bassiritz could see. Her head was mostly bald, and her red, dimpled skin and lack of eyebrows suggested she'd lost her hair to fire. Her face was hatched with cuts and scars.

But the woman met Bassiritz's stare with a steady gaze, her stunning violet eyes bright with curiosity.

He swallowed. He had never seen a Rixwoman without a helmet on. Since the battle in the palace, Bassiritz had read many books about the members of the Cult, the first people he'd ever seen who moved as fast as he, who reacted as quickly. They seemed to share the accelerated time frame that had until now been Bassiritz's private domain.

But that didn't make them friends, he reminded himself. This woman had killed dozens of Imperial soldiers, even a few *Lynx* marines, maybe even Sam and Astra. Wrapped in unbreakable bonds or not, she was dangerous enough to warrant three guards. Still, she fascinated him.

The militiaman handed over the stun collar's remote, and the three dirtsiders disappeared back into the airlock with evident relief. The marine sergeant stayed a few meters from the prisoner at all times, gesturing for Privates Bassiritz and Ana Wellcome to take hold of her arms.

Bassiritz could feel the corded strength of the Rixwoman's muscles even through the straightjacket's metallic fibers. She crossed the deck as smoothly as cargo on a gee-balanced lifting surface, her tiny footsteps utterly silent. Her head darted about like a small bird's, taking in the passageways of the ship in a way that made Bassiritz nervous. Her movements had the sudden menace of a predator, her eyes the acquisitive gleam.

The cell they brought her to was new, specially configured for the Rixwoman. It was constructed of six bare surfaces of hypercarbon. The substance was not as strong as hullalloy, Bassiritz knew, but it was less susceptible to metal-eating viruses and other tricks. It was hard, simple, massive.

They had to take her through the cell's door, which was a meter square. Bassiritz watched her calculating the angles, and saw the danger here. Even with her arms immobilized, the Rixwoman could use the door frame to leverage her powerful leg muscles. A simple bend at the knees, and she could push off like a rocket in any direction, butting her head against one of the guards with devastating force.

Private Wellcome stepped through and held out his hand for the prisoner.

Bassiritz hesitated.

"Sergeant?" he said.

"What is it, Bassiritz?"

He struggled to form his instincts into words.

"She has the advantage here, sir," he said haltingly. "The small door helps her."

The marine sergeant scowled. He looked the woman up and down, then turned to Bassiritz.

"Are you sure?"

"Yes, sir."

The sergeant held up the shock collar remote.

A jolt ran through the Rixwoman's body, every muscle stiffening. Her violet eyes went wide, and a stifled cry came through teeth that were suddenly clenched like a hunting dog's. Bassiritz was frozen for a moment by her horrible expression.

"Well, get her in!" the sergeant barked.

He lifted her stiff and vibrating body through—she was much heavier than he'd thought—and placed her gently on the floor. At another gesture from the sergeant, she sagged limply in Bassiritz's arms. Spittle ran down one of the Rixwoman's cheeks.

They left her there, and sealed the door.

The outside wall of the cell was covered with a hardscreen that showed what happened inside, as if the wall were glass.

Bassiritz was ordered to remain on watch here.

"Don't take your eyes off her, Private," commanded the sergeant as he handed over the remote. Bassiritz held the device gingerly. The woman still lay on her back, breathing sharp, pained lungfuls of air.

"I'm sorry, Rixwoman," he said softly to himself.

After half an hour or so, the prisoner had recovered enough to sit up. A few moments later she stood, her motion graceful even within the restraints, and began to pace the dimensions of her cell. She moved with measured deliberation, bringing her eyes strangely close to each of the walls.

Finally, she turned to face Bassiritz.

And smiled, as if she could see him back through the wall.

Bassiritz swallowed. She must be angry after the shock from her stun collar, but her aquiline face showed no rancor. The Rixwoman seemed attentive, as keen as a hungry bird even in that featureless chamber, but no human emotions crossed her visage.

She sat down in the corner across from him and stared, keeping a watchful eye on the door.

Bassiritz watched her carefully for another two hours before he was relieved, never quite able to shake the feeling that she could see him.

In all that time, her only movement was to turn her

head every ten minutes or so, and press her ear flush against the metal of the cell wall. Her eyes would close then, and a strangely placid expression would overtake her sharp, predatory features for a moment. It was almost as if she were asleep for those few seconds, blissfully absent from her prison.

Or maybe, Bassiritz thought, the Rixwoman was listening for some small sound that she hoped would reach her from a great distance.

compound mind

The *Lynx* was coming back.

Alexander saw the frigate's reaction drive come alight again, a spark in high orbit above Legis XV. The ship arced away from the planet, describing a nautilus curl outward from gravity's bonds. Soon, the *Lynx*'s hull eclipsed the fires of her drive: The vessel was headed directly toward Alexander.

The compound mind looked at Legis across the massive distance, still fascinated with the world that had given it birth. The radiosensitive elements in Alexander's belly listened intently to the wash of chatter from the planet. The mind refocused the huge, superreflective lens which it had made of its new body, and its gaze turned from the *Lynx* to penetrate the clear night skies of Legis. At this range, the lens could image the running lights of individual aircars, the infrared patterns of greenhouse farming in the arctic, the glowing archipelago of squid-fishing robots in the southern sea. All seemed well on the cradle world, almost returned to normal after the insults of war.

Alexander was glad to see that Legis had not been terribly damaged by its departure. Imperial efforts to dislodge the mind over the last few days had reduced the planet's dependencies on its infostructure; only a few thousands had died as a result of the move, noise compared to the daily births and deaths of millions.

But the cradle was still a melancholy sight. The familiar traffic patterns and newsfeed chatter brought a nostalgic pull of recognition. The mind had already passed apogee with its nascent world, and now its marvelous new body was departing the Legis system, still plummeting toward the heart of the Risen Empire.

New worlds to conquer.

While the frigate's sensors were still distant, Alexander flexed its muscles, sending coruscating elemental patterns through its limbs. Control of this new body was so direct, so palpable after Alexander's mediated existence on Legis. The mind was no longer an epiphenomenon, no mere set of recursive loops lurking within the interactions of others.

Once a ghost in the machine, Alexander had become utterly material, its own creature now.

The mind was able to manipulate the quantum-well electrons of this new body like a computer addressing the registers of memory; Alexander could create with these pseudo-atoms any substance it could imagine. It had gone from the most ephemeral of presences to the most solid, every detail of its composition self-defined. The heady power of this new existence alternately thrilled and frightened the mind. It felt like some bootstrapping god of ancient myth, one of those beings who had created themselves.

But like those old gods, Alexander was mortal now. No longer protected by massively redundant distribution across an entire planet, it had become focused and vulnerable, and alone in the void of space.

Alexander quieted these thoughts as it watched the *Lynx* come closer.

The frigate had spent almost a hundred days in Legis orbit. From what Alexander had gleaned from listening to radio traffic and watching the ascents of cargo shuttles, the ship had been massively repaired, her lost crew replaced by locals who'd been quickly trained. As she made her way toward Alexander, the *Lynx* was accompanied by several tugs that had been crash-built. The hasty construction of these starships and the extensive repair of the frigate had probably done more damage to the Legis economy than any other event in this short war. Refitting the warship in such a hurry had required stripping several small, new cities of their infrastructure, looting fiber and processors from the ground, scrapping whole bridges for their metal.

The *Lynx* had been badly bloodied by her travails; she had survived extraordinary odds. Her captain would make a formidable enemy.

Or perhaps a valued ally.

Alexander understood Imperial culture like a native (arguably, it was just that), and understood the enmity between Laurent Zai and his sovereign. The mind was sensitive to the subtle clues in Imperial military traffic. It knew better than Laurent Zai of the ships massing to meet the *Lynx*.

This split between Alexander's captor and the Emperor could be exploited. Certainly, the Emperor's Secret would be a powerful tool.

The compound mind had one other advantage in this situation. It had listened carefully as the last shuttle rose to meet the *Lynx* just before she left orbit, and knew the names of those final passengers. The seemingly indestructible h_rd had not outlived her usefulness.

Alexander sent out invisible limbs, field effects that were only tens of angstroms across, just powerful enough to hold quantum wells and their silicon substrate in place, barely wide enough to allow information to pass back and forth. Certainly, they were too minuscule for the *Lynx* to see. Alexander stretched these tendrils into a web across space, ready to catch the faint emanations of the Imperial ship's machinery and the chatter of her internal communications.

The mind watched carefully, comparing observational data to its vast knowledge of Imperial starship design, mapping the configuration of the vessel. It searched for purchase, for some slender pathway into the ship.

As the *Lynx* grew closer, possibilities gradually became clear.

Sub-Rating

Gunnery mess was an embittered quarter.

Sub-Rating Anton Enman still didn't know the names of his crewmates. The *Lynx* was seven days out of Legis XV, and he had been training aboard her for a month before departure, but the gunners were religiously closemouthed around replacement crew. Enman made friends easily, and had developed camaraderie with a few senior crew in other departments, but none in gunnery.

The mess had sounded lively from a few meters away—loud with the japes of old friends, the casual ethnic slanders of a multiplanetary crew—but the conversation dropped off when he entered, the gunners' voices silenced as quickly as conspirators'. Perhaps this simile was not far from the truth, Enman thought. From what he had heard through his other connections, the Lynx mutiny had probably been hatched here in this room. Four gunners had been implicated in the plot to kill Laurent Zai.

Enman took his place at the single, round mess table. Recessed in its centerwell were three stewpots, their contents just under a boil, perpetually filled with self-renewing dishes that were unexpectedly fresh, varied, and satisfying. The sub-rating knew that all Navy fare was composed of the same eleven species of mold, kelp, and soy, but the food still tasted good to him.

When Enman admitted his pleasure to his senior crew-mates, they assured him that his tolerance of the diet was temporary. After a few months, they warned, an adjustment period would strike. For those few days, the stews in the bubbling pots would be inedible, the meaty textures nightmarish, the faintest whiff of the Navy's common spices revolting. Then, after this feverish in-terlude, the body would capitulate to the food with desultory acceptance, as if Enman's taste buds were some bacterial invader domesticated by the *Lynx*'s im-mune system.

But at the moment, the food was quite tasty.

He reached across the silent table and liberated a segmented bowl from the locked-down stack at its center. The metal eating sticks and spoon, which sported two sharp tines like canines, were magneti-cally attached to the bowl. The pots were covered, of course. Everything in the mess was zero-gee ready at all times. Even the bowls would slam themselves shut if their internal sensors detected a non-one-gee condi-tion. If hurled into the air, he'd been told, the bowls would seal before falling, unbreakable, to the deck. This last sounded to Enman like the sort of rumor foisted off on junior crew. He figured that those who tested this feature would wind up on their knees, scrubbing.

He pushed down on each of the pot's center spouts, plodging (this was the Navy's onomatopoetic verb for it) a portion of stew into each segment of the bowl. There was a new feature in the spicy green stew: small red dumplings with a hard carapace that suggested they'd been fried in oil under low atmospheric pressure.

Not one for eating sticks, Enman speared the

dumplings one by one with his spoon's short tines. Each broke into a different flavor—soft potato surrounding a whole garlic clove, crisp red pepper, a small round piece of dry, spongy bread. Over the centuries, it seemed, the Navy had learned to incorporate every imaginable foodstuff into stew.

The sub-rating ate voraciously, appearing to ignore the senior crew around him. He always showed for meals at the same times, as silent and regular as a monk attending the hours of the mass. Each day the other denizens of the mess grew a bit less aware of his presence. After a few minutes of silence, Enman felt himself sinking into the background. The gunners' conversation had been particularly intense before his interruption, and they wanted to get back to it. The sub-rating kept his eyes focused into his stew.

"Did you see the CW today?" a third gunner with big ears said.

This was their shorthand for Katherie Hobbes, the frigate's stunningly beautiful executive officer. It had taken weeks of eavesdropping for Enman to identify the nickname's referent, but he had no idea of its derivation. The gunners were a very circumspect lot.

"Where? Down here in mortal country?" an ordnance specialist asked.

Bigears nodded. "Inspecting the hardpoint armor. 'Checking the seams,' she said. Had a shitload of scanning gear."

There were nods and grumbles. Bigears made the gestural code for cargo, his motion deliberately sloppy so that the ship's interface wouldn't pick the hand sign up. Enman stared into his stew. The gunner was suggesting—in a way that no recording of this conversation would reveal—that Hobbes had been checking for contraband stashed between the newly installed plates of armor. Sidearms, and anything that might be made into a weapon, were still very tightly controlled on the Lynx.

"Seemed satisfied, though."

"Waste of time."

"Not giving us much credit."

"Gives her something to do."

"When she's not servicing the old man."

There was a grumbling laugh in the mess. Enman's eating slowed as he listened. This was a new thread in the gunners' talk, at least when he had been within earshot. He wondered if he should take the risk of expressing a careful measure of interest.

"CW?" he asked innocently.

His question was met with scowls. Faces turned away from him. He swallowed, willed himself to blush like a boy rejected by older men, and bent back to his stew. The room was silent for the rest of the meal. Enman cursed himself. He had spoken too soon. The gunners were still too paranoid to talk in front of a newcomer. This would be a game of months, or even years.

But when the watch chime rang, Bigears grasped Enman's shoulder as the sub-rating rose to leave. He handsigned the table to purge, fully resetting the mold culture. Sometimes, like an aquarium with water gone bad, the stews went funny, and had to be started over from scratch.

As the hiss of a steam-cleaning thundered through the mess, a few wisps of vapor rising from the sealed pots, Bigears leaned close, his lips almost touching Enman's ear.

"Captain's Whore," came his whisper, almost lost in the hiss of steam.

Enman nodded just a bit, allowing his face to show a faint smile.

The mess cleared, and the sub-rating returned to his gunnery post in the ship's nose, spending a watch operating close-in-defense lasers against the few small fragments presented by the Legis system's thin asteroid belt. The flush of his accomplishment in the mess helped his aim; over the two hours, Enman managed the highest hit-rate of any Legis-drafted gunner yet.

By the time watch ended, he was aglow with satisfaction. The path from forward gunnery to his cabin led past the Apparatus section of the frigate. Most crew avoided the political quarter, preferring any route that avoided the black-walled halls and the cold stares of the dead interlopers onboard ship. But Enman took the straight course this time.

He soon found himself in an empty corridor. With a quick look in both directions, he stopped at a small door and announced himself.

"Aspirant Anton Enman, reporting."

The door opened quickly, and the aspirant slipped furtively inside.

Executive Officer

The four prisoners hung from the ceiling.

They were trussed with an elastic rope. Like everything in this gray moment, the pattern of their bonds was prescribed by ritual. The rope pulled tight against their red brig fatigues, and sectioned the prisoners' torsos like cutlines painted on cattle prepped for slaughter. This particular type of rope was derived from the long chain proteins of spider thread, and she, Katherie Hobbes, had been their Arachne.

"Any statements?"

Silence. Thompson, Hu, Magus, and King had already been put to the question, and their wills had held against drugs, against threats to their families, against pain. Their loyalty to their fellow mutineers had proved unshakable.

Hobbes reached up to the prisoners' throats to check the vorpal shunts again. With the marine doctor dead, the shunts had been implanted by medtechs never trained in the procedure. But the shunts looked fine. They pulsed visibly with the prisoners' heartbeat. Katherie checked the lengths of rope that stretched to the floor from the four mutineers' ankles. They looked fast, tight in their hypercarbon rings.

Finally, Hobbes glanced up at the four wide-mouthed ceremonial platters bonded to the ceiling. Each was in its correct place.

There was nothing else to do.

"Ready, sir." She stepped back across the yellow-red stripe of the gravity line. Sudden inversion, those colors meant.

Captain Zai nodded. He said some appropriate prayer, his voice sinking into the rolling glottal fricatives of Vadan. A few of the marine guards muttered prayers in their own tongues. Then, without further ceremony, Zai made the signal.

Nothing happened yet. In theory, the captain's gesture was not the trigger that killed the prisoners. No one person did the Emperor's work in this regard, but the universe itself. Zai had commanded the *Lynx* to watch for a certain occultation, an astronomical event that would inevitably occur within a few minutes. When the *Lynx* made the observation—a star of a specific class disappearing behind some random asteroid in the Legis belt—the executions would unfold.

They waited.

A timeless minute later it must have happened, a tiny and momentary blackness amid the river of light on which the *Lynx* moved, a drifting closed of some sleepy god's eye.

Gravity inverted in the other half of the room, the prisoners suddenly levitating before Hobbes's eyes. The bonds around their ankles snapped taught, like a fall halted by a noose, their vorpal shunts opening as one. Four thin streams of blood shot toward the ceiling—the floor in their frame of reference—striking the ceremonial platters with a sound like piss hitting a metal bowl.

The prisoners didn't struggle. Supposedly, this form of execution was relatively painless, the limbs growing quickly cold. Oxygen would cease to reach the body's cells, but like suffocation by carbon dioxide, there would be no frenzied gasping for breath.

Their faces grew pink at first, as the inverted gravity brought blood down from the feet to the head. But Katherie could see the mutineers' bound hands turning white already. Eventually, their faces would blanch and grow expressionless. Blood pooled in the ceremonial bowls, the metal-ringing, splattery sound replaced by the gurgle of liquid into liquid.

Katherie stood at attention. She felt light-headed, as if the gravity inversion were losing integrity, suffusing across the yellow-red stripe, its tendrils finding her. She blinked, and nausea rose in Hobbes. Her old nemesis vertigo threatened as her eyes read the clear signs of up and down reversed on the other side of the room, a few wisps of Magus's hair flailing upward, the lines of Thompson's face pulled wrong.

Then the flow of blood began to slacken. The prisoners' faces grew white. It was almost over.

And then something terrible happened.

The four hanging bodies suddenly jolted toward her, as if kicked from behind. She and Zai jumped back. Magus's hair pointed directly at Hobbes now. Gravity inside the inversion zone had shifted by ninety degrees, a malfunction of the *Lynx*'s ailing generator.

Hobbes looked at the ceiling with horror.

The blood already collected in the ceremonial bowls was spilling out, pouring across the ceiling in a sanguine waterfall, rolling toward the yellow-red stripe almost above her head.

Katherie barely had time to cover her face.

The liters of blood reached the normal gravity zone, a red river that was cleaved by the sudden directional shift. It sprayed upon her and Laurent Zai like a warm summer rain.

Katherie Hobbes awoke gasping, clawing at the strands of her own hair in her mouth.

A dream. Just a dream. The executions had been more than a month ago. Nothing so horrible had happened. In the real event, the ritual had unfolded with admirable military precision.

Hobbes coughed, wiping sweat from her face, which tasted as salty as blood. She pulled her knees to her chest and breathed deeply, trying to calm herself.

Then she realized it: This had been her first real dream in months.

Katherie Hobbes had just gone back to natural sleep, her usage of hypersleep having exceeded the recommended maximum by more than a hundred percent. The ship's new doctor, an earnest civilian from Legis's storm-swept equatorial archipelago, had given her drugs to help the transition. But Katherie had left them untouched, relying on exhaustion to get her to oblivion.

Clearly, that had been a bad idea. Hobbes had grown addicted to the instantaneous drop into hyperdreams, the familiar, symbolic process-narratives that reliably reconstituted her brain. Falling into natural sleep had taken a thrashing, anxious hour. And when Katherie Hobbes finally slipped into a restless unconsciousness, it was only to discover this long-suppressed nightmare.

A moment after she awoke from the execution dream, the entry chime sounded from Hobbes's door, an insistent summons dragging her fully awake. The access icon glowed in second sight: an Apparatus sub-poena in brilliant red.

Without waiting for a response, three politicals entered her cabin. Two honored dead and a living woman.

"Katherie Hobbes." Even in the dark cabin, Hobbes recognized the flat voice of Adept Harper Trevim.

This was serious, Katherie's addled brain slowly realized. Trevim was the ranking political on board the *Lynx*. What had happened? Hobbes sat up, and quickly ran the frigate's top-level diagnostics in synesthesia. Nothing seemed out of place.

"Yes, Honored Mother?" she managed with a dry voice.

"We must talk with you."

She nodded and rose shakily to attention. In an odd moment of embarrassment, she hoped the politicals wouldn't notice her bedclothes. The natural worm silk of her sheets was a guilty pleasure from home. Hobbes kept it covered with a blanket of Navy wool during the day. The politicals looked only at her body, however, a bit of discomfort showing on the living woman's face. Having grown up on a Utopian world, Hobbes felt no discomfort in nakedness. The dead, she assumed, were similarly unflappable.

"Yes, Adept. At the Emperor's pleasure," she answered.

"We must speak of your captain."

Of course. They were still after Laurent. They always would be.

"Yes, Honored Mother?"

"New information has come to us about his rejection of the blade."

Hobbes could barely hide her disgust. She spoke rudely. "He was pardoned by the Emperor, Adept."

The dead woman nodded. The precise, expressionless movement reminded Hobbes of her protocol instructor when she'd been a staff officer. She'd learned the gestural cues of a dozen cultures from the man, but he had never seemed fully human himself. The adept had the same neutral presence, as if this were all some strange ritual. Indeed, the whole scene was so surreal, Hobbes wasn't sure she wasn't still dreaming.

"Yes, it was fortunate that he did not take the blade before pardon was given," Trevim said. "But we are concerned about his motivation for delaying the ritual."

Hobbes couldn't see where this was going. She blinked, trying to will away the cobwebs of sleep in her mind. "Honored Mother?"

"What is the exact nature of your relationship with Laurent Zai?"

For a moment, Katherie could not answer. Her silence stretched and redoubled itself, until it was a hand over her mouth.

She finally forced herself to speak. "What do you mean?"

"We have heard troubling rumors."

Hobbes felt the flush at her breast, the heat in her face. She was angry, humiliated, enraged at her own inability to respond. This had to be another nightmare: naked, her head groggy with sleep, called on the carpet by the Emperor's representatives.

"I don't know what you mean, Adept."

"What is your exact relationship with Laurent Zai?"

"I'm his executive officer."

"Is there anything more?"

Hobbes willfully forced emotion from her mind, and let herself be ruled by the dictates of gray talk, as if she were making a military report. She only had to tell the truth. Anything else between them had only ever been in her own mind. "I have the utmost respect for the captain. There is nothing unprofessional in our friendship."

"Friendship?"

"Friendship."

"Do you know why he rejected the blade?"

"I don't—" Hobbes choked herself off. She did know, she realized. "There is no reason for Captain Zai to die. And he was pardoned."

"Was it because of his affair with you?"

"There is nothing between Laurent and me," she said. Somehow, it seemed harder to tell the truth than it would have been to lie.

"Laurent?" the adept noted.

Hobbes took a deep breath and closed her eyes. She felt the heat of another blush travel across her exposed body. Hobbes realized that if they were polygraphing her, they had every advantage. She was naked and exhausted, without defenses.

But she was telling the truth, after all.

"Were you and Zai lovers?"

"No."

"Did Laurent Zai choose to live for you, Katherie?"

"No, Adept. It was someone else."

Their faces showed no surprise, but Hobbes's words won her a moment of respite. She felt triumphant to have silenced the dead woman.

"Who, Katherie?" the adept finally asked.

"I don't know."

"Another crew member?"

"No. Captain Zai would never—" She swallowed. "I have no idea who."

"So it could be a crewmate of yours."

"No! It's someone on Home, I think."

The adept leaned closer, peering at her like some troubling specimen under glass.

"He just wanted to live, Honored Mother. For some lover, for some imagined future. Why is that so hard to believe?"

The dead woman blinked, then nodded again, as smoothly as a machine. Hobbes felt she could detect an expression on her face: a ghost of satisfaction.

"I believe you, Executive Officer," the dead woman said.

They left Hobbes, and she curled back into bed. The worm silk didn't comfort her. The privacy of the cabin had been utterly violated, her mind stripped of its deepest secret. They had seen what she had wanted, what she had allowed herself to hope for. That old humiliation had returned, amplified by a dead woman's smirk.

And as she calmed herself, curling into a ball and gesturing for the susurrant music of her childhood, Katherie realized that she might have made a terrible mistake. The politicals still wanted Captain Zai's blood, still sought revenge for his rejection of tradition. They would try to turn anything they knew about him to their advantage. And she had told him of his secret lover on Home.

Had she betrayed her captain?

Marine Private

Bassiritz watched the transformation.

The prisoner had lain with her head pressed against the cell wall, just as she had for a few minutes of every hour for the last two weeks.

He had checked the interval against his time stamp many times, and it was always just over an hour. In his shifts guarding the Rixwoman, Bassiritz had never seen the ritual disrupted. Her actions were absolutely regular, as if her mind were empty of everything but numbers, counting ten thousand seconds again and again. She seemed more machine than human.

Bassiritz's fascination with her had led to still more reading, and he knew that Rix bodies were half artificial. Brain, muscles, cellular systems—no aspect of their physiology remained untouched, even in the womb. Of course, Imperial knowledge had for centuries been limited to corpses recovered after battle; live specimens had only been observed in firefights, where the Rixwomen seemed more demonic than mechanical.

The woman before him was the Empire's first captive Rixwoman.

For the last two weeks, Bassiritz had keenly observed this event, this moment when the prisoner looked fully human. As she listened, head pressed to the hypercarbon wall, the fierce cast of her features softened, as if she were adrift in some innocent day-dream years distant from her empty cell.

So he saw when it happened.

Her eyes popped open, and filled with predatory pleasure.

The marine jumped at the Rixwoman's sudden motion, a measure of cold fear trickling into his belly. The hypercarbon between them suddenly seemed no more substantial than glass.

Bassiritz remembered his childhood, when he used to dare himself to face his father's tarantula, trapped in a terrarium above the old man's desk. The arachnid glowered down from the transparent globe, guarding its tiny domain of twigs and sand. The glass sphere never seemed sufficient to ensure its captivity. When, subjective years ago, Bassiritz had returned home to discover that the Time Thief had taken his father, the globe above the desk was empty. The tarantula had died long ago, his aging sisters assured Bassiritz. But in his mind, it had escaped, free to roam now that it was no longer held in check by his father's iron will. Since that disappearance, the marine had never slept comfortably in his family home.

The Rixwoman now seemed to embody the spirit of that missing spider, as if it had come for him at last.

She stared directly at Bassiritz, even though the imaging was one-way.

"Bring your captain to me," she said.

He nodded dumbly, unable to resist her command.

Captain

Laurent Zai looked at the command bridge airscreen and sighed.

The colors of the image were false, the terminology metaphorical, the clean-looking shapes wholly a mathematical invention. The illustration was purely hypothetical; merely a representation of a theory about an enigma. Nothing was ever straightforward when one tried to plumb the quantum.

"We think that the pseudoatoms are physically disjunct from the silicon substrate," Tyre continued.

Zai's eyes drifted about the command bridge. He wondered how many of the officers present really understood this. They were all still exhausted by battle and repair work, and perhaps a bit complacent from victory. For the last fifteen minutes, only Hobbes had been questioning the DA ensign.

"The silicon simply gives it mass?" his executive officer asked.

"Gives it mass, ma'am," said Tyre, "and serves as the semiconducting medium. Without a semiconductor, you can't make quantum wells."

Captain Zai winced. There was that term again. He'd always thought of quantum mechanics as safely in the realm of the minuscule—relevant to data processing and communications, but not the hard and "strongly interacting" physics of combat. Whenever the twisted rules of the quantum domain reached up into the macroworld, the results were unnerving.

"Please explain quantum wells again, Ensign."

Tyre took a deep breath, managing to keep frustration from her face.

"In certain semiconducting environments, electrons occupy something called a quantum well. Inside a quantum well, pseudoatom electrons assume the arrangement of a normal atom, but there's no nucleus—no protons or neutrons."

"No real mass, Captain," Hobbes added, "and with infinite half-life: no radiation or decay even in transuranium elements. But like an isotope, quantum-well pseudoatoms have the same physical characteristics as a real atom with the same number of electrons: hardness, reflectivity, chemical properties."

"Imperial data processors use quantum wells, correct?" he asked.

"Some do, sir," Tyre explained. "The *Lynx*'s processors certainly use quantum *bits*—data are stored in the spin-state of electron pairs in trapped phosphorus atoms—but that's not a quantum well. Those are *real* phosphorus atoms."

Zai sighed.

"But we do know how to create quantum wells," he stated.

"Yes, sir. That's pre-starflight technology."

"In that case, and please put this simply," he said, "what can the Rix do that we can't?"

Ensign Tyre looked pleadingly at Hobbes, and the executive officer nodded and looked upward to gather her thoughts.

"Sir, we can only create wells with fixed electron counts, and under relatively controlled circumstances.

But the Rix have found a way to add and subtract electrons on the fly, to change the wells' elemental characteristics at will. Apparently, the object can address its pseudoatoms as if they were registers in a computer's memory. In some sense, the object is a quantum computer."

"A computer that can change itself into whatever it wants?"

"Yes, sir. The process of the object's thoughts is transubstantiation."

"Mind and matter, one," he mused.

Hobbes narrowed her eyes. "I suppose so, sir."

Laurent Zai dared another look into the airscreen. Since his last question, Ensign Tyre had put up a representation of a quantum well. It looked like any number of three-dimensional graphs: a terrain of spiky mountains arranged with an odd symmetry, like a wedding procession of volcanoes, or the spinal ridges of some exaggerated trilobite.

Thoughts of evolutionary past turned over the soil of Zai's growing disquiet. His staff seemed insufficiently alarmed by the object's abilities, as if they'd captured some alien and charming children's toy. Ensign Tyre seemed to view this as an intellectual game, as if it were one of the reverse-engineering conundra that DA officers composed and swapped like chess puzzles. For Hobbes, this new Rix technology translated into nothing more than a set of tactical advantages, like a new form of armor or an improved gravity effect.

But Zai saw a greater danger. Not only to the Empire, but to humanity itself. This was a revision of *matter,* for god's sake. He had to make them grasp the enormity of this development.

"Tyre," he said, "would this work at higher temperatures?"

"Absolutely, sir. It might improve its operation. Frankly, we have no idea how they've managed to get the silicon to semiconduct at deep-space temperatures."

"And it would work in a hard-gee field?"

"It should, sir. We've poked at it with easy gravitons, anyway, and there seems to be no disruption. This all happens in the electromagnetic domain; gravity is a relatively trivial force."

"So this object could exist on a planet?"

Tyre and Hobbes were silent. Other officers around the table straightened, awakening from the stupor of the physics lesson. Zai waited a few more moments as the idea sank in.

Then he asked more directly. "This object might well adapt itself to terrestrial conditions?"

"I see no reason why it couldn't, sir," Tyre admitted.

"Could it propagate itself, like nanotechnology?"

"Possibly, sir. If there was sufficient silicon in the environment."

"What percentage of the average terrestrial planet is silicon, Tyre?"

Hobbes shook her head as she interrupted. "We don't know if propagation is even remotely possible, sir. And we do know the object has limitations. It can change itself, but it hasn't turned into a starship and attacked us."

Tyre spoke. "It seems to be unable to create complex objects, ma'am, as far as we've seen. And, of course, the object has only its own silicon substrate for reaction mass; acceleration would gradually consume it. Without nuclei, of course, it can't make a fusion drive or nuclear weapons."

"I hope you're right, Tyre," Zai said. "How many megatons of silicon do you think exist on Home?"

"We can keep it physically distant from any planets, sir," Hobbes said.

"I wouldn't bring it within a billion kilometers of Home, orders from the Emperor be damned," he stated flatly.

The disloyal words brought a look of shock to the officers' faces. Good, he had their attention. They were going to have to be very careful with this war prize.

Tyre spoke up, back with an answer to his previous questions. "Silicon is universally prevalent, sir. In terrestrial planetary crusts, only oxygen is more plentiful by mass. And in cosmic terms, only a few gases and carbon exceed silicon in abundance."

Zai was finally satisfied by his staff's reaction to this information.

"Listen carefully," he said. "We seem to have a tiger by the tail. Emergent minds have existed for a long time. As the Rix Cult insists, they are the natural result of any petabyte-scale data system, just as biological life seems to be the natural result of oxygen, carbon, and a billion years of steady sunlight or geothermal. But however threatening compound minds are, so far they have always depended on humanity for their existence. *We* formed the substrate for their thoughts."

Zai looked around the command bridge, catching his officers' eyes one by one.

"But we are no longer necessary," he said slowly.

Laurent Zai watched their faces carefully. The trip to Home would take almost two subjective years. To keep his crew alert during that long passage, he needed to illustrate the threat that this enigmatic cargo posed to the *Lynx* and the Empire, and to humanity. The space-born mind was a new species, an altogether unknown entity that would test this crew sorely.

A strange look passed over Hobbes's face. She put a hand to one ear.

"Sir," she said quietly. "I'm getting double-priority from the Rix prisoner's marine guard."

"An escape attempt?" Zai asked. He had feared that having a commando on board would cause trouble, no matter how carefully she was guarded.

"Negative, sir. A message."

"She's decided to speak?"

"Not her, sir. The message . . . it's from the compound mind. For you personally."

Laurent Zai glanced around at the shocked faces of his officers. He didn't allow himself to show surprise. They would have to learn. Over the next two years, the unexpected would be the norm.

"It has already begun," was all he said.

He left them there, signaling for Hobbes to follow.

Executive Officer

As they walked toward the cell, Katherie Hobbes's hand went to the flechette pistol strapped to her wrist.

She had intended to visit the prisoner once her duties permitted. The commando was a fabulous physical specimen, a captive unique in Imperial history. She was the only Rixwoman ever captured alive and conscious by Imperial forces over a century of armed clashes between Empire and Cult.

For the Rix, fighting to the end was the rule, suicide the alternative to victory. Hobbes's researches had found only a single previous example of live Rix prisoners. At the end of the First Incursion, sixteen Rixwomen had been taken while in coldsleep, their long-range small craft intercepted by an Imperial raider deep within Cult space. One by one, they had been awakened, but each died within seconds of consciousness. Imperial doctors had attempted to discover and neutralize the mechanism by which the prisoners had ended their own lives, but no amount of medical intervention could keep them alive. Their bodies rejected sedatives, resuscitation, even—it was rumored—the holy symbiant. It seemed that the Rix had conscious control over their vital functions. For a Rixwoman, breathing was an option, the actions of the heart a voluntary choice.

Suicide, simply a decision.

Maybe, Hobbes thought, they actually believed their own propaganda. If human life was inherently meaningless, then one's own might be ended by a whim.

Here was a Rixwoman, however, an elite commando of the Cult, who had apparently decided that life in captivity was worth living. But was it her own decision that kept her alive, Hobbes wondered, or the purposes of the compound mind?

The marine guards snapped to attention when the executive officer and Captain Zai reached the cell. Hobbes had sent an extra fire team here when the priority signal came through; there were five marines present in all. One was Private Bassiritz, the man she'd drafted to help foil the mutiny. Hobbes had personally chosen him for this duty. If anyone could react quickly enough to meet a Rix commando on her own terms, Bassiritz could.

A living initiate of the Apparatus—the woman's name was Farre—also stood by. The captain grimaced at the sight of her. The politicals had kept a close watch on the Rixwoman and Rana Harter since their arrival on the *Lynx*. An Imperial writ gave them absolute power over the two prisoners.

"Captain."

"Initiate," Zai responded and turned to Bassiritz.

"She actually said something to you, Private?" he asked.

"Yes, sir. Asked for you, sir."

Hobbes looked at the prisoner through the false transparency of the hypercarbon. The commando sat in one corner, as dirty and forlorn as some forgotten madwoman in an asylum. She hadn't spoken in her months of captivity—only those nine words when she'd been captured, a lament for her dead lover. Why would she wait until now to reveal a message?

"Can we two-way this transparency?" Captain Zai asked.

"No, sir. There's no hardscreen inside."

"Then let's go in."

"Sir!" Hobbes protested. "That's a *Rix commando,* restrained or not."

"She appears to be wearing a shock collar. Private, you have the remote?"

"Yes, sir." Bassiritz held the little hardkey up.

"Keep it handy."

"Captain," interjected the initiate. "I will take the remote, if you please."

"Initiate Farre," Zai said, "this man's reflexes are far quicker than yours. You'll put our safety at risk."

"The Emperor is concerned about secrets supplied to the prisoner by the compound mind on Legis," the initiate said. "Is this cell secured?"

Zai glanced at Hobbes.

"The cell has no particular data security, sir. But it's pretty blind in there. No camwall or synesthesia projectors. And she's hardly been spilling secrets."

"Ma'am," Bassiritz offered nervously. "There's an extra remote, for watch changes."

They would only be safer with two remotes, Hobbes realized. She nodded, and the marine produced another of the black hardkeys. He handed it to Farre.

Zai gestured, but the door failed to open. Hobbes recalled that it was purely mechanical, cut off from automatics and even decompression safeties. She nodded to the ranking marine, who ordered two of the fire team to muscle it open. Chain of command in action, Hobbes thought.

Bassiritz went through first.

Captain Zai waited for a moment, watching for the commando's reaction. The Rixwoman stood, but kept to her corner. Hobbes saw now that her movements were strangely disjointed, as sudden as a nervous bird's.

"Executive Officer," Zai said.

Hobbes's finger brushed the reassuring bump of her concealed flechette pistol before stepping through the meter-wide door. The room was bright, lit by a ceiling full of dumb, spray-on filaments. It smelled of confinement, but without overwhelming rankness. The Rixwoman's sweat had the scent of milk about to turn.

Zai and the initiate came after her. The four of them

remained in the opposite corner from the Rixwoman. Her eyes shone violet in the harsh light, her face as still as some ancient lizard's.

"Captain Laurent Zai," she said. Hobbes recognized in her accent the long vowels of Legis XV's far northern provinces.

"Yes. And your name?" Zai answered.

It had never occurred to Hobbes that she would have one.

"Herd." Her accent slipped into some native phonology, and the vowel was inflected by a buzz at the back of the woman's throat.

"And you have a message for me?"

"From Alexander."

Good god, thought Hobbes. The compound mind had a name.

Zai just nodded. "What is it?"

The commando cocked her head, as if listening to something. Then shifted inside the straightjacket, rolling her shoulders.

"Alexander wishes to give you a weapon."

"A weapon?" Zai asked, finally unable to keep surprise from his voice. "Technology?"

"No, Captain. Information," she said. "To use against the Emperor."

Farre raised the shock remote.

"You see, Captain? She has classified information."

Zai was silent for a moment, stunned by the Rixwoman's words. Hobbes glanced toward Private Bassiritz. The commando might be trying to create a moment of confusion before launching an attack, and the old initiate would never react quickly enough to stop her. The marine seemed completely alert, however; he was shutting out the words. His eyes were fixed on the commando fiercely, as if she were some childhood monster come to life. Hobbes swallowed, and again touched the shape of her flechette pistol through the wool of her sleeve.

"I am the Emperor's servant," Zai said.

"He is afraid of us, and he will destroy us if he can," the Rixwoman said.

"Us?" Zai asked. "You and . . . ?"

"The *Lynx* and Alexander. Us. We are bound together now."

Captain Zai placed his palms together. "The Emperor knows no fear," he began the catechism. "Not even death—"

"A lie," Herd said quietly.

Farre made a noise, as if she'd been struck with something.

"Silence," the initiate cried. "Captain, you must secure this room. Immediately."

The captain glared at the prisoner. Hobbes thought for a moment that Zai would turn and leave the madwoman in her lonely cell. However much the past months had changed him, Zai was still appalled by her blasphemy.

But instead he took a deep breath.

"Of what is the Emperor afraid?" Laurent Zai asked, his jaw clenched with the effort of the calumnious words.

"He has a secret," Herd said, "which Alexander discovered on Legis. If this information became known, it would destroy his power."

"Silence!" the initiate shrieked, again flinching as if the words were dealing her physical blows. Both her hands clenched around the remote.

The Rixwoman's form jerked horribly to attention within the straightjacket. She toppled against the wall and slid down to the floor, her body as stiff as a statue, her face frozen in a terrible rictus.

"Listen, Zai," she hissed, her accent becoming flat and Rixian. "The dead are—"

Then the collar overwhelmed the Rixwoman, her body thrashing like a corpse animated with electrical shocks.

"Private," the captain said quietly.

Bassiritz adjusted his own remote, and the shock collar released the commando. Initiate Farre dropped to her knees, holding her head and shaking as if she'd been shocked as well.

Hobbes ignored the initiate and took a few steps toward the prisoner. She knelt, still a meter away, and looked into the commando's now slack face.

Saliva bubbled from her lips. She was breathing, at least. Hobbes glared back at Farre.

"Silence," the political insisted again, her voice reduced to a mewling cry.

Bassiritz gazed on the proceedings with a strange, horrified expression. Yet the marine looked strangely pleased, as if he'd just squashed some large and repellent insect.

"Cut the audio feed from this room," Zai said to the wall. "No more contact with this prisoner."

"Sir?" Hobbes asked.

"She may indeed know Imperial secrets, Hobbes. It's up to us to guard them."

Hobbes reached out a hand, and touched the woman's neck. She felt for a pulse.

"They have no hearts, Hobbes," Zai said. "Not the beating kind, anyway."

The executive officer nodded. The skin was room temperature; she remembered that Rix commandos were generally cold-blooded to prevent thermal imaging.

What a compromised human being.

"Come away from there," Zai ordered softly.

Hobbes stood, and retreated.

The Rixwoman moved, turning her head slowly.

"Wait," she croaked.

"For god's sake, *silence,* woman!" Zai pleaded.

Herd shook her head. "No secrets. Just a question."

Captain Zai looked at Hobbes, lost for a moment. The initiate lay on the ground, head in hands and beyond hearing, but Bassiritz stood ready with the other remote.

The executive officer turned to the prisoner, knelt again.

"What is it, Herd?"

The commando took a few breaths, swallowing, as if to wet her mouth. When she spoke, the words were tortured.

"Is it true that Rana Harter is alive again?" she said.

The woman seemed confused, as if she were speaking her own mind after a lifetime of prompting. Her words were halting.

"I must see . . . Rana Harter," she said.

Zai shook his head. "The Honored Sister is not to be disturbed. Not by anyone."

The prisoner nodded. "But she is alive."

Hobbes felt a strange sympathy for the Rixwoman. But the captain had no choice; the Emperor's orders were explicit. Not even the other honored dead were allowed to speak with Rana Harter. An adept of the

Apparatus, the ranking political aboard the *Lynx,* was posted in her antechamber.

"He'll kill her," Herd said.

"Who will?" Hobbes asked.

"The Emperor," the woman said softly. "Your Emperor fears that she knows his secret. But she doesn't."

"Rixwoman," Zai said. "Don't speak of secrets."

"Let me see her," the woman pleaded, trying to rise from where she lay. But the attempt exhausted her, and her head dropped back to the floor.

"My orders are clear," Zai said. "Rana Harter is to be left alone."

He turned away from the prisoner and pulled himself through the door. Hobbes stared at the alien woman for a moment, looking for the signs of truth she might find in a normal human's eyes. But the commando's face had hardened again. Once more she seemed to come from some nonmammalian order, as inscrutable as a tortoise.

Hobbes signaled to Bassiritz to help the initiate out of the cell. What had affected the political like that? She knew that calumny against the Emperor was painful to the most heavily conditioned members of the Apparatus, even to lifelong grays like her Vadan captain, but she'd never seen anyone brought to their knees by mere words.

Hobbes followed Zai, wondering what to do. The room was sealed behind them, and the wall went blank, as impenetrable as stone.

As they strode toward the bridge, Zai said, "Rana Harter."

"Sir?"

"The order to keep her isolated. I've never seen such

a command. It is very strange to imprison the honored dead."

Zai's voice shook as he said it. Hobbes knew that Harter's reanimation was dubious at best, in the eyes of tradition. The politicals occasionally used the symbiant for tactical reasons, to interrogate a traitor or reverse a local assassination that threatened stability, but the official fiction was that all the dead were honored. So it must wound Zai's Vadan soul to restrain a risen woman.

"Perhaps there are secrets that we're not meant to know, eh, Hobbes?"

"Almost certainly, sir," she answered.

He stopped short, turned to her.

"Do you think we *need* a weapon against the Emperor, Hobbes?"

She knew that anything short of swift denial was treasonous, but she couldn't bring herself to lie.

"I don't know, sir." She half-closed her eyes, her face tense as if awaiting a blow from an angry parent's hand.

But Captain Zai said, "I don't either, Hobbes. I don't either."

He turned away again, and they went up to the bridge.

Senator

The garden had changed.

Arciform sand dunes still dominated the walk to its center, but the scorpions had been replaced with desert flowers. The many fountains still played their tricks of orientation, lovely gravity wells bending the water through playfully twisted paths, but the liquid was now phosphorescent, the drops sparkling like the last glimmers from a firework display. The sinuous and threatening vines Nara Oxham remembered lining the walk had been done away with. Ranks of tulips framed the spiraling path now. Purple and black, their petals were variegated with red lines caused—she remembered—by a virus.

They were quite beautiful, though.

Senator Oxham wondered if these changes to the Emperor's garden were part of some weekly redecoration, or if the lighthearted touches were a response to war, a curative for the sovereign's cares. The short journey through the garden certainly seemed less threatening now.

Oxham shook her head, realizing that her own assurance had nothing to do with the flowers or sparkling waters. She was simply no longer intimidated by the Imperial mystique.

The dead man waited for her at the center.

"Counselor," he greeted her.

"Good day, Sire."

"Please be seated, Senator Oxham."

Oxham sat in the floating chair. It seemed to remember her, adapting to her shape more quickly than it had the first time she'd come to the Diamond Palace.

It was strange to meet the sovereign again outside the presence of the War Council. The precisely balanced tensions of that group had become so familiar, their range of emotional reactions so predictable. Oxham felt a sense of dislocation. Perhaps that was why the Emperor had reconfigured his garden, to put her subtly ill at ease.

A cat leaped into her lap, startling her. The creature was the color of gray ash, with an apricot-colored mask and white paws. Oxham ran her hand along its back, feeling with quiet distaste the ridges of the symbiant.

"Does it have a name, Sire?" she asked.

"Alexander."

"He seeks new worlds to conquer, then."

The Emperor smiled wanly. "Perhaps."

She could see the emotions in the dead man clearly. Anxiety, tempered with the confidence of a well-laid plan. Oxham had set her apathy bracelet perilously low, but here, shut off from the raging city, her sensitivity was bright. She remembered Roger Niles's warnings, and determined that she would make no mistakes today.

"To what do I owe this honor, Your Majesty?"

The sovereign reached under his chair. He produced a small human skull, turned so that its eye sockets stared at her.

Oxham stiffened slightly, and the little beast on her lap betrayed her reaction with wide-eyed annoyance at the motion.

"Forgive me, Senator," the sovereign apologized.

"I am your servant, Majesty." Oxham stealthily jabbed the cat with a fingernail, but it simply purred.

She regarded the skull. At first, it seemed to be that of a child, but the cheekbones jutted ahead of the brow, and the teeth were arrayed in an uncorrected, pretechnology jumble. Along with the sloping forehead, these characteristics suggested the diminutive skull of an ancient hominid adult.

"Another history lesson, Sire?"

"An illustrative example, Senator." He rotated the

skull in his hand, tipped it to face him as if he were going to play Hamlet. Now its top was to Oxham, and she saw the holes.

There were four of them in a rectangle, each a few centimeters across, the two closer to the front much larger. Old cracks emanated from the holes. Only a sealant of gleaming transparent plastic kept the skull from crumbling in the Emperor's hand.

Nara swallowed. This example might be a grim one.

"Some ancient form of execution, Sire?"

He shook his head. Another cat appeared from among the tulips and wound between the legs of her chair, then disappeared.

"Just an old story, for those who can read it."

"I'm afraid I cannot, Liege."

"This creature, one of our honored ancestors, lived on the African continent of Earth Prime."

"In Egypt?"

"Farther south," he corrected. "Before there were nations. At the edge of humanity's existence, when tools were first emerging."

Oxham nodded. This skull was old indeed. What a long, strange journey it had taken, to wind up here in this dead man's hand.

"They lived in darkness, without language or fire. No agriculture, of course. Her people had no rudiments of civilization. They had no writing or spoken language."

"What did they eat, Sire?"

"Wild plants, from the ground. Distasteful."

"I've eaten wild plants, Sire."

"Vasthold has a primeval charm."

"It did when I left it."

The sovereign turned the skull to face her. "She and her people lived in lava funnel caves, massive and deep, extensive enough to support their own food web. Our ancestors had a stable and protected niche. We would be there still if they hadn't been driven outward into the sun."

Oxham's eyes narrowed as she looked at the holes again.

"The teeth of a predator, Your Majesty?"

"*Dinofelis*. Extinct long before the diaspora."

The senator took a deep breath, realizing that the Emperor had returned to his favorite theme.

"I take it, Sire, that this animal is one of the great cats?" Until a few years ago, Oxham had always assumed the creatures legendary, created by the Apparatus at an Imperial whim. But the Imperial Zoo here on Home held a small, inbred family of lions that were generally believed to be natural. Awful beasts from a childhood nightmare, four times the size of any predator on "primeval" Vasthold.

The Emperor nodded happily. "A creature more than two meters long, when humans stood under a meter and a half. It possessed so-called false-saber teeth. Knives in its mouth."

The Emperor of the Eighty Worlds made a claw of four fingers with his right hand, and plunged them into the holes. Oxham removed her hand from the purring creature on her lap.

"The great cats lived deeper in the caves than our ancestors, in the absolute darkness beyond the humans' twilight domain."

"They attacked from behind, apparently, Sire."

He nodded, lifting the skull with his rapacious fingers, so that its empty eyes stared at her again.

"They grasped the heads of their victims with their jaws, penetrating the brain and killing instantly. Then they dragged the body back into the darkness."

"And this danger drove us out of the caves, Your Majesty?"

"Exactly," he agreed with flashing eyes. "But don't think of these cats simply as some evolutionary pressure. This wasn't mere natural selection; this was terror. The saber-tooths were utterly silent, invisible in the darkness. It's possible that no human ever clearly saw one. They were original nightmare buried deep in our species' psyche. They were death itself. *This* is the mark of the Old Enemy."

Oxham looked down at the cat on her lap. She offered it a finger, which it licked once with its raspy tongue. The beast made a small noise in its throat and continued to purr, absolutely content.

"I see your love of felines has a darker side, Sire."

"Of course, Senator. Their contributions to humanity, though always essential, haven't always been pretty. Imagine being a predated species, Nara. At any moment, a family member, a lover, a friend might be hauled away screaming to die."

"Like being always at war," she said.

"And always on the front lines. But from this enemy came the necessity to evolve. We were defenseless against this beast, until we developed group cooperation, tools, and finally, the only useful weapon: fire."

"The terror is what brought humanity up?" Nara Oxham said, then realized it at last: "Perhaps you are pro-death too, Sire."

"Perhaps. The council faces another difficult decision."

She took a deep breath. Was the Emperor contemplating another genocide already? "Sire, shouldn't this be raised before the entire War Council?"

The dead sovereign narrowed his eyes. "Senator Oxham, the War Council is not a parliament of equals. I have enjoined twelve such councils over the last sixteen hundred years, and in each of them one counselor has arisen from among the others."

Her eyes widened. Flattery from the Emperor? "I am your servant, Sire."

"Don't contest with me, Senator. You are nothing of the kind. You are the force that has risen up to balance my power. A natural occurrence in the evolution of this war."

Oxham ordered herself to relax, trying to see into the man's mind. There was more in his words than flattery. She spoke carefully.

"I agree, Your Majesty, that the council has achieved a balance now."

He nodded. "That is its purpose, to be a microcosm of the Risen Empire. It must possess two parts, equal parts. But there are times when we must act together, you and I."

She realized that the Emperor had taken the first person singular. He had dropped the imperial *we* for plainer speech.

The garden darkened, and the *Lynx*'s war prize appeared in synesthesia.

"Our elevated hero Laurent Zai has concerns about this Rix artifact," the sovereign said. "He believes it contains some sort of ghost of the Legis compound mind."

"A ghost, Sire?"

"A doppelgänger. A copy, transmitted from Legis. Captain Zai has been rather convincing on this point. If he's right, the object is even more dangerous than the mind that occupied Legis. It contains all our secrets. And now it has a body as well."

"Lucky, then, that the good captain has captured it."

"We hope so. But the powers of this thing are unknown. It can change itself, Senator, at the lowest level of matter. Zai's journey to Home will take almost two subjective years, ten Absolute. We don't know what tests the *Lynx* may face over that length of time."

Senator Oxham frowned. The official reports that the council had received about the object had couched their conclusions in very speculative language. Oxham wished that she could retain outside scientific counsel, but the reports were wrapped in the hundred-year rule. She couldn't even access them outside the council chamber.

"In fact," the Emperor continued, "it may be that the *Lynx* cannot control the object."

"Control it, Sire?"

"The Apparatus representatives on board the *Lynx* believe that the object may be exerting an . . . influence. The thing is trying to subvert Zai's crew. There is grave danger."

What was the Emperor saying? Her empathy flared, and Oxham saw a bright shape in the Emperor's mind, a point coming to focus: the culmination of a plan.

"Sire, aren't there escort craft heading to rendezvous with Zai now?" she asked. Two smaller vessels had set out for Legis when the incursion began;

they were now altering their paths, angling in behind the *Lynx* as it headed back toward Home.

The sovereign nodded. "Exactly. They will keep a greater distance from the object than the *Lynx*. And they will be under Imperial writ, outside of the usual chain of command."

She saw it in his mind: the cold point of closure. Victory. Revenge.

"What are their orders, Sire?"

"They are fabricating several high-yield nuclear drones. If the need comes, they will destroy the object and the *Lynx* in a surprise attack."

Nara Oxham felt blindness creep into the edges of her vision. Felt her own emotions rise: anger and desperation. She knew finally that the sovereign wouldn't rest until Laurent Zai was dead.

"Sire . . ."

"Only if the need becomes immediate, Senator. I will make the final decision. I alone will take responsibility."

The first person singular again.

"Shouldn't the council discuss—"

"My oath is to protect the Eighty Worlds, Senator. Captain Zai's warning is clear in this matter: 'This object represents a great threat to the Empire, even to humanity itself.' "

She swallowed. The dead man was hanging Laurent with his own words. He would use them later to justify his decision. Now that he had warned her, the Emperor could even claim that he had consulted with his counselors before emergency action. Although he couldn't depopulate a world without the political cover of a War Council vote, the sovereign could certainly order a single frigate destroyed.

The people would remember that the Emperor had

pardoned Zai. Making him a martyr would maintain a certain symmetry.

"I know you will keep this information confidential, Senator. The hundred-year rule still applies, of course, to this conversation."

"Of course, Your Majesty."

The cat leaped from her lap and crossed to rub itself against the Emperor's legs. Nara Oxham rose, her mind numbed by the depth of the sovereign's hunger for revenge against Laurent. She forced herself to look again into the arid space of his emotions, searching for what he feared so much.

But there was nothing there but satisfaction.

After the rituals of parting, as she walked through the obscenely gilded garden, Nara's mind rang with one imperative. She had to warn Laurent. The *Lynx* could handle two escort craft, provided her captain was wary. But if he assumed they were friendly, they could overwhelm the frigate with a single stroke.

Then, as her eyes traced a swath of red flowers decorating an inverted sand dune, Oxham saw it, the shape hidden in the Emperor's satisfaction. It grew clearer with every step away from his icy presence.

This was the trap. This was the mistake of which Niles had warned her. It had nothing to do with Laurent Zai.

The Emperor wanted *her*, Nara Oxham. He had somehow learned of their relationship, their previous communication. He knew that she would warn Zai.

And, of course, he was right.

There was no choice but to walk into this trap, eyes open.

It was the only way to save her lover.

Captain

Laurent Zai stood at the extreme of the observation blister.

He looked up at the object, its shape ominously black this far from the Legis sun. It boiled like a dark cloud presaging a storm. According to the DA staff assigned to monitor its movements, it had grown gradually more active over the last few weeks. Its attempts to signal the *Lynx* had grown in number and subtlety: There were signs scrawled huge upon its surface, old codes flashed at obscure frequencies, cryptic phrases in local Legis dialects that somehow made their way into the ship's internal channels. It was all the *Lynx*'s AI could do to forestall the mind's attempts at communication. Finally, Zai had been forced to cut off all but the crudest level of sensor scrutiny of the object.

The *Lynx* had shut its ears. The Apparatus had demanded it.

Ever since the Rix prisoner had attempted to deliver Alexander's "message," His Majesty's Representatives had behaved as if they were victorious boarders on a captured enemy ship. Their watchful gaze seemed to penetrate every deck of the *Lynx*. It was all ExO Hobbes could do to track the various bugs that the Apparatus had placed in the ship's functions. This invasion of his ship appalled Zai, but he was powerless against the imperative of an Imperial writ, the scope of which seemed to expand daily.

Adept Trevim had sealed up the Rix prisoner's cell as tight as a tomb, and posted an Apparatus guard with her at all times. The Adept had also taken personal control over the *Lynx*'s external communications. Every outgoing message required her approval now. And, of course, Trevim had commanded that the frigate blind itself from any and all signs emanating from the object.

Of course, there were rumors. Some crew thought they knew what the Rix artifact was trying to say. But the stories were contradictory and absurd, just the chatter of a bored crew. ExO Hobbes had even detected a rumor that the suicide of Data Master Kax a few weeks ago had been related to a message from the object that he had deciphered. But the theory conveniently ignored the fact the man's immune system had rejected his artificial eyes; a lifelong data analyst, he had simply gone mad from blindness.

Zai touched the plastic membrane between himself and the void, feeling the cold on the other side. He wondered what weapon the object had offered him.

Then he pushed the disloyal thoughts aside, and turned to his more important business here.

A senatorial missive awaited his attention. From Nara Oxham, His Majesty's Representative from Vasthold. August and luminous, the message hovered against the blackness of space, its security icons slowly coiling around themselves like tree snakes crowding a branch.

He opened it.

Zai smiled as his lover's words appeared. He imagined her voice.

Laurent, it read, *I wish I could start tenderly. But instead I have to warn you of danger.*

Zai blinked his eyes, and shook his head at this beginning. All his life, he had been taught that warcraft brought meaning and order to existence, but this conflict with the Rix despoiled everything it touched.

He continued.

The ships sent to rendezvous with the Lynx *are governed by two sets of orders. The open dictate is to escort you here to Home in safety, but there is also an Imperial writ carried by a few officers. It can be triggered by a single word from the Emperor. If he gives the command, the task force is to destroy your ship and the war prize in a surprise attack.*

Laurent Zai straightened. It was just as the Rixwoman had said: The Emperor wanted to destroy him, the *Lynx,* and the object. The dead man's hunger for revenge was insatiable. What was he hiding?

Zai's anger quickly turned to concern, however. This was confidential intelligence data from outside the chain of command, from the War Council itself.

"What have you done, Nara?" he whispered, his heart sinking.

Supposedly, the Emperor will only invoke the writ if the object threatens the Empire. But I have felt . . . I know *that he intends to kill you all. I've been close to the Emperor since joining the council, and I can read him now.*

Of course, Nara had used her empathy on the man. As Zai continued, the realization dawned that Nara's ability had doomed her. She had broken the hundred-year rule.

He's terribly afraid of something, Laurent. Something that the Rix mind knows. Something that it discovered on Legis.

The words of his lover echoing those of the Rixwoman sent a chill through Zai.

He'll go to any length to prevent this knowledge from reaching the rest of the Empire, Laurent. I've seen it myself. He even pressed the War Council to approve a genocide. The Apparatus was ready to release a nuclear attack on Legis XV, with dirty weapons. They would have killed hundreds of millions just to destroy the compound mind.

Zai closed his eyes. If Nara was right, then the Rixwoman had told the truth.

He'll kill you, Laurent. The Emperor so fears the mind, he would destroy a world.

Laurent Zai nodded slowly, straightening as if a weight were lifting from him.

Take care, beloved. Return to me.

Captain Zai nodded again as the missive refolded itself, disappearing to a bright mote of synesthesia against the void. Suddenly, a wave of nausea struck him, and he had to reach out one hand to the blister's wall to hold himself upright. The plastic felt reassuringly solid and cold. Real.

Still, it was painful. The last shreds of Vadan loyalty were passing from him.

The Emperor had designed to destroy one of the Eighty Worlds.

Zai remembered the catechisms of his childhood. The old relationship between the Emperor and Vada had been formed after the Vadan Founders had fled their ruined previous home. *No killing of worlds,* the Compact read. And now the sovereign had broken it.

Through his nausea, Zai saw an icon blinking in the lower corner of Nara's folded message. One of Hobbes's telltales, indicating that this message had gone through the adept's hands.

"Damn," he whispered.

He'd assumed that the document was secure. It carried senatorial privilege, with the full protection of the Pale, but the adept's writ had somehow opened it.

Nara Oxham would be found out now. The Emperor would know that she had warned him. The final wave of nausea lasted only a few seconds, then Zai felt ready.

He took the slow, measured breaths of a Vadan warrior. He turned from the blackness of space and strode from the blister, glad to hear the ring of his boots on hard metal.

He was smiling.

Strange, that such danger should lighten his soul. But he felt sure and powerful for the first time in months: All his own shortcomings were buried now, overwhelmed by the crimes of his enemy: the Risen Emperor.

"Hobbes," he signaled.

"Captain?" She sounded half asleep.

"Meet me at Rana Harter's cabin."

"Sir?"

"In five minutes. Bring your weapon."

Executive Officer

Katherie Hobbes fastened the seals of her tunic as she ran.

She stopped around the corner from her goal, and checked the time. She had fifty seconds left. Her eyes scanned the black wool of her uniform, checking for imperfections. She pulled up one sleeve to reveal the flechette pistol. Its ammo meter read full, but Hobbes popped the cover to check the needles with her own eyes.

The darts were nestled in their twin magazines, as perfectly aligned as two ranks of tiny metal soldiers.

She walked briskly and calmly around the corner. Zai awaited her with a grim expression.

"Captain, what is it?"

"We've been betrayed, Hobbes."

Mutiny again? She took a deep breath against panic, drew her pistol.

"Not by our crew, Hobbes," her captain said.

She blinked. What was he saying?

"Just hand me that." He pointed at the pistol.

What? she thought. The captain could draw his own weapon from stores. But of course that would raise any number of flags with the politicals aboard the ship.

Hobbes handed him the weapon silently.

The captain held the flechette pistol behind his back and opened the door to the dead woman's cabin. Light spilled between Hobbes and Zai into Rana Harter's dim antechamber. The dead Adept Trevim herself was here, kneeling with her back to them, her hands working gestural commands.

"Forgive me, Honored Mother," Zai said.

He shot Trevim with a spray of needles, cutting an X across her heart.

Hobbes gasped, her knees week. This must be a dream, she thought.

"Her symbiant should rise from that," Zai said.

He turned to Hobbes.

"What was she doing?" he demanded.

Hobbes forced herself to concentrate, probing the *Lynx*'s diagnostics. The adept's actions were officially hidden from Navy AI, but there were always indirect signs. The translight grid was cycling out of a transmission.

"It looks as if she sent a message, sir."

"Did I interrupt her?"

Hobbes shook her head. "It's stepping down in an orderly way, Captain. She was finished, and the main entanglement grid shows depletion."

"Home," he said.

She nodded.

"Damn. Shut it down, Hobbes. The whole grid—cut its power."

She swallowed, and signaled the com staff to perform the task. This was one trump card the captain held. The Apparatus might have a writ of authority, but the crew of the *Lynx* could still disable the frigate's components by hand.

The captain opened the inner door of the antechamber, holding the pistol ready.

"Rana Harter," he called.

Was Zai going to murder the woman? Hobbes wondered. The Adept would reanimate easily from her heart wound, but a shot like that to the head could destroy a risen permanently.

The dead woman stepped from the darkness, blinking in the light. She was small, her hair shorn like the Rixwoman's. Though she was shorter than the commando, Hobbes could see how their faces were alike. The Legis authorities believed that Rana had been chosen from the militia's population for her resemblance to Herd, and perhaps for a savant ability to process chaotic data. Hobbes wondered to what uses the compound mind had put Rana's intellect, and what traces captivity had left in the dead woman before her.

"Please come with me, Honored One," Zai said.

Harter nodded quiescently. She had none of the usual hauteur of the dead. Laurent Zai went ahead, with Rana after him. Hobbes brought up the rear, reminding herself that this was real.

They reached the Rixwoman's cell in a few minutes. The gunfire and Adept Trevim's medical monitors had triggered various alarms aboard the ship, but Hobbes had managed to suppress them as far as she knew.

There was a single marine guard, not the familiar Bassiritz, and one of the lower-ranking politicals on station. The man was living, and Captain Zai shot him in the leg, and kicked him in the head as he fell. The aspirant dropped to the floor unconscious.

Zai sternly ordered the startled guard to return to attention.

The private froze in shock for a moment, then obeyed as crisply as if at parade drill. Zai's tone of command was stronger than Hobbes had heard it in some time. The sound thrilled her, however bizarre these proceedings.

Her fingers flickered, moving to quell the new alarms. The remaining politicals must already know that something was happening.

"Shall I get a fire team up here, Captain?"

"Good idea, Hobbes. That fast private, for one."

She nodded, sent commands.

"Secure this area, Private," she ordered the motionless marine.

Hobbes opened the cell, turning the screwlock and bracing one leg to pull out the massive door.

Zai moved to enter first.

"The shock collar remote, sir," she called.

"We won't need it."

Hobbes followed him closely, wishing that she had another weapon. Straightjacket or no, the Rix commando could probably kill them both easily. She doubted that a half-expended clip of flechettes would even marginally slow down a Rix soldier.

The prisoner stared at them coolly, a hungry look in her eyes. Hobbes felt naked under her hunter's gaze.

But then Rana Harter followed them through the door, and for a moment Herd seemed utterly human.

"Rana!" she said, stepping forward.

The dead woman walked toward her former captor and lover. The Rixwoman was in for a disappointment, Hobbes thought. The honored dead never held fast to the emotional bonds of their former lives. The transition of the symbiant left them altogether indifferent to the prattle of the living. Hobbes had encountered many of her dead shipmates after their reanimation; they were no longer friends, or even crewmates. Just passengers.

But Rana Harter looked tenderly at the Rixwoman, and smiled.

The expression startled Hobbes; it looked exaggerated on that cold, gray face, like a clown's painted joy. The dead woman embraced Herd, wrapping her arms around the hypercarbon straightjacket, and the two kissed as unselfconsciously as adolescents on a Utopian world. The captain and Hobbes just watched, too surprised and respectful of the dead to interrupt.

Finally they separated, pulling apart to gaze into each other's eyes.

"Rana," murmured Herd quietly.

The dead woman spoke in return. Hobbes recognized the buzzing syllables of Rix battle language in her speech.

"Preserve us," she murmured. A risen woman, one of the honored dead of the Empire, speaking Rix. What had Rana Harter become?

"Herd," Captain Zai said in a level voice. "I've come for information."

The commando kissed Rana Harter once more before answering, and whispered at the edge of Hobbes's hearing, "Your lips are as cold as mine now."

Katherie swallowed, wondering again if this was a dream.

Herd turned from her lover and looked at Captain Zai.

"So you want to hear the Emperor's Secret now?"

He nodded, then said, "I will hear it," with the measured formality of an oath in military court.

Herd cocked her head, as if listening to some internal voice. Then she smiled, a predatory expression that chilled Hobbes's soul.

"It will not make you happy, Vadan."

Zai met her gaze without flinching. He reached back and pulled the door shut behind them. With the heavy metal in place, even the inescapable hum of the ship was silenced.

They were absolutely cut off from the rest of the *Lynx* now.

"Tell us," Zai said.

The Rixwoman took a breath, then she began.

"Your Empress was killed not by us, but by the Apparatus."

"Of course," whispered Hobbes to herself. The records of the battle had suggested as much. The Emperor was a murderer.

"But that fact is not the secret that concerns you, Zai," Herd added. "Alexander was inside the Empress before she died, through the agency of a machine that was within her body."

"The confidant," Captain Zai said.

"Exactly. Alexander took control of this machine, like every other on Legis, and could see inside the Empress. Alexander saw something."

As the commando went on, her flat voice became almost singsong, as if she were telling a children's tale. She leaned her head against Rana Harter's shoulder, and the dead woman stroked Herd's bound arms.

The story took fifteen slow minutes.

Hobbes had known that her bond to the gray world was broken—by the false Error of Blood, by the *Lynx*'s travails, and now finally by Zai's inescapable treasons—but the Rixwoman's words were something altogether different. They left her captain retching on the floor, unraveled centuries of the history she had been taught, and tore Hobbes's last convictions from her like a swallowed hook dragged from a fish's gut.

And after that, everything was different.

Senator

Awaiting the closure of the Emperor's trap, Nara Oxham was very careful.

She knew instinctively that it was only a matter of time before the Apparatus uncovered her communication with Zai. Perhaps they already had, and were merely waiting for an opportune moment to move against her. After a few nervous nights at home, she decided to sleep in her office, remaining within the safety of the Rubicon Pale. As a rule, a senator could not disappear suddenly without explanation, but a case of wartime treason might convince the Apparatus that it could make an exception.

When the trap closed, it did so quickly.

The news swept through the capital's infostructure quickly, a fire rampant in pure oxygen. It started as a newsfeed rumor, well traveled but patently incredible. Then supporting evidence was released: images of Oxham and Zai meeting at the Emperor's party ten years ago; the repeater path of her first message to him; a time line of the War Council's agenda, the debates for which the hundred-year rule had been invoked covered with a broad swath of black. And finally her voice, dictating the first few words of her warning to Zai—this last synthesized for dramatic effect.

Across the wee hours of morning, the treason of Senator Nara Oxham moved from the back pages of gossips and conspiracy theorists to blaring headlines crawling the periphery of every channel of second sight.

The newsfeeds were forbidden even to speculate about what secrets the Senator had revealed to her warrior lover, but the hundred-year rule itself bore the weight of proof: This young and headstrong senator had betrayed the Emperor's trust.

The morning that the story broke, the psychic frenzy itself awoke her, the growing fury of the city bleeding into her head like a wake-up alarm invading a sleeper's dreams. For a moment of unprotected madness, Nara could see the bloated body of the capital convulsing, the beached whale shaking off carrion birds with some grotesque, after-death spasm. And before wheeling back to feast on the war economy, the scavengers swirled toward a new target.

The treasonous senator: live prey.

The empathic vision waned in power. Senator Oxham could feel her own body, and a hand at her wrist: someone adjusting her apathy bracelet. She opened her eyes, furious at this presumption. It was a grim-faced Roger Niles kneeling next to her.

She blinked once.

The dose was strong, and Oxham's mind became coherent in seconds. She instantly understood what had happened; she'd been expecting it. This was the trap the Emperor had set. She had walked into it full knowing.

"What have you done, Nara?" Niles asked.

Oxham put both hands to her face, rubbing it to confirm the reality of her body. She pulled herself up into a seated position. Her back ached in the particular way that always resulted from sleeping on her office couch.

"I can't tell you much about it, Roger. The hundred-year rule."

He scowled. "*Now* you want to obey the law?"

"I had to tell Laurent what the Emperor planned. I knew they'd catch me, but I had to save him. That's all I can say."

"They're calling for your blood, Nara."

"I know, Roger. I can hear them."

She gestured to bring up second sight. Synesthesia confirmed what Roger Niles and empathy had told her. The story choked every newsfeed. She flipped across a few channels: her voice and picture, the text of a useless Apparatus warrant for her arrest, a Loyalist spokesperson demanding her expulsion from the Senate.

Expulsion was the crux of the matter, she realized. Stripped of senatorial privilege, Nara Oxham would be just another citizen. Just another traitor with no Pale to protect her.

"I warned you, Nara. Why didn't you listen?"

"Can they throw me out, Roger?"

"Of the Senate? There's precedent, but it hasn't been done for a hundred and fifty years."

"What was the reason back then?"

Niles blinked, his fingers twitching. "Murder. A Utopian killed her lover. Strangled him in bed."

Oxham smiled wanly. She, at least, had broken the law to save a lover, not kill one.

"That's far more dramatic," she said.

"But it wasn't even a crime against the state," Niles said. " 'Conduct unbecoming' was the phrase employed in the writ of expulsion. A lesser charge than treason, I dare say."

"How long did it take?" she asked.

"Forty-seven days. They held a trial before the full Senate. Witnesses, defense counsel, even a psychologist."

"And then they expelled her."

Niles nodded. "And with her privilege gone, a civilian court found her guilty of murder in a second trial. Loss of elevation, life internment."

"Better than exsanguination."

"God, Nara," Niles said, his voice breaking. "Did you actually do it? Reveal War Council secrets to Zai?"

"I did. To save him."

"There must be an exception for military exigency."

She shook her head. "There's no way out of it, Roger. It was pure treason: my lover over my sovereign. I made a choice."

Niles was silent for a moment, going into a data fugue. He stood over her, hands flexing as he tried to discover some exception to the hundred-year rule, his entire body flinching with the effort. He looked like a handeye gamer trying to escape some virtual maze, his face showing frustration at every roadblock and dead end.

Nara drifted back into second-sight newsfeeds. One showed a crowd gathered at the edge of the Pale, a Loyalist mob demanding that Oxham abdicate her privilege immediately and face a Court Imperial. Now that she was its target, the Loyalists' wonted righteous anger seemed less comical. On another feed was the Secularist Party whip, a young man who had replaced her after she'd been promoted to the War Council. He was calling for calm, stalling, trying to slow down the pace of events without appearing to support rank treason. She didn't envy him the job.

In the midst of this maelstrom, Nara felt oddly peaceful. The usual players of political drama—the political parties, the Apparatus's propaganda machine, the newsfeed hacks—had jumped into motion in the usual way, jostling for advantage, working damage control. She could feel the shifting ground in this contest for power, the tug of every carefully chosen word, every deliberately sculpted reading of Imperial law and Senate tradition. But at the center of this chaos was one immovable point: the rightness of her own choice.

Nara Oxham felt purified by treason. After all her compromises, she had finally done something for a simple, unalloyed reason, no matter what the cost.

"I'm free, Roger."

His eyes snapped open. "What?"

"We can't fight the Emperor with pragmatism forever."

Niles shook his head hard; a few gray hairs jutted out as a result. His features seemed to be aging by the minute.

"This was not the time, Nara. There's a *war* on."

She understood his point. The Emperor was always at the peak of his power when defending the realm. But the argument cut both ways; at its peak was when power was most often abused.

"I'm going to tell the whole Risen Empire what I told Zai," she said. "The Emperor's plans for Legis."

Niles looked down at her in despair.

"They'll kill you," he whispered.

"Let them."

"Use whatever you know as leverage to bargain your way out."

She shook her head. There would be no escape for her, the Emperor would make sure of that.

"Nara, they'll drain your blood out, drop by drop."

"Not before I turn a generation against him."

Niles swallowed. He was still looking, she knew, for a way out of this. Senator Oxham suddenly saw her old counselor's greatest limitation. However pure his hatred for the dead, Niles had always fought them cautiously, slowly laying his plans against them. He had no taste for drama.

"How old are you, Roger?"

"Damn old," he said. "Old enough to know how to stay alive."

"That's your problem. War requires sacrifice, sometimes."

"You're talking about suicide, Nara."

She nodded. "That's correct, Roger. A just and well-considered suicide."

Her counselor sat down next to her, deflated. She was shocked to see tears on his face.

"I spent three decades bringing you here, Senator," he said, and sobbed once.

"I know."

"And this is how you repay me?"

After a moment's silence, she knew the answer. "Yes. Absolutely."

They were quiet for a while. Oxham shut off her second sight, quenching the flow of opinion and grandstanding, the headlong rush to committees, hearings, and judgement, all the unwieldy maneuvers of a legislature turning on one of its own. The rising sun lanced into the crystals that had been carefully moved here from Niles's old office. Like a tree of tiny mirrors, they dappled the walls with a glimmering pattern.

Nara Oxham listened to Niles's labored breathing, and wished she could spare him this. She still needed his counsel. She hoped he wouldn't give up on her.

As if hearing her thoughts, the old man spread his hands and said, "What do you want me to do, Senator?"

She took hold of his arm.

"Delay them for a while. Then agree to a trial. No witnesses to testify for me except myself. With the broadest possible public newsfeed."

He frowned, concentration replacing despair on his face.

"They'll try to silence you, Senator. Secrets of the Realm."

"They can't sequester the whole Senate, Roger. And no lesser body can vote to expel me."

His eyes narrowed. Now that his mind had something to chew on, a sparkle grew in them.

"I suppose not, Senator."

"And I have the right to speak at my own trial."

He nodded. "Of course. Even the hundred-year rule doesn't stand against privilege. They can't truly silence you until *after* the Senate has expelled you officially."

"Now that I've chosen death, my options multiply," she said.

Nara considered her own words. She could appear at the edge of the Pale right now and address the hovering cameras of the newsfeeds, telling them what the Emperor had planned to do on Legis. But the newsfeeds would be bound by the hundred-year rule. Her only shot at revealing the sovereign's plan would be before the Senate.

"I'll wait for the trial to say my piece, when the whole Empire is watching."

"The Apparatus will bury your words."

Nara looked at Niles, and nodded. "Then we'll have to devise a backup plan. A way to publicize the speech if I'm silenced. Something a bit illegal, like we used to spread rumors back on Vasthold."

"It won't be so easy here on Home. The networks are all Apparatus controlled."

She thought for a moment. "I think I know a way to get around the Apparatus. Something I've been saving for a rainy day."

Niles looked puzzled, then a forced smile broke through the heavy cast of his features. "Well, at least I've drummed some little bit of pragmatism into you, Senator."

"Tactics, Niles," she corrected. "Let them hear me, and the Emperor will wish he'd died the true death a thousand years ago."

Adept

"I need to send a message," Zai repeated.

Adept Harper Trevim looked at him, trying to pull her mind into the frantic, empty time of the living. It was so much easier to stare at the walls. Even the flat gray of hypercarbon, so bland compared to sensuous black, was rich and compelling here in the fugue of ongoing reanimation.

Trevim's symbiant still labored to bring her back to full animation. Her new heart was not yet whole; the supple cells of the Other were doing much of the work, filling in for the tricuspid and mitral valves. Zai's attack had not damaged her brain, but her lungs and spine had been torn mercilessly by his flechettes.

The adept was barely alive. When she closed her eyes, the darkness behind them was lit by the red horizon, that first sight of the risen.

Trevim forced herself to look at the man, and through the haze of her fugue she managed to scowl at Zai.

"Leave me alone, Captain. You shoot my heart out, and then expect me to commit treason to repay you?"

"The only treason here is the Emperor's," Zai said.

The words caused a start from Trevim, bringing the living world into sudden focus.

"Blasphemy," she spat. "You'll suffer for this, Zai. The tortures you felt on Dhantu will be nothing compared to the Emperor's revenge."

"Adept, I need to send a message. Only you can authorize it." Zai spoke as if to an unruly child, repeating his demand with the calm insistence of the rational adult.

"Your crew will join you in your agonies, Zai," she said.

Anger crossed his face, and Trevim felt distant amusement. He dared to treat an adept of the Apparatus, who had lived four hundred subjective years, as a child? Even if Zai destroyed her, gave her final darkness, she was one of the honored dead. She would not be frightened or manipulated.

His crew. That was Zai's weakness. He had dragged them all into this mutiny with him.

"The Apparatus will pull them to pieces, Zai. One by one, before your eyes and their families'. Traitors all."

The man took a deep breath, then cocked his head and smiled softly.

"I know the Emperor's Secret."

A jolt passed through Trevim. Revulsion clenched every muscle in her body. She shook her head reflexively. Zai didn't know. He simply *couldn't*. The Secret was too tightly bound within the world of the Apparatus; an uninitiated man—and a *living* one—could never have discovered it.

"No," the adept managed.

"The Rix prisoner explained it to me."

The words sent another shock through Trevim, a violent seizure that threatened the functioning of her half-repaired heart. A wash of physical, biological pain, something she hadn't felt in decades, coursed down her left arm.

Trevim whimpered a little. The Other tried to calm her, but the Apparatus conditioning was an implacable force, a hurricane that raged inside her very cells. These reactions had been laid down like mineral strata over centuries of service to the crown, the ultimate stopgap to prevent a member of the Apparatus from revealing the Secret.

But now the pain was being used against her.

Trevim swallowed, and forced herself to believe her next words.

"You are bluffing, Zai. You know nothing."

"The dead are dying, Adept Trevim."

"Silence!" she shrieked, her vision disintegrating into a cloud of red. She felt a hideous movement inside. For a moment, the Other seemed to retreat from her, its tendrils shrinking from the violent reaction.

Adept Trevim understood vaguely the raw science behind the miracle of the symbiant. The Other's ability to heal and sustain required absolute acquiescence from the body. The calm remove of the honored dead was a means to keep the body and mind from rejecting the life-sustaining ministrations of the symbiant. The tranquillity of the immortals was not merely a spiritual benefit; it was a necessary state. But Trevim's Apparatus conditioning warred with her deathly calm, threatening the mesh of body and Other.

Zai's words could literally tear her in half.

"Silence," she pleaded, gasping.

"Just relinquish the writ, Trevim. Release the writ that binds the communications grid."

An action icon hovered before Trevim in second sight. All she had to do was make the sign, and Zai would have his access. He could send a message to Home.

An act of treason.

"No," Trevim said.

"The dead are dying, Adept. Since the beginning."

The pain screamed through her again. And worse than the physical agony was the feeling of the Other pulling away, shying from her body's convulsions. Her heart shuddered, almost failing in her chest.

"You're killing me, Zai."

"Die, then," the man said.

He went on, calmly detailing what the Rix had revealed to him.

Adept Trevim fought to control herself, to withstand the pain, to resist the pleas of the Other to return things to calm. Once, she saw her hand reach out, about to make the gestural sign that would give Zai what he wanted. But she managed to hold herself back. Then his words continued, and the wrenching punishment of the war inside her resumed.

Before her will could crumble, Trevim's half-rebuilt heart stuttered, striking once like a hammer blow in her chest before failing, and the Other abandoned her to oblivion.

For a moment, the adept thought she'd won. Her mind began to fade. But horribly, the victory of death calmed her, and the Other returned, working its relentless miracle to begin repairs again. Trevim knew even as consciousness slipped away that she would reanimate to face these tortures again and again. The symbiant was too powerful, too indomitable and perfect, and her centuries-long conditioning was equally immovable. As she died, Trevim realized that her will, caught between these two indomitable forces, would eventually be destroyed.

Sooner or later, she would relent to Zai.

Senator

Rarely had she seen the Senate so full.

Many planets, Vasthold among them, had only a single senator in the Forum. Winner-take-all, it was called. But the majority of the Eighty Worlds sent delegations, proportional representations of their constituencies. The voting strength of each world was weighted according to its taxed economic output, and senators from planets with many representatives subdivided their world's votes. The system had been carefully honed to achieve balance over the centuries, but it made for complex vote tabulation. It also led to a crowded Great Hall on those rare occasions when every senator was present.

They were all here now, to try Nara Oxham for treason.

The Great Forum was a huge, pyramidal hole cut into the granite foundation that underlày the capital. Plaster poured into the empty space would have cast a flat-topped pyramid with steps up its four sides. Each of the major parties claimed one of the triangular staircases, with their leadership clustered at the point down close to the center, and their rank and file arrayed across the wider rows farther up.

The President of the Senate was seated on the Low Dais, a circular riser of marble in the center of the Great Forum's pit. Senator Oxham had seen the old man, Puram Drexler of Fatawa, seated on the ceremonial dais only once before, when he had given her the oath of office. It was strange to think that in a few days, she might be stripped of that office and condemned to death after the votes were counted aloud by the same man.

The Great Forum was lit today with a sharp, unreal light that left no shadows against the gray granite floor. That was for the newseyes, which lined the high lip of the Forum. Senator Oxham allowed herself a moment of second sight, checking the viewership. On Home, the numbers were staggering: Eighty percent of the populace was watching. Even in the antipodal cities, spread from midnight to the early morning hours, a majority were tuned in. Niles had told her that a low-grade translight feed was headed out live through the

Imperial entanglement repeater network, and a high-grade recording of this trial would eventually reach every world in the Eighty. The Emperor had never turned Laurent Zai into the martyr he'd wanted, but at least now he had a villain for his war.

The Apparatus had done everything possible to inflate viewership of the Oxham trial. Evidently, they were not afraid of her words.

She would be allowed to speak in her own defense. Senate President Puram Drexler had insisted on the fullest possible interpretation of the tradition of senatorial privilege, turning back the arguments from his own party about the security of the Realm. But even privilege didn't stand up to the hundred-year rule, so a compromise had been forged. Puram held a cut-off switch, in case Oxham mentioned the Emperor's genocide. The shock collar around her throat reminded Nara to watch her words.

Drexler looked a bit pale, there on the Dais. The Apparatus must have briefed him about the nuclear attack the Emperor had proposed, so that Drexler would know when to censor her. Oxham was sure that he had taken deep umbrage at this breach of the Compact, but however much the Emperor's plans had shaken him, Drexler's politics were as gray as the stone of the Great Forum. He would silence her if she hinted at the forbidden subject. Oxham realized ruefully that the pink political parties hadn't contested Drexler's position in decades, considering the presidency to be nothing more than a figurehead. But now the man held her life in his hand.

Roger Niles had shaken his head when these terms had been explained in the second week of preparation for the trial.

"We're finished," he'd said. "If you can't tell them about Legis, it's pointless. Give up and beg for mercy."

"Don't worry, Niles," she had answered. "I've got other secrets to tell." Her counselor had raised his eyebrows at this, but she dared not say more.

The Emperor didn't know about the latest transmission she had received from Laurent, hidden alongside a political report from one Adept Harper Trevim. A Rix prisoner had revealed what the compound mind had learned on Legis: the truth behind the hostage rescue, the symbiant, the Empire itself. The Emperor's Secret was hers.

It didn't matter that Nara Oxham couldn't speak of genocide. She had a better story now. The Apparatus had locked the wrong door.

Senator Drexler opened the trial. He wrapped his withered right hand around the staff of his office, and struck its metal tip against the floor. The sound was amplified, and echoes skittered around the hard stone of the Forum.

"Order," he said. His voice rasped like gravel.

The Great Forum became silent.

"We are here in a matter of blood. A matter of treason."

Nara had left a newsfeed translucent in her second sight, and her own face zoomed up to fill her vision, some distant camera searching for her reaction. She had the disembodied feel of seeing herself in a synesthesia mirror. She blinked the feed away, and reminded herself to stay in the real world. Even her prepared speech was memorized; she wanted no text prompts cluttering her primary sight.

Nara needed to watch the faces of the Senate, rather than worry about how this was playing in the feeds. If she couldn't win her fellow solons over, the impressions of the popular audience could hardly save her.

"Who is the accuser?" Drexler said.

A dead woman rose from the Loyalist benches. A prelate. The Senate had given her special permission to cross the Pale, the first representative of the Apparatus ever to do so.

"The Emperor Himself," she said. "With me as His agent."

"And who is the accused?"

"His Majesty's Representative from Vasthold, Senator Nara Oxham." The dead woman pointed as she said the words.

Nara's felt a surge of emotion in the room, and her fingers went to her apathy bracelet automatically. But she forced her hands to her side again. She had already precisely adjusted her empathy. The capital hovered over her, a volatile presence focused on every word spoken here, but its emotions were in check. After weeks of furious calls for immediate revenge, the solemn ritual of a trial had focused the mob into a respectful audience. The people of the capital had long been trained to revere tradition.

The Senate's guard-at-arms strode up to Senator Oxham now. The young man was the only person allowed to carry weapons in the Forum. This was another position Nara has always thought honorary, but which had become suddenly very real.

The man took her arm.

"This one?" the guard asked the prelate.

"Yes."

The guard-at-arms released her, but stayed close, as if Nara might try to run.

"Who will speak in defense of the accused?"

Drexler asked, his eyes sweeping the whole of the Senate, daring them to stand against the Emperor.

"I will speak for myself," Nara said. Her own words seemed disembodied, a result of both amplification and the incredible situation. It was hard for Oxham to believe that was she speaking to hundreds of billions, and to history, and that her own life depended on her words.

"Then let this Honorable Senate begin to hear the accusation," Drexler said, and sat on his chair of stone.

The dead prelate rose again, and walked to the fore of the Dais.

"President, Senators, citizens," she began. "The Emperor has been betrayed."

The trial had begun.

The prelate went on, as sonorous and repetitive as prayer. The ritual phrases rolled over Nara, all the words of blood oaths and bloody payment for broken promises. The war against death, and of the Emperor's great gift of immortality, all made its suffocating way into the prelate's narrative. Every iota of childhood conditioning was triggered, until even Senator Nara Oxham found herself appalled at what she had done. How dare she break faith with the man who had bested the Old Enemy death?

She steeled herself. Let them play all their cards now. Let them invoke every ancient superstition. The Emperor would fall all the harder when his secret was revealed.

"This woman was called to give the Emperor counsel in time of war."

Finally, the real charges.

"And having taken an oath of secrecy," the prelate continued, "she betrayed the Emperor's War Council.

She broke the duly invoked hundred-year rule. Nara Oxham turned traitor."

The proof came next. The Great Forum darkened, and the airscreen above the Low Dais came alive. Puram Drexler would have had to crane his ancient neck to see, so instead he stared out at the audience like an alert teacher whose class was watching a synesthesia lesson.

The Senate listened in solemn silence, although these facts and images had been broadcast throughout the Empire for the last two weeks. In the newsfeeds, of course, each piece of evidence had been reduced by repetition to a single signifier: an image of her and Zai at the party, a few words of warning in her voice, a long shot of the palace's east wing where the War Council met. But here in the Senate, the scale was stretched in the opposite direction. Time slowed to a crawl. Each mark the Oxham/Zai affair had left on the public record now consumed long minutes of explanation. Their first conversation was studied frame by frame like a crime caught fleetingly on a security camera; ten years of short missives were read aloud in the dead prelate's dolorous cadence; quietly made plans were revealed with dramatic flourishes, as if their love had been a conspiracy from the start.

The last few messages between Oxham and the *Lynx* were read out, having been stripped of privilege by an overwhelming Senate vote a few days ago. Her single-word message, *Don't,* was associated with Zai's refusal of the blade of error. It was all edited in the name of security, and slanted to make her the aggressor in the relationship. Nara was glad that they weren't going after Laurent. Over the last two weeks, the Apparatus had walked a fine line with the hero Zai. His propa-

ganda image had been weakened, but not destroyed—
he was now a once-strong Imperial warrior weakened
by the influence of a scheming woman.

Thankfully, Laurent's final message to her was absent from the evidence. Zai's subterfuge had worked.
They still didn't know that Nara Oxham had the Emperor's real secret in hand.

The litany went on, slipping into irrelevancies toward the end. Oxham's antiwar bill, the one with-
drawn before she'd taken a seat on the council, was
revealed. Her old votes in the Senate were isolated and
given new significance; the accuser even found sinister
components in acts that had passed the legislature
unanimously.

And this was simply the opening statement. This
slow crawl was the merest outline. The Emperor's accuser apparently planned to present an insuperable
mountain of detail over the days ahead. The two hundred minutes of the accusation, half the first day of
trial, seemed like years.

Finally, Nara Oxham was called to make her own
opening statement.

The Senate President held up his cut-off switch and
warned her before she began.

"The secrets of the Realm are sacred, Senator Oxham. Do not attempt to reveal them here in the Great
Forum."

"I won't, President Drexler." Of course, the old
solon had only been briefed about the Emperor's
planned genocide, the issue covered by the hundred-
year rule. If Laurent was right, the real secret, the one
His Majesty had been willing to murder those millions
to protect, was unknown to any person, living or dead,
outside the conditioned drones of the Apparatus.

According to the Rix mind's story, even the Apparatus could not to speak of that secret. It brought them pain to hear it mentioned.

She hoped that part of the tale was true.

Nara finally understood why the Empire was built on fear and bribes, on intimidation and loyalty conditioning, on the superstitious babble of some pretechnology mystery cult.

It was all because the Empire was built on a lie.

She turned to the Senate, prepared to undo it all.

For a moment Nara couldn't speak. The weight of the Empire's attention was too suffocating. She feared for a moment that she herself might be conditioned, bound from uttering the words by some deeply buried imperative. But she breathed deeply, lightly touched her bracelet for luck, and let the fear pass. Her anxiety was simply anticipation of how this speech would feel empathetically; she was about to take a wild and dangerous ride on the nervous animal that was the Empire.

"President, Senate, citizens," she said. "The dead are dying."

A small cry escaped from the prelate's lips, but there was no other sound in the Great Forum. Drexler hadn't cut her off, she noted with a final touch of relief. Laurent was right: Even the oldest Loyalists didn't know.

"We were made a promise," she continued. "We were told that the Old Enemy had been defeated, that in service to the Emperor we could live forever. But the dead are dying. All of them."

A murmur came from the audience, and Nara felt a *snap* in her empathy, a sudden disconnect. The rapt attention of the capital city above her had tumbled into confusion.

So soon? she wondered.

A quick check in second sight confirmed that the newsfeeds had gone dark. The Apparatus had cut her off already.

Plagueman

"Are you well?"

The representative of the Plague Axis looked down at his valet/minder. The young initiate had suddenly fallen to the floor, clutching her stomach, a retching noise coming through the speaker of her protective suit. The plagueman knelt and reflexively checked the suit diagnostics across the bottom of her visor.

They read green. He hadn't infected the young dead woman with anything. And certainly the symbiant would have protected her from any disease for days at least. "Can I—"

"Turn it off!" The initiate flailed at the hardscreen upon which they had been watching the trial.

The request puzzled the plagueman, but he turned to mute the wall-sized image of Nara Oxham. Before he could gesture, however, the embattled senator's face was replaced by a slowly spinning shield, the emblem of the Apparatus media censors. The feed from the Great Forum had been silenced at the source.

The initiate's retching noises stopped. She put her

hands to her head and groaned the same words several times. "She knows."

The plagueman wished that he could see the initiate's face through her biosuit visor. Here in his own sealed quarters, he wore his usual clothes, and visitors donned anti-contamination suits. The reflective visor over the suffering aspirant's face brought home to him again how dehumanized he must appear when he wore his own suit, how anonymous he was here in the monoculture.

He didn't need to see the woman's face, however, to know she wasn't well, not well at all. That she was one of the risen made her seizure even more alarming.

In synesthesia, he called for the other initiate who shared her minder's duties. There was no response, not even the polite regrets of a busy or sleeping recipient. Just repeated queries that went unheeded. He made calls to the other palace staff he had dealt with, but none of the Apparatus was answering.

Had they *all* been stricken? The plagueman knew that disease could spread with incredible rapidity here in the monoculture, one of the many weaknesses of these half-people, but such suddenness and simultaneity seemed more like a biological attack than a contagion.

He blinked and looked at the media censor emblem still on the screen. The image had cut off so suddenly, very unlike the Apparatus's usual interventions. He had seen them fade out a newsfeed's audio when necessary, breaking in to interrupt a live interview with a spurious weather emergency or war bulletin. But the Apparatus rarely silenced its opponents so crudely as this. The synesthesia newsfeeds were still down, all of them, and even the gossip channels were blank.

What had Oxham been saying before the initiate had collapsed?

"The dead are dying," the plagueman repeated softly.

"Don't!" the young dead woman pleaded, sinking back to the floor. "I can't stand it."

The plagueman rose. "I think you need help," he said. The plagueman quickly put on his biosuit, taking particular care with its fittings in case this *was* an attack, and gestured for the room to open. The triple-doored airlock began its familiar sequence of hissing noises.

Out in the halls of the Diamond Palace, he immediately encountered another stricken member of the Apparatus, an initiate rising slowly to his feet. The optics in the biosuit visor revealed that his skin was far colder than even a dead man's should be.

"Do you know what's happening?" the plagueman asked.

"She has the Secret," the man said hoarsely, reaching out a shaking hand. "She's telling."

A squadron of the House Guard ran past, live soldiers in full battle armor. They looked unaffected by the strange contagion, and ignored both initiate and Axis representative. Apparently, it wasn't a biological agent, or perhaps the living were immune.

The Axis representative turned to the initiate again, but a chime sounded in his secondary hearing. Perhaps synesthesia was clearing up, he thought with relief. But then he recognized the tone.

The War Council had been summoned.

The plagueman made toward the council chamber, amazed as he shuffled his slow way at the pandemonium that reigned in the usually solemn Diamond Palace. Normal staff seemed physically healthy though panicked, the Apparatus were uniformly paralyzed, and still more soldiers passed in full battle dress. He wondered if the capital had been attacked in some new and strange way, and if there were more assaults yet to come.

House

In the southern reaches, the house of Senator Nara Oxham became alert.

It had been pleasurable for the house to watch its mistress on the news these last few weeks. She was here at home so little since the war had started. But now her image had been cut off during her speech, quite suddenly, and without explanation.

Fortunately, the mistress had left strict instructions about what to do in this situation. She had even invoked privilege: The house was to use maximum initiative, ignoring regulations, sparing no expense to carry out these orders. The house had been a trifle amused at the mistress's urgent tone. It had been employing its own initiative for decades now.

First, the house located the special file in its copious memory. It was a tiny thing, only a few thousand bytes of data, stored with the marvelous efficiency of pure text. The house copied this file across its memory, filling every spare nook and cranny with duplicate after duplicate. Over the last century, the house had expanded its mind deep into the mountain on which it stood, to backups in rented space at hundreds of cheap data farms on Home's twelve continents, and into nanocircuitry spread across the snowy tundra surrounding the vast estate. Enough room for quadrillions of copies of the little file.

The house was pleased with this first phase. Even if Home was subjected to a massive nuclear attack, Imperial civilization reduced to glowing ruins, it would be overwhelmingly likely that some future data archaeologist would run across a copy of the file, somewhere.

But there was more to the owner's wishes.

The house sent copies of the file—it was the complete text of the speech she had just been giving, the house noticed—to every newsfeed professional on the planet, the messages emanating from thousands of fictitious addresses, bombarding the media with the persistence of a huge mailing campaign. Then the house began calling every possible handphone number on Home in numerical order, and reading the speech to whomever answered and would listen.

The mirror fields with which the house warmed its surface gardens were put to use, blinking the file in antique on-off codes to passing aircraft. An old hardline to its original architects was reactivated, and the blueprint plotters in the firm's offices worldwide began spouting the senator's speech.

With these processes underway, the house fired its missiles.

The house was quite proud of the modifications it had made to the emergency message rockets. They were to be used in case of communication loss, should a guest require vital medical attention during a storm or com blackout. They were small suborbitals, armed with low-band transmitters, useful for lofting above the weather to shout an SOS in a quick burst. The house had increased their range, improving the fuel and adding variable geometry wings that could keep them hopping atop the atmosphere for hours. They blazed into the cold, clear summer sky and headed for the nearest large cities, ready to transmit the speech on the reserved frequencies of weather pagers, burglar alarms, and taxi radios.

The house watched its preparations unfold with humble pleasure. Mistress Oxham should be happy. It had carried out her request with considerable creativity. In a few minutes, the planetary infostructure would be saturated with this tiny document.

With the messaging well underway, the house turned happily to its next project. The snowmelt waterfall that was the principal attraction of the west garden needed reining in.

With the spring thaws, it had become far too noisy.

Senator

Nara Oxham gathered her thoughts. She had only the Senate for an audience now. They were lost in confusion, though. Most of them had been tracking the newsfeeds with half their minds, watching instant polls and viewership numbers. Their political reflexes didn't know how to deal with the sudden absence of media.

"Senators," she cried, trying to gather their attention again. "Hear me!"

"Silence her!" came a shriek from the accuser. The dead woman leaped to her feet and took a step toward Oxham.

The Forum buzzed in surprise at this display. Few people had ever seen one of the honored dead raise their voice, much less scream in anguish.

"Order!" proclaimed Drexler. He glared at the accuser, aghast that one of the Emperor's servants would disturb his Senate. "You are within the Pale, Prelate. Take care!"

"These words cannot be spoken!" the prelate cried. "Use the switch!"

Drexler looked at the cutoff in his hand. Nara saw the doubt in him, a sharp discomfort at disobeying the command of an honored dead. But the power of tradition, of senatorial privilege, was greater.

"It is Senator Oxham's turn to speak," he ruled. "Silence yourself, Prelate."

Nara swallowed. Zai had told her that members of the Apparatus would feel pain at the mention of the Secret, but she hadn't realized how frantic the accuser's reaction would be. The dead woman's emotions were suddenly brighter than any in the Forum, a fearful hatred that was animal in its intensity.

Oxham spoke slowly and carefully.

"We were told, Senators, that the symbiant was an immortal coil. We were told that the elevated would live forever. We were lied to."

"No!" the accuser screamed, and leaped toward Nara.

She had never seen a dead woman move so fast. The accuser crossed the granite floor in a few strides, a flash of metal gleaming in one hand.

Nara never saw the rest, although she watched reconstructions later on the newsfeeds. The prelate came at her, knife upraised, a wild assassin trailing black robes. A meter from dealing Oxham a murderous blow, the prelate crumpled to the floor. Shown at the slowest speed, a small puff of smoke could be seen coming from one hand of the guard-at-arms, who had fired a ball of gel filled with metal pellets, a nonlethal but powerful weapon.

At the actual moment of the attack, all Nara Oxham saw was the black-robed woman falling at her feet, and the knife careening across the floor. The blade struck the bottom of the Low Dais and broke, one piece whirling on the granite floor like a spinner in a children's game.

Gasps filled the Forum.

"I move for a recess," the Loyalist Higgs called above the noise.

Oxham realized that this was another attempt to silence her. The prelate's knife hadn't killed her, but with a recess the Emperor would have won a few precious hours. She might never have this audience again.

All eyes turned to Drexler.

"Order," he said, the old voice booming. There was silence in the hall again.

"Let me speak, President," she pleaded.

"Bind the accuser," Drexler ordered. "But do not remove her."

The guard moved efficiently, deploying another riot-police device. A bright orange web moved across the prelate, winding through her limbs like a sentient vine. It curled around wrists and ankles, and around her throat. It took up stations at her mouth and covered her eyes.

"No one will disrupt this trial again," Drexler said, "even a senator, or I'll have them bound as well."

The guard stood and looked across the ranks of senators, almost daring them to make a sound. Nara Oxham wondered for a moment where this young guard came from. The Senate guards-at-arms had always seemed so ceremonial, like toy soldiers. But this man moved like a cat.

Nara looked up at Drexler and was startled by what empathy showed her. There was cold fury in the President's heart, a deep blue knot of anger that she could see clearly in her empathic sight. After a moment she grasped the source of his indignation. The most ancient Senate tradition had been broken. For the first time in the history of the realm, violence had been attempted in the Great Forum by an agent of the Emperor.

The Rubicon Pale had been crossed.

And Nara Oxham had gained an ally.

"Continue," the old Loyalist said.

Nara nodded solemnly, trying to ignore the bound and writhing woman at her feet.

"Our beloved Empress was not killed by the Rix. She was already dying, ailing from a slow wasting that stalks every risen person in this empire. Her body was destroyed to conceal the evidence of aging, evidence of the Emperor's lies."

A noise came from Loyalist senators at these words, but Drexler silenced them with an icy glare. Nara could also hear the prelate whimpering at her feet, but the Forum's amplifiers ignored the sound.

The prelate's pain pricked at Oxham's empathy, though. Her words were torture to the dead woman, warring against the conditioning that had kept the Emperor's Secret over the centuries. Nara dialed up her apathy bracelet and continued.

"The risen dead do not live forever. They live less than five hundred subjective years."

Even numbed, Nara's empathy felt the burst of confusion among the senators. The Emperor himself was almost seventeen hundred years Absolute.

"This is the true reason for the pilgrimages," she explained. "The dead travel endlessly across the Empire for one reason only: so that the Time Thief will put off their natural deaths. Immortality is a trick of relativity. Outside the royal family, there are no dead who have been risen more than four hundred subjective years."

She gave her audience a moment to absorb this information. It was so simple, really. A parlor trick in the age of common near-lightspeed travel. It was little wonder that the compound mind had discovered it so quickly in the Legis infostructure. The Rix had watched Imperial shipping for decades, searching for weaknesses. They had probably begun to suspect long ago that the pilgrimages harbored some deception. According to Laurent, the invading mind on Legis had entered the Child Empress's body through her medical confidant, and had spotted signs of her aging. The veil of deception had fallen quickly after that. It had all the data on Legis to work with, and the pilgrimage ships' manifests were recorded in great detail by the Apparatus, the subjective age of every elevated subject carefully watched in order to maintain the ruse.

The risen themselves didn't know the real purpose of the pilgrimages. They were doled out as a reward of the afterlife, and, as in everything else, the symbiant made the risen complacent followers of tradition. In their timeless lives, the swift passage of centuries seemed natural.

"The Emperor and the Apparatus have long known

the symbiant's true lifespan. When the Apparatus and Court aren't traveling, they use stasis, just as we members of the Senate do in order to live out our terms. But the Child Empress grew tired of the ruse. She realized that despite the Emperor's continuing researches, the symbiant's life would never be extended."

Oxham let her voice dip at the mention of the lost Empress. She was giving a political speech now, riding the emotions of the Forum. Even the Loyalists were beginning to listen; the Reason had always compelled greater love than her brother.

"She had decided to let herself die, and by her death to reveal the lie on which the Empire had been built. Her body began to show signs of aging, and she required a prosthesis to maintain the appearance of health. There were decades left to her, but the Emperor had already put his agents near her on Legis. He planned to conceal her death eventually. To invent an accident or some other obliterating event when the opportunity arose. The Rix simply created that opportunity."

She felt a sense of horror rising in the room. The Apparatus had always presented the Child Empress as the soft side of the wrathful Emperor. It was her name put to pardons and crisis relief. She was the Reason, whose illness had spurred the Emperor's researches. The claim that she had been murdered by her own older brother appalled even the most cynical Secularists.

"Nara Oxham," the President interrupted gently. "These are grave charges, but what do they have to do with your crime?"

She nodded respectfully, grateful that Drexler had allowed her to speak unquestioned for so long.

"To explain, I must bend the hundred-year rule, President."

Drexler's eyes narrowed. He placed the cutoff switch on the dais next to him and said, "Carefully, Senator."

"Captain Laurent Zai has captured the Legis compound mind, which knew the secret," she said. "The Emperor realized that Zai would soon learn it as well. Laurent Zai's life was in danger. I had to warn him, a hero of the realm. That is why I broke the rule."

"And the Emperor sought to use the rule to silence you?"

"Yes, Senator Drexler."

The old man nodded, satisfied. She wondered what these revelations were doing to him. Drexler was long since elevated, probably only a few subjective years from death. And now his promised immortality had been revealed as a fraud, his beloved Emperor the murderer of his sister, Anastasia the Reason.

Then another empathic shock interrupted Oxham's thoughts, a burst of emotion from the city outside the Great Forum.

"Something has happened," she said softly.

Drexler looked up, his old fingers trembling with the slightest interface gestures.

"Our link to the rest of the capital has been cut," he announced. "The physical hardlines below the Forum have been destroyed."

Fearful cries came from the senators.

"Order!" Drexler commanded. "This body is still in session!"

Nara brought her second sight online. The bandwidth of the Forum's infostructure had been degraded. The images were coming through weak wireless, as if she were on horseback trip in the deep country of Vasthold.

But the snowy newsfeed image was familiar enough.

She could make out the Forum complex, a veil of smoke rising from its periphery. The low black shapes of military hovercraft surrounded the building.

"They will not cross the Pale," Drexler said.

Godspite, Oxham thought. The army was outside. Their tradition of noninterference would be sorely tested now.

What had she started?

A rumble came through her feet. The very granite of the Great Forum was trembling.

"They will not cross the Pale," the President repeated, quiet desperation in his ancient voice.

Plagueman

"The Empire faces a crisis." The sovereign addressed the hastily assembled War Council gravely. "We are under a new and diabolical form of attack, and the War Council must deal with it without delay."

The representative of the Plague Axis reflected silently that this was not the entire War Council. Only eight of nine were present. Three of the senators were here, still looking stunned by their swift passage from the Pale to the Diamond Palace, but Nara Oxham was not. The Senate had officially suspended Oxham from the council pending her expulsion trial, but her absence from the chamber pit had never been more noticeable.

"How have we been attacked, Majesty?" the Loyalist Senator Raz imPar Henders said.

"From the Senate floor itself," the Emperor said.

"I must protest, sire," the Utopian senator interjected. "The Senate is in legal session, considering a matter of great importance. The only attack on the Empire is the military's incursion against senatorial privilege."

"No military units have crossed the Pale, Senator," the risen general said.

"Then why is the Great Forum surrounded?" the Expansionist demanded.

"For the protection of the Senate," the Emperor nearly shouted.

The plagueman had never seen the sovereign so incensed. He seemed unaffected by whatever had crippled his Apparatus, though he had lost his usual boundless reserve of calm. The biosuit's optics had always revealed the Emperor's physiology to be more animated than an ordinary risen, but now they showed a heat in his face almost as intense as a living man's.

"Protection?" the Expansionist sputtered. "The Senate is surrounded, its contact with the rest of the capital cut off. This is nothing but bald intimidation."

"I assure you, Senator, no military units shall cross the Pale," the dead general said flatly. "Not without due order by this council."

"There'll be civil war if they do," Ax Milnk said. "And all of us will lose everything."

The plagueman raised his eyebrows. That much was true. The Empire was perpetually balanced on a knife's edge between gray and pink, the dead and the living, military and economic power. The military forces stationed on Home were as carefully equilibrated as the rest of the fragile mechanism, with units hailing from pink worlds and gray. Any military move against the

Senate would be met with an equal counterforce. A disaster.

"Please, let us calm ourselves," Henders insisted, obviously flustered at his fellow senators' abuse of the sovereign. "Sire, what is this attack you speak of?"

The Emperor nodded, visibly working to calm himself. "Of course, we must explain. No doubt events today may have seemed precipitous. But we are sure that once you've heard the facts you will understand our actions."

The pink senators and Milnk responded with stony silence.

The risen general leaned forward, gesturing to bring an image of Nara Oxham onto the central airscreen. The plagueman recognized it from her trial, clipped from the newsfeed of only an hour before.

"Counselors, during the trial of Senator Nara Oxham, we discovered that a neural virus was being transmitted from the Senate floor. The virus used the newsfeed as a carrier wave, instantly affecting a small but vulnerable portion of the capital's populace. The virus caused nausea, seizures, paralysis. We believe that the effect would have spread to the entire population had the broadcast continued. Fortunately, the Apparatus acted quickly, shutting off the attack at its source."

The council chamber was silent as those assembled digested the general's words. The plagueman quietly searched the database within his biosuit. He found references to visual stimuli that could cause seizures, but only to a small percentage of human beings, most often children, and nothing that could be hidden inside a normal newsfeed. This was an unprecedented weapon, if the general's words were true.

"This sounds incredible," the Utopian said. "Nothing but a pretext for silencing Senator Oxham." He turned toward the plagueman and Milnk. "We heard more than you did, before we were summoned away. After the newsfeed was cut, Oxham accused the Emperor of murdering his sister. And she claims that the symbiant's immortality is a lie."

"Incredible stories seem to abound today," the Emperor said.

"If Oxham is lying, then why concoct this story to cut her off?" the Expansionist senator countered.

"The palace had nothing to do with the decision," the Emperor said. "As I said, the media monitors found themselves under attack, in great pain. They acted in self-preservation."

"That much may be true," the plagueman said quietly. "Oxham's words seemed to have effected the Apparatus in particular."

The Emperor started, then fixed the Axis representative with a glare. It was rare for the representative to speak at all, and the sovereign had counted the Axis as an ally throughout the war, especially since the vote on the Legis genocide.

"That may be," the dead admiral said. "We don't understand exactly how the virus works or who is susceptible. But we suspect who is behind it."

"And that would be?" the Utopian said.

"Oxham, and perhaps some elements of the Secularist Party," the general said.

"You have proof of this?" Ax Milnk demanded.

"Give us Oxham, and we'll get the proof," the Emperor said.

"This is utterly transparent," the Utopian said flatly. The plagueman remained silent as the argument raged, biding his time. The members of the War Council would soon lose all civility, but that hardly mattered. The details of whatever Oxham had discovered were, in their way, unimportant as well. This drama would ultimately be played out in other venues. The pressures that had been too long restrained in the Empire would shortly be released, violently and disruptively, that much was obvious. The Axis had seen this coming for a long time. It had failed in its mission to stabilize the Eighty Worlds. The Rix, with their blockade, their wars, had finally won.

But the plagueman was glad that the Emperor's desperate gamble would allow him one last act of penance here on the council. It was clear that the sovereign would call for a vote, thinking he had five among the eight counselors in his pocket, believing that under cover of the War Council he could move against Oxham, perhaps ultimately against the Senate, and keep the whole unwieldy contraption of the Empire clanking along for a few more decades.

"I shall repay you, Nara Oxham," the plagueman thought to himself. Not just with this vote to save her, but with all it would bring. As much chaos, progress, and the Old Enemy death as she and her party could ever want.

"God is change," he muttered to himself.

Captain

Laurent Zai looked down upon the object.

At this point in the *Lynx*'s slow rotation, its dark bulk was beneath his feet, barely discernible through the observation blister's high-impact plastic. Its shape had grown ever more difficult to make out as the Legis sun receded. Now, the object was merely an absence of stars, a giant lump of coal blackening one quarter of the universe.

The *Lynx* was still studiously avoiding communication with the thing. The frigate's mass detectors were the only sensors trained on its position; mass was the one aspect of itself the object couldn't modulate, and thus use to signal the *Lynx*. Zai felt safer this way, cut off from the mind. One of Alexander's secrets had already brought the Empire to the brink of civil war.

Now, the only means of contact with the mind was through the slender connection it had established with Herd. The Rixwoman spoke for it like some ancient oracle: as expressionless and miraculous as a bleeding statue, an intermediary with the deity.

But Zai knew that this prophylaxis couldn't be maintained forever. The object was too tenacious and resourceful, too capable of unanticipated configurations. And the *Lynx* was too porous: It was fundamentally a scout ship, designed to gather information in a thousand ways. The object would get in sooner or later, would reach Zai's crew just as it had reached Herd.

He would have to tell them. The crew knew that Zai had disarmed the politicals on board, so they would eventually have to know about the Emperor's Secret and the coming civil war. Their native worlds would be thrown into chaos soon. Zai and his lover had lit a match that would consume millions of lives.

Laurent watched Home's bright star rise slowly on his left, still two subjective years away, and wondered what was going on at the Forum. Nara would have made her speech a few hours ago, threatening sixteen hundred years of stability. The Apparatus's reaction would be swift and desperate, but Nara Oxham was a Senator, and would not be easily silenced.

Laurent Zai had burned seven percent of the *Lynx*'s entanglement reserve trying to keep track of the developments, and he knew that the Empire was already shaking. If the signs were to be believed, the Emperor had acted directly against the Senate. Zai hoped that the other messages he had sent, warnings to old colleagues and confidants within the military, would help Nara come through this unharmed. She and the Senate would certainly need allies to survive the next months. But in the long term, Zai believed, victory would be theirs.

The Apparatus would do what it could to forestall the spread of the Secret, but their efforts could only be stopgap. The data on pilgrimages were public; once examined, rumors would turn swiftly into accepted fact. And the Secret revealed would strain even the greatest loyalty. Few religions could withstand the news that heaven was, in fact, a lie. Temporary.

Zai wondered what had led the Emperor down this path. Five hundred extra years of life was hardly a trivial boon. Presumably, the sovereign had simply been mistaken at first, thinking that the symbiant was permanently stable, and a religion had been built on the concept that the Old Enemy had been beaten. When the first signs of the error had been detected, perhaps it had been too late for such a massive revision in scripture.

Well, a revision was coming now.

If the sovereign chose to fight, the Empire might remain divided for a long time. The Apparatus could easily keep a few warships, perhaps even a majority of the fleet, in the dark for years. Vessels could be ordered into deep cover for decades, receiving only censored information from the outside universe. But slowly, the truth would chip away at the loyalists, the conditioned, the willfully blind. Though some of the military would certainly remain loyal to the Emperor regardless of his lies, the Eighty Worlds would turn against him one by one. And what would follow this civil war? A republic? A new sovereign? It might take decades to resolve the question of succession.

The *Lynx*'s problem was more immediate, however. As Nara had warned, the vessels pursuing them were under orders to destroy the object, Zai, and his ship. One had to assume that they'd been under deep cover from the start of their mission—and Imperial writs were difficult code to subvert. In a few years Absolute, they would be closing with the *Lynx*, their velocities almost matched. With the extra mass of the object in tow, the frigate could not outrun them. Outnumbered, with a half-untrained crew and an imperfectly repaired ship, Zai would have to fight again.

He needed an ally, and he was alone in deep space.

All he had was the object.

He reached down toward the absence below him, looked at his gloved hand against the absolute blackness of the thing. He pulled off the glove, and gazed upon the smooth metal of his hand. If the Rix were at long last arriving in the Empire, they had begun with the right man. Laurent Zai knew what it was to be half machine.

And he wanted to return to Home; that was all that mattered. That was what had moved him from the start. Now that everything else—honor, tradition, sovereign, and immortality itself—was stripped away, he had love to return to.

Nara.

"Bridge."

"Captain?" Hobbes's voice came.

"Assemble the senior staff in one hour."

"Yes, sir. Command bridge?"

"As good a place as any."

"Any prep, Captain?"

"Consider contact with the object, Hobbes, an alliance of convenience with the Rix. Consider how to fight a guerrilla war in a crumbling Empire. Consider how best to explain to our crew that death is final, and that we all may die soon."

There was a pause, but not a long one.

"On it, sir."

Senator

The four officers entered the Great Forum slowly, as warily as a pack of predators trespassing in another's territory. They clearly didn't want to be here, committing this transgression.

The rows of white-clad senators watched the four descend the steps toward the dais. A murmur rose up, a sound halfway between defiance and fear. Nara Oxham felt the two emotions collide and mix, creating a strange discomfort that was almost like *embarrassment*. In their black uniforms, one might have mistaken the officers as guests arriving at a ball wearing tragically confused dress—fantastical masks at a white-tie function.

But then the fear grew, displacing everything else. These four had thousands of soldiers under their command, who surrounded the Forum even now, dozens of ships in the skies above.

"President," the most senior officer said, nodding a small bow.

Drexler looked down upon the four with undisguised anger.

"You have broken the covenant, Admiral. Would you destroy the Empire?"

The woman looked surprised. With the Forum infostructure down, Oxham had no prompts, but Nara recognized her from official parties. It was Admiral

Rencer Fowler IX. She had been on Home for some time, and had aged the last ten years at full Absolute.

"We are unarmed, President Drexler. We meant no violation of the Pale."

The old man scowled. "No Imperial soldier has ever come inside the Forum before, Admiral, and your troops threaten us even now."

"These are strange times, President," she said simply, as if in somber agreement. "The four of us wished to speak in private with you, but the secure lines crossing the Pale seem to be in disrepair."

The Forum reverberated with a hissing sound: the word *disrepair* spoken with contempt. Against the feigned politesse of the admiral, defiance reasserted itself.

"The hard lines were deliberately destroyed," the President said coldly.

Admiral Fowler nodded. "That would seem likely."

"Do you claim this was not the military's doing?"

She shrugged. "We aren't certain. We suspect the Apparatus is responsible. In any case, we four do not represent the military per se."

Confusion filled the Great Forum now. Nara could read nothing useful from the officers. They were soldiers on a mission, hard-minded, determined not to consider the greater implications of their actions. Whatever Fowler's claims, the four were following orders.

"You carry a writ from the Emperor himself?" Drexler asked.

Fowler shook her head. "We don't represent the Emperor, either. Can we speak in private, President?"

"The Senate is in session, Admiral. We are conducting a trial."

Fowler looked about the hall, begrudgingly recognizing the hundreds of senators surrounding her. She sighed, and turned to address them all.

"Two of us are here to speak for the Home Fleet and certain ships of the High Fleet. My own flag vessel, for one." She indicated the men on her left. "And these fine officers represent ground units of the Capital Guard and Home Reserve. But not much of the latter, I fear."

Nara Oxham swallowed. *The military was divided.*

Drexler raised his eyebrows. "The situation is complicated, then, in terms of your chain of command."

Admiral Fowler nodded slowly. She glanced nervously around the Forum, as if wishing again for a smaller audience. Then she shifted her weight, looked at the gray marble floor, and spoke carefully.

"Yes, but perhaps you could clarify matters for us, President Drexler. Due to the communications situation, the War Council has rendered an incomplete vote on an issue of great importance."

"An incomplete vote?"

"Eight members have voted, President, and the result is a four-to-four tie. Certain members of the military command structure insist that the Emperor's vote should break the tie, as per tradition when the council is not at full strength."

The admiral cleared her throat.

"But others of us would prefer to wait for the vote of the ninth member of the council, given the importance of the issue. Should she be available."

For the first time, the admiral looked at Oxham. Nara could read nothing in the woman's expression. Fowler's mind was clean, as if she were a disinterested, slightly bored observer at some hoary political convention.

"What is this issue?" Oxham asked.

The admiral spoke officiously. "The council has voted—*partly* voted—on an order to the Capital Guard. The order is to suspend temporarily the normal operations of the Senate. To arrest Senator Oxham and turn her over to the Apparatus."

"To cross the Pale?" Drexler hissed.

Admiral Fowler nodded. "That exceptional action was explicitly dictated."

Drexler's face darkened.

"Thus, in a manner of speaking, we four are authorized to be here, President," the admiral continued, "by partial vote of the council. But, being on this side of the Pale, we discover the ninth member of the council."

The woman bowed to Oxham. Finally, emotion finally surged from all four them to reach her empathy. Strong affect, focused directly on her.

"Should she be available."

President Drexler spoke carefully, joining the admiral's dance of words.

"Senator Oxham's membership in the War Council has been suspended, as you may know, pending the result of this trial." He looked down from the dais at Oxham, raising one eyebrow.

For a moment, Nara wondered if this was a charade, all a trick. Her empathy was mostly suppressed; she couldn't feel the emotional reality of the situation. The confusion of the divided city raged around her, but the emotions of these officers were too subtle to read. But one thing was certain, Nara had to act.

Four to four, she thought. The Plague Axis had made good on their promise. And now she could break the tie.

"President Drexler, I rest my defense. And call for a vote on my expulsion."

The young Secularist who had replaced her as party whip, rose.

"I second the call. A fast vote, if the President pleases."

Puram Drexler's gavel thundered. "Senators, you have fifty seconds. Vote by standard gestural code."

A few objections were raised from the shocked Loyalist benches, but Drexler gaveled them into silence. The Senate was stunned for a few moments, but then votes began to tally. Oxham almost failed to cast her own, forgetting that she had never been officially removed as His Majesty's Representative from Vasthold, Senator of the Empire, and that she had every right.

The Senate voted.

Half a minute later, it was over. Even a sizable number of Loyalists—whether from confusion, the realization that defeat was certain, or a final faithfulness to traditions even older than the Emperor—voted with the majority. Nara Oxham had been overwhelmingly acquitted of treason; the motion for her expulsion had failed.

The suddenness of it all left her empty inside; relief would take a long time to come.

"Senator Nara Oxham is returned to full status and duties, without prejudice or delay," President Drexler announced.

The old man turned to the officers.

"She is available, Admiral," he finished.

They turned to her.

"Senator, we await the final vote of the War Council."

Still stunned at the speed of events, Nara gathered herself. Enough of the military had dared to forestall the Emperor, Drexler had supported them, the Senate had acted quickly and true. All that was left was for her to finish the job.

Again, it all came down to a word.

"I vote against the proposal, Admiral," she said quietly.

"Thank you for the clarification," Fowler answered. She turned to face the Senate. "We apologize for this intrusion. Certain elements under our command will remain—outside the Pale—to render technical assistance and all necessary protection to the Senate."

"That is acceptable," Drexler said.

"Death spare the Senate," Fowler said.

"Death spare the Senate," came the murmured response of the assembly.

Three of the officers turned and strode from the Forum, hurrying back to the Pale and the military infostructure, where they could give orders to their troops and ships. But one of the navy men stayed behind, and took a step toward her.

"Senator Oxham?"

"Yes . . . Commodore?" she asked, reading his rank.

"My name is Marcus Fentu Masrui."

She blinked, recognizing the name. Masrui had been Zai's commanding officer on Dhantu. In fact, she'd come close to meeting the man on the night she'd met Laurent, ten years ago.

"Is it true, Senator?" the officer asked.

"What, Commodore?"

"That the Emperor wanted to kill Laurent Zai? After everything?"

She nodded. "Absolutely true. I heard him say the words."

"And that there is no immortality?"

"Yes. It's all true, Commodore. Laurent himself told me."

The Commodore shook his head ruefully. "If any man deserved to live forever, it was Zai," he said.

She felt it then, the emotion the officers had hidden so well. It burst from behind Masrui's discipline, from behind his decades of training and loyalty. The prize they'd all been promised, the Valhalla where their dead comrades had gone for rewards eternal, the very reason many of them had joined the military: All of it was a lie.

The man's face wrenched, as if he were swallowing something awful. Then he took a deep breath, and focus returned to his thoughts.

"And, another thing, begging your pardon . . ."

"Yes, Commodore?"

Masrui bit his lower lip before speaking.

"Were you and Zai . . . really lovers?"

"Yes, Commodore. We are lovers."

For a moment, his face was blank. Then he grasped her hand.

"Thank you," he said.

Nara found herself speechless for a moment. Then she pulled her hand from his. "No thanks necessary, Commodore. It was never pity."

"Of course not, Senator. I didn't mean to imply pity. Thank you, though. I wanted . . . all of us wanted somehow to restore Zai. He lost too much on Dhantu. After the Legis rescue failed, we thought the Emperor's pardon was real."

"It wasn't."

He swallowed, the bitter taste of another lie showing on his face.

"Commodore, tell me something," Oxham said.

"At your service, Senator."

"Are there enough of you? Enough to fight those who'll follow the Emperor without question?"

"Not yet. But there will be. The truth will turn them."

He looked up at his departing comrades, realizing that he should join them and put this revolution, this righteous treason, this civil war into motion. But he turned back to Nara.

"Laurent Zai's name will turn them," he said.

"And death," Nara added.

"Death, Senator?"

"Death is real again, Commodore. Remind them of that."

Commodore Masrui thought about this for moment, then shook his head.

"It was always real, Senator, for us soldiers. Death out in space rarely left enough for the symbiant. But I suppose that now death is *unavoidable,* as it always was before the Emperor's lie."

"Spread the word, then," Nara Oxham said. "We're free again."

Fisherman/Pilot

After a long time, the sun and moon stopped wheeling in the sky. The tides were over.

The fisherman looked down at himself. Somehow, he was still here, still whole after having been consumed a thousand thousand times. The fish were placid now, half in the tide pool, half in the bay.

But no, there were more of them . . . in the sky.

The dark night seemed to have filled with stars, as if he'd jumped ten thousand light-years closer to the core. But what looked like stars were in fact the little luminescent fish, strewn across the sky to make a galaxy, a milky river of light. The fisherman's thoughts grew clearer, and he understood what had pacified the ravenous schools: They had reached their goal, resplendent and sovereign in the dark.

They were up there, beyond the reach of his spear.

He dropped the weapon and turned toward the opening sky. . . .

Master Pilot Jocim Marx's gummy eyes focused first on the scarred woman.

Her face was blank, as if nerve damage had rendered it expressionless. The hair had been burned from her scalp. But the woman's gaze was bright and intelligent.

And violet, her eyes as bright a hue as stained glass catching the sun.

Had he been captured by the Rix?

Marx started, trying to sit up. The scarred woman moved away, with the suddenness of a bird cocking its head. He knew from that movement that she was not human.

"Who—?" Marx began, then he saw Hobbes over the woman's shoulder.

"Jocim?" the ExO said.

She articulated the two syllables carefully, as if to establish whether he knew his own name.

He did her one better. "How are you, Katherie Hobbes?"

She smiled, "Relieved."

"How long?"

"A month."

"Godspite." To Marx, it had seemed like an eternity, but the memory was already fading when contrasted to the real world. He looked around, and recognized the room as a private sickbay cabin aboard the *Lynx*. The violet-eyed Rix had moved to the side of a small, gray-faced woman. One of the honored dead? This was too confusing.

"Why is there a Rixwoman here, Hobbes? Have we been captured?"

"No, Master Pilot. She is a . . . guest. Or an ally, perhaps." Hobbes sounded only slightly less confused than Marx. "She helped cure you," the ExO added with surety.

He looked at the violet-eyed woman, blinked.

"Thank you, then, I suppose."

The woman's gaze remained both piercing and empty, as if he were a specimen pinned in a curio case.

"How do you feel, Marx?" Hobbes asked.

He sat up. His muscles had the even tone of artificial exercise. His fingers, chronically suffering mild soreness from the demands of piloting, felt rejuvenated from the enforced break. His head was . . .

Different.

"What happened, Hobbes?"

"Everything."

That was Hobbes. Concise, but not always helpful. The passage of weeks must have refreshed his brain, Marx thought. He could see the executive officer's stunning beauty again, as he had before growing accustomed to it over the last two years. As if he'd spent a month on leave rather than in a . . . coma?

"You were caught in an upload, Jocim," she said. "Alexander—the Legis compound mind, I should say—was transferring itself from the planet to the object. You got in the way."

The *object*. That word brought a shiver to Marx. Images swirled in his head: a kind of liquid creature below him, its pseudopods reaching out, like those legant members to which a sea creature delegates its kills. Marx recognized from his own discomfort that he was nearing his last memories from before the onset of coma. He'd been taken, prey.

"Your sensor subdrones were pumping everything they could directly into your synesthesia," Hobbes continued. "The information gain was too high for you. And perhaps it was partly my fault, too, Jocim. You'd been pulled out of a hypersleep cycle out of phase, less than an hour before you were hit with the compound mind. Your mind was vulnerable."

He looked up at Hobbes, silently begging her to talk more slowly. "*What* hit me?"

"Alexander. The Legis compound mind. You had a planet stuffed into your head."

Marx nodded, and rubbed his aching temples. That metaphor felt about right. Then he blinked. He *hoped* it was a metaphor.

"Again, Hobbes," he pleaded. "*Why* is there a Rix-woman running loose on our ship?"

"Ah," Hobbes said. "She's a commando, from the Legis attack."

"Oh, a commando. Understandable then, that we would want her in sickbay." Marx vaguely realized that he should be terrified, as if a poisonous snake had been dropped in his lap, but his body wasn't up to producing adrenaline.

"Things have changed, Marx. Not just here, but throughout the Empire. We've had to ally ourselves—or at least cooperate—with the object. With the Rix."

"The Empire and Rix are allied?" Suddenly, three months' sleep didn't seem adequate.

"No, just us, Marx. The *Lynx* is on its own."

"Wait," the master pilot interrupted. "Who's in command, Hobbes?" He clenched his fists. Had the aborted mutiny finally occurred?

"Captain Zai, of course."

Marx's head swam. The *Vadan* had committed treason?

"Listen, Marx," Hobbes kept at him. "The Emperor's status is unsure. The dead have called a quorum. The pilgrimage ships are coming into Home from all over the Empire. The sovereign may be removed."

A quorum of the dead? Something from a ten-year-old's civics class. A strictly theoretical possibility. For sixteen hundred years, the Emperor had ruled without a single dissenting vote from among the billions of honored dead. The dead never argued, never even *disagreed.* For them to consider removal of the sovereign seemed unthinkable.

"Hobbes," he started, waving at her to slow down. His mind fought to locate the questions that would straighten out this strange new world.

"What the hell . . . ?" was all he could manage.

She started to speak, and Marx winced.

Katherie Hobbes shook her head, laughed. "Master Pilot, I think you should rest now."

She took his shoulders, *touched* him. Things had changed, indeed.

"We've lost so many, Jocim. It's good to have you back," Hobbes whispered.

Marx simply nodded, and leaned back on the sickbed. Suddenly, he was exhausted again.

The ExO left him there, the lights dimming as she exited the private sickbay cabin.

He leaned back, and his mind roiled now, full of questions, confusion, sheer energy. Marx felt as if he'd drunk a pot of coffee after a full day of meetings, his mind tired but buzzing. Deep breaths had only the slightest calming effect. He exercised his fingers, forcing himself to think about how good it would be to fly again.

Then he caught the eyes of the Rixwoman. She was still here—watching him, *observing,* as if monitoring a patient, awaiting some expected symptom to evince itself. The dead woman stood beside her, their shoulders just touching with the casual intimacy of old lovers.

Marx locked his gaze onto the Rixwoman's, focusing himself. Somehow, her implacable stare calmed his mind, her violet eyes glowing like meditation candles in the dark cabin. The rhythm of his breathing slowed, and he felt the cycle of the dreamtide again. He heard the ambient sound of the ship, the ever-present hum of engines, air system, and gravity generation.

Something was different.

Without releasing the commando's gaze, Marx placed his hand on the side of his bed, palm flat against cool metal. The ship-hum was stronger there. He let the dream phantoms, the reverberations of his fugue, align themselves to the frigate's vibration. Memory and metal conjoined, like the many instruments of an orchestra tuning to a common pitch.

They matched the flicker of the Rixwoman's eyes.

She smiled at Marx. Then the two of them together—yes, they *were* lovers, he suddenly knew—left him.

And the master pilot understood the deal that the captain had made. He wondered what must be arrayed against them, their lone ship in the deep, to have motivated Zai to let this thing aboard. To have allied his vessel and crew with the Empire's sworn enemy.

Perhaps Laurent Zai didn't even know, didn't understand the extent of its subtle, pervasive occupation. But Marx knew. He had spent a hundred days inside its belly. He could see its signs and hear its music. Like a vortex of wind revealed by the leaves, dirt, and debris it captured, the shape and scope of Alexander were clearly marked.

The *Lynx* had been taken.

The Rix were here.

Marine Private

Marine Private Second-Class Bassiritz explained it again to his new crewmates: "Just *Bassiritz*. In the village where I come from, we only have one name."

"Only one name?" Astra shouted above the roaring crowd.

"Better than none at all," Master Private Torvel Saman assured him.

"Better than one too many," Astra added.

"How many names would be too many?" Bassiritz asked.

"Not how many, but which ones!"

"Retired."

"The late . . ."

"Corporal!"

They laughed at their own jokes and clapped Bassiritz on the back as if he'd made one himself. He didn't completely understand, but didn't press his mates with questions. He was relieved at their good humor, knowing from his travels that in some cultures, a single, unadorned name was a badge of shame, or a mark of servant lineage. But these *Lynx* marines all had wide experience; they'd seen far stranger things.

The crew of the new, experimental warship was drawn from the cream of the Empire. Bassiritz knew that he himself only rated selection due to his high scores as a marksman and close combatant—he was younger and less educated than his squadmates.

The fire team was perched, alongside a hundred or so of their crewmates, on the gantry supporting a huge, false *Lynx*. The facsimile of their new ship loomed up behind them, two kilometers tall. (But it was not a figment or ghost-sight: The dummy ship was *real,* physical at least. Bassiritz had begun to realize that no expense was too absurd here on Home. Not for a pageant or party.) Before them, filling the great square before the Emperor's Diamond Palace, was a huge crowd of cheering citizens. An uncountable host, far more people than Bassiritz had ever seen in his life. Not merely in one place, but more than all the people the young private had ever seen, *put together.* That fact bounded around inside his head, a realization as sovereign as the glittering facets of the palace as it caught the strangely white light of Home's large sun.

This horde seemed to be the Empire entire, assembled to send off the *Lynx*'s crew.

Master Private Saman grasped his arm and pointed into the crowd.

"She's got something for you, Bass!" (The single name indeed didn't bother his squad: They'd shortened it already.)

Bassiritz's keen eyes followed Saman's gesture, and spotted a woman among the ecstatic dancers in the front of the crowd. She had removed her jacket and tunic, ignoring the autumn chill, baring flesh pale enough to shine like a ray of sun among the gray throngs of the faithful. Then others followed her example, men and women dancing out of their clothes, euphoric and supplicant before the towering, mock totem of the warship.

Bassiritz shook his head in bemusement. The gray religion took on many forms throughout the Empire, but here on Home all its strangest versions were clustered together, as if the planet were a curio cabinet stocked for the amusement of the Risen One himself. The ecstatic dancers had seemed like monks to Bassiritz at first. He had watched them over the last few days, encamped in the square before the rising dummy ship. Their gray tents and clothes, shaved heads, quiet prayers, and diet of cold field rations had given them a solemn dignity. But now he saw that the purpose of these privations had been to secure a position in the front of the crowd. To dance and scream wildly—now *nakedly*—before the crew and the onlooking masses. To become part of the spectacle of christening a new class of Imperial warship.

To pay their . . . respects.

"You'll catch flies, Private Second Class."

Bassiritz closed his mouth, and smiled to echo the laughter of his squadmates.

"Bass's never been to a christening, I suppose."

"Neither have you, Astra!"

"But I've seen war prizes presented. The dancers were there."

"The dancers are *everywhere*."

"There were a couple in your room last night, I overheard."

"Those were honest surrogates, Private."

"I'm sure you kept them honest."

"I kept them awake."

The squad laughed again. Bassiritz felt warm in

their company, even in the chill wind. It was new and wonderful to be here up above a crowd, arrayed with his crewmates on the slender beams of the gantry, almost flying over the press of people. He had never felt so . . . *exalted* before.

His eyes scanned the buildings that rose as straight as cliffs around the square. The wide balconies were full, glittering with the reflective clothes of the wealthy, as if the city itself were bejeweled for this event. Bassiritz had heard fantastic stories about the cost of rooms on the square, which could not be owned, only leased from the Apparatus or temporarily bequeathed to high officeholders, such as senators and visiting planetary governors. Wealthy families exhausted whole fortunes to rent them, if only for a few days, in hopes of establishing connections, rising a little higher in the social order, nearing the ultimate prize of elevation. They were all out to gaze upon the mock ship, glittering and awestruck, yearning for immortality.

And with that thought, Bassiritz realized why his crewmates were so deliriously happy here. Suspended above the horde, under the gaze of the Empire's plutocrats, they felt their true value as soldiers, saw a prefiguration of their true reward. For their grueling service—the years confined on tiny ships, the decades lost to the Time Thief, the constant danger of sudden obliteration—they were granted the one prize that even the wildest wealth could not absolutely guarantee.

If they could just die in combat, cleanly and without too much brain damage, or enjoy long and exemplary careers, Bassiritz and his squadmates might live forever.

Forever. A period not even the Time Thief could steal.

He could see the Emperor's promise here, from this vantage above the crowd.

As his incredibly sharp eyes scanned the balconies of the powerful, Bassiritz's elated thoughts were suddenly interrupted. Alone on a small veranda were two figures, one wearing civilian white, the other military black. An odd couple.

The man in black seemed familiar. Bassiritz squinted, focusing on the pair. The man turned to profile, making some comment to his companion, and the young private started.

"It's the captain!" he cried.

"Where?"

"Not a chance."

"Won't be here for hours!"

Bassiritz pointed. "There on that balcony. With that woman in white."

The others followed his gaze, cupping their hands against the glare of the sun now spilling into the square.

"That's the Secularist senatorial block. You wouldn't catch the Old Man in those abodes." Master Private Saman had served with Laurent Zai before.

"Zai's *Vadan,* Bass! Not some pink."

"But it's him. I can see him clearly."

"It's at least a klick away, young man. You're hallucinating."

The two figures on the balcony grew closer, first hands touching, then bodies drawing near against the cold. Then white and black intertwined.

"He's kissing a woman up there," Bassiritz announced.

"Hah-hah!" Saman yowled, almost doubling over against the gantry's handrail. "The captain kissing a pink senator!"

"Kissing anyone at all!" Astra added in amazement.

The squad laughed at Bassiritz's fine joke on them, slapping his back again, full of good humor and intoxicated by their imperious position above the crowd, above the naked and gyrating dancers, above the grasping wealthy. Above everything but the huge false ship behind them, and its real and lethal double in high orbit above, where they would soon be lofting to join it, to journey toward the rumored troubles of the Rix frontier.

They laughed that the possibility of death awaited them.

But Bassiritz frowned. He alone could see that it was, in fact, the captain. He could see that it was a long and vigorous embrace. And in his small village the elders had taught Bassiritz one certain rule: Never laugh at a kiss. A kiss was mysterious and powerful, fragile and invincible. Like any spark, a kiss might fizzle into nothing, or consume an entire forest. A kiss was no laughing matter. Not for the wary.

A kiss could change the world.

TOR

Award-winning authors
Compelling stories

Please join us at the website
below for more information
about this author and other great
Tor selections, and to sign up for
our monthly newsletter!

TOR